TRIAL AT MONOMOY

Trial at Monomoy

JOHN MASTERS

p

PIP
POLLINGER IN PRINT

Pollinger Limited
9 Staple Inn
Holborn
LONDON
WC1V 7QH

www.pollingerltd.com

First published by Michael Joseph 1964
This PIP edition published 2005

A CIP catalogue record is available from the British Library

ISBN 978-1-905665-00-6

CONTENTS

CHAPTER ONE

FRIDAY

Lynn Garland turned the object over with the toe of her boot. It was a seaman's life jacket, Swedish make, and it had been in the sea a long time. Whatever story it had to tell was ended long since. She walked on, northward along the Great Beach, the Atlantic Ocean on her right, the tall ridge of the dune on her left.

It was early morning, in February. A small wind blew gently against her right cheek. The sun was coming out of the Atlantic behind Pollock Rip, raising the lightship to float in sharp silhouette above the green and silver line of the horizon. Closer, the wreck of the *Pendleton* looked like a barn set in the sea, the red paint flaking from its walls.

A bottle rolled to and fro, gentle and slow like a pleasantly drunken man at the edge of the near-frozen wavelets. Lynn went to the edge of the water and picked it up. The glass was clear, the bottle empty. She threw it into the sea and walked on.

She looked at her watch. There was an hour before the bus left for Chatham and Hyannis . . . thence Boston; and an appearance before the permanent subcommittee of the Teachers' Association. She must allow herself ample time to wash and change. And time to make sure, twice at least, that she had not left her notes behind. *Statement of case, by Miss Lynn Garland,* Monomoy High School, suspended from teaching by the School Committee on . . . only three days ago. It felt like a month. She led a full life – too full, according to the principal – but nothing seemed to *matter* as much as teaching, and no other occasion held the thrill of that daily moment when she entered the classroom and all the young faces turned to hers. In every class there were a few who saw how the vocabulary and grammar of the English language were welded to the spirit of the English-language writers; a few who knew beauty through language; a few, a very few, who began to create meaning and excitement under the warmth of her encouragement. So, in every class, the lights burned and there was no darkness for her, and she could say, 'I am a teacher, a teacher of the word, the Sacred Word of Shakespeare and Thoreau.'

7

A teacher under suspension for upholding Thoreau's standards. And why not? Being right was what mattered.

And yet it bothered her. She had a little house here. For some reason no other place had ever been or become 'home' to her; but Monomoy was. What could the Teachers' Association do for her? Could they do anything at all while she was still receiving her full salary?

She shouldn't fight so much. Roll with the punches, the sports-casters kept saying, as though that were a noble thing to do. Not noble, perhaps, but wise. At what point did wisdom become opportunism?

She must be back from Boston in good time for Town Meeting. It was disgraceful that she had not been able to raise enough signatures to have the petition about winter concerts put on the Warrant.

Perhaps it was as well. 'You must not spread yourself too thin, Miss Garland,' the principal had said. That made sense, particularly when a really important fight was shaping up, a fight that affected everyone, not just herself. And affected the physical foundation of the country, too, for surely a nation that failed to protect its dunes and beaches, and turned its places of refuge into building lots, could not for long retain its hold on its people's imaginative loyalty?

She tossed her head, throwing the heavy hair out of her eyes. But why did one have to fight, always, with such peculiar-looking allies? Last night, for instance, the meeting in the high school to arouse enthusiasm and organize another mass meeting, and *that* to organize support for the proposed Monomoy Park and National Sea Shore . . . radiator pipes clanking, remains of an algebra problem on the blackboard, Harvard professor with strong middle-western accent droning on, a total of twelve people present, including the professor and herself; ten women and two men. The other man was Elliott King, chairman of the School Committee that had just suspended her – and also the biggest builder and contractor in town. It was easy to see why he had sat in the front row with a sardonic grin, taking notes. One could almost hear his thoughts – bunch of crackpots, long-hairs, foreigners, out-of-staters. Unfortunately, how near the truth! (Who was there? Mrs Miller, kept twelve cats. A retired music teacher, member of the American Vegetarian party and therefore automatically to be labelled *Communist*. Miss Coker, who attended everything but heard nothing. And the professor churning out facts and figures like a sausage machine – availability

8

of fresh water; number of different bird species that used the southern part, the Handforth Tract; past history – when the Army took it, when the Air Force got it, when they said they didn't want it any more.) But it was enthusiasm that had to be engendered, not yawns. She remembered leaping to her feet. 'The central issue here is not how we use the Handforth Tract but how we decide our future. Whether we have a park and bird sanctuary or whether we have a few hundred houses doesn't really matter. What *does* matter is whether the people of Monomoy decide their future as a community, or have it decided for them by the selfish interests of a few powerful men who are concerned only with personal profit.' *That's* what she'd said, looking Elliott King straight in the eye, too!

The grass on the forward edge of the dune was grey with frost, here and there stiffened by spray into a small forest of spears. The sky was pale blue and she heard no birds. The sound of a motor broke into the peace, and she looked up. A huge vehicle came down from the north towards her, running smooth and fast on the hard, tilted sand. After a moment of wonder she recognized the Coast Guard DUKW. For another moment she thought the big amphibian would roll by, splattering her with water, without acknowledging her existence. As it came near, it slowed quickly and stopped. She didn't know the man at the wheel: the other, standing up, was the man in charge of the Monomoy Life Boat Station, John Remington.

He touched the peak of his arctic cap as he leaned over the side. 'Good morning, Miss Garland . . . Pretty cold on the feet, walking, isn't it?'

'Not with good boots on,' she said.

His jaw tightened. He was not a big man in height, but broad-built above with cowboy hips below, seemingly impervious to the cold in a thin denim work jacket.

'I beg your pardon,' he said stiffly. 'I walk the beach whenever I can, and I have found my feet get cold in winter, whatever boots I wear . . . O.K., Jobell.' The DUKW rumbled on south.

Why did I answer so curtly? she asked herself. I didn't mean to. But I have an allergy to uniforms and uniformed men. Furthermore, I have a chip on my shoulder, there's no use pretending I don't. The problem is – how to get rid of it without lying down and being a nice pussy? Heaven forbid that a man should ever think of me as just *that*. She walked on, half smiling.

Half a mile down the beach John Remington, still standing in the DUKW, saw a bottle rolling at the edge of the tide. He

9

hesitated and then said firmly, 'Stop!' Seaman Jobell braked hard and John vaulted to the sand. He picked up the bottle and saw that it was empty. No action to take, nothing to report. Jobell was trying to hide a grin. John scrambled quickly back up and nodded, without speaking. The DUKW moved on.

The Garland woman would have seen the incident too, if she'd looked round. O.K. – let her laugh at a man for looking in bottles in this age of radar, satellites and nuclear fission. He wasn't college educated the way she was, but he knew the sea. He knew that sometimes desperate men *did* still send out messages in bottles. Now that the Coast Guard didn't have men walking every inch of the beach every day, who was to find the messages?

He saw a torn, faded, life jacket on the sand – but he had seen that before. It washed up the day before yesterday . . . Let them call him Salt Horse behind his back. A man had a job to do in this life and there wasn't anything else to it, he just did it, the best he could.

Jobell would think Miss Garland was nuts, to be walking the beach at this hour of a February morning when she had a warm house to stay in. Men like Jobell and Tyson and Knighton didn't stop to think, maybe, she had that good glow in her skin just because she walked the beach. As for beginning to understand why anyone should want to be alone and silent when they could be in a yelling crowd . . . But fighting the School Committee, fighting the Selectmen, she was nuts, at that. Maybe wearing pants was a clue. She wore them a lot, and she had a pretty good shape, but even the best-looking woman had a woman's ass.

They were under the Gap now. 'I'll get out here,' he said. 'Take her on round.'

'To the beacon, or all the way to South Point?' the seaman asked.

'The beacon,' John said. 'Do the rest tomorrow.' He scrambled up the sand slope until he reached the foot of the concrete steps built into the dune. In summer wooden steps covered that last ten feet too, but every fall they were pulled up and stored. He went up the steps on the double, two at a time, and arrived in the Gap. Here, for a space of a hundred feet, the Great Dune dipped closer to sea level. The flat space was paved with asphalt, and constituted the Coast Guard parking lot. The tall bulk of a wooden boathouse occupied the north-east corner. They used to keep the oared surfboat in there on its carriage, and a steep ramp used to lead down to the ocean, beside the steps. So they could launch the surfboat direct into the ocean, or take her the other way, down Boat Street to Longships Bay. And there used to be a team of horse at call; and if the horses were sick, why, the men were numerous enough and strong enough. No more. All gone. The Old Boat House was a garage. Rescue operations on the ocean side were left to the Chatham boat whenever possible, and the ramp had vanished. There was a New Boat House on the bay, at the corner of the Green.

From the north side, broad steps climbed steeply out of the Gap toward the bulky station house, perched on the lip of the slope. From here, looking upward, you could see its deep concrete foundations and understand why this new one, about twenty years old, had been built of cinder blocks rather than the traditional wood and lath.

John ran up the steps and entered the front door under the sign, UNITED STATES COAST GUARD, LIFEBOAT STATION, MONO-MOY. There'd be papers for him in the cramped little office, but they could wait. Better still, let McGill deal with them. He ran on up the stairs, past the seamen's mess deck on the second floor, on up to the third, the lookout and operations room.

Two men were staring through the east windows at the sea and the yellow ball of the sun slanting up over Pollock Rip. They turned as he came in. One was Wallace, the seaman on duty. The other was a civilian, about six feet tall, about seventy years of age. His blue eyes were set deep in a bony head and his hands were big and bony, and marked with the white scars of fishing-line burns between thumb and forefinger on both hands, and across all the knuckles. This was Walter Crampton, retired fisherman, Second Selectman of Monomoy.

John said, 'Good morning, Walter. Be with you in a minute.'
'Sure.'
'Anything to report, Wallace?'
'Nothing special, Chief. There's maybe a storm brewing off Florida. On that top signal.'
John read quickly. The Tiros satellite had photographed an exceptionally large storm area off the eastern coast of Florida. Another, smaller storm was moving very slowly eastward through the Mississippi Valley.

'Have a look at this, Walter,' John said. 'This is the same weather pattern that gave us that bad nor-easter in March, two or three years back. This could be bad, too.'

Walter Crampton read the message carefully. Sure, there was going to be a storm, there were always a couple, every winter.

11

Sure, it could be bad. But *his* house was shipshape, the way his boat used to be. Couldn't do more than that.

From the bank of radio and radar equipment in one corner a hollow voice boomed, 'Monomoy Coast Guard, this is CG 36614 departing Coast Guard pier, en route Outer Mark, exercising. Over.'

Remington picked up the mike on the set. He said, 'CG 36614, this is Officer in Charge, Monomoy Coast Guard. Proceed on mission. Report at Outer Mark. Over.' He took a telescope from its rack and went to the west window. Walter followed slowly. His joints might be a little creaky, but he didn't need a telescope to see from here to the Coast Guard pier.

There she was, the 36-footer, about ready to go, Randall at the wheel, one young fellow on the bow and another on the pier, the mooring rope unfastened from the bollard, and held loose in his hand. The tide would be running sharp northward about now, and would pull the boat out faster than the boy expected. There, the gap was widening fast . . . The young seaman took a flying leap, rope in hand, landing like a cat on the turtle deck forward. There he stumbled, and would have gone clear over the side, if the other kid hadn't caught him.

Remington muttered, 'I hope Randall's bawling Tyson out, goddam kid stuff, on a Coast Guard ship. Tyson's grinning like an ape. Now he's scraping up snow . . .'

'I can see,' Walter said. The kid was throwing a snowball at some other kid on the pier. The 36-footer backed out into the bay and began to turn. Remington watched, the frown clefts that were permanent between his eyes now deep and angry.

Remington said, 'Sometimes I think these kids nowadays are a different breed of animal from the rest of us. Not just younger, like we used to be, but different. They don't speak the same language . . . There's nothing makes you feel so good as doing a job right, eh?'

'No.'

'Well, do you think these kids believe that? Or will listen when you tell 'em?'

'No.'

Remington raised the telescope again, to watch the manoeuvrings of the boat as it went down the marked channel between the red and black bouys. Walter took a turn round the room, looking out all the windows in turn. Chief Remington was a good seaman and a good fellow, as far as any government man could be, but he let things, and people, rile him too easy.

12

You got a different view of the town from up here – even of the sea. Small waves were breaking on the shoal bank a quarter mile out from the east beach. There was broken water on the Stone Horse Shoal, too. Close on the north the lighthouse tower edged into the view, broad-barred red-white-red. That light occulted every four seconds. Straight out, east, you could see the Pollock Rip lightship today, a touch of red against the dark water – *occulting every five seconds*. That was government for you, those two lights only a few miles part, and practically the same flash. They sure as hell looked the same when you were heaving up and down in a lobster dory, in the tail of a nor'easter.

North and south the Great Beach was empty. No one on it, not even Mrs Handforth scattering birdseed to seagulls, or the schoolteacher hiking along in trousers. Just the sand, and patches of snow in the hollows of the dune, and a touch of north wind raising up eddies of dry sand and snow in the bent grass.

Back at Remington's side, Walter looked down on the town and bay. The high school seemed raw and unfinished, though it was almost ten years old now. The Longships Hotel looked like an old-fashioned man-of-war, even now, when it was shut up for the winter. Its rows of black shutters looked like gun ports. To the left of Sachem Island the 36-footer was passing Buoy 14, and the coxswain had just opened her up to full speed, now he was out of the restricted area. Monomoy House was white-painted brick, but it shone a sort of gold, almost, way out there across the bay, with the sun right on this face. There was a boat in Clam Cove, under the house, the place that old Mrs Handforth insisted was where the Vikings landed. *She* called it Viking Cove and expected everyone else to. Let 'em, if they wanted to. Not him, though. It was hard enough swallowing Longships Bay, and they'd done that when he was a kid, about seven maybe; changing it from Big Bay.

Remington turned to him. 'How's Daisy, Walter?'

'About the same. But she fails some every day.'

The doc said she ought to be in hospital over in Hyannis, but there wasn't room for people who were just dying. She didn't want to go either. Bad enough to miss Town Meeting, the first she'd missed since 1921

'I'm sorry,' Remington said.

Walter Crampton nodded silently. He was sorry, everyone was sorry, but when your time came, it came. Daisy wouldn't go easy, though. She never had. Married forty-three years and now near the end. It seemed impossible but of course it wasn't.

13

He said, 'I came up to ask whether you fellows are going to do anything about the Diadem Bay oyster beds.'

'You mean the Nantucket men coming over?'

'Yes.'

'You know we can't do a thing unless they break sea laws or create a disturbance.'

'Yes,' Walter said, 'I reckon there'll be one soon enough.'

'We'll just have to wait for it,' Remington said.

At midday an old man paraded around Monomoy Green with a hand-painted placard on top of a pole. He had a mop of grey hair, a droopy grey moustache, and hot, dark eyes. He wore galoshes, brown wool trousers, a red-and-black lumberman's jacket and a dirty blue wool scarf. The scarf was folded round his neck and tucked in badly, like a coarse ruff. The placard, in red paint, modified Roman script, said JUDGE NOT THAT YE BE NOT JUDGED.

A few fisherman were gathered idly outside the Town Hall. One shouted, 'Hey, George, what's on your mind now?'

The old man stopped, and said, 'The horseshoe crabs.'

'Again? Jesus!' the fisherman said.

'Listen, my friend, I'm asking you and everyone here to think. Suppose we squash every beast or animal that causes us the least little harm. Squash them without a thought. Then what is to stop someone, something bigger than us, and more powerful, from squashing us? We treat the horseshoe crab like a criminal, because he eats a few clams . . . What harm do *we* do? Suppose the horseshoe crabs came out of the sea, in millions, and tried us for pollution, for waste, for cruelty? Suppose they had a Town Meeting tonight, down there under the bay, and put a bounty on every human tail?'

'That reminds me,' a man said, and walked away. Laughter boomed round the group.

'Good old George,' someone cried.

'I am serious . . . I want to ask you to help me, tonight, at Town Meeting . . .' His foreign-accented voice disappeared under laughter and quips.

Two men watched the scene from outside the firehouse, at the north-west corner of the Green. One was the police chief, the other the First Selectman. The First Selectman had a long Yankee face, a humorous mouth and a mottled cheek, and wore a cap with earmuffs. He seemed to be in his mid-forties.

'Any trouble, Frank?' he asked the police chief, jerking his head towards the group, where the old man was now gesticulating violently, the placard waving in the air.

The chief shook his head. 'Nothing, Nelson. Might be if the rest of the artists were here, but I don't think there's another one staying over in town this winter.'

'They've been leaving for some years,' the Selectman said, 'going to P. Town or the Vineyard.'

'The horseshoe crab *lives* here!' the old man cried.

'So do we!' one of the men shouted, his voice unfriendly.

The elms that used to line the Green on all four sides had caught the blight. Nelson had to have them cut down the year before. It gave a better view of the four Queen Anne houses on the west side, and of the water of Longships Bay seen between them, but to Nelson it made the Green look like a boxing ring, the elm stumps a series of squat posts around it.

The old man clutched the pole with one hand, and waved the other. It was hard to see whether he was supporting the pole or the pole was supporting him.

'Has he had a few?' the First Selectman asked.

'No. He don't drink much. Not for a couple of years. Getting old. Like the rest of us.' The police chief rubbed a gloved hand over his heavy, dark chin.

A third man joined them. This man was big, blond, rugged, about forty, All-American. His big hand pounded the First Selectman on the back, then the police chief. 'Hi, Nelson! Hi, Frank!'

'Hi, Elliott.'

'What's on the crazy Greek's mind now?'

The First Selectman said, 'George Zanakis? He's not crazy. Just Greek . . . Well, what did you find out?'

The big man's voice dropped, though the genial, open expression on his face did not alter. 'The story is, Local 28 of the F.M.C. are going to send some organizers down tomorrow,' he said.

'What's F.M.C.?' the chief asked.

'Furniture Makers and Carpenters – it's a small union. I don't think they'll give us much trouble.'

The chief puffed out his cheeks. 'I heard it was going to be the Teamsters. Boy, that's a relief!'

The First Selectman smiled. 'These fellows are nearer our size, I reckon. I talked to Jim and Walter already, Frank. You just be there and invite 'em out of town, same as we did last year with the bunch who wanted to organize the laundry. Speak

15

soft, don't hurt anyone, just invite 'em to get going, and not come back.'

The big blond man beat his gloved hands together, grinning. 'If you want any help, Frank, I'll be glad to put on a badge, and shove a nightstick in my belt.'

'We can do it, but thanks anyway, Mr King,' the chief said. 'Just so long as it ain't the Teamsters.'

Three miles away Mrs Elaine Handforth sat at her escritoire in Monomoy House with pen in hand. She had iron-grey hair and a long neck. Her skirt reached half down her calf and she wore a cameo brooch at her throat, and pince-nez. She looked out of the window beside her, south across the wide mouth of the bay. Over there she could see the scattered houses, eight in all, of West Village. Smoke curled from a few chimneys, but there were no other signs of activity. Farther left – east, as she looked – she saw the low dark roof of the Charter House. That roof needed repairing, and she'd told the Selectman about it twice now, and still they hadn't put it on the agenda for Town Meeting. Perhaps they were hinting, in their stubborn Yankee peasant way, that she ought to pay for it out of her own pocket, as the house had been her family's gift to the town. She nodded her head. Very likely. She would have to deal with that later. First . . .

She dipped the pen in the inkwell and wrote confidently – *Dear Miss Garland . . .*

A blue jay swooped on the bird feeder and a dozen tits, sparrows, and chickadees scattered in alarm. Elaine Handforth frowned slightly. Really, the jays ought not to be so aggressive. But there was food for all, the little ones would just have to wait.

It was a pleasure to talk to you after the lecture last week. I shall certainly speak to the Selectmen about your idea for starting winter concerts in Monomoy.

The girl's mother was one of the Boston Shotwells. The father – a collateral of the New York Garlands. Probably a grandson of Cornelius Garland, the one who spent his share of the Garland money on a British actress. No money anywhere now, of course, but that didn't alter the blood. Good blood, both sides.

As you know, in winter, I usually spend Sunday mornings feeding the birds in one of the more inaccessible parts of the peninsula. She glanced at the calendar. *This Sunday, I propose*

16

to walk along the trace of the old railroad bed. I will be so pleased if you care to accompany me, and afterwards return here for luncheon.

At that time, perhaps, she might arrange another meeting for two weeks later. Better not try to plan too far ahead. Robert would not be down until April and it was essential to have a good look at the young woman. Blood was vital, but upbringing had some importance. She seemed civilized enough, but in two or three short meetings one could not tell. Perhaps she took herself too seriously. That might well be, since she'd managed to get herself suspended from teaching. Perhaps she was becoming something of an old spinster, at – what? Thirty? Thirty-one?

The blue jay swooped again, light blue against the iron sea and the white patches of snow on South Point. She raised her pen and pointed it. 'Naughty rascal!'

She signed her name – Elaine Le Fevrier Handforth. She blotted the ink, folded the paper carefully, found a matching cream envelope and began to address it – Miss Lynn Garland, 31 Nickerson Street, Monomoy. As it was Friday already, the letter should be delivered by hand. She pressed a bell beside the escritoire.

Rising, she walked to the east side of the big room. There was another bird feeder on the sloping lawn outside these windows, and many more small birds round it – mostly juncos here, she noted. The view stretched east across Longships Bay, over the sand-and-hummock waste of Sachem Island, to the town. Monomoy was a huddle of white and red and dark grey in the winter light, two-dimensional, a town painted on the dun wall of the Great Dune.

Behind her, the door opened. Without turning, she said, 'Arthur, there's a letter on the escritoire. For delivery by hand, please.'

'Yes, Mrs Handforth.'

A little later the door closed quietly again.

Chief Boatswain's Mate John Remington, sitting in the living-room of his own house, glanced at the clock on the mantel. Five o'clock. About time he left for the Pryors'. He got up, thinking, I ought to be feeling happy to get out of this empty house; but I'm not. I like it here, even though I'm alone. I get lonely, sure, but not here. In crowds you can get lonelier than anywhere, when you suddenly realize there isn't a single guy there thinking the same way you are.

17

He picked up the telephone, and dialled quickly. 'Remington here. Anything on that storm?'

The dutyman answered, 'I've got something here, Chief. Timed 1510. Want me to read it out to you?'

'Go ahead.'

He listened carefully. The two storm areas continued to move slowly forward. If they went on the way they were going, they'd meet off the Carolinas in a couple of days' time.

'Right. Thanks.' He hung up, frowning.

Ten minutes later he pressed the chime bell beside the Pryors' front door. He waited a long time, then heard scurrying feet, and the door jerked open.

'Oh, I do apologize, John, I wasn't ready . . . there's always so much, somehow, and . . . Betty never hears a thing . . . come in . . . or doesn't want to. Nelson's in the shower.'

John shut the door carefully behind him. Mary Pryor was a faded blonde, pretty, plump, disorganized. 'We'll be eating as soon as Nelson comes down,' she said, 'after a highball, that is. He couldn't live without that. Do you want one now?'

John shook his head, smiling. As always, Mary looked as though she had not seen a hairdresser for a long time. She wandered round the room, emptying an ashtray here, twitching a curtain, picking up a newspaper and stuffing it under the coffee table, talking to him over her shoulder. 'I tried to get a girl for you, but really, at this time of year . . . Not that I like the summer people, most of them.'

'I'm just as happy,' he said. 'Happier.'

She sat down on the edge of a chair by the fire. The anxious blue eyes, older than the face, swung to his. For the first time she looked full at him. 'It's been some time now, hasn't it?'

'Two years,' he said. 'But I'm not in the market, Mary. If I meet someone . . . I'll be damned careful,' he finished, biting off the words.

Nelson Pryor, First Selectman of Monomoy, came into the room. 'Hi, John . . . Mary didn't give you a drink yet? Darn it, honey, how often . . . Well, I'm going to have one.'

Nelson's hair was thin and brown, grey streaked. Without his overcoat his small storklike stoop was more obvious. He poured himself three ounces of rye, dropped a lump of ice into the glass and drank quickly, jerking his head back decisively.

'That's better,' he said. He poured another shot and sat down.

'Nelson – ' his wife's voice was almost a wail – 'dinner's nearly ready. I only have to take it out of the oven . . .'

18

'With you, that means twenty minutes, hon,' he said, smiling. He had a good mouth, wide and humorous, and soft brown eyes behind the glasses. 'So you'd better start now, if we're going to get to Town Meeting in time.'

'I won't be coming tonight,' she said. 'I'm sorry, Nelson, I meant to, but then things piled up, and now . . .'

'O.K., O.K.,' he said, waving his glass irritably. 'Give us a call when dinner's ready.' She went out of the room.

'Always the same,' Nelson said. 'Sewing drapes, scrubbing the sink or the oven, addressing envelopes for the PTA, some damned crap. You marry a woman you can live with, drink with, talk to . . . I'm not a college man any more than you are, but I read, and there are things going on I'd like to talk about, here, in the evenings, but hell, after a few years it's not a woman you've married, it's a walking subcommittee, a domestic machine in skirts . . . You coming to Town Meeting tonight? We got most of it done last week.'

'I was there,' John said. 'As I remember, we cleared Article 60.'

'Well, we got a few odds and ends to tidy up and then we'll get to Article 74, the future of the Handforth Tract. That could take hours, but we don't want a vote. We're just going to bring it into the open, then postpone it for a special Town Meeting, all to itself, in a couple of months.'

'How's it going to go?' John asked.

Nelson Pryor looked up with a sudden sharp turn of the head. John thought, Boy, you had to remember all the time, when you were talking to a politician, that there was no such thing as an innocent question. Everything was loaded, or greased, or both.

Nelson Pryor said, 'Well, I can tell you, Elliott King's all out to have the town get the land back, so he can build houses and maybe a few factories on it, and what Elliott King wants badly enough, he usually gets. Not always, but usually. This time, you got to remember there are several million bucks to be made and split up – carpenters, plumbers, hardware dealers, stores, gas stations, banks – everyone'll make some. But it isn't only the money. Elliott *believes* in development. Parks are for the birds. That's his joke, not mine. He's not a bird, he's a man . . . On the other side, well, right at the moment it looks like a few do-gooders, organized by that schoolteacher, Lynn Garland. But it won't be as easy as that. There are plenty in this town would like to keep it from changing, for one reason or another, even

19

if they'd make more money by the change. We grew up here, you see.'

'Then you're for the park?'

'I didn't say that! I'm First Selectman – that's all.'

Mary Pryor's high, anxious call rang through the house. 'Billy! Betty! Dinner's almost ready.'

John said, 'Remember that March nor'easter?'

'Three years ago? Sure.'

'Well, the same sort of weather pattern's forming now, off Florida and in the Mississippi Valley.'

'Does it worry you?'

'Yes. I think I'll skip the rest of my liberty, and get back to the station tomorrow.'

'Out of that house and back with the boys?'

'It isn't that, Nelson . . . I think the town should do what it can to get ready. If the storm is as bad as the last one, maybe you might even put the Civil Defence in charge of the precautions. Of course, we can't be sure . . .'

Nelson Pryor interrupted with a touch of impatience. 'Sam Budden took off yesterday for a fishing vacation in Key West, as if he did anything else much here. We can't bring him back. Anything we do would cost money.'

'It could be money well spent,' John said.

'Just you wait,' Nelson said with sudden bitterness, 'just you wait. Get a little older, and you'll see that people would rather put their eyes out than *see* something that's going to cost them money.'

'Nelson! Dinner's ready. Betty! Billy!'

A male voice answered from upstairs. 'Coming, Mom'; and a girl's, 'All *right*!'

Nelson got up slowly. He jerked his head upward. 'Boning up on his English. All hours of the day he does it – in any light, in no light. So next time he'll pass the English, in spite of Miss Garland, and then the Coast Guard Academy will fail him for bad eyesight.'

They went into the small dining-room and Bill Pryor, the First Selectman's only son, was there, a tall boy, holding back, his mother's chair. Betty Pryor, a plump girl with a marked resemblance to her mother, and, at the moment, the same harassed frown, slipped into her place and the meal began.

The High School auditorium was filling up fast as John Remington took a seat. Jim Carpenter, the Third Selectman, was already on the platform, together with the Selectman's assistant and the town clerk. Walter Crampton and Nelson Pryor were walking up the aisle together, nodding to friends.

A woman sidled in next to John and smiled briefly at him, 'Good evening, Mr Remington.' She was fortyish, short, plump, with reddish hair.

'Good evening,' he mumbled. Now who in hell . . . ?

'Mrs Quimby,' she said, 'Charlotte Quimby – Mr Morgan's secretary. He'll be along soon, but he had some sort of engine trouble. He phoned from Hyannis . . . So I'll take notes till he gets here. I'll just put my coat and gloves on this chair, and save it for him.'

John nodded vaguely. Harold Morgan was a contractor and builder. This Mrs Quimby he now remembered meeting a couple of times. She came here once as a summer visitor, returned to stay, got a job . . .

A hand fell powerfully on his back and a full male voice said, 'Hi, Chief. Good to see you taking an interest in our little local affairs.'

John stood up. It was Elliott King, punching him in the chest now. Behind, in the aisle, Mrs King waited – sallow, brown-eyed, thin, her wide mouth turned down at the corners.

John said dryly, 'I'm a property owner here, remember.'

Elliott said, 'Heck, yes! I always think of you as the Chief, in uniform. Well, be seeing you.' He waved his hand and moved on. His wife ducked her head and followed him down the aisle. John wondered what a big, good-looking fellow like King could ever have seen in her.

A tall woman with iron-grey hair, pince-nez and an un-fashionably long skirt swept slowly down the aisle. Her lips were fixed in a half smile and she nodded to right and left as she came. The murmur was almost continuous – 'Good evening, Mrs Handforth . . . Good evening, Mrs Handforth . . . Hand-forth, Handforth . . . '

Two or three times she stopped and said a few words, then nodded, smiled, moved on. John grinned to himself. Feudalism was dead in these United States, so they said. The news hadn't reached Elaine Handforth. There seemed to be plenty of people eager to play the game with her. As she reached the foot of the platform everyone on it stood up. The three Selectmen came forward to the edge, and reaching her hand up, she shook their hands one by one. The Selectmen returned to their seats, and sat down. Mrs Handforth walked back several rows. Someone moved over a seat to give her a place on the aisle. She smiled pleasantly, and sat down.

Martin Fox, town counsel and moderator, walked slowly down the aisle and on to the dais. The hum of voices began to die away. Fox lowered his heavy body into the centre chair and turned to mutter a few words to Nelson Pryor on his right. The voices died lower. Fox took the gavel in hand. Every seat in the auditorium was occupied and men stood two and three deep along the walls. In close silence Fox banged the gavel three times.

'Before Town Meeting reopens,' he said, 'the chairman of the School Committee has asked me to let him make a statement . . . Mr King.'

Elliott King's broad back rose from a front row seat and moved forward. He leaped easily to the platform, and turned, his arms out in the gesture of a champion. 'Folks, you all know we've had a little trouble in the school. Some of the kids thought their teacher was being too rough on them, making the examinations too hard, and why, they decided to make just like grown people, and go on strike and everything.' He paused, smiling confidently. A low laugh spread through the audience. Elliott raised his right hand – 'In the Marine Corps, when we had trouble, someone would say . . . well, I can't tell you what they'd say, but everyone would get the hell back on the job, but fast. This isn't the Marine Corps, this is home. We got good kids, and good teachers, and don't let anyone tell you different . . . We want to tell you this thing looks like a personality problem. Nothing to be ashamed of. I guess we all got personality problems, like when I see a pretty girl, and Dorothy sees her too and, next thing you know, I'm getting a plate broke right over my head.'

There was laughter, and pleased feminine giggles. Charlotte Quimby dug her pencil point sharply into her note pad and muttered, 'Ham!'

Elliott King continued, 'You all know we've suspended one teacher and a couple of kids, temporarily. That's to lower the temperature all round. And that's why I'm on my hind legs now, asking you folks to keep calm, don't crowd in on us – give us a chance to get this thing settled. That's all. Thank you, Martin.'

He jumped down from the platform amid general applause. He returned to his place, smiling affectionately at his wife before he sat down beside her. The gavel banged and the Moderator said, 'Town Meeting will continue. Article 61.'

Flo Monsey, town clerk, was on her feet, reading the Article: 'To see if the Town will vote to raise and appropriate a sufficient, sum of money to construct, grade, harden, fill, and surface the entrances, exit, and a portion of the land off Fifth and North Commerce Streets purchased by the town from George Wellborn on October 14, 1961, for a parking area.'

The Surveyor of Highways, George Lathrop, explained the expenses. No questions. Vote taken. Affirmation.

Article 62: 'To see if . . .' Something about changing a street name. *Article 63* – purchase of a typewriter for the Assessor's Office. *Article 64* – an adding machine, for the Accounting Department. *Article 65:* 'To see if the Town will raise·and appropriate the sum of $10,000 to pay for a study and survey for a Town sewage plant, the same being necessary to protect the clam beds from further pollution.'

John Remington eased himself into a more comfortable position. This was where the infighting began. The Third Selectman, Jim Carpenter, was on his feet. Carpenter was plump and smooth, and wore big horn-rimmed glasses. His upper lip was long and his ears big; he was about thirty-five.

He began to speak, with a lawyer's precision, slowly. 'The clam beds referred to are the ones along the north side of Longships Bay. They have been deteriorating in quality and the number of clams has been falling off, too. We had a full investigation made last year, as you know, and the report was that the shellfish were being affected by sewage seeping into the bay from the town. I think I'm right in saying that no town on the Cape, except Hyannis, has a sewage plant, because it isn't necessary. The whole Cape, including Monomoy, is sand, and cesspools do the job. But Monomoy has been growing fast, these past few years, and will grow more. The report suggested that there isn't enough room between the ocean and the bay here for all the sewage the soil now has to take care of, so there is seepage, and that is what is affecting the shellfish. The Board of Selectmen recommend this preliminary action be taken, and the Article passed in the form it has been put to you.'

He sat down, carefully rearranging his papers. Already a tall thin man was on his feet, 'How much is this sewage plant going to put on the taxes?'

Jim Carpenter answered from his seat, glancing now and then at a paper spread on the table. 'The survey will cost less than one dollar per thousand of assessed valuation. We don't know what the plant will cost till the survey's been completed.'

'A million dollars, likely,' a voice called from the hall.

Carpenter said, 'It would be unwise to guess.'

A big, bald-headed old man rose. 'How does anyone *know* the clams are going to get better if we do spend the money? Seems I heard that oysters went from the Jersey shore and it wasn't proved it was pollution. They just went. Suppose we spend a million, a million and a half dollars and then don't have anything?'

John controlled an impulse to leap to his feet with an answer. He was a householder, but he was also a member of the U.S. Coast Guard, on active duty in this place . . . But, they were so petty! No one starved in Monomoy, or came near it. Plenty of people, even in the poorer sections, had two automobiles. Everyone had a television set. Yet here they were, backing and filling, looking for any excuse not to do something that ought to have been done ten years ago. At that time, it would hardly have cost three hundred thousand.

The discussion continued. After fifteen minutes, as though at a signal, a woman suddenly rose and moved that the matter be shelved for another year. Her motion was passed by a three-to-one majority. Charlotte Quimby sniffed loudly. John lit a cigarette in disgust. The trouble with civilians was not that they made the wrong decisions – it was that they refused, if they could manage it, to make *any* decisions.

The Moderator called, 'Article 66.' Flo Monsey read aloud. It was a proposal to raise the bounty on horseshoe crabs from 2 cents to 4 cents a tail. When she had finished reading, Walter Crampton, the Second Selectman, stood up. The overhead lights could not reach into the deep caverns of his eye sockets, so that his eyes seemed unfocused, peering out into the depths of space rather than at the audience.

'Last year, at 2 cents a tail,' he said, 'we paid out for 7,940. That's $158.80. The horseshoes did a lot of damage all over. We want to double the bounty. We'll get more than double the horseshoes. Probably have to pay out a thousand dollars. It'll be worth it.' He sat down.

A fisherman was on his feet. 'So move,' he drawled. Someone shouted a second.

'Wait, wait! I will be heard!'

The voices rose along the right-hand wall, near the rear of the hall. 'George, what in hell have you got in that . . . ?' 'It's *you* that's been stinking the joint out!' 'Hey, Zanakis, you collecting skunks?'

The Moderator banged his gavel, the disturbance continued. Half the people in the hall were standing, turning. George Zanakis struggled forward along the wall, a sack over his shoulder. His grey hair stood up in a halo and his moustache drooped. He had large, white false teeth, not well fitting, that snapped with a life of their own as he pushed forward through the grinning, lumber-jacketed men along the wall. The Moderator's gavel banged loudly. 'Be seated, everyone, please. Mr Zanakis, can't you make your point from where you are? You'll be heard, don't worry about that.'

The old man scrambled up on to the platform. 'People have to see, too, Martin,' he said in a loud voice. 'I won't be long.'

George Zanakis emptied the sack carefully on to the Selectmen's table. Four horseshoe crabs slid out. Jim Carpenter held a handkerchief to his nose.

Zanakis took the biggest crab by its spike tail and stepped to the edge of the platform. His eyes, smarting and blinking under the lights, searched all round the audience. There was quiet.

'I'm an artist,' he said. 'I know about today, but there is also tomorrow, and yesterday . . . Look at this. We call it a horseshoe crab because we have to give everything a name. All right, it's a horseshoe crab. It is, too, a creation of God, a part of God. It hasn't changed in ten million years. Ten million years ago, you know what we were? Microbes, tadpoles, swimming around in the sea with no brain, no sense, no thought, nothing. At that same time the horseshoe crab was swimming around, like this. He was here first, see. Now, because we want to make more money, to buy more television sets, more automobiles, you want to condemn him to death . . .'

'He's takin' food out of my kids' mouths!' a man's voice called out roughly. A murmur of agreement filled the hall.

George Zanakis waved the horseshoe crab to and fro. 'But what right does anyone have to condemn to death a living thing? Not just death – extermination, of a whole species?'

The horseshoe crab sank as his arm sank. The round, armour-plated nose scraped gently on the floor. He stood there a long time, staring at the people. 'I see,' he said softly, 'I see, your minds are already made up. What gets in our way – kill it. Go ahead, then. Kill! But we will pay. We are on trial.'

'By the horseshoes?' a voice called. 'Don't worry, George. We'll appeal to the Supreme Court!'

George Zanakis put the dead crabs back into the sack and left the platform.

The Moderator put the Article to the vote. John watched the old artist all the way back along the wall, into the crowd at the door, and out. Vote – affirmative.

The Moderator's voice cut in on his thoughts. 'Article 67.' Flo Monsey read a long article to do with increasing the size of the police force and, of course, raising the money to do so. Nelson Pryor called on the police chief to explain the proposal.

Frank Damato was portly, forty-fivish, dark-jowled, with wide dark eyes. The lights quivered on his full, fleshy lower lip.

'Fellow citizens,' he began. He cleared his throat and spread his hands. His voice rose a half octave. 'It's like this. We got three beaches to patrol from May 15 to September 15. Ocean Beach on the ocean side, North Beach on the bay, and Town Pond, where now we got rafts to keep an eye on.' He pulled out a big handkerchief and wiped shiny sweat from his face. 'It's the summer people, especially the college kids, that make the trouble. Them, and the beatniks. The beatniks only go to two places, Provincetown and here . . . Beer cans, whisky bottles, all hours of the night. It isn't only the beaches, either. The roads, too, and some of the lanes that are dead ends. Look at Beacon Road, why, any summer night there's liable to be two dozen automobiles parked along there, clear down to the Beacon.'

'Some even in winter,' Charlotte Quimby muttered. John caught her eye and she whispered, 'It's natural. You're only young once. What do they expect?'

Decent behaviour, John thought, that's what people had a right to expect.

'And speeding,' Damato went on; 'the kids drag down West Village Road . . . We just need more police. We need one more patrol car and four more patrolmen, permanent, starting May 15.'

Nelson Pryor stood up beside the police chief. 'The Selectmen strongly urge passage of the Article. It will add $1.22 per thousand to the tax – based on the present assessed value of the town.'

The Moderator recognized Mrs Handforth.

The angular figure rose slowly. She addressed the Selectmen in a clear voice that could be heard for its decided quality, though she spoke low. 'I agree with the proposal,' she said. 'Monomoy has a reputation to uphold. If we do not wish to become another Hyannis, we must discourage that type of behaviour.' She sat down.

The Moderator said, 'Thank you, Mrs Handforth. Is there any . . . ? Miss Garland.'

The schoolteacher's voice, easily recognizable by its 'foreign' accent, rose from somewhere behind him and John did not turn round.

'It isn't the business of the police to spy on people's private lives,' she said. 'We have traffic laws, and laws against robbery, and we have enough police to supervise them. There's no law that says a boy can't sit in his car on Beacon Road, or drink beer on Ocean Beach at three o'clock in the morning. If we try to stop that, of course we'll want more police. And new laws, too.'

John Remington frowned down at his hands. Damato was only trying to do his job. Of course police were needed to see that the beaches weren't used as . . . as combination taverns and cat houses. The way some of the summer people behaved was a damned scandal, and the richer the worse.

Two women spoke in favour of the proposal, mentioning the protection of their children from moral contamination. A man asked for the tax figures to be explained. Vote was taken; the Article passed. Chief Damato passed down the aisle, mopping his brow.

Article 68 . . . 69 . . . 70 . . .

Article 74: 'To see if the Town will vote to send a resolution to the President of the United States, requesting him to transfer the piece of land known as the Handforth Tract from the Department of the Defence to the Department of the Interior, to be set aside as a National Park, Sea Shore and Wildlife Refuge.'

Nelson Pryor rose and pushed his glasses farther down his nose. 'Well, as I guess most of you know, we're not going to vote on this article today. We're going to ask the people to postpone decision to the special Town Meeting, which has already been announced for April 10. All we want now is to make a few things clear. First, when we vote on April 10, it's probably going to settle it, one way or the other. Both the U.S. senators from Massachusetts have told me that no one in Washington's aiming to go against our vote, whatever it is. So, we've got to vote carefully. We've got to know the issues. People are already forming groups for and against the park, and that's fine. There'll be a hearing by the Department of the Interior, probably a week before our special Town Meeting. Jim, do you want to unroll that map?'

The Third Selectman got up and jerked at a string. A large hand-coloured map of Monomoy unrolled on the back wall. A chevron-shaped red line cut through the narrow isthmus a little south of the town. Nelson Pryor stooped beside the map, pointing – 'This red line is the northern boundary of the Defence Department land . . . and that's the same, give or take a few acres, as the old Handforth Tract. Before 1940 about three quarters of it belonged to the Handforth family, the rest to other private citizens. In 1940 the Department of the Army took it, paying compensation, and built the emergency airfield' – his long finger pointed – 'and a few huts, which have since fallen down. Last year the Department of Defence decided they had no further use for the land. Its disposal is for the President and Congress to decide. It can be sold by auction. It can be bought by the town. Or it can be handed over to another branch of the federal government. Which is it to be? That's what we shall be deciding on April 10 . . . Right now I'm going to ask a few prominent citizens to say what they think about this matter. That'll give us all some ideas . . . Mrs Handforth.'

Mrs Handforth said, 'I have several questions. What will happen to West Village – if the park comes into being?'

Nelson Pryor said, 'I'm told it will have to be abandoned, and the people moved out. That's seven families . . .'

'Six, Nelson,' a voice called from the body of the hall. 'The Travers moved to Orleans last month.' Nelson Pryor nodded acknowledgement.

Mrs Handforth said, 'Thank you. And the Charter House?'

Pryor looked at the map, but did not point. Everyone in this audience knew where and what the Charter House was – a small house, the oldest on Monomoy, standing on the shore halfway along the southern edge of Longships Bay. In it, set under glass, the town preserved the Monomoy Charter. Pryor said, 'Charter House can be moved, Mrs Handforth . . . Jim Carpenter thought we might set it up in the middle of the Green. We can find a good place, for sure.'

'Thank you. And Beacon Road?'

Nelson said, 'Beacon Road will be closed to the public. I suppose there'd have to be a gate, because the road itself has to be kept up for the Coast Guard. That's right, isn't it?' He looked vaguely toward Chief Remington.

John rose to his feet. 'That's right,' he said. 'We have to be able to get vehicles to the Diadem Cape beacon.'

Elaine Handforth said, 'Thank you.' Still standing, she took off her pince-nez, put them carefully into a case, closed the case, picked up her handbag from the seat, opened it, slipped the case inside, pulled out a handkerchief, and blew her nose. The people waited in silence. Elaine Handforth replaced the handkerchief in the bag, closed it, put the bag on the chair and faced the Selectmen.

'The southern part of Monomoy is one of the most important and famous shorebird areas in the United States. There is some nesting, but not a great deal. It is a place of refuge for thousands, sometimes millions, of birds during the spring and fall migrations . . . It has always been a place of salt marsh, fresh-water marsh, bent grass, without houses. This town, and the rest of Monomoy, would change out of all recognition if that land were to be developed and covered with houses. The change would not be for the better. We do not want any more people here. There are enough already. In summer, there are too many . . . Unless new facts become known in the next few weeks, my son and I – we have discussed this – would like to see the Handforth Tract become a park and wildlife sanctuary.' She sat down.

Nelson Pryor said, 'Thank you, Mrs Handforth . . . Elliott King.'

Elliott King stood, half turning toward Mrs Handforth. 'Ma'am,' he said, 'I'm sure you won't take it amiss if I disagree with you . . . I'm a contractor, a builder. Me and Harold Morgan, we're the only contractors here, you all know that. If that land, the Handforth Tract, comes open for development, it stands to reason Harold and I are going to build a lot of houses, and make a lot of money . . . until Uncle Sam gets after us.' He laughed infectiously. Most of the audience laughed with him.

Elliott King became serious. He spread his hands. 'I love birds,' he said, 'but I love kids more. People . . . sure, there are bad ones, the type we don't want in Monomoy, but there are good ones too. Young people, just married, looking for a home, a place to raise a family the American way, the New England way. The whole population's growing, and people have to live somewhere. We can't say, go camp in the woods, stop getting married, stop being born . . . And Monomoy. You know me, I'm a stranger, I'm from Boston. I've only been here sixteen years. Monomoy's a wonderful little town. But why can't it be a wonderful *big* town? Sure, I'll make money, but so will everyone else – more people to buy food, furniture, electricity, gasoline. More automobiles. Why, we'd have to raise the Selectmen's salaries, buy Frank Damato a bigger gold hat, double the police force . . . and all this with *lower* taxes. I'm going to be happy to accept whatever the people of the town – *my* town – decide . . . but, gee, I don't know who *can* stop this town growing. I don't know whether it's right to try . . . that's our land, that's part of Monomoy . . . I say, let's all look to the future . . .'

He sat down. A sprinkling of applause grew to a heavy roll of clapping. John shifted his weight in his seat and glanced at the clock. Twenty past ten . . . Nelson Pryor said, 'Father Bradford.'

Father William Bradford was thin and tall. He was about thirty-five, but nearly bald. He said, 'I want to make clear to everyone, Catholics and non-Catholics alike, that this is not an ecclesiastical decision. The Church is not taking sides. I am giving my own thoughts . . .' He paused briefly, and John thought, Close your eyes, and you could be listening to J.F.K. Not surprising, when you realized that Bradford was Exeter and Harvard; but surprising, all the same, coming from a Roman Catholic priest.

Father Bradford continued, 'I am as interested as anyone in the fate of the birds. But people are made in God's image, birds are not. Supposing that there is a need for homes on Monomoy, I would have a hard struggle with my conscience if I were to prevent them being built for the sake of birds. Surely it is better for children to be born and grow up here, in this lovely place, than in the slums of big cities?'

He sat down to respectful applause. 'Reverend Day,' Nelson said.

The Reverend Arthur Day was shorter than the priest, and considerably older, and had a wrinkled bloodhound face. His clerical collar was too large for his thin neck. His soft, harassed brown eyes wandered over the hall as he spoke – 'I do not speak for our Church, either,' he said. 'The Congregational Church of Monomoy. It's me, myself, I'm speaking for . . . Except, I don't think there's anything in the Bible to prevent people making parks if they want to . . . I mean, the Bible can be made to say anything you want to make it say . . . people who have all these children without thinking where they're going to live, without a sense of responsibility, so that they become a burden on the state, the taxpayer, I mean, *other* taxpayers . . . I don't see why we should spoil what we have built and looked after, for their sake . . . No one has to live in slums. There are many places they can go. They don't have to come to Monomoy . . . I agree with Mrs Handforth. Monomoy's big enough. We have enough sin as it is, without doubling the number of sinners . . .' He laughed uncertainly, to show that he had make a joke. Some of the audience laughed, with equal uncertainty. He sat down.

Nelson Pryor glanced at the sheet of paper in front of him, and called – 'The chairman of the Monomoy Park Association.' John turned round to see who that might be. Lynn Garland rose to her feet. She liked sticking her neck out, John thought. Or maybe just liked the sound of her own voice.

Lynn Garland said, 'This question should be settled by our votes, as Mr Pryor says. But it is already being influenced by money. The money of those who want to build. They will spend money – they *are* spending money – to persuade, bully, bribe . . .'

The Moderator banged his gavel and said flatly, 'Withdraw that word, Miss Garland.'

The woman hesitated, then said, 'I withdraw it. I should have said – to attempt to influence by *any* means. The Monomoy Park Association needs money to show the other side of the picture . . . to show what will happen to the water table if the southern half of the peninsula is thrown open to developers. To show how the sewage will have to be treated then, and what it will cost. It will be much more than a million dollars. To show what new schools will have to be built, and how they will have to be paid for. To show the new roads, the widened roads, the extra police, the extra judges. To show what will happen to Monomoy Town – the traffic to the southern part would have to come through the centre of town. Houses will be torn down, lawns bulldozed, trees destroyed . . . Of course everyone will make money. It's that money we must sacrifice for the sake of air, light, and peace. What will the future be like if we go on the way we're going? Take Antarctica – We can make it a world park, or we can go in there and build and dig. Then to the moon, the same way. It doesn't stop anywhere – but it begins here.'

She sat down. The applause was thin and scattered. John stirred uneasily. Charlotte Quimby looked at John, began to say something, changed her mind, and instead pulled another pencil out of her pocketbook and eyed the point with professional interest.

John thought, She's a nut; but when you think carefully over what she says, you agree with it. The important thing was, she wasn't trying to make a fast buck. 'Duty' wasn't the word for what she meant, but it wasn't 'what's-in-it-for-me' either. But he'd heard fellows say that this park stuff was just a front, that what people like Lynn Garland really wanted was to keep the U.S.A.'s population and strength down, so that it would fall behind Russia.

Nelson Pryor glanced to his left along the table, and Walter Crampton stood up. 'It ain't usual for Selectmen to talk much in Town Meeting,' he said, 'but I got something to say – This is a free country. A man wants to go out and buy himself a piece of land, build a house, no one has the right to stop him. There's been talk about having zoning here, and I don't hold with it. Next thing, someone will come along and tell me what shape house I got to have, what sort of boat, when I got to get my hair cut . . . Now there's this land. If anyone wants to buy it, to make a park out of it, well, let him. That's his business. But not the government. We got too much government, poking their noses into a man's business, taking everything one man's made by the sweat of his brow, for taxes, and giving it to another, who's maybe an idle good-for-nothing. The government shouldn't hold nobody up, and it shouldn't push nobody down.'

He sat down to murmurs of applause and agreement. I agree, John thought. Then, almost at once, he thought, I don't really know what he said, but I know what he meant, and that's what I agree with . . . I think.

Half a dozen more citizens made brief statements: The park proposal was an attempt to impose federal control on the state, even on the town. Monomoy needed growth, industry, commerce, tourists. Monomoy needed peace, quiet, and a place to park your car in Commerce Street around noon in summer.

At midnight the Moderator, looking tired, banged his gavel and said he thought the subject had been amply aired. A few minutes later Town Meeting ended.

Outside the stars hung sharp and cold in a silent sky, and his breath blew out in long grey puffs in front of him. John Remington walked fast down North Hill Street toward his house. The long finger of light from the lighthouse swept over his head, for a moment illuminating the top of the Great Dune. Frozen snow crackled in the gutter outside his garage door.

The night was too fine, his head too full of thought and stale air and the smell of people. He couldn't sleep yet.

He opened the garage door. Five minutes later he was heading south on South Commerce, his breath congealing on the inside of the windshield so that he had to wipe it clean with his hand. After the last house, the last lights, the road ran south through the rolling sand hills of the Handforth Tract, curving back and forth for no obvious reason. The bulk of the Great Dune followed steadily south, alongside, on his left hand.

Money, money, money. Everyone wanted more, and then more . . . his own Janet, running away for the sake of a Cadillac. Elliott King, piling it up for no particular reason. Lynn Garland, even, because she thought people had too much money, maybe meaning she didn't have enough.

On a sweeping right-hand curve the headlights picked out a car parked a hundred yards off the pavement, under the steep of the dune. For a long two seconds he looked at a head, a woman's head, staring eyes, wild hair, in the back window of the car. There was a pair of arms round her shoulders. Then she sank slowly out of sight, and his lights passed on.

That was a '56 Chevy, with fire stripes, extra exhaust, a Continental spare tyre, and a raccoon tail dangling from the antenna. Charlie Tyson's car. Who was the girl though? Wasn't Charlie going steady with Betty Pryor, Nelson's daughter? It hadn't looked like Betty, but at a time like that, you couldn't tell. Betty was seventeen and Mary had no control over her, so it might have been her.

He grimaced in distaste. O.K., sex is fine, but Charlie Tyson talked about getting to be an officer, about being the greatest seaman, the greatest driver, the greatest – period. But work for it? Study? Read, instead of screwing girls? Hell, no!

On the right the dim bay curved close, on the left the Great Dune sank quickly towards the earth, and vanished, and now the ocean hurried close on that side. The road led on, like a tight-rope walker, delicately between sea and sea, towards the steady pulsing flash of the Diadem Cape Beacon. There it ended. John parked the car at the foot of the beacon and got out. For a while he stared up at the light, counting . . . flash . . . one, two . . . nine seconds, flash, one two . . . She was all right. The glass seemed undamaged. He bent and examined the fuse and timing box at the foot of the beacon. It was locked, padlock intact, no signs of tampering.

Straight ahead, low over the ultimate point of land, the Diadem Cape bell buoy sent out a rapid red flashing. The bell clanged at long intervals, responsive to the slow heavy swell passing into Diadem Bay. On again, straight over the bell buoy, the Diadem Lightship marked the other side of the Race, and the edge of the Diadem Shoal, with a triple group flash every twenty seconds. . . Yes, she was on time.

The water looked like ice tonight, still and cold. Tide making,

33

the whole body of water gliding smoothly in from the Sound.
Least, it was smooth enough here, close to land. Out there in the
Race it would be a chaos of angled rips and cross-crests.

This was the kind of night he always imagined it was when
the frigate H.M.S. *Diadem*, 32 guns, went on to the shoal.
March 12, 1744. The shoal was marked on the chart, without a
name, then. He should have lived in those days. Things were
harder to do then, from steering a ship to building a house; the
question was always 'How?' Now there didn't seem to be a thing
that couldn't be done, and easily, too. But the question was
harder: *Whether*? . . . What kind of a crazy world it would be
if everyone thought and acted like Zanakis the old painter!
Why, then, was it Zanakis' hot eyes that stared at him now, in
the cold night under the beacon? Didn't Miss Garland mean
the same thing, when she talked about preserving light and air,
as Zanakis preserving the horseshoe crabs?

He turned quickly, got into the wagon, and headed back.
After a couple of miles his headlights shone on a man, standing in the middle of the road, waving one hand, shielding his
eyes with the other. This was the curve where he'd seen Charlie
Tyson's car on the way down, and this was Charlie Tyson.

John wound down the window and leaned out. 'What's the
trouble?'

'Chief? . . . That must have been you that passed a while
back.'

'It was.'

The young man grinned sheepishly. 'I'm sanded in. I don't
want to . . .'

'I thought you were an expert beach buggy driver. That's
what you've told me often enough.'

Charlie Tyson pouted slightly. He was a good-looking boy,
athletically built, with a flat-top cut, and bright, small blue eyes.
'I had my mind on something else,' he said, and hurried on. 'I
don't want to leave the car here, there's a couple of goons in
town who go round these roads looking for cars and stripping
them. The young lady's got to get back, or her pa will tan the
hide off her.'

'I'll take her back,' John said. 'And Harry's Amoco is usually
open till all hours. He ought to be here in half an hour or so. If
not, you'd better start walking.'

'Thanks, Chief . . . JoAnn, the Chief's going to give you a
ride home. Come on over.'

A girl appeared out of the darkness. John recognized her

now – JoAnn Griffiths, daughter of a fisherman. She was the same age as Charlie, about nineteen. She stood now in the light, short and square, her jaws moving with a steady cowlike motion as she chewed gum. She had walked out of the darkness without shame or shyness. Now her dark-blue eyes searched slowly for him, behind the bright light. 'Thanks,' she said.

She opened the door and slid in beside him. John waved curtly to Tyson, and drove off. The girl smelled of cheap perfume, chewing gum, and consummated sex. In the glow from the instrument panel he was aware that her short skirt was pulled up above her knees, showing plump thighs and the darkening texture of the nylon at the top of one stocking.

'You live on Front Street, don't you, beyond Sixth?'

'Yeah . . . Nice car you got here.'

'A '59 Plymouth station wagon? It's O.K.'

She fingered the chrome knobs in front of her, pushed in the lighter, watched until it sprang out again, and then sank back. She said, 'My dad will give me a hiding.'

'Maybe you deserve it,' John said, trying to speak lightly. What was the good of acting the heavy father to a girl who wasn't any relation, a girl you'd hardly seen before?

'Yeah,' the girl said. She chewed evenly. After a minute she said, 'Charlie won't get into trouble, will he?'

'Charlie Tyson? No, he's on liberty. But it'll cost him ten bucks to get his jalopy towed out of there at this time of night.'

'Yeah. Well, just so long as he doesn't get into trouble.'

'It looks as if you're going to, though.'

'Yeah. It don't bother me . . . Charlie don't need no more trouble. He had a fight with his girl, see, Betty Pryor. That's why I went with him.'

'Oh.'

They were in the town now. Harry's Amoco stood on the corner of Nickerson and South Commerce, and Harry was there, working on a Buick in the lighted garage. John got out and spoke to him and he glanced at his watch, but agreed to go. John drove on.

As he turned off North Commerce on to Fifth, leading toward the bay front, the girl said, 'You got troubles, too, mister?'

He started. 'Me? No. Well, I suppose so. Everyone has, don't they?'

'I guess so . . . anyway, you're nice.' She relapsed into a silence that had suddenly become warm with friendship. She did not move closer to him, or adjust her skirt, or in any way act

35

coquettishly; but he felt, on the instant, that she was a nice girl, and it was pleasant to be driving her home. He pulled up outside the house. 'Well, I hope it isn't too bad . . .'

'You and me both. Thanks for the ride.' With a wave of her hand she slid off the seat, and walked towards the row of houses on the opposite side of the street. She walked slowly, but confidently. As he turned the car the headlights swung past her and she looked toward him, the big round breasts outlined, the eyes very deep and dark, and waved her hand.

CHAPTER TWO

SATURDAY

A few minutes before ten in the morning Charlie Tyson hurried
into the station washroom and tried to clean his hands. He'd
broken a finger-nail getting the engine back into the 22-footer's
well. That was bleeding a little, and he couldn't get the grease
out from under the other nails. His stomach felt hollow, the way
it used to when he was a kid and his dad would say, *Charlie*, in
a certain tone of voice, *I want to speak to you*. Hell, he wasn't a
kid any more. Play it cool. Look the bastard in the eye and
show nothing, nothing at all. At ten o'clock he went into the
little office. Remington was standing by the window, his peaked
cap on the desk beside him. McGill was there, looking stern.
Remington said, 'Tyson, you didn't grease the trailer axles when
you were told to. Right?'

Charlie said, 'I forgot, and . . .'

'Then you lied to McGill about it. Right?'

Charlie said nothing, but stared at a point six inches above
Remington's head. Ought to be staring right at him, looking
cool, uninterested. He couldn't do it.

'Thirty days loss of liberty privileges. That's all, Jimmy. No,
you stay here, Tyson . . . Sit down.' Charlie sat down sullenly.
Remington sat on the edge of the desk. Remington said, 'Do you
remember telling me, when you came here, that you wanted to
be an officer?'

'Yes,' Charlie said grudgingly.

'And I told you you'd have to take night school if you wanted
to make the Academy?'

'Only for maths,' Charlie blurted out.

'All right, only for maths – but what have you done about it?
Nothing, right? . . . Well, I want to tell you that good grades
aren't the only thing you need to be an officer. An officer doesn't
have to be very bright—' he smiled; Charlie kept his face cold.
They weren't going to get around him that way.

'—just conscientious. You're not. You seem to think you're
going to do everything right, without practising. Be the star on
the team without doing what makes a star – practice, think,
rehearse, keep in training. I know you're young yet—'

37

Jesus Christ, if I hear that word once more, I'll . . .

'Now's the time to form the right habits . . . And while I'm on the subject, your private life is no business of mine, but you know you got that girl in trouble last night.'

Charlie said suddenly, 'Even she can't know that yet.' He could not keep back a grin.

'Don't be a smart ass, Tyson,' Remington snarled. 'Miss Griffiths said her dad would beat her, and I guess he did. That's what I mean about a sense of responsibility. It isn't only your job in the Coast Guard, it's the way you live, the way you look at life.'

Charlie made up his mind. 'Me and JoAnn's going to get married,' he said.

The Chief's hands tightened, his tanned face darkened and his blue eyes bulged. Charlie found the palms of his hands cold and damp.

'You're going to marry JoAnn Griffiths? Then how are you going to get to the Academy? They don't take married men. You know that . . . I thought you were going steady with Betty Pryor.'

'She ditched me.'

'So you're marrying JoAnn to spite her, eh?'

Charlie said nothing. Not to spite anyone, just to get out from under, to be a man away from this pile of chickenshit. Just to be a man, your own boss, do what you want to do, jive it up a bit, drink a little beer, get laid when you want to.

'You're full of crap, Tyson. And you'd better smarten up, fast! Now get out of here and grow up.'

Charlie got up and went out. Cool, he'd played it cool. They'd got nothing out of him. Before his mind's eye there suddenly appeared an officer's peaked cap, with the big gold badge of the United States Coast Guard, and the scrambled eggs of a commander. But the crap you had to swallow to get it.

In the hall he stopped in surprise. JoAnn Griffiths was sitting in one of the chairs. 'What are you doing here?' he asked.

'Come to see him.' She jerked her head at the office door. 'The other fellow, Mr McGill, told me to wait here.'

Charlie rearranged his face to be tough and cool. He said, 'Look, you don't have thank him for nothing—'

'I know.'

'I told him – about us.'

'What about us?'

'About us getting married. He nearly blew a gasket.'

'Yeah . . . Anyone else in there?'

'No. Go on in. Only, what gives?'

'Things,' she said. He watched, frowning, as she knocked perfunctorily on the door and at once opened it. Then he turned and hurried away before the Chief could see him.

The Chief was sitting at his desk when JoAnn went in, but stood up when he saw her. He looked surprised, then maybe a little pleased, too, and she felt good about that, and smiled at him. She'd seen him in the town often enough, but never *looked* at him, because he had never looked at her. He wasn't so tall, but he had a chest like a barrel on him, and curly brown hair. He was like a cowboy, or a man in a Marlboro ad, except he had no tattoo on the back of his hand.

He held out a chair for her. Then he opened the door which she'd closed, and left it open. 'What can I do for you, Miss Griffiths?' he said.

'JoAnn,' she said automatically. When people called her Miss Griffiths it gave her the creeps. She'd turn round to see who they were talking to.

'It's about my brother Dick,' she said. 'He was driving the car with your fellow last night, what was his name? The one who was drunk and fighting the fuzz in Provincetown.'

'Harrington.'

'Yeah.' She shifted the gum to the other side of her mouth and made it smack loudly. 'Dick's got a job in Hyannis. They'll take his licence away, drunken driving.'

The Chief said, 'So they should, JoAnn.'

'Yeah,' she said, 'but if Dick can't get to work, he'll lose his job. That leaves me doing a solo, unless Pop finds a job that's good enough for him.'

'What do you want me to do about it?' he asked.

'Well, I thought maybe you could talk to Mr Damato about your fellow. Mr Damato's a buddy of the chief in Provincetown. They play ball together – you know – and Mr Damato wants to keep in good with the Coast Guard, so he'll do it, for you. When you speak to him about your fellow, you mention Dick too, see, and they'll let him off, too.'

She watched the shadows move across the man's face. He was good-looking in a rough sort of way. Not like the singers, but then he was older. A lot of hair on the backs of his hands where the tattoo wasn't.

He said, 'I'm not going to speak to Chief Damato, JoAnn, I

sent Randall up to Provincetown early this morning to see that Harrington is properly treated. I'm going to see that he gets a fair hearing – and that's all. If he did get drunk and resist arrest, if he did fight the police up there, I'm not going to try to get him off.'

'It don't look good to have a Coast Guard fella thrown in jail.'

'No, but if he's guilty as charged, he will be, and he will deserve to be.'

'Deserve to,' she repeated to herself. How could a guy *deserve* anything just for getting drunk? But the man looked sad and noble when he said it. 'O.K.,' she said, and started to get up.

'Wait a minute. How did it go with your father last night – this morning?'

'Oh, I got a whoppin'. Not too much.'

'Aren't you a little big for that now?'

'Yeah. Dad can't think of anything else. It's better than Mom screaming *whore* at me all the time.'

'Charlie Tyson just told me the news about you two.'

'Charlie talks too much.'

'I wasn't supposed to know about you getting married?'

'I ain't going to marry Charlie.'

He stared at her. 'You're not? He just told me . . .'

She waved her hand. 'Yeah. He asked me, last night, right after, when you saw us. The first time. He said, "We'll get married." I didn't say anything. He doesn't want to marry me, Mr Remington, and I don't want to marry him. He wants to marry Betty Pryor.'

'But . . .'

She got up. 'Don't you worry,' she said. 'Were you ever married?'

'Yes,' he said shortly.

'What's happened?'

'She left me.'

'She musta been a jerk,' she said softly. So that was why there was the sad thing round his eyes and the lines in his forehead.

He looked at her. 'Thanks,' he said, smiling. 'Sorry I can't do anything for your brother.'

'That's O.K. I guess I oughta be sore, but I'm not.' Unwillingly she turned to go. It would be nice to stay and talk, but now he was looking impatient and upset. Some other time, maybe. She gave him a last, long smile and went out. He closed the door behind her.

40

John Remington reached his desk, sat down, and picked up a pencil. The telephone rang. 'Coast Guard, Monomoy,' he snapped.

'Remington?' John recognized the gravelly staccato of his immediate superior, Chief Boatswain Harrison F. Helm, in charge of all lifeboat stations and lighthouses on Cape Cod, and the lightships of its shores. 'Helm here. The Diadem Lightship reports three boats from Nantucket dragging in the oyster beds. A Monomoy boat went up close and they saw oars being waved and someone throw something, it looked like a spike.'

John said, 'Those beds are seeded by Monomoy, Mr Helm. They haven't done it for at least two years, though.'

'I know. Diadem reports the Monomoy boat's got radio and she's standing off, waiting. I guess you'll find some boats leaving from Monomoy right now, and Diadem says they can see two more coming over from Nantucket. You'd better get out there.'

'Aye, aye, Mr Helm.'

'Take it easy, Remington. Just keep 'em apart. Tell 'em to save it for the judge.'

John replaced the receiver and called, 'Jimmy, launch the 36-footer. I'll take her out. I want three seamen, armed.'

'O.K., Chief.' McGill's voice echoed through the station. 'Wallace, Ritchie, Tyson . . . boat job, pistols . . . Kaiser! Kaiser! Where the hell's Kaiser?'

'In Chatham, with one of the transmitters.'

'Lerroux then! . . . O.K., you go. Truck's ready, Chief.'

John called, 'Come in here a moment, Jimmy, while I tell you what's going on.'

In police headquarters, on the Green, the telephone bell jangled suddenly at his elbow and Frank Damato started nervously. 'Police,' he said.

The voice at the other end was old and anxious. 'Frank? They're here . . . Warren Mercer speaking. They're here, at the main gate.'

'How many of them?' Frank asked. His collar felt tight. Why? He wasn't afraid of any union punks.

'We can see five. There may be more. They have two cars.'

'All right, Mr Mercer. We'll be right out.'

'We don't want any trouble, Frank. Nothing in the papers, no violence . . . you know.'

'I know, Mr Mercer. Don't you worry.' He held down the

receiver, then dialled a number. 'Nelson? This is Frank. They've come – half a dozen, at the Warren Mercer Company. I'm going down now . . . O.K.'

He put down the phone and called through the open door to the dispatcher, 'Bill, that job at the Warren Mercer Company's come up. Who's nearest?'

'Palmer, out by the Yacht Club when he reported in a few minutes ago.'

'Tell him to meet me at the corner of Sixth and North Hill in five minutes. Get Crable, Mackey and both Pitts in right away.'

'O.K.'

The phone rang and he picked it up quickly, 'Police.' He listened with deepening anxiety. It never rained but it poured. Now there was going to be a fight in Diadem Bay. He interrupted when McGill, at the other end, paused – 'We can't do nothing about it, Jimmy. Our boat's laid up in the winter, you know that . . . Oh, O.K. then. Those Nantucket men have no right . . . well, yeah, leave it to the judge. Right. Right. Thanks.'

He picked up his hat, with the gold chinstrap and the Massachusetts coat of arms and the word CHIEF. He'd have two cars, and five patrolmen, not counting himself. That ought to be enough. He pulled his pistol from its holster and made sure it was loaded, with one empty chamber opposite the barrel. Trade-union men were tough cookies. Why did they have to come here, to Monomoy, where no one wanted them? Why couldn't they stay in Boston or Providence, or wherever the hell they came from? In those places unions were respectable. People liked them, people belonged to them. In Boston or Providence, he'd probably belong to a union himself, if he weren't a policeman. On the Cape, it was different. No one wanted unions. They were un-American, like socialized medicine, and . . .

The dispatcher's voice broke in. 'They're here, Chief, all but George Pitt. And he's parking now.'

They gathered in the dispatcher's office. Frank heard the stamp and shuffle of them, and that distinctive click and rattle as one of them checked his pistol. He went through to them. 'All set?' he asked gruffly.

They nodded. Crable said, 'Sure, Chief.'

'Well, this is the job I told you about yesterday. Just the same as the laundry last year. Take it easy. We'll go down in my car. Crable, you drive.'

Palmer was waiting near the factory, sitting in his patrol car.

Frank went over to him. 'We're going on foot from here. As soon as we're round the corner there, take your car to the corner, where you can see the main gates. We're leaving my car here. Keep an eye on that too.'

Palmer nodded and Frank said, 'Let's go, fellows.'

They were all wearing the heavy blue great coats with the two silver buttons in the belt at back. They were good-looking fellows, all tall and strong. Not one of them, except himself, had an Italian name, and he was the chief! God bless America, Frank Damato thought with fervent, nervous pride, striding along in the centre of them. Then they rounded the corner from Sixth into North Commerce.

His uplifted spirit sank. A crowd blocked the sidewalk – maybe twenty, thirty men gathered round the factory entrance, and a few women. *Madre mia*, why did people have to come when they were least wanted? When a cop did something good, like rescuing a child from a top window, stopping a runaway horse in the old days, you could be good and sure no one would be there to see it! When the job was tough and dirty, the kind that gave people a chance to yell bully, son of a bitch, fascist, or other names, then they'd be there.

The crowd opened up for them. Frank saw two parked cars, one behind the other, a few feet up the street. Good, that was a *No Parking* zone. Three men were standing in the open factory gateway. Beyond them was Harry Rippon, the factory guard, looking old and frightened. Three men got out of the parked cars and came slowly forward.

The men in the gateway had a big pile of pamphlets at their feet. Frank, glancing down, saw the single big word on the top line ORGANIZE . . .

He said, 'Those your cars, mister?'

The man in the centre of the three wore a collar and tie, and a snap-brim hat. He was thin, sharp, quite tall. 'Yes, officer, they are.'

'That's a *No Parking* zone,' Frank said.

'Oh dear, dear me, what a shame,' one of the other men cried in falsetto.

The crowd stirred with laughter and Frank Damato felt his neck grow red. The man with the snap brim, the leader, threw the joker an angry look. To Frank, he said, 'We'll move them right away, Chief. We're not lawbreakers,' he added with slow emphasis, 'we're American workingmen. Mac, go and get the cars off the street.'

'And I want to speak to you inside,' Frank said.

'Me? Inside where?'

Frank nodded at the factory yard. Three big trucks were backed up to a side door, being loaded with Warren Mercer Company original Cape Cod furniture. A lot of people were crowding on to the steps outside the main entrance. There were faces at every window. All were silent, watching, waiting.

'Inside the factory,' Frank said.

The man said, 'I can't go in there. I've just been thrown out on the orders of Mr Warren Mercer. Whatever you have to say, you can say here, Chief.'

'All right,' Frank said. 'Get into those cars, all of you, and leave town. Leave town, and don't come back.'

Throughout the long tense silence someone breathed hard in his ear. The five union men stood in a tight group, the leader in the centre. Behind them Frank saw the long neck and spotty face of Joe Steele. And young Stan Jenkins. And Gene Begg. *Cristo santo*, the Steele Band was here. Dirty punks, trouble-makers, drugstore cowboys . . . they were like those vultures they had in the Old Country, which his father used to tell him about, that came floating overhead as soon as there was anything dead, and sometimes before, the old women believed.

'Just a minute, Chief,' the leader said, very polite and reasonable. 'We are officials of the Furniture Makers and Carpenters Union, Local 45. What law are we breaking?'

Frank said, 'Now just get into those cars and get out of town, or I'll have to throw you in jail for causing a public disturbance.'

One of the union men said in a loud clear voice, 'Dirty, stinking bastards. How much does old Mercer pay you for this?'

The crowd murmur increased. Hard to tell how many were on each side. There were a few strong union men in Monomoy, but not many. Old man Mercer was a pretty good employer. He made them work 5½ days, but he paid well, certainly better than guys got in similar plants in Hyannis and Buzzards Bay.

None of the men moved to obey his order. Frank sighed, and eased back his shoulders. 'O.K. You're under arrest.'

He took a step forward. The crowd surged, voices rose, someone fell against him. He struggled to keep his balance. Patrolman Crable stumbled, fell, suddenly yelled out in pain. Then he jumped to his feet, scrabbling for his gun with his left hand, his right hand pouring blood. Frank had seen the boot grind into the back of Crable's hand while he was down. Whose boot? He started to look up the leg, trying to find the face that had belonged to that cruel, vicious boot . . . but oh, no, Christ, no, he couldn't. There were other things to do, to be done now, fast. 'Put that gun away, Crable,' he said, 'we don't need guns. These men are going quietly, aren't you?'

'We didn't push the cop over,' the leader said. He too had turned pale. 'It was one of those fellows.' He pointed. 'They're trying to turn this into a riot, so you can shoot us down. Are they in your pay, too?'

Frank said, 'Get going now. *Right now.*'

Crable said suddenly, 'They're going to jump us.'

The union men crouched, hands tensed. The crowd edged back. A woman screamed. The Steele Band edged forward. Jenkins, Steele, Begg, he saw. Howard over somewhere behind him and . . . and . . .

Crable had his gun out again, so had the Pitt brothers. Just one little thing would start the shooting now. Just one little thing, like Joe Steele throwing the half-brick he had in his hand, the arm drawing back . . .

'Hey, what's going on? Chief Damato? You want any help?'

Frank sighed, long and slow through pursed lips. It was Randall, the B.M.2 at the station, and one of the seamen. They were wearing winter dress blues. They carried no weapons, but they looked big because of the badge on Randall's cap, and the lettering on the battleship-grey truck – UNITED STATES COAST GUARD.

The union leader said bitterly, 'So the Coast Guard's taken up union busting . . . O.K., we'll go. We'll go now, Mr Company Cop. But we'll come back, with reporters – flashbulbs – the works! Everyone's going to know how you turn a peaceful organization meeting into a riot – with these goons.'

The union men began to pick up the pamphlets. Frank thought, I should tell them the Steele Band are no friends of ours. What in hell was the use? Who'd listen?

Randall was asking, 'What's he talking about? What was that about union busting? We're not supposed to get into anything like that.' He sounded nervous. He was a queer, unhappy guy, behind the uniform.

'Nothing,' Frank said. 'Lucky you were passing. You've come at the exact psychological moment.'

Randall said, 'We've just been to P. Town. We got a guy in jail up there for fighting the cops.'

'Anything I can do,' Frank said, taking off his cap and wiping

45

his head, 'you just ask. The Provincetown chief's a good friend of mine. You tell Remington.'

'O.K.' Randall said, 'but Remington doesn't hold with fixing things. He's a square. But from Squaresville.'

The crowd dispersed, the ordinary spectators one way, and four or five men, mostly in the high teens or early twenties, the other. Frank saw Joe Steele, Stan Jenkins, Gene Begg, Harry Howard and, and . . .

Patrolman Crable's voice grated in his ear, 'Chief, you know who tripped me up?'

'I thought it was Begg.'

'It was Begg. And you saw who stamped his boot on my hand, turned his heel round and ground it into my hand?' He held out the hand. The blood had begun to congeal in heavy streaks and blobs. Raw flesh showed in half a dozen gouges.

'That needs looking at,' Frank said quickly. 'We'll get you to Doc Aiken right away . . .'

'It was Chris,' Crable said. 'Chief, it's no good looking the other way. It was Chris, your son. This isn't the first time. The next time we catch him doing this kind of thing, any one of us, we're going to beat him to a pulp. I swear it. Do you hear what I'm saying?'

'Yes, yes,' Frank muttered. 'I hear . . . it is terrible.'

Chris was such a good boy, once. So beautiful. *Madre mia,* so beautiful. And now, *Gesù Cristo*!

Charlie Tyson flicked the wheel a half turn right, met the pressure, held, started to come back. They were coming up to Black Can 5, opposite West Village, and feeling the swell from the Sound. The old cow began to roll and heave. Three fishing boats had left town a few minutes ahead of them. The last of the three was a clear mile ahead by now, turning sharp round the Outer Mark and heading south. The other two were almost level with the 36-footer, and half a mile to westward and headed due south instead of north-west. All three boats were crowded with men. Hell, Charlie thought, there must be fifty men in those boats. The Nantucket boats would have as many. There'd be a pitched battle, and he'd be in there, with his pistol – *bam, bam*!

'Steer tighter for the buoy,' Remington snarled, 'we've got no time to waste.'

Charlie didn't answer, but inched the wheel to port. O.K., if the bastard wanted to shave the buoys, Charlie Tyson was the man to do it for him. The surge of the sea pushed the bow to starboard. He corrected with a quick, fierce twist. The blunt bow came round sluggishly, and kept coming. The buoy disappeared. There was a long clang-bang-bump.

'Jesus, Tyson,' Remington said, 'when are you going to . . . ? Well, I guess you got to learn, like the rest of us.'

Charlie glowered through the spotted windshield. Goddam floating cows, 9 knot maximum, slower than a slow wave from the Sound, always slower than the current in the Race. No radar, radio about a hundred years old, no depth meter, no proper shelter . . . He stamped his feet on the coxswain's flat.

An idea struck him. Hey, they could save two miles by cutting across the sandbank that extended north-westward, under water from South Point. That would bring them almost up to the hurrying fishing boats.

He said, 'Chief, it's half tide, why don't we cut across now, right after Red Nun 4. There ought to be a foot to spare, on the bank, and . . .'

'We'll go to the Outer Mark and turn there,' Remington snapped.

'Yes, *sir*,' Charlie muttered.

Bastard, stupid old bastard. Chickenshit bastard.

Remington said, in a voice he was trying to make gentle, 'The tide's falling, Charlie. Never take a risk on a falling tide . . . remember, until someone makes accurate soundings, no one knows what the winter storms are doing to the bank there. We might get across, sure, but this isn't a lifesaving job. You mustn't take any risk at all with a lifeboat unless you have real cause.'

Charlie Tyson didn't speak. There wasn't any place for a hep guy in this outfit. You had to be old and square, but square!

'Steer tight, against the current for Christ's sake, Charlie!'

Half an hour later they passed South Point, heading south-east now. From there John saw the gathering of boats on the oyster beds. He counted nine and whistled softly. Impossible to tell at this distance which were from Nantucket and which from Monomoy. Well, that didn't matter. He wasn't aiming to fight for Monomoy against Nantucket.

He said, 'I'll take her, Charlie. Tell the others to come aft.'

He took the wheel and spread his weight evenly on both legs, knees slightly bent. Steering a 36-footer was a lot like riding a big, clumsy horse. The other crewmen came out of the survivors' compartment forward, Wallace tucking a pack of cards into the pocket of his coat. They crowded into the draughty shelter of the low windshield.

John said, 'All we're going to try to do is keep 'em apart. You steer, Wallace. I'll go to the well deck, you watch my signals. The rest of you, come with me. You too, Leroux – unless the engine quits. Remember, don't draw your pistol unless I give the word, or unless someone's actually trying to kill you.'

Wallace, a steady sensible man, took the wheel, shifting a wad of gum from one side of his mouth to the other. John picked up the megaphone and went forward to the well deck.

36614 ran straight into the current, the wind more or less astern, riding as easy as a 36-footer ever did. Now he could tell which boats were from Nantucket and which from Monomoy. The Nantucketers had pulled up their drags, but showed no signs of turning away. The Diadem Lightship bore south-west, three miles, the bell buoy due south, a mile and a half. He pulled out his notebook and recorded the position, the time, and the weather.

As he looked up he saw all four Monomoy boats swing sharply and head for the nearest Nantucketer – one of the three that had actually been dragging. Naval tactics, he thought. They were going to cut her out and board her.

Now he was among them himself. The skipper of the Nantucket boat, *Louise*, taken by surprise and cut off from his comrades, swung towards the 36-footer for protection. John signalled a turn to port and lifted the megaphone. '*Seagull* ahoy!' he shouted, calling the name of the nearest Monomoy boat. 'You too, *May*, *Highflyer*, all of you! Get back to your own ports, do you hear me? You're just heading into trouble here.'

A man on the *Seagull* waved derisively. The captain of the *Louise* shrugged his shoulders and pointed at the four Monomoy boats now circling on the other side of the 36-footer.

John glanced back and made a tight circling motion with his hand. Behind the windshield Wallace acknowledged the order. The 36-footer began to turn in a tight circle, between the *Louise* and the Monomoy boats. At the end of one full circle, the remaining Nantucketers had swept round and joined *Louise*. Once again the two hostile flotillas were united, one on each side of the 36-footer.

John lifted the megaphone. 'Get on home before you get into trouble! You can't settle this out here, only in a proper court of law. Go on . . .'

The boat veered hard to starboard and the engine revs rose

sharply. John, looking round, saw that one of the Nantucket boats had cut astern of him and the rest were attempting to follow, and Wallace had taken the only action he could. The 36-footer answered sluggishly, as always, to the helm. While John swore violently, the Nantucketers' manoeuvre succeeded. Four of their vessels reached *Highflyer*. Men poured over the gunwales. Fists flew and heavy sea boots thumped and echoed on the decks. Charlie Tyson, hanging to the metal rail on top of the survivors' compartment with his left hand, watched with his mouth fallen open. His right hand kept sweeping to the butt of his pistol. John said sharply in his ear, 'Keep your hands off that gun, kid.'

He turned and gestured, slicing with his hand. Wallace nodded, and the nose of the 36-footer thrust remorselessly between the *Highflyer* and the rest, sheering them away from her like barnacles off a hull. The Nantucket men began to leap back from the deck of the *Highflyer* to their own boats. One man failed to get away – three men grabbed him as he tried to jump, and pulled him back into the *Highflyer*. A big hand caught him by the throat, a fist swung into his face, then another. Lerroux grappled *Highflyer's* rail with a boathook. John bellowed furiously, 'Let that man go! Do you want a murder charge?' He made ready to jump across.

The *Highflyers* let go the Nantucket man. Dazed and bleeding he stumbled over the gunwales and into the well of the 36-footer. 'Get in there, lie down, and shut up,' John snapped.

Stupid, obstinate bastards . . . During the few moments in which he had been fully involved with the *Highflyer*, a similar operation had taken place in reverse. A hundred feet astern of him, the Nantucketer *Phantom* was hemmed in and boarded by two Monomoyers, one on each side.

Thirty men pushed and shouted and struggled on *Phantom's* deck. A knife flashed and John's heart jumped . . . but it was to cut the drags free. They went overboard. But once knives were drawn, whatever the purpose, killing was likely to result.

He ran aft and grabbed the wheel from Wallace. 'Get for'ard!' he shouted. 'Hold tight.'

He swung the 36-footer and headed for the three grappled boats. At half speed, 4 knots, he crashed between the *Phantom* and the Monomoy boat on her port side. The creak and crunch of smashed wood made a new, shocking sound, that seemed very loud over the shouting, the putter of the marine diesels and the slap and sigh of the sea. All the fishermen were crying out

49

now, waving their arms at him. Tyson's running over the buoy would be nothing to what *he* was doing to the paintwork. A little harder, and he'd sink one of the fishing boats. Their skins were frail, at least compared with the reinforced structure of the lifeboat.

He headed for the *Highflyer* group. They swung hastily apart as he came through. 'Go home!' he yelled, and turned the wheel fast, heading back towards *Phantom*. The 36-footer chugged through the narrow gap between *Phantom* and a boat on her starboard side. 'Listen!' he shouted. 'You all head for your own ports in ten seconds flat, or I'm going to start ramming. And I'm going to call up a cutter to arrest every man jack on every boat out here. The *Casco's* standing by in Woods Hole. Now, get going!'

The flotillas were already pulling apart . . . slowly, not directly away from each other, but in wary half-circles, as though unprepared, yet, to show the enemy their sterns.

Seagull straightened out of a slow turn to port, and headed for South Point. *Mary*, *Highflyer*, and *Maiden VI* followed. The Nantucketers all turned together and headed for their island.

John spoke into the mike: 'Monomoy Coast Guard, this is CG 36614. Fishing boats from Nantucket and Monomoy are heading for home ports. We have a civilian casualty aboard. I don't think he's bad. I propose to take him back to Nantucket and get the names of all captains and crews involved, while I'm there. Inform Group Commander, over.'

'Roger, over.'

'Have a petty officer at the fish pier to take the names of all the Monomoy men, when they come in, also to inspect and record details of damage and injury as claimed. The boats are *Seagull, Mary, Highflyer, Maiden VI*. Got that?'

'36614 – O.K. Over.'

'Better get one of the Selectmen to be there, too. Out.'

He fumbled in his pocket and found his pipe and tobacco. Calling forward he said, 'Ritchie, come and take her. Follow the Nantucket boats, half a mile astern.'

Jim Carpenter glanced at the clock as he picked up the phone.

'Jim Carpenter,' he said. Nearly seven o'clock, and dark long since.

'This is McGill of the Coast Guard again, Mr Carpenter. Chief Remington will be landing in about ten minutes, at the New Boat House.'

50

'Thank you. I'll be right down.'

He put the papers he had been working on into the wall safe and got into his overcoat. There was one day totally wasted, what with waiting at the Coast Guard station to hear more about the fight at Diadem Bay – the 'oyster war' they were already calling it; then discussing with Crampton and Pryor what, if anything, the Selectmen should do; then waiting at the fish pier, and spending two hours with the crews when they came back. They'd been in a rage, hot against Remington and the Coast Guard as much as against the Nantucketers. Probably they were mad, really, because Remington broke up a good fight: but you didn't pick up votes by siding with the Coast Guard against your local fishermen, however stupid and quarrelsome they might be.

When he reached the pier the 36-footer was close in, and clear under the searchlight from the boathouse. The sound of her engine, muffled by the heavy air, thudded in isolation, without echo, like damped drumbeats. It came alongside, and Remington stepped off. He peered at the men on the ramp. 'You're in charge now, Randall. Go ahead.'

He turned to the Selectman quickly, his face unsmiling. 'Mr Carpenter, what can I do for you?'

Jim Carpenter found himself nervous. 'Uh, do you want to come inside somewhere, Chief? There are a few questions I have to ask, on behalf of the town. We can go into the Town Hall, or the police station . . .'

'Not now, Mr Carpenter. I must stay here till the 36-footer's hauled up. I have to take a look at her hull.' He had taken a notebook from his pocket, and now made brief notes on time of docking and weather conditions. He put the book away, stuck his hands into his pockets and stood, immobile, watching.

Jim Carpenter shifted his weight from one foot to the other. He and Remington were about the same age. Their original background wasn't too different – he from a poor Catholic home in Boston, Remington from a poor Protestant home somewhere out west. Their basic outlooks weren't too different. Through graduation from high school, their education had been similar. Why, then, did he feel that they came from different planets? But here, in the open air at the edge of the sea, he felt soft-skinned, weak-bodied, large-headed, almost repulsive. Remington smelled of salt and tar, and drops of water gleamed like pearls in the heavy wool of his jacket. Remington wrote slowly, not from lack of practice, or of skill – but from deliberation, from a sense of responsibility towards small, real things. And what did Remington feel about himself? That he was an enlisted man, a horny-handed sailor without a college education, helpless on shore, inside houses and courtrooms against the wiles of a lawyer . . . ?

The 36-footer seemed to be in position. 'O.K.,' Randall called. 'Slow now.'

The boat started slowly up the ramp on its cradle. Remington watched intently. Beyond, also silent, another man watched. Jim recognized Bill Keating, skipper and part owner of the *Seagull*. Keating had been very hot against the Coast Guard when he came in.

'Hold her!' Randall called. 'O.K.'

Remington turned. 'Hullo, Bill. So you got back safe.'

'You were rampaging about like a goddam mad bull out there,' Keating said. His voice was sharp, but without bitterness.

'Yeah,' Remington said. 'How many boats do you think would even be afloat by now, if I hadn't?'

Keating grunted. After a minute he said, 'You done about three, four hundred dollars' worth of damage.'

They weren't even looking at each other, Jim saw, but standing side by side, watching, as Randall began to inspect the 36-footer's bottom.

'That's about what you did to the Nantucketers' drags, I reckon,' Remington said.

Keating cackled loudly. 'We sure showed them sons of bitches, eh?'

Remington walked into the boathouse. Keating called after him, 'We ain't made up our minds yet, John. We're thinking of suing you and the Coast Guard . . . Don't look like the 36-footer got more'n a scrape or two.'

Remington paused at the boathouse door. 'That's about it. But no thanks to you.'

Keating cackled again. Jim Carpenter sighed with relief. Only a few hours ago he would have sworn that there'd be a dozen lawsuits against the Coast Guard and Remington. That wouldn't do anybody any good, in the long run. Besides bringing the ridiculous 'oyster war' into the headlines, it would create bitterness between the Coast Guard and the local community, which might take a generation to heal.

He followed into the boathouse. John Remington was on one knee under the hull, water dripping on to his face and coat, running his hand along the curve.

52

And why did Keating, who was full of bitter anger at three, start laughing at seven? Just because time had passed? No, because he was talking to another sailor, instead of to a lawyer.

The probing questions he had meant to ask Remington while the man was still tired; the damaging admissions he had intended to wring from him, for later use on behalf of the Monomoy fishermen . . . it all seemed petty now, petty and pointless. There would not be any lawsuits against the Coast Guard. Against the Nantucketers, maybe – but that was a different kettle of fish.

The telephone rang and a seaman answered it. Jim heard – 'Chief, Mr Helm's up at the station.'

'Tell them I'm inspecting the 36-footer,' Remington answered irritably. 'I'll come up when I'm finished.'

Jim Carpenter stepped forward. Remington, upright now, walked slowly round the stern of the boat, inspecting the stern-post and rudder. Jim said, 'I want to thank you for what you did, Chief, and . . . if there's anything I can do, any help . . .'

'Sure, sure,' Remington answered absently. He was writing in his notebook again, and Jim slipped out of the boathouse. None of the Coast Guardsmen seemed to notice him go. He felt that they had not noticed him come, either.

Jim drove slowly up Boat Street. Even after work hours, there were too many cars for the narrow, old streets to take. Monomoy was getting overcrowded. But at least you could smell the sea in any part of town, and in any street you could feel the sand underfoot, blown down from the Great Dune. Things were real in Monomoy. On the whole, people were real, too.

He waited for the traffic light at Third Street. What do you mean by a crazy remark like that? he asked himself. About the people being real here? Well, Remington and Keating were different from himself, right? They felt real, he didn't. Right? Right. But why? What made a man feel unreal to himself?

He put the car in the garage and let himself into his house. From upstairs his wife called, 'Is that you, Jim?'

'Yes, it is I,' he answered.

She came downstairs. She was wearing a black wool dress and she'd had her hair done.

'Damn it, Barbara,' he cried, 'you promised not to change your hair till I finished the painting!'

She tossed her head. 'I'm not going to go about like a gipsy

53

any longer, just because of your – It should have been done three days ago. You'll just have to get a professional model.'

He said, 'We've talked this over a hundred times. I cannot paint nudes, *and* be a Selectman. Not in Monomoy.'

She said, 'Then we must leave Monomoy. You've been talking about it ever since we came here.'

'I know,' he said, 'but, Barbara, I think it's real here.'

She stared at him. 'Real? And New York isn't? Boston isn't?'

He said, 'I don't think anyone's real till he knows who he is, what he's doing. Darling, sit down – let's . . .'

She said, 'I have to do my nails. We're late already.'

She was gone, vanishing upstairs, first the platinum head, then the well-tailored, carefully controlled body, then the legs, shining and smooth in the stockings, then the high-heeled shoes.

Jim dropped into a chair. How could he make her understand what he meant by reality? And did he really mean that? Or was it a sort of mental aberration, brought on by the atavistic romanticism of the scene at the boathouse – the lifeboat, the crew in heavy coats, the dark water, the flat Yankee accent of Keating, the cold New England winter night . . . a sense of the elements. Water. Life. Death. These things could not, in the last resort, be equated with nail polish, hair curlers, dinner invitations, or even legal decisions. Legal decisions might arise from them, but could not have an independent, real life of their own.

But art did. Barbara disapproved of art. Especially of the only form that he was any good at.

He looked at his watch. Half an hour late for the Firemen's Buffet Supper. Not to mention the Firemen's Buffet Booze. Tonight he could do with a couple of stiff ones. Right now he'd better go and talk to the kids. They'd start yelling downstairs, 'Daddy, daddy!'

John Remington ended his verbal account of the oyster war. Chief Boatswain Harrison F. Helm stared a long time at the chart on the opposite wall then he said, 'Good.'

He examined the chart. A minute later he said, 'Who were you talking to in Boston, about King and Morgan?'

John blinked at the change of subject. A couple of months ago an officer at District Headquarters had asked him his opinion of the contractors and builders on Monomoy. 'It was Lieutenant Commander Upham,' he said.

Helm said, 'It's leaked. Better to keep your mouth shut.'

'He asked me my opinion, and . . .'

'Better not to have one. You won't, when you've got twenty-nine years in.'

Helm returned to his examination of the chart. John thought back to his talk with Upham. The Coast Guard was considering replacing the Diadem Lightship with a lighthouse, probably on the point of the Cape. Obviously a local contractor would get the job. It seemed reasonable for the officer to ask his opinion. For the good of the service John answered: Things went wrong with the houses Elliott King built. The work was usually good to look at, well presented and, in small ways, unreliable.

Helm said, 'Your disciplinary figures are seven per cent above normal, mister.'

John thought angrily, I know, I know! But why? Were these uncommonly wild men he'd got? They didn't look it. Their past records didn't show it.

'It might be Monomoy,' he said slowly. 'It's a dull place for young men. They have to drive a long way to get action. When they find it, they're apt to go overboard.'

It sounded thin. He would have done better to keep his mouth shut. The Chief Boatswain said, 'This station was all right under the last man. And the one before him. Satisfied with McGill? Randall? Gardner?'

'Yes,' John said promptly. 'It has nothing to do with them.'

Mr Helm's voice, which had carried a rough edge of hostility, softened slightly. 'Two years since your divorce, Remington. You're younger than Dowling at Race Point, Levin at Nauset . . . Why do the young fellows work better there than here? Because you can't interest 'em in their job?' He stood up, reaching for his cap. He stabbed a thick finger at John's chest. 'Maybe you're not interested in *them*, only in the U.S. Coast Guard. Can't be done, Remington. They go together . . . You're in an exposed position here, if that storm hits. Been thinking about it?'

John said, 'Yes. I think we'll be able to do our job . . . I'm worried about the town, though. There's plenty they ought to do, I think, but they won't.'

Helm headed for the door, growling, 'Don't take any wooden nickels.'

A minute later McGill came in. 'What did the Old Man say?'

John shook his head. 'Nothing . . . Anything happen while I was out?'

'One of your high society ladies called. Wanted to know whether you'd have dinner with her tomorrow night. *Late* dinner.'

'Who?'

'Mrs Bryant. She heard about the storm early this morning, and drove down in a hurry to check on her house. And to ask you to have dinner, of course.'

'Can it. What did you say?'

'I told her you'd call back.'

John nodded. Alice Bryant was a rich woman from New York. She owned one of the houses on the Green, Number 3. She was married, but didn't let it bother her. From a couple of looks she'd given him last summer he thought she wouldn't mind a little fling with him. Well, he could afford to take a few hours off, as long as he stayed on the peninsula.

McGill said, 'Oh, and Harrington got back.'

John looked up. McGill seemed apprehensive. John said, 'They let him off?'

McGill said, 'Released him. No evidence.'

John said, 'What do they mean? Two o'clock this morning they're good and mad, he's hit a cop over the head with a bottle, they have every kind of witness, there isn't a chance in hell of getting him off. Now . . . ?'

McGill shifted his feet. 'Harrington says Elliott King sprung him – and the Griffiths boy. That's what the cops in P. Town told him.'

'Elliott King?' John said slowly. 'That *operator*?'

McGill said quickly, 'I guess it was really the Griffiths kid King wanted to spring. I guess. JoAnn Griffiths went to him this morning, after you turned her down.'

John exploded. 'Who in hell does he think he is, interfering with the administration of justice . . . and for one of *my* men?'

'Gee, Chief, I don't know. Do you want to see Harrington?'

'No,' John snapped. 'Yes, tomorrow – charged with being AWOL.'

'O.K., Chief. You looked pooped.'

'I am. But I'm going to the Firemen's Buffet. King'll be there.'

From across the room Dorothy King stared at her husband's broad back. Boy, did he look good tonight! Were they eating out of his hand tonight! Men and women alike, the men smiling, the women simpering, admiring from a distance. *How long, how long?*

Frank Damato came in out of the cold, rubbing his hands. He looked at her, smiling warmly. He'd seen her looking at

Elliott just now, and was thinking. How nice to see a woman who just plain worships her husband. She sipped the glass of sweet sherry. *The truth will set you free.*

'Pardon?'

She looked up, and found herself face to face with the Coast Guard petty officer, John Remington. She realized that she had said it aloud, the truth will set you free. The blush spread over her neck and face. She wanted to stare at the floor, twisting one toe.

She said, 'I was thinking that if you could hear everything people say tonight, you'd hear the truth . . . I mean, what is behind the things people said last night, at Town Meeting.'

John Remington said, 'That's about what Mrs Quimby said yesterday. I don't know. I've found people pretty honest. They're mostly what they seem to be.'

'They're not!' she said violently. His head jerked a little in surprise. 'Some aren't,' she said, in a lower tone. Mr Remington was a nice-looking man, a Westerner with the distinctive drawl and, added to it, the bite of command. He had a big chest and powerful arms, but that was no proof. She ought to know. The thought grated like a hurt tooth. She said, 'Take Elliott, for instance. You wouldn't think he was a subtle sort of man, would you?'

It was dangerous to talk, even to hint. Something in the air was forcing her to. Perhaps it was the storm the radio had warned about.

Remington said, 'Your husband? . . . No, I wouldn't, Mrs King.'

'Well, he is,' she said. 'If you went to Boston, and talked to the right people . . . politicians, people with pull, people like that . . . you'd be surprised.'

That was enough. Remington was looking unhappy to have heard it, or was it merely because he had heard it from her. Go on, she screamed silently. You know I'm a dutiful, loyal, loving, mousy little wife, picked out of nowhere by the mighty, brave, handsome, bluff, male Elliott King, contractor, go-getter, Marine Corps hero. You know he could have had any girl he chose. You know I worship the ground he walks on. Then ask yourself why I'm telling you this. Ask me!

John Remington said, 'It's a real privilege to be invited to these firehouse parties. Would you care for a drink? A glass of wine, maybe?'

'No, thank you,' she said flatly, and could not find a smile.

57

Walter Crampton stood in the engine barn next door, his short mackinaw coat still on his back, but unbuttoned. One of the combination fire trucks loomed over him in its glory of scarlet and brass, another made a backdrop. The barn doors were closed. Outside, the street lamps shone on the empty Green. The finger of the Old Church steeple rose into darkness.

Walter swirled the bourbon in his glass. Nelson Pryor, opposite, leaned against the rescue truck. Neither spoke.

Walter thought, the doc says Daisy can't last another couple of days. Maybe so, but he remembered . . . about '16 or '17 maybe it was, anyway, before we got married. He was out with Dad beyond the Diadem Shoal, and they were upset by a big wave that came crossways at them out of the Race. Two fellows disappeared right away, never saw 'em again, but there was Dad and him and Billy Brunswick hanging on to the bottom of the boat. She was upside down and just awash. After a while Billy Brunswick started saying, We can't last much longer. It was February and colder'n hell, so cold it hurt to breathe. Dad didn't say nothing, and he didn't know what he was thinking. *He* didn't say nothing, either, and if he was thinking anything, he didn't recall what it was, not even right after. He just hung on. Billy Brunswick's voice got thinner and thinner, saying it over and over, we can't last much longer, until he couldn't hear it any more, and he knew he'd gone. They were there two hours more, Dad and him, until the Coast Guard found them.

Daisy would be like that, only more so. She had all the guts in the world.

John Remington came through the open door from the main meeting room. Walter had noticed him talking to Dorothy King . . . poor fellow was glad to escape. Well, that's why they didn't encourage women in the car barn.

'Hi, John,' Nelson said, 'you got a drink? Good. You deserve it, from what I hear about what you did out there in Diadem Bay. Goddam fools.'

'It ought to be settled between you and the Nantucket Selectmen,' John said.

Walter thought, There's nothing to settle. Diadem Bay is Monomoy water and always has been; but Nelson said, 'Sure, sure, I was speaking to them this afternoon, and we've made a date. You heard that our local witch has put her whammy on you now?'

'Who?'

'Miss Garland. You haven't heard? About how the U.S. Coast

Guard engaged in strikebreaking this morning? Outside the Warren Mercer plant in Monomoy?'

Remington's face was darkening. 'No. I haven't heard.'

'Well, this friend of mine called me from Boston, soon as he read this in the evening paper. He was joshing me. It was an eye-witness account, telephoned to the paper by Miss Lynn Garland, schoolteacher. There was a lot of police brutality, it seems, and then the Coast Guard came along and helped chase the union men out of town.'

'That's not what happened,' John said.

'I know. Don't worry about it, John. No one's going to take one little damn bit of notice. But ain't that Garland woman something? . . . She's the one who failed my Billy, you know.'

'I know.'

'Why'd she have to fail those kids?' Nelson said moodily. 'God damn it, what's the difference? Just put passed on their papers, and let 'em go. What's worth all the trouble? Parents keep ringing me, as if I could do anything. So they go to Elliott.'

Walter Crampton said, 'I don't like her. I think she's a socialist. And I'm sorry for Billy. He's a good boy. But if there's a grade the kids are supposed to reach, then she's right to fail them if they don't reach it.'

Nelson said, 'Sure, Walter, but the way she set the exam it was a matter of opinion. She didn't give them those true-or-false papers no one can argue with. She gave them essays, and marked 'em on what she calls style, content, logical expression. Hell, it's just her opinion against theirs.'

Walter thought, the trouble is that only opinion matters. Facts can be twisted, facts don't mean a thing. Like suppose the fact is a man has a master's ticket, but your opinion is he's no damned good – which is more important to you? And here was Elliott King coming in, a plate in one hand and a glass of whisky in the other. There was another example, because the fact was Elliott was a hero and a rich man, but as for his own private opinion – well, that could be something else again.

Elliott King greeted them heartily. 'Hi, Nelson. Hi, Walter, you old mooncusser. Hi, John.' He clambered up on to the long firestep of the truck, where the firemen stood when it went out, and sat down.

Remington thought, I shouldn't raise the matter here, when

they're all having a good time. I should be more tactful. The hell with that. I'm a chief boatswain's mate, not a politician.

He turned to Elliott King and spoke carefully. 'I believe you sprung Seaman Harrington out of Provincetown jail.'

Elliott waved his glass. 'Sure! Glad to. Think nothing of it.'

John felt his neck getting redder. He said, 'JoAnn Griffiths asked me to use my influence to spring her brother and Harrington. I refused, because I don't want my people – or civilians – to think that service in the United States Coast Guard gives any privilege to break the laws.'

Elliott King put down plate and glass. 'So I trod on your toes, eh? If I have to, I'll do it again, see?' His voice was a little rough and he stared at John, his head lowered, like a bull.

Nelson Pryor said, 'Hey, John – Elliott – take it easy.' They both ignored him.

John said, 'It doesn't help me to maintain discipline on my station if an outsider does what I have refused to do. Why didn't you ask me first?'

Elliott King pointed at him suddenly. 'Did you ask me before you shot off your mouth in Boston about the kind of work I do?' In an affected, mincing voice he piped, 'All work carried out by Elliott King, though within legal specifications, seems to deteriorate very rapidly . . . If the Coast Guard builds a lighthouse on Monomoy, Remington, I'm going to get the contract. You're not going to stop me, no, sir.' He pushed his face close to John's. 'How much did Harold slip you to talk that kind of stuff? How much, eh?'

'Elliott!'

John grabbed Elliott by the shirt, his right fist tensed and his belly taut. He dragged him off the firestep on to the floor. The shirt material ripped in his hand and a button flew as Elliott jerked a pace back. His expression was almost comically astonished, as though a cigar had exploded under his nose.

'Take it easy,' he said. 'Hey, take it easy, feller . . .'

John moved forward. 'Apologize, or . . .'

'Well, Chief, we don't want to fight . . . I'm a bigger man than you, heh, heh . . .'

John growled, 'Apologize, Mr King.'

'You shouldn't have said that,' Nelson said.

'O.K., I'm sorry. I lost my temper . . . All I ask for is fair play. I'll tell you, Chief, I *knew* you didn't want Harrington sprung. And I didn't really care a damn about Griffiths. But I wanted to show you that you can't live, or work, around here without reckoning with me. Now, we're all square, eh? No hard feelings, eh? Here.' He thrust out his hand. After a slight hesitation John took it. The big hand squeezed and released, squeezed again. Elliott's left hand came round and caught him by the shoulder, squeezing powerfully on the muscles. With difficulty finding a smile, he nodded and broke away.

Elliott King was alone with Nelson at last. It had taken a long time, what with Remington getting mad. Walter talking about it afterwards, and other men sticking their heads in to say hi. By now Nelson looked as though he'd had about two too many, as usual. Then once in a while he'd really cut loose. You could always tell when he'd done that by looking at Mary's face the next day. It would be kind of raw, her eyes red and small. Sometimes you didn't have to wait till the next day, because you'd helped carry Nelson out of a tavern or put him to sleep on someone's couch. It was a wonder they kept on electing him First Selectman. Damn it, you'd got to remember that he got elected *because* he wasn't any better than any other guy. He didn't just pretend to be ordinary, like a lot of politicians – he actually was. Right now he was stewed, but not badly enough so he couldn't understand what he heard.

Elliott said, 'How much land do you hold, Nelson?'

Nelson Pryor said, 'Here, in town? Just the lot the house is on.'

'Outside town.'

Nelson drank. 'It's no secret. Twenty-five acres.'

'On Bayside Road, about three miles out?'

'Yeah. It'll be valuable, one day.'

'Only if the town develops. I'll lay it on the line, Nelson. No sense in fellows like you and me beating about the bush, after all the years we've known each other . . . Are you thinking that if the park goes through, it'll take a lot of land off the market? And so what's left becomes more valuable? Including your twenty-five acres? And when the auditorium's built, more people will want to come here, and build, summer homes at least?'

Nelson took a big swig. Elliott knew he had correctly guessed at Nelson's line of thought.

He went on earnestly: 'It won't work out that way, Nelson. Unless you get extra tax money from more houses, I mean hundreds more houses, and from industry, you aren't going to be able to build the auditorium . . . or the sewage treatment plant

... or the new yacht basin ... or the new parking lot. This town doesn't have the choice of standing still. It's got to go forward, or back – way back, back to where people begin to leave. Then there'll be plenty of room for the birds ... Your land will have more value if the whole peninsula is developed than it ever will any other way.'

Nelson said violently, 'Jesus, sometimes I wish I didn't own anything, not one goddam thing!'

Elliott said, 'Ah, you don't mean that!' He leaned forward – 'Another thing I want to talk to you about – that Garland woman. We're going to get rid of her. She's a trouble-maker. I've been making some inquiries about her and I don't think we'll have any trouble easing her out. She was shacked up with a Commie called Bernard Kauffmann, in New York, seven, eight years back. Remember, McCarthy got after him? He was teaching at N.Y.U., and eventually took the Fifth, resigned, and disappeared? Well, this girl was living with him.'

'Seven years ago?' Nelson mumbled. 'I'd hate to have to answer for everything I did seven years ago.'

'It's just what we need,' Elliott said impatiently. 'Then the Teachers' Association won't try to protect her. We'll fix it all, in the School Committee. You needn't do a thing.'

'O.K.,' Nelson said. He drained his glass. 'Hell, people have got to learn to look after themselves. I'm going to get myself a drink.'

'Hold on a minute, Nelson. She's for the park. She's leading the group who are for it. You've got to remember that, remember who's for the park – nuts, crackpots, do-gooders, Communists. You don't want to stand up and be counted with *them*. There's no votes there, Nelson. The other way around. There's a dozen votes against you every time one of those people agrees with you ...'

'Sure, sure,' Nelson muttered. He stood away from the truck, steadying himself with one hand. 'God damn it,' he said explosively, but in a low tone. Then he went through to the recreation room and Elliott was alone.

Not for long, he thought comfortably. People would see him alone in here, then they'd come in, one by one. Probably Frank Damato first, or maybe Jim Carpenter. He wanted to talk to Carpenter. Carpenter was the one Selectman it was hard to read. He was well educated, of course, and a lawyer. Boston Catholic, part-Irish background ... ambitious, secretive. He had something on his mind, but what? He ought to find out.

Well, it was Frank Damato, after all. Elliott banged the step beside him. 'Come on up, Frank. Good view, fresh air . . .' He laughed loudly. Frank Damato clambered up and sat down beside him.

Elliott let his hand fall on the other's knee, and squeezed hard. 'I hear you did a great job with those union guys this morning.'

'It was nothing,' Frank mumbled, 'only that Miss Garland told the paper in Boston we were acting like a bunch of Nazis or something and if the Attorney General gets to hear about it . . .'

'Don't you worry,' Elliott said, 'I'll ring a guy I know, first thing tomorrow. You won't hear any more about it.'

'Thanks, Elliott,' the police chief said.

Elliott said, 'Any little thing.'

Frank Damato cleared his throat. 'You know, Elliott, we're going to need more men again next year, and another patrol car. I wanted to put it all in this year, but Nelson says "not so fast." Now, I don't know whether we'll get the rest, even next year. Not unless Nelson pushes for it good and hard.'

Elliott twisted his empty glass in his hands. 'You know Nelson, Frank. He's not a pushing-type guy. Mind, I'm not saying a word against him. He wouldn't be First Selectman if he pushed hard all the time . . . I think we can get you what you want. I'll talk to a few fellows, and maybe have a look at the figures again. There are ways we can get the men, and the car, without showing the full cost on the year's budget . . .'

Damato broke out: 'I don't want them so I can push people around, like that Miss Garland said.'

'Don't worry about her.'

'I got a job to do, that's all. Kids aren't supposed to neck on the beach – drive up and down the streets at sixty, seventy miles an hour – make fires outa driftwood and dance around them and sleep onna sand like a bunch of gipsies. Rich kids, too, college kids. My pop woulda whipped the shit out of us if we'd done anything like they do. It's not all in the law, what they're supposed to do, because who woulda thought kids would be riding round all night and sleeping on the sand when they had homes to go to? Then some of the parents come to see me, complaining, asking, why you giving them a hard time? They're only young once. People like Mrs Bannister and Mrs Graham and Mrs Hurst and Mr Osgood, real important people, they ask me that. If we had more men, the fellows wouldn't have to act tough. We could sort of keep an eye on the kids instead of like now, when one of my fellows sees a party on the beach, and his radio's telling him to get on down to an accident on North Commerce, and someone's having a baby out in West Village, so he runs out of his car and yells at the kids, break it up, get going, what the hell you think you're doing! Then *I* get into trouble.'

'I know,' Elliott said warmly, 'it isn't right. I want you to know there's one guy for the police in this town, one hundred per cent.'

'Thanks, Elliott,' Chief Damato said, his gloom unabated.

Harold Morgan stood in the recreation room, staring moodily across the room into the car barn. Elliott was in there, with Damato now. Pushing, shoving, wheedling, grabbing, Elliott never rested. He was a grabby guy, that was all you could say about him.

'Eh? Oh, yes, about George Zanakis . . .'

It was the Coast Guardsman, John Remington, and they had been talking about Zanakis, eating in the corner there among a group of grinning firemen. They were joshing him about horse-shoe crabs, and Remington asked whether he was really a nut, or just acted that way, and how come he got invited to firehouse parties? Well, the answer to the last was that he had once done a fine painting of the fire trucks leaving the old station for a fire, and given it to the firehouse, and by heck, some visiting big shot sees it and offers them 5,000 bucks for it, so they think differently about him. A man who can make 5,000 bucks that easy is never really a nut.

'He's from Brooklyn originally, I believe his father was born in the old country – Greece. He came to Monomoy about 1916 and built himself a house – that same shack near the fish pier he lives in now. No one knew why he came, to live in a little shanty like that. He'd just made a fortune and everyone was after him to paint pictures . . . Remember *The Druggist*? No, you wouldn't. Well, it was an ad, some drug company, a big painting of a bearded druggist making up a prescription in a back room, surrounded by bottles and so on, and a couple of young kids waiting. I don't remember anything being as famous, except those sisters with the long hair, and *September Morn*. Right after that, he came here . . . A fisherman who used to live close to him down there told me he'd burn everything he'd painted, once a month. Black smoke would pour from the chimney and George would be dead drunk for two days. Then he'd start again. He teaches art classes every summer, makes enough to get by the rest of the year. My wife always had a soft spot for him, always was worrying over whether he was getting enough to eat, about him living in that shack with no heat all winter.'

To tell the truth, Julia wanted another man to push around. Let's see, he'd married her in '33, and buried her across the Green there, behind the church, in the winter of '58. Twenty-five years of being told what to eat, what to wear. All his clothes bought for him and his ties chosen for him, not just in the store but in the bedroom, every morning when he started to dress. And, at firehouse parties, anything like that, either he didn't get to go or she was there, too. 'Just one drink now, Harold!' Her voice echoed sharply in his ear. Wonderful woman. Wonderful, being free these past three years.

John Remington was speaking, 'That's a very efficient secretary you have, Mr Morgan. I sat next to her at Town Meeting.'

The blood rushed to Harold Morgan's head. 'She's . . .' he began. He controlled himself. 'Yes, she's efficient,' he said, 'very efficient. She's forty-three,' he added, 'and a widow.'

Women made plans for you, like generals or something, he thought gloomily. They closed in on you. They handed you on, from one to another. When he used to leave the house, he left Julia – but Miss Burroughs was waiting at the office, ready to see that he didn't smoke more than three cigars a day, hiding the key of the cupboard where he kept the whisky. Julia dies, and later Miss Burroughs retires . . . but she chooses her replacement, this 'nice widow lady' from Troy, New York, whom she's met in the town, on holiday : Mrs Charlotte Quimby.

Harold ran his hand over his bald head. People had always been ready to laugh at him over Julia and Miss Burroughs. Now they were laughing over Mrs Quimby. Let them laugh, he thought resentfully, but how did you escape?

Mrs Quimby started work right after Labour Day. About October she started putting on perfume. November, more lipstick. December, the black stuff round the eyes. Sitting with her knees crossed so he could see above the knee. Leaning on him. There was a narrow passage, back of the office, that led to the lumber-yard. Ten, fifteen times he'd gone out that way and met her, coming toward him, so she'd pressed herself back against the wall, her front sticking out, and he'd had to squeeze past.

He drained his drink, and went to the long table, where the bottles were set out. Maybe he'd run away, to Tahiti, some day. Right now – 'Bourbon and branch,' he said ritually.

Father Bradford sipped his highball and thought, Day and I ought to be going. The clergy weren't expected to stay late, and surely Day must have had all the tomato juice his stomach could take, particularly as the poor man liked whisky. That was one of the minor but still real weaknesses of the heretical churches. Most of the parishioners drank sociably, but they didn't like their pastor to do so.

'How's the porcelain collection coming?' Father Bradford asked.

The Reverend Arthur Day said, 'Just before Thanksgiving I heard of a pair of very good Sèvres pieces, at an auction in Dedham, and managed to get them cheap. Ah, well, Sèvres is never cheap, but, shall we say, reasonably . . . I hope you didn't take my remarks at Town Meeting amiss?'

'Not a bit,' Father Bradford said, smiling. 'I think we both agreed that it was not a subject for official church guidance . . .'

Poor old Arthur looked like a dejected bloodhound. He, Bradford, had an idea why, but only time could prove him right – or wrong.

Father Bradford continued, 'From the strictly material point of view of my own comfort, I wish the park would go through. I already have more parishioners than I can handle, and I'm sure the bishop will not authorize the creation of another parish.'

Oh dear, he shouldn't have said that. Poor Arthur was looking glummer than ever. But it was a fact that the Catholic population of Monomoy was increasing, partly by the Catholics' higher birth rate, partly by Catholic immigration from Boston, and partly – a small but important part – by conversion. It was so difficult to avoid treading on tender toes: tender, because Day's congregation was steadily shrinking.

Arthur Day said, 'I suppose, in your position, *we* would build another church. It's a well-to-do and generous community . . . but, while the Old Church is standing, it would seem almost sacrilegious to have another on the peninsula.'

Touché, Father Bradford thought. Congregational parishioners included nearly all the town's leading citizens and rich men. The church itself, built by a disciple of Wren's, was famous all over the United States. How many million coloured postcards had travelled across the nation and the world, showing the delicate white spire piercing the line of the Great Dune, precisely in the V of the Gap. The photo was taken from Sachem Island, black Buoy Number 15 in the foreground. Here in the United States his own Church could not pride itself, as in England, that the sacred, stately edifices were originally built by and for Catholics. The Old Church at Monomoy was Protestant from first to last. His own church, a brick horror at the poorer, crowded north end of North Commerce, offended him every time he looked at it – and the Reverend Mr Day knew it.

Suppose New England went Catholic altogether, Father Bradford thought. Why should we not then take over these churches, the pride of the land? The idea was not impossible. One day, assuredly, God's truth would prevail . . . That would be a triumph as great, in its way, as the conversion of Constantine. Who would hold the first High Mass in Monomoy Old Church? Suppose it were he, by then cardinal and archbishop. Then perhaps his Bradford ancestors would hail him as Priest of God, instead of whispering endlessly in his ear, Traitor, traitor, popish traitor . . .

John Remington thought, Time to go. The party was breaking up. Some young fellows had begun to sing, and most of the wives had gone home. Up at the station there might be a late report on the storm. He'd see that, and then hit the sack. He said good night to his host, Fire Chief Merrill Crosby, and let himself out by the side door. He stood a moment on the edge of the Green, breathing the cold air. The spire of the Old Church rose straight ahead, pale against a blue velvet curtain. To his left Town Hall was dark behind its pillars, and above it the beam of the Monomoy light circled the town. On the right, a blue lamp shone outside the police station, and yellow-bright windows on the ground floor showed where the night clerk sat at his desk. Beyond, the four big houses stood foursquare and solid between the Green and the bay. Beyond again, the Coast Guard New Boat House, large as it was, looked insignificant against the towering, lightless bulk of the Longships Hotel behind it. He turned up his collar, crossed the Green, and walked fast up Boat Street.

JoAnn Griffiths sat on a stool in Doug's Diner, at the corner of Boat and North Hill, and sucked up another half ounce of Coke. The big hand of the clock on the opposite wall had swung round, and round, since she came in. The soda jerk, and what a jerk, kept making cracks about what did she expect for two Cokes, would she like him to make up a bed in there, and he was about ready to close, too, see? She hardly minded waiting.

67

Some girls did. She didn't. It was warm in Doug's, her fanny stuck out over the edge of the stool, and guys gave it a big pat every time one passed, but she took no notice. It didn't mean a thing, it just happened, like the long hand of the clock going tick – wait – tick – wait . . .

The soda jerk said, 'See here, JoAnn—' But she'd seen him coming up the street then, his coat collar turned high, and she slipped her fanny off the stool and went out.

He saw her as she came out the door, practically into his arms, and said, 'JoAnn!' He was pleased to see her, though he was frowning. She could always tell.

'I want to talk to you,' she said. 'Can we go to your house?'

'No!' he said, real salty. Then, 'What is it? Walk up to the station with me, or you'll catch cold.'

'O.K.,' she said. They began to walk across the parking lot. 'Are those your kids, that you had photographs of on your desk?'

'Yes,' he said. 'Now what . . . ?'

'They're cute. What are their names?'

'John Junior, he's nearly nine now, and Betty – she's seven.' Then he said, like it hurt, 'They're in California.'

She said, 'Did she go away with another fellow?'

'JoAnn . . . You just don't ask people that sort of question.'

'I only wanted to know,' she said.

'What did you want to speak to me about?'

She searched her mind. There must have been some particular reason. Men like Mr Remington always asked for reasons. Once they'd got one, it was all right. They were at the front of the steps now. Mr Remington had stopped.

She said formally, 'It was about my brother. I had to go ask Mr King to get Dick out of trouble, so he wouldn't lose his licence, because we need the money, Dad said, so I did. I'm sorry.'

'I know,' he said. 'I don't blame you. Is that all?'

There was another thing. Oh, yes.

'Charlie Tyson,' she said. 'I called him right after you all got back and he was off duty. I told him I didn't want to marry him.'

'Well, I'm glad to hear that,' Mr Remington said.

'I told you, I didn't want to marry him,' she said. 'I never said yes. He was just trying to get even with Betty Pryor.'

Mr Remington said, 'So you wait all night to tell me. I'm grateful to you, JoAnn, but you must think of your reputation.

People might get wrong ideas about us . . . well, about you, particularly.'

'They think I do it with everyone anyway,' she said, 'so what's the difference.'

'Look, you've got to go home now. And I've got to go into the station, and go to sleep. You'll be all right, walking home?'

'Sure, Mr Remington . . . well, good night.'

'Good night.'

CHAPTER THREE

SUNDAY

Lynn Garland dried her cup, and took another look out the window. It was still a lovely morning, fresh and cold, the sun shining and a few clouds scattered like sheep across a pale sky. Mr Crampton's car was not in its usual place at the foot of the street, but Mrs Crampton's bed still blocked the upstairs window. Lynn could clearly see the old lady, propped up on several pillows, looking down at the empty street.

Mrs Handforth's big, black Packard drew up in front of the apartment, Mrs Handforth sitting up very straight in the back. Lynn gathered her field glasses, dropped her bird-recognition book into her handbag, and hurried downstairs.

The chauffeur opened the car door and Elaine Handforth patted the seat beside her. 'Get in, my dear . . . Good, I see you are wearing sensible shoes.'

The car glided up the street and turned left. Lynn noticed that Mrs Handforth was also wearing stout tie-up Oxfords, with a brown tweed suit. A bright red arctic cap, of the type worn by motorcycle police in cold weather, lay on the seat.

Mrs Handforth said, 'I see you telephoned the Boston papers about the fight at the Warren Mercer Company.'

Lynn said, 'Yes.'

'What made you do that? Are you a part-time correspondent for them here?' Her manner was friendly but assured. Obviously she considered the First Lady of Monomoy had good right to ask such questions.

Lynn said, 'I got the impression that it was going to be hushed up, and I don't think that's right.'

The big car rolled silently past Elliott King's lumberyard at the old railroad station, past the Catholic church, past the Warren Mercer Company.

Elaine Handforth said, 'You decided what was right to do, and did it. Good. The people are so lost without leaders, aren't they?'

Lynn murmured vaguely, not knowing just what the old lady meant. Apparently, there'd been another fight yesterday, one she had not seen, in Diadem Bay. It must have been a strange and

70

perhaps beautiful thing to watch – from a distance at least – the boats swooping and turning like gulls, white water under their sterns . . . Was anyone going to telephone Boston to tell of John Remington's skill, of the Coast Guard's patient work to prevent real trouble there in the bay?

'Stop on the right there, Arthur,' Mrs Handforth said. She put the red cap on her head, pulled down the earflaps and carefully tied the strings under her chin. The chauffeur opened the door and they got out. They stood at the edge of Town Pond, half a mile beyond the northern outskirts of Monomoy. The Chatham Road ran on north into pine and scrub oak woods. At the north end of the pond, the long-since abandoned roadbed of the Cape Cod Railroad crossed the highway and plunged straight into thickets of birch and ash and swamp myrtle.

'We'll be about two and half hours, Arthur,' Mrs Handforth said. 'At the other crossing.'

'I know,' the chauffeur said. He was a small, grey man, full of patience. He climbed back into the driver's seat of the high Packard, and drove away. Lynn hitched her handbag on to her shoulder, brushed the hair out of her eyes, and hung her binoculars round her neck.

'Ready,' she said, smiling.

Elaine Handforth did not move. It had been Leverett's idea to make Town Pond into a fresh-water bathing spot. What stupid arguments the Selectmen had put up against it! Who wanted to bathe in fresh water? Who would pay the salary of the life-guard? Who would prevent immoral frolicking in the changing huts? But Leverett kept prodding and finally it was done. Goodness, nearly thirty years ago.

It was a pleasant winter Sunday, and the people seemed to be enjoying themselves. Skaters dotted the pond, and others sat at the side, putting on their skates or resting. Young Fred Butcher had a black eye. Perhaps he'd got it in that oyster war yesterday. And why had that blown up so violently, and why hadn't she known about it? There was no doubt about it, without a husband one was bound to miss a great deal . . . Close to her three families were carrying barbecue equipment down to the ice. Well, there was little danger of fire today. On the far side of the pond an old man skated alone in long graceful sweeps, his hands behind his back. She raised her binoculars: Upham, from the cannery, he'd a major operation for stomach cancer last year. Four boys swooped across the ice, sticks flashing, their puck skimming toward the Butchers. Elaine frowned. The west end of the pond was reserved for hockey players. She'd speak to Nelson Pryor.

She led off along the railroad bed. A few of the ties had been removed, but for the most part they lay, dark and rotting, in their places. She walked carefully, methodically sweeping the woods from right to left with her eyes. On a day like this, really, they should have gone to the Diadem Cape, and watched the seabirds. There might be a million of them resting between there and the Diadem Lightship. Only last month she had recorded an Iceland gull (accidental visitor, rare), and a fulmar (winter visitor, rare). But with the seabirds one could not both walk and observe, and the exercise was so necessary for a woman of her age. Besides, she reminded herself, neither bird watching nor exercise was the prime object of today's expedition.

They walked easily, side by side. Their shoes made a soft swish in the moss and grass of the roadbed, a muted crunch on the ties. The sounds of laughter, and boys' shouts, died away behind, absorbed by the trees. The cold smell of ice filled the wood.

A flash of white on her left caught her eye and she watched until it stopped. A downy woodpecker, male. The bird watched her, his head cocked. She whispered, 'Hullo, there!' The bird flew deeper into the wood.

Half a mile farther two bird feeders stood in a small clearing on the right. She unstrapped the bag of sunflower seed from her shoulder and filled the feeders. At once she moved away and, after twenty paces, stopped and turned. The birds had come back already, the little dears . . .

'Purple finch,' Lynn Garland whispered, 'on the right.'

She focused her glasses. So it was! Blue jays, noisy in the churchlike silence, swooped argumentatively, ruffling their feathers. A cardinal . . . they'd been coming north much more than they used to. When she first came here, after marrying Leverett, she'd only seen one every two or three years.

Tufted titmouse. Chickadee. Tree sparrow. White-throated sparrow. House sparrow. A wren . . . that was rare.

'Winter wren,' the girl beside her whispered.

Quite right. She nodded approvingly. The girl had good eyes and a good memory, and spoke with confidence, but not brashly. She had class. You couldn't conceal good blood, any more than one of those sparrows could pretend it was a cardinal.

After twenty minutes they moved on again. Almost at once,

72

on the left, the woods opened on to Indian Pond. Three men, widely scattered, sat on stools, fishing through the ice. Through her binoculars Elaine carefully examined the far line of woods. Ever since the jeep was invented lazy people had been driving to places that should have been free of them. They ought to be prevented.

Next, she examined the fishermen. Bill Stanford; a man she didn't recognize; Walter Crampton. Walter looked up, recognized her, and raised one hand. She waved her hand in reply. A good man. Without him the Board of Selectmen would be like a boat without a rudder, young Carpenter thinking only of his personal advancement, Nelson waiting to see what the people wanted or what would be easiest. It was a pity Walter was against the park, the Handforth National Park and Bird Sanctuary, but it didn't matter. Too much unanimity looked bad, and, with a little guidance, the right thing usually got done in the end.

On again, this time with a definite, strong, pleasurable anticipation. Here it came, now, on the right, the water lapping the low embankment – Quasatuit, the most beautiful pond on the whole Cape. She remembered coming past in the train, in the days when there was a train; leaving Chatham station, winding round Stage Harbour, the boat sails shining in the sun; then into the steep cutting of Morris Island, suddenly out on to the flat marshland, the ocean on the left and Nantucket Sound on the right; then past the sandy cone of Monomoy Hill, and once into the woods . . . and through the woods . . . and suddenly, after two or three miles, this small pearl, white birches silent on the far side, leaves floating on the dark surface, like polished mahogany. It was like a framed picture, presented in the train window, held for a few fleeting seconds, just long enough for comprehension and wonder and love, then the curtain of the woods was drawn quickly across it again.

She gazed at the pond and the girl waited patiently beside her. At last, Quasatuit remembered again for her, she moved on. Only a mile and a half to the road now and, in her experience, very few birds. She slowed her pace, and turned to the girl. 'Tell me, why did you leave Radcliffe before graduating?'

John Remington put down the last of the telegraph messages, walked to the east window and stared out to sea, his hands jammed into his pockets.

The fleecy clouds began to cluster and darken. A long swell

73

rode in from the south-east, diagonally across the current, which always ran south on a rising tide, north on a falling tide. A line of spindrift marked the edge of the ocean and the barometer had begun to fall. The weather map showed the storm's low-pressure system covering the whole area from Bermuda to Hatteras.

He spoke over his shoulder. 'Get McGill up here, please.'

The First arrived, panting, five minutes later. 'I was in the Old—'

John interrupted him. 'Jimmy, if that storm really starts to move, it'll hit us tomorrow or the next day. We're going to be ready, as ready as it's humanly possible to be. I want to double-check every installation we're responsible for – every light, every buoy, every horn and bell and beacon. I want every gas tank and fuel tank inspected, checked for leaks, and filled. Every motor and generator stripped, cleared and tuned. Compasses, vehicles, boats, rigging . . . everything. How many men are off the station?'

'Four, Chief . . . and Randall.'

John stared at the ocean, walked across the room, stared at Monomoy House. 'Recall them all,' he said. 'They're going to grouse like hell, Jimmy. But we're not civilians. We *can* do what we think ought to be done, and we must.'

'Sure, Chief.'

'The Weather Bureau says, look out. I'm going to treat this as an emergency, as of now. Anyone doesn't like it, he can write to his congressman.'

John kept staring out the west window after McGill had gone. How would the temperatures run? That was the big question. If the storm brought really low temperatures, to freeze equipment and load decks and roads with ice, then they'd be in for a hard time. But very low temperatures usually didn't carry much snow, not in these latitudes, and so close to the Gulf Stream. The storm would more likely bring heavy snow, perhaps even rain.

He glanced at the unfinished paper work on his desk. To hell with it. Let it wait. This was a time for a lifeboatman to look to his lifeboat.

Lynn Garland said, 'My fiancé was killed in Korea.'

There, that would stop the inquisitive old woman. But Elaine Handforth said, 'Who was he?'

'Cabot Collins.'

'What a tragedy that was. We knew him quite well. Your engagement was secret, of course . . . And then you couldn't face Cambridge any more?'

'No,' Lynn said.

It was the simplest answer, but it wasn't true. It was merely a formal representation of the truth, which itself was too complicated, too abstract, to be captured in simple answers. They had both completed their junior years, that June of 1950, she at Radcliffe, Cabot at Harvard. Then came Korea, and he went into the Air Force at once. Six months later, he was dead.

'Then you went to New York?'

'Yes. Yes. I went to New York.'

New York. Just twenty-one; a virgin; a raw hole where there had been a conventional, happy-ending future; bursting with strong but unaimed emotions. She joined pacifist groups, heard with passion of agreement every voice screaming against a world which allowed these things to happen; finally began to cry out, herself, against a world which allowed Cabot Collins to be young and handsome, rich and well-born, intelligent and self-confident, without having worked for any of it. She met Bernard Kauffmann, and at once became his mistress. Why? God knows, except that he wasn't young, handsome, rich, well-born, or self-confident; and, in large matters, not very intelligent in spite of his professorship.

Elaine Handforth said, 'But you graduated?'

'At N.Y.U.,' Lynn said. 'I took my teacher's certificate there, too.' She almost added, Yes, that's where Bernard Kauffmann was a professor.

She remembered Bernard's eyes when they first met, the anguished uncertain eyes belying the certainties of his talk. Herself sitting at his feet, listening, watching his eyes. His fear – of the police, of the FBI, above all, of the Party, the inscrutable party that he worshipped and would never understand. She moved into his apartment when he asked her to hostess a small gathering. That began the growing-up years. Two years of finding unpaid bills stuffed into drawers; of trying to get them paid; of new fears; of his sudden sexual attacks on her, infrequent and puny, when he rushed like a child who has lost its temper upon her, with petty, inefficient frenzy.

Mrs Handforth said, 'My son, Robert, telephoned yesterday. I told him he should come down to help prepare the house in case this storm comes. Besides, he usually comes down once a

75

month . . . I've been worried about him ever since he went to New York a year ago . . . just after Leverett died. New York is so unsettling . . . He's a good boy, about your age . . . but he needs *guidance*.'

She'd seen Robert Handforth about, often enough. He was at least 6 foot 3, with sandy hair and skin, freckles, a narrow face and high forehead. His chin slightly receded and he had a high-bridged nose. Altogether, he was almost a caricature of the in-bred aristocrat, except for the dark, troubled eyes and the sensitive, always slightly twisted mouth. Mrs Handforth said, 'I would like him to meet you, Miss Garland. I think you are a very sensible young woman, and you have character. And breeding, of course.'

There, it was out and plain. She, Lynn Garland, had been picked for inspection as a possible candidate for the post of guide and wife-mother to Robert Monomoy Handforth. Elaine did not need to mention that he was already rich and would be very rich when she died. There was the partnership in Chapelle and Handforth, Investment Bankers. There was the Boston mansion, now simply closed up. There was Monomoy House . . .

Lynn said, 'I don't know whether we'd agree on much. He'll probably think I'm a Communist or something.'

Mrs Handforth said, 'I wish you were. I wouldn't be at all worried about them if they were led by Garlands and Cabots and so on. I'm sure that's why William Bradford became a Catholic. We're their natural leaders. Without people like us, they're a rabble . . . I think you and Robert will get on very well.'

Lynn thought, What has happened to my self-respect, that I don't object more vocally to being selected, like a side of beef, and taken home for inspection? What has happened, she continued, is that I am being pulled about six different ways. I am a normal woman, Robert Handforth is a normal man and, from what she had seen, a kind and essentially simple one. She wanted a home, and a husband, and children, the way most women did.

But she also wanted *her* kids back, the kids in the classroom, the ones whose eyes she looked into, watching for the spark, the girls and boys on the threshold of maturity whom Elliott King was keeping her away from the kids who had taught her that she was a teacher and showed her that Monomoy was her home . . . Then, she wanted social justice for all. And a world fit for babies, birds, and horseshoe crabs. And . . .

76

Mrs Handforth said, 'You're thirty-one. It's time you began to think of settling down. It is not schoolteachers, or spinsters, who guide affairs the way they should go . . . Here we are.'

They came out of the woods. The Packard was waiting, Arthur Tolley ready at the door. Fifteen minutes later the wheels crunched to a halt on the gravelled drive of Monomoy House.

It stood square on the top of North Point, to right and left the sea. It was of brick, foursquare, three stories high, the brick white painted and then sandblasted. At every window the wood-work was white, and the shutters, turned back against the brick, were black. The lawn swept down on the left towards Longships Bay and a small private jetty.

Half a dozen bird feeders dotted the grass. Elaine picked up a big paper bag from just inside the front door and said, 'I'll refill the feeders. This weather makes them all so hungry.'

Lynn went with her, a song humming itself, unbidden, in her head. *This nearly is mine!* Lovely tune, silly words, lovely idea.

Mrs Tolley waddled toward them across the grass. 'You didn't see the telegram, madam? It was lying right there, beside the bird seed . . . They telephoned it, of course, and I wrote it down and put it there.'

Elaine Handforth took the slip of paper, put on her pince-nez, and read slowly. She said, 'Robert's coming. Why didn't he telephone, the silly boy? This was sent from New London. He'll be here any minute.'

Mrs Tolley said, 'I've set the table for him, too.'

'Thank you.'

Mrs Tolley returned to the house. Elaine followed slowly, shaking her head. 'Now why didn't he tell me yesterday he was going to come? He sounded then as though he didn't wish to. Something about a show he had to see . . . Now, my dear, the bathroom's through here . . .'

After washing, Lynn reached the great living-room before her hostess. It filled the whole southern half of the house on the ground floor, with windows facing east, south, and west. It was a room of light as well as space, the parquet floor gleaming and a spray of antirrhinums on Mrs Handforth's desk in one corner. An Adam fireplace occupied the centre of the north wall, and over it a big concave mirror in a gilt frame, with an American eagle. The walls were cream painted, and the furniture was of waxed, unpainted oak.

Lynn heard the sound of a car engine and went to the east windows. A black car had stopped by the front door. Robert

77

Handforth was opening the passenger's door. A girl got out. She was tall, too – dark complexioned, very chic; a short car coat, open; long legs, dark-tone stockings; a grey wool sheath dress.

Lynn stepped away from the window. Why hadn't he told his mother he was bringing a girl with him? She smiled to herself, and only the approaching sound of footsteps enabled her to suppress a laugh. So much for Elaine's matchmaking. So much for her own silly, momentary visions!

The door opened on Robert's voice. 'Darling, this is the—'

The tall girl walked in. Her skin was the colour of pale coffee, the nose small in her face, her mouth wide and her lips large and red. Her eyes were coal black, very large and slightly almond-shaped. Or was the Oriental effect caused by her eye make-up? Her black hair was thick and loosely waved, her bust high and firm, the breasts widely separated. She was probably twenty-seven or twenty-eight years old.

Robert said, 'Oh, I beg your pardon! It's Miss Garland, isn't it?'

The tall girl smiled, white teeth gleaming in the dark face. She moved forward with lithe, dancer's steps. 'I'm Louise Lincoln.'

'How do you do? . . . Your mother invited me to lunch. We've been bird watching, along the old railroad bed.'

'That's one of her favourite walks,' Robert Handforth said. His voice sounded nervous. He lit a cigarette, went to the window, adjusted his tie, coughed. Miss Lincoln stared at Lynn with a wide fixed smile.

Elaine's distinctive footstep, firm but slow, approached. She came into the room, smiling, hands spread. 'Robert . . .' She stopped, still smiling.

'Mother, let me introduce . . . Miss Louise Lincoln. Louise, my mother.'

Elaine's voice was warm. 'I'm so happy to meet you, Miss Lincoln . . . Robert, you naughty boy, why didn't you warn us? Not that it matters. Mary always cooks enough for half a dozen. Did you have a good drive down? You must be tired. Robert, why don't you show Miss Lincoln . . . ?'

Robert's voice came out hoarse and loud. 'Mother, Miss Lincoln and I are engaged to be married.'

'Why, Robert . . . that's just wonderful . . . but you'll still want to wash all that road dirt off yourselves, won't you? Off you go!"

78

The dazzling smile fixed on her face, the tall girl followed Robert out of the room.

Elaine Handforth's calmness vanished. Her face might have been reflected in a plastic mirror, the plastic melting and changing shape under enormous invisible heat. Her hand fell on Lynn's arm, the hand became a claw, the fingers gripped. 'You must stay the night. The week-end! I'll send Arthur to get your clothes. Don't say a word to anyone!'

She released her grip and walked rapidly away. At the end of the room she turned, her hands together. The myriad pieces of light that had formed the known pattern of her face changed, and moved continuously so that she became a different person every moment, now anguished, now furious, now frightened, now lost.

Her eyes narrowed, and she stared sightlessly past Lynn's head. 'She must be his mistress?'

Lynn said, 'Perhaps . . . I think . . .'

'Why don't people accept the fact nowadays? A wife and mistress acknowledging each other's place. It used to work. My great-grandfather did it. The mistress was an actress, well known, Lucille something. People just shrugged and felt sorry for his wife. She didn't feel sorry for herself. She had the mansion, the money, the children, a few lovers . . . Could you face that. now?'

Lynn felt dizzy. 'Face what? *She* is his fiancée.'

'Yes, but suppose . . . later. I'll think of something.'

They returned, the girl coming in on the long lilting legs, Robert stoop-shouldered, trying to squeeze his long thin body into nothing behind her.

Elaine said, 'A cocktail, Miss Lincoln? A glass of sherry? Robert, would you . . . ? Sit down here, Miss Lincoln. Now, tell me all about yourself.'

Robert, at the cocktail cabinet, said, 'Louise is a dancer, Mother, an actress. Her stage name is Avaloka.'

'Avaloka,' Elaine Handforth said slowly. 'Avaloka. What a lovely name! It's Hindu?' ,

'Annamese,' the girl said. Her voice was soft, slightly slurred, with nothing of the American Negro in the accent but something in the timbre.

Elaine said, 'My husband went to Annam years ago. He was quite a globe trotter. It must be lovely country . . . but I suppose you left there when you were quite small.'

'I . . .' the girl began. Elaine swept on over her, 'Avaloka

79

from Annam!' So beautiful, so romantic! 'Thank you, Robert. Lynn, has Robert made you a drink?'

'Yes, thank you,' Lynn said, looking down at her martini. She did not usually drink at midday, but now she needed something strong. The tall girl stared toward the sea. Perspiration shone on her upper lip and in the corners of her nose.

Elaine Handforth said, 'I have it! We'll give a little dinner party tonight, just a few friends and neighbours, to meet Avaloka.'

'Mother . . .'

'Now, don't try to deny a lonely old woman a little party. I'll have to do some telephoning at once. We have ten or fifteen minutes before lunch will be served. Why don't you show Avaloka the house, Robert? Lynn, please stay and help me with the numbers. My eyes, you know . . .'

'Mother . . .'

'No, no! I won't be denied! Run along now!'

As soon as Robert and Miss Lincoln had left the room Elaine wheeled on Lynn. 'Do you think there's any hope of breaking up that engagement?'

'I don't know.'

'I think not. Like most weak men, Robert's fantastically obstinate. He's made up his mind. Very well. For people like us there's only one crime, one stupidity. That is – that is – to show fear!' Her voice had become firm and strong, and again calm. She walked to her escritoire. 'We must look the rest in the eye, and dare them! . . . The Pryors,' she said, and began dialling.

'Mary? This is Elaine Handforth. Robert has come down from New York with a fiancée. Yes, a perfectly lovely girl, an Annamese princess – I can hardly pronounce her name. Do please break any other engagement and come to dinner . . . That's most kind of you. Seven o'clock. Good-bye . . . Now, didn't I hear that Alice Bryant had come down to check on her house? Look her up, please. A woman of no background, but amusing, if you like that sort of thing.'

Mrs Bryant accepted, but there seemed to be some complication. Mrs Handforth said, 'You have a guest? Bring him, too, by all means. Mr Remington? The Coast Guard Chief? Certainly. He's a charming man.' She hung up and looked at Lynn. 'She was going to have Mr Remington to dinner, à deux. I must say, I wouldn't normally invite a chief boatswain's mate to a dinner party of this kind – but why not? Now, Father Bradford . . .'

Lynn Garland sat writing at the big desk in the right corner of her living-room. A well-authenticated legend told that Thoreau had once sat at it, and for that she had paid more than she could afford for it. She wrote a word, looked at it, and shook her head. She brushed back the hair falling down the right side of her face. Constructing the carefully phrased statement that the Teachers' Association had advised her to submit wasn't so easy. Crumpled paper filled the wastebasket. Perhaps she had been too hard on Billy Pryor and the rest of them, after all.

The doorbell rang and she half turned, wondering. Four o'clock on Sunday afternoon? She called, 'Who is it?'

'John Remington,' a voice answered, muffled, from behind the door.

Lynn got up slowly.

The voice continued, 'I would like to speak to you for a moment.'

She opened the door. He was standing there, in dress blues, peajacket buttoned, cap in hand. His weather-burned, mahogany face was like an Indian's of his own West, granite and unsmiling. She said, 'Come in.'

He walked in, closing the door carefully behind him. She backed off a few steps, so that they stood facing each other in the middle of the floor. From his pocket he produced a folded square of paper, and handed it to her. He said, 'It says there that you gave them that information, miss.'

So that was it. She ought to have guessed sooner. She hardly glanced at the paper before answering, 'Yes, I did.'

Someone at the desk in Boston had exaggerated her message, and also misunderstood part of it. But not seriously enough to change the meaning, and it was a coward's trick to cry that you had been misquoted.

Remington said, 'I don't think this report is fair, or honest.'

She said, 'I'm sorry.'

That was all she meant to say. The rest, the fact of a fundamental divergence between their points of view, hardly needed spelling out. But he stood so straight and dignified that after a while she added, 'It's been slanted up rather unfairly, but even that is only justice. What other weapons do they have to fight against police with?'

He said stiffly, 'Lying is never right . . . I telephoned you several times this morning, but there was no answer. So I came for myself.'

'You thought I was just not answering the phone? I was out

. . . as you were yesterday when I tried to call you, to tell you what I was going to tell the newspaper. I thought you ought to know.'

'Why didn't you speak to McGill? He's in charge when I'm not there.'

'He would only have referred me to you . . . asked me to wait. I couldn't wait. You were at the oyster war. I was wishing, this morning, that someone could have seen that, and written to the papers about that too. *Everything* ought to be out in the open.'

'We're not looking for publicity, liss. We only want to do our duty without being called names for it.'

'I hear the fishermen called you lots of names . . . Look, that newspaper report is not exactly what I said. I knew your men didn't actually threaten the union organizers, and I said so. The rewrite man made it sound as if they had.'

'It made a better story,' Remington growled.

'I would ask them to retract but it wouldn't be any use, and it's better not to say anything more. Let sleeping dogs lie, the way the Selectmen and Mr Damato want them to. I am sorry I was misquoted, Mr Remington, but I meant what I said to you, just now . . . about its being right, in the long run. The union men were having unjust methods used against them. Anything that puts a counterweapon in their hands makes towards real justice.'

'I don't agree,' he said. 'What you're saying is, the end justifies the means.'

She hesitated, began to answer, then stopped. She did think that. In cases of extreme social injustice, for example: Is it not almost a duty to steal, if there is no other way to keep alive? What of the duty of rebellion? But she couldn't get into all that now. She had her report to finish.

She said, 'It's something I'd like to talk about with you another time. Tonight, for instance.' She smiled tentatively. 'We're both dining at Monomoy House, I believe.'

'Oh,' he said, 'you'll be there? . . . Well, that's all I had to say. Thank you.'

He nodded slightly and went out. She couldn't be sure whether his face had shown some softening, or merely disgust that he was to be saddled with more of her company.

John Remington walked up Second Street and turned left towards his own little house. Dark clouds covered the sky now and it felt as though the barometer was still going down. The wind blew steadily, moderately hard, from the north-east. He'd better make sure his shutters were tight, storm windows secure, and everything shipshape.

And decide what he ought to wear tonight. Alice had told him the men would not be wearing tuxedos. The question seemed to amuse her. He had one good dark suit, but it wouldn't look like much against the other men's. He didn't know who the other men were going to be; but at Monomoy House you had a pretty good idea they weren't going to be tramps . . . or enlisted men. He chuckled. Except me! Well, he'd wear uniform, in case some emergency came up. It would look better.

He was close to his house now. A Sunday afternoon hush had fallen over the town and no one was about. Not on the streets, but – he turned – a group of people were wandering round the back of his house, where there was no road or trail. There were four men and a woman, going slowly across the dune a hundred feet or so from his back door. Now they stopped. From that height they were looking down into his kitchen and one bedroom. Peering through the increasingly heavy gloom, he recognized Steele; Caroline Merchant; Gene Begg; the big ape Bill Vernon; and Chris Damato.

He walked up beside his house, past the garage, and at the far corner stopped, hands on his hips, staring up at them. Joe Steele called down, 'Hey, Little Boy Blue, you lost your sheep?'

The joke convulsed Bill Vernon with booming laughter. The others did not crack a smile. Steele and his sister wore twin sets of black leather jackets, tight jeans, and high cowboy boots. Their faces reminded John of dogfish.

'Get going,' John said, 'I don't like punks looking in my back windows.'

'Screw you,' Steele said.

'Do you want me to call the cops, Steele?'

Chris Damato laughed, once. He had been practising that cold, single laugh a long time, John thought. Steele said, 'Oh, but Mr Remington, we're on the side of the police, aren't we? Didn't you hear how we helped the fuzz and the Coast Guard put down a riot?'

'Get going,' John said, 'and keep away from my house. And the station.'

'Or we might be found beaten up, some place on the dune?

Well, Little Boy Blue, how'd you like to know that some of your guys would be just as happy to beat *you* up? Eh?'

'I don't need any help,' John said angrily. He started up the slope, his fists doubled.

He saw Damato and Vernon look at Steele for orders. Caroline Merchant stepped a few paces back. Steele said, 'Not this time, admiral. Not this time.' The five of them moved on along the slope without looking back.

John watched them go. Slowly his fists relaxed. God damn it, what the hell was wrong with Monomoy? Or the U.S.A.? Or the world? Where was that world he had once known, and his parents used to talk about, where kids spoke politely to older people, where people avoided trouble instead of looking for it, where the object was not to destroy and use up things, but save them? Shaking his head, he went into his house.

At a quarter past six Lynn's telephone rang. She had just finished drying herself after a bath. Naked, she picked up the receiver.

'Miss Garland? This is Barbara Carpenter . . . You'll think me very inquisitive, but I heard you were going to dinner at Mrs Handforth's tonight . . .'

The voice trailed into silence. 'Yes,' Lynn answered, 'I am.'

'You were there at lunch, too, weren't you?'

'Yes,' Lynn said, 'I was . . . after a bird-watching walk.'

Really, she thought, idly shaking out her hair. Would Mrs Carpenter like to know next what she had been wearing, or what she was going to wear?

'I mean, you were there when Mrs Handforth sent out the invitations for tonight – did the telephoning. I heard it was at lunchtime.'

'Yes.'

'You see, Jim and I have been out all day and only got back half an hour ago. The children were here with a baby sitter most of the time, but she says she took them out early in the afternoon, and . . . you see, Mrs Handforth invited us to her last dinner party, before Christmas, and we couldn't go because little Jerry had an upset stomach, it was quite severe. The doctor came three times that day . . . but Mrs Handforth said she would invite us to her next party, without fail. "You shall come to my very next dinner party" was what she actually said. She doesn't usually forget things, and it would be so awful if we had been invited and didn't turn up . . .'

Lynn said, 'It's rather a special occasion, Mrs Carpenter, and very sudden, too. Robert Handforth came down from New York, bringing his fiancée with him, and Mrs Handforth invited a few people to meet them.'

'I heard that the Coast Guard man, John Remington, has been invited.'

Lynn hesitated a moment. To tell Mrs Carpenter the whole truth about that would start a whole new round of winter gossip. She said firmly, 'Yes, Mr Remington was invited.'

'And she said nothing about us?' The voice sounded petulant now. 'Oh, well . . . well, thank you, anyway. Good night.' The phone clicked.

An hour later Mrs Handforth's Packard arrived to pick up Lynn. In the street the beam from the lighthouse flashed against the housetops, a light broken every four seconds by a momentary spasm. Mrs Crampton lay propped in her high bed in the upper window at the foot of the street, where Arthur Tolley turned the big car. Mr Crampton sat beside her, a book in his hand. The car headed out along North Commerce, then Front, then Bayside . . .

Sunday night . . . Radios blared in lower windows that were closed against the strengthening wind, but still the sound came faintly through to Lynn's ears. From passing cars she heard the twang and jump of twist music. The kids huddled, pressed in them, faces eager, forward pointing, the engines roaring, car and kids alike impatient to be out, off the peninsula, pouring on the coal down the Mid Cape Highway to jukebox Hyannis, the Big Town. A sudden glimpse of a bridge table in a front window, and a woman beginning to draw the draperies. Twenty cars outside the Fisherman's Tavern, behind the darkened cannery. A steady stream of lights coming up in the back window, passing, going on north toward Chatham, the Cape, the 'outside.'

Lynn sat back as the car left the outskirts of town. Let's see, ten people for dinner. How would Mrs Handforth arrange the seating?

Frank Damato looked gloomily round his parlour. No other place to go, for him. If he makes too much noise here, Maria barrels in from the kitchen and throws him out. But a man's got to drink sometime, eh? If he's the police chief, where's he gonna go, eh?

He tossed off the small jigger of whisky on the table beside him and picked up the glass of beer. Sometimes the furniture was like animals, closing in on you. Good stuff, well made though, good and solid, dark, and good dark red curtains, the best.

The police chief can't go into a bar, not to tie one on. So he sits at home by himself looking at the goddam wall and wondering why he took the job, why he ever wanted it. Everyone knocking his brains in.

He sat at the head of the table, his coat off, showing red-and-blue-striped braces as well as a belt. He had pushed the peaked cap with its gold chinstrap to the back of his head. From the back of the house he heard running water and the clash of metal pots.

Now Remington was mad at him because he sprung the Griffiths boy and that seaman in Provincetown. Did Remington think he wanted to get those punks off? They struck a police officer! But then Elliott King comes to him and starts talking about extra police and the fine weather and all kindsa crap but what he means is, Play ball, Frank, or else. Elliott King knows a lot of big shots, don't get fooled, he knows a sight more than any of the Selectmen. So what's the police chief going to do, when all he wants is do a good job? Does he get the extra men and patrol cars or does he send the Griffiths boy and the seaman to jail?

He might talk to that Remington, quiet-like. He wore a uniform, too, he's got responsibilities, he's in the same boat. So tell him to go careful with Elliott King. Elliott's tough . . . wonder whether Remington did take anything from Morgan. No, he wasn't that kind of guy. *Anyone* was that kind of guy. He, Frank Damato, ought to know, for Chrissake.

Take Scully's Bar, Front and Fifth. Harold Morgan owns it but has a guy run it for him. As long as Harold gets his cheque every month, he's happy. In winter Scully's is on the level, but in summer that guy hires three, four waitresses and gives 'em little rooms, at the back, upstairs. They're not pros but he knows how to pick 'em. The summer people go there, private school kids trying it for the first time, businessmen, big shots. It has an Old New England atmosphere, it advertises. My ass. But it's a high-class establishment, there's scandal, and the guy who runs it slips me a few bucks every week, too. I don't want his stinking money but I have to take it, that's what kills me. *I have to*, because he said, sort of smiling nasty, right at the beginning, You take it, Frank, because there's going to be a dozen hookers swear you do, anyway.

86

And now Elliott wants me to jump on Scully's, this coming summer. If there's enough scandal, he thinks Harold will leave town, because Harold's sensitive. Then there'd be only one contractor in Monomoy. And Elliott King knows exactly how much the guy gives me every week and he can prove it.

The world's full of sin, and badness. Last summer the Steele Band beat up a couple of guys right outside *the church*! Imagine that! All the people inside thinking of God and the Holy Virgin . . . least, down by our church they would be, and I guess at the Old Church they think of Jesus Christ and the Holy Ghost even if they don't go much for the Holy Virgin. And I always take duty outside the Old Church because that's the custom for the police chief and it was tough enough getting the people to take a Catholic chief, back when I made it, without looking for more trouble. In church, just for a few minutes, just once a week, *some* people ain't thinking of what they can get, who they can screw out of a buck, and *that's* where Joe Steele and his team of punks have to start a fight.

Chris wasn't in *that* one. About the only time he wasn't . . . That's one thing about Elliott King. He loves children. He loved Chris when he was a kid. Chris used to love him, admire him. Then three, four years ago, pfft. Suddenly Chris don't admire nobody, don't listen to nobody.

He wiped his eyes with the back of his hand and poured out another shot of whisky.

What burns me is, that kid don't realize where we come from, how far we've come. My dad was a waiter, didn't speak no English, he was *pasta*, Christ, I was ashamed to have my friends in the house. In Hyannis, that was, before it got big like it is now. Nine kids we got, me and Maria, the four big girls, then Chris, then the four little girls, and not one of them got the brains like Chris. He can speak good, too, if he wants to. That boy could be President of the United States!

Nelson Pryor said jovially, 'I'm a bourbon man.'

Robert Handforth poured a carefully measured jigger. Nelson thought he'd stay close to the liquor cabinet for a few minutes. This drink looked like a cockroach had pissed in his glass.

Mary gave him a warning glance, and he frowned at her. Her hair looked awful. The other women looked fine, even Lynn Garland. *Her* hair hung down across her forehead, as usual, but it looked as though it was meant to. Elaine Handforth's hair was getting thin, and it was grey, and untidy, but – it looked right. Alice Bryant, ah . . . her hair always looked great, even when she'd just come out of the sea, even when it was spread out on a cushion in her living-room, on a summer evening, the house silent, the dusk just coming. He turned away from her and took a big gulp of his drink, finishing it. Surreptitiously, he poured himself another.

The Princess Avaloka was a coloured girl, if ever he saw one. How had she managed to put that Annamese princess routine over on Elaine, for Christ's sake? Hell of a good-looking woman, though, and the way her great dark eyes went up at the corners, there just might be bit of truth in it. She was talking to Father Bradford, looking up into his face with a wide, white smile.

John Remington came toward him. 'How's the storm, John?' Nelson asked him cheerfully. As soon as he had spoken he knew he should have kept his big mouth shut. Remington fixed him with an intent, aggressive eye, and said, 'I think it's going to hit here, and I think we ought to make what preparations we can. I'm a householder here, too, remember.'

'Sure!' Nelson said, smiling. 'Though I reckon it would take a tidal wave to bring the water up to your place.'

Remington's face was serious. 'It may be as bad,' he said. 'This is a real big storm, Nelson. I've just heard I've lost a good friend in it, a B.M.C., same as me, he got swept overboard from a cutter on routine patrol.'

Nelson drank lovingly, the mellow liquor warming and loosening the muscles of his throat. He said, 'I'm sorry to hear that, John . . . And while your service buddies risk their lives, we civilians squabble over a few lousy oysters, that we're too stingy to look after properly anyway, eh?'

Remington looked momentarily startled. Then his face set. 'Well,' he said, 'I wasn't thinking that right now – but I have. Nelson, last time there was a hurricane warning here, you had a plan to hold an emergency meeting of the Selectmen, with the fire, police, highway chiefs, me, a few others. Honestly, I think you ought to do that now.'

'First thing in the morning,' Nelson said. 'First thing in the morning I'll ring the station, and then we'll all make up our minds, eh? How about that?'

The Coast Guardsman hesitated, and then said, 'O.K. Fine.'

Remington wanted him to say O.K. right away, but what could he do at this time on a Sunday night? What kind of a ruckus would he kick up if he went calling everyone out now, even to arrange for tomorrow? And suppose the storm went away in the night or turned west to hit Virginia? That's what they usually did. Not many hit the Cape at this time of year. It would probably pass by. Hell, sure it would!

Remington said, 'There are things which we can do that don't cost money. Make sure that all fuel and gas tanks are full. Make sure the snowploughs are in good order, arrange to have a call on Elliott and Harold's dozers and tractors. Get the stores to stock up on canned goods, milk, canned vegetables. The power could go off, so . . .'

'Are you still talking about your old storm? Nelson, I declare he did nothing but rant about that storm all the way here.'

Alice Bryant stood between them, cocktail glass in hand. She was wearing a plain white dress, with a sapphire clip on the left shoulder. The column of her neck rose white and firm from the narrow shoulders, and her head was set jauntily on it, the ash-blonde hair falling in an easy wave. The pale-blue eyes had small wrinkles at the corners, wrinkles hinted at a smile or a pout in the corners of her small, red mouth. The watch in its thin sapphire bracelet on her wrist must have cost a thousand bucks.

'It worries me,' John Remington said, not smiling.

'Oh, come on, what can we do? Stock up on snowshoes?'

'We might do just that,' Remington said sombrely.

She took his arm and squeezed. 'You have such a sense of responsibility. That's what we like about him, isn't it, Nelson?'

'Sure thing,' Nelson said.

What had she liked about *him*, then? His political power in the town? The way that certain look glazed his eyes when he watched her stretching out her legs on beach or couch? The fact that he was there at one particular moment? She'd be laying Chief Remington tonight, and God damn it, it hurt. Why? He didn't love her. He wasn't sure that he even liked her very much. So why should one lay, five minutes on a couch, in summer twilight, two years ago, prick like a small sharp needle under his heart? Because he was ashamed? Or because he wanted it again?

He poured himself a drink. Mary was giving him that goddam pleading, warning look. It put his back up. Look, Mary, he could say to her, if I don't take another drink, I'll be thinking of Alice Bryant's crotch, and I'll be plotting and planning to get into it, see? Whereas if I have another drink I shall be thinking of the drink, and about the storm, and this Avaloka woman and Robert Handforth, and Lynn Garland and her suspension from teaching, and the union trouble at the Warren Mercer Company ... and the drink ... and the next drink ... so finally, if Alice does give me the old come-on, I won't be able to do a thing about it. Furthermore, your slip is showing and sure as eggs what you're bending George Zanakis' ear about is the last PTA meeting, or maybe how you sewed up Betty's dress after she ripped it dancing the twist last week, as if that old Greek goat cared one small damn.

This is going to be a bad night, he thought. I always know.

At the dinner table Lynn found that Elaine had placed her between Nelson Pryor and Father Bradford, opposite Avaloka. In this room the curtains were of dull maroon velvet, the walls cream, the table and chairs mahogany. Silver and flowers shone down the centre of the table and a huge spray of hothouse carnations stood on the sideboard.

Mary Tolley began to serve the main course, a rack of lamb. Arthur Tolley half filled Robert Handforth's glass with red wine. Robert sipped, nodded, and mumbled something. Arthur Tolley filled the others' glasses.

Conversation became general. Lynn thought that Father Bradford's clerical collar looked very odd, when, at the same time, you were listening to his extra-flat Harvard accent. But, then, he was always full of contradictions. He had been a Notre Dame quarterback, and looked it ... but that Harvard accent! The Prince-of-the-Churchly way he drank his wine and his suave Italianate bantering with Mrs Handforth did not go with the grey eyes, the almost bald head, and the long, craggy face proper to a direct descendant of Governor Bradford.

Nelson Pryor's voice rose above the general murmur. 'Our Betty's out with Charlie Tyson again. I thought he was dating JoAnn Griffiths these days.' The words came out slightly blurred, and Mary Pryor looked up anxiously.

John Remington said, 'JoAnn's a good girl ... a nice girl.'

Lynn thought, JoAnn nice? Good? She'd heard a lot of things said about the girl, but never that.

'And Charlie Tyson,' Nelson said quickly, 'what about him? Is he a good kid, *for our Betty*?'

John Remington said, 'He's young ... he's a good kid, but immature yet.'

Nelson said, 'I see. Well, thanks for telling me.' He turned to his hostess. 'We were talking about the park just now ... I heard they made up their minds in Washington, what they're going to call it – the Diadem Cape National Sea Shore and Bird Sanctuary.'

Elaine Handforth said sharply, 'Ridiculous, Nelson!'

'The Diadem Cape National Sea Shore and Bird Sanctuary.'

Elaine said, 'They promised! The man who came down and talked to me promised! So did Senator Quinn. I was clearly given to understand it would be called the Handforth National Park!' Her voice rose stridently and the guests stared at their plates. 'This is disgraceful! How do you know, Nelson?'

Nelson Pryor mumbled, 'Elliott King told me. He heard from his political friends. It's definite, he says. That is, if the park goes through, of course.'

'Disgraceful,' Elaine said. 'This puts quite a different complexion on the matter.'

They all began to talk at once, to tell her that the people would always know whom the land really belonged to, what its real name was – all except Robert Handforth and the tall, dark girl. Those two had been pushed, politely, into the background from the beginning. Silent and ill at ease, they had been a captive audience for talk which – near Mrs Handforth at least – was always of Monomoy. Now they looked at each other, and the girl's smile did nothing to disguise her isolation.

Alice Bryant made a joke, and chattered on, light, witty, sophisticated. The tension over Elaine's outburst eased. Alice leaned across the table and spoke to John Remington. Lynn sensed a promise in the way she parted her lips, in a tiny intimate gesture of her hand. She would sleep with John Remington tonight, because she was bored. Where was the punishment for women like that? Women to whom clothes and comfort meant everything, the world's miseries nothing? Women who used their qualities of brain or body solely for their own pleasure?

Elaine Handforth's voice rose above the others. 'And now, as you all know, we have a little announcement to make . . .'

Suddenly they fell silent. Suddenly the smile vanished from the dark girl's face. Elaine said, 'I am privileged to announce the engagement of my only son, Robert Monomoy Handforth, the sixteenth of that name, to the Princess Avaloka, of Annam.'

Father Bradford swirled the brandy carefully in the deep-bosomed snifter. Dinner had ended, they were gathered in the living-room, and Miss Garland was talking with Mary Pryor.

91

The young woman had a mobile face, and more illuminating than she probably imagined. Every time she looked at Alice Bryant, for instance, her expression subtly shadowed. That was reasonable. Alice was a vain and shallow woman, sensuous in the full meaning of the word, and predictable in the way a small river is predictable: you know that it will always find and follow the line of least resistance.

But Miss Garland's disapproval might be more personal. It might be due to jealousy; which meant that she had a romantic interest in Chief Remington. That, too, was reasonable. He was a divorced man, alone and lonely, with good prospects in his profession. But hadn't one of the Coast Guardsmen mentioned how angry he had been over Miss Garland's report to the papers in the Warren Mercer Company trouble? That relationship needed watching . . .

Elaine had taken it very well, considering. It was hard to believe she had had *no* warning, explicit or implicit. But, looked at from Robert's point of view, that was the only possible way. Robert had never been exactly frightened of Elaine, as he had been of that old bully of a father; but she was an integral part of the system of pressure against him. He could never have found the courage to talk about it with her. Anyone other than a Handforth – or a Bradford – would simply have married the girl and told his parents he'd done it. To Robert that, too, was impossible. This was the way it had to be. There was more to come, too. That was clear from Robert's inability to concentrate, from the way he didn't seem to be listening even to his fiancée as she whispered to him on the sofa. A beautiful, a very striking woman, fine, intelligent eyes . . .

Robert stood up suddenly, and his voice was loud enough for everyone in the room to hear. 'Mother . . . I'm selling my partnership in the firm.'

Father Bradford nodded thoughtfully. One more chain snapped.

Robert cried, 'I never wanted to be a banker. I hated every minute of it.' His voice rose, his prominent Adam's apple moved rapidly up and down. 'I tried to tell you . . .'

Just a year since Leverett Handforth died, Father Bradford thought. Why hadn't he done it sooner? Because this girl gave him the desire, and the strength?

'Let's not talk about the past,' Elaine said, laying her hand gently on her son's arm. 'What are you going to do now?'

'I'm going into the theatre,' Robert said.

Avaloka spoke up suddenly. 'Robert's going to go into production.'

'I've been studying it with Saul Jordan for six months now,' Robert said. 'We're only waiting for a good play, and then we'll go in together. I know a lot of theory already, but I've got to find my feet in practice.'

Father Bradford thought, It will stand as good a chance as any, with Jordan's fame and talent and Robert's money. And of course Avaloka will get her big break in the show . . . and become a star . . . and that will be the end of the kind of domestic life Robert is probably dreaming of.

Elaine spoke privately, her hand still resting on her son's arm. 'I should have guessed. Your room was always full of books about the theatre, plays, pictures of actors and actresses.' She let her hand fall slowly to her side. 'It's quite a surprise, though.' Her wandering eye fell on Avaloka, paused – was there a baleful flash in it? – passed on.

Father Bradford decided that he had been putting the cart before the horse. Robert did not meet Avaloka and because of her decided to go into the theatre. He went to the theatre because that was what he yearned for, and there he met Avaloka.

Leverett Handforth must have been more cruel, or more insensitive, than even . . . his own father. Ah, that was a shameful comparison. Twenty paternosters, and beg forgiveness for implying such a thing . . . Now he must speak to Robert, say a few congratulatory words, and then, soon, it would be time to leave.

'Tha' brandy's empty, Father. Lemme ge' you another.'

Nelson Pryor leaned over him, his speech really blurred now, the thin grey-flecked hair mussed, the spectacles awry, the eyebrows raised in a childlike astonishment.

'I'm a bourbon man, myself,' Nelson went on. 'You made a big change, too, Father, didn't you? Jus' like Robert. This is a night for True Confessions, eh? I've always wanted to ask you . . . why did you do it?'

One of those small social tides that sweep guests up and down living-rooms had left the two of them isolated. Mary Pryor was watching with strained anxiety from the far end of the room, but George Zanakis was talking to her, and she could do nothing.

'Why?' Nelson persisted. 'Or is it personal? I don't want to be personal.'

Father Bradford didn't have to ask what Nelson wanted to

know. The question was, How could the direct descendant of a Pilgrim governor become a Roman Catholic? It ought to be an easy question to answer, and a priest could not accept that the revelation of God's Truth was personal in the way that, say, a boy's relationship with his earthly father was personal. A priest should be proud to tell how the truth came to him. Yet he had always found a peculiar reluctance to speak about this matter, and an awkwardness, so that a flush reddened his neck, and he knew it had come, but he could not control it, and that annoyed him.

He said, 'One day, I thought about what I really believed, as a Congregationalist . . . and found nothing. Then a Harvard friend—'

'When did your father die?' Nelson said, swaying forward, his eyebrows rising still farther.

Father Bradford felt the blush spreading to his face. 'It had nothing to do with my father,' he said sharply. 'My father was alive . . .'

'I bet he was disappointed,' Nelson said. 'No offence meant. Only, it's human nature, isn't it? . . . I mean Frank Damato would be pretty cut up if Chris, even *that* dirty little punk, joined *our* church, wouldn't he? And so would I, if Betty or Billy . . .'

Father Bradford went on hurriedly: 'This friend introduced me to a priest. We talked. He did not convert me, though. I converted myself. After six months I knew there was no other truth.'

'And then you decided to be a priest? I mean, you found something good, you wanted to tell everybody else, right?'

'I didn't feel a vocation for the priesthood until after I transferred to Notre Dame.'

'Boy, that musta been the day, the day you told your dad about *that*, eh?'

How could anyone like Nelson Pryor understand what it had been like? Growing up in that great house, Exeter and Harvard ahead, the family business stretching all round, for ever and ever, and father so kind, so understanding – and understanding *nothing*. His father just about went to pieces when he said he was leaving Harvard for Notre Dame. Leaving *Harvard*? It was far worse than leaving the Congregational Church.

Nelson waved his glass, spilling whisky on the carpet. 'I'm stewed,' he said distinctly, 'otherwise I wouldn't be talking to you like this . . . always wanted to . . . I bet they gave you a bad time at Notre Dame, too. All the micks and dagos and bohunks . . . So you played football, to *show* 'em, eh? Remember that time – *Life* magazine? You showed 'em that a New England Pilgrim Yankee could make their goddam football team, eh!'

Father Bradford winced. Yes, he'd shown them, in the pride of his youth and pride of his family. Every thought and suspicion that crossed Nelson Pryor's owlish eyes were true— He was a Bradford of Massachusetts. Why should the Church be run by immigrants, by nothings, and nobodies? Why should it skulk in back alleys on the wrong side of the tracks, its parishioners labourers and waiters, cooks and cops?

Nelson swayed forward, 'Now, Father, what about the girls, eh? You know the story, 'bout a priest and a rabbi, see?'

Thank heavens, the tide had turned. Mary Pryor came fast, hurrying across the floor. 'Nelson, it's time we went home.'

It was time they all went home. Father Bradford was glad he didn't have to answer Nelson's question. He liked women. They were a temptation, and always had been.

'Nelson!'

Mary Pryor jogged her husband's arm with nervous impatience. Nelson turned slowly, and went on turning. He said distinctly, 'Half the time . . . everybody's lying.' He fell with a heavy crash to the floor. The glass leaped from his hand and shattered. Whisky flowed in a short, dark flood across the parquet.

John Remington knelt beside him. 'Out cold,' he muttered. 'He didn't hit his head. I saw. He ought to be O.K.'

Mary Pryor began to cry, the patchy powder at once streaking down her cheeks. Elaine Handforth took her by the arm and said, 'It's perfectly all right, my dear. Poor Nelson, he does overwork so much . . .'

Father Bradford carefully put down his brandy glass, long since empty, and helped lift Nelson. 'We'd better carry him to his car,' Remington said, 'but then . . .'

'I'll follow in mine,' Father Bradford said. 'I'll give you a hand at the house.'

'And I,' George Zanakis said, 'I will follow also.'

Mary Pryor wept on, noisily.

George Zanakis switched off the ignition and stepped down. For a moment he stared at the dark, high-standing bulk of the Model A. She cost – what? – $400, something like that, when he bought her. Now, thirty years later, people were offering him two and three thousand. It was crazy. Everything, everybody crazy, no sense of values. If you came across truth, or worth, it was by mistake, and the only way to deal with it was to get drunk.

He switched on the light in his hut, and stared, uncomprehending, at the painting on the easel opposite. Who had painted that? Who'd left that cheap, sentimental daub on his easel?

By God, it was his own. In this light, come upon suddenly, its badness clamoured aloud. The idea was bad, the technique was bad.

He yawned and took off his coat. The windows rattled steadily, and the house frame creaked.

Poor Pryor. A good man there, somewhere, spoiled by politics. Why didn't he leave it to the Elliott Kings, the Carpenters? . . . Quite a job they'd had, getting him to bed, but Father Bradford was strong, and he himself . . . he was not strong, but he was expert. He'd had plenty of practice, long ago, carrying drunks of all sizes and sexes up and down stairs much narrower than the Pryors'.

Nelson would be asleep now, rather than unconscious, Mary weeping like a leaky gutter beside him. And the Coast Guard fellow cuddled up with Alice Bryant. And Father Bradford brewing up more of those tasty certainties that all the churches sold to poor, frightened, lost humanity. And Robert Handforth creeping down the corridor to get into bed with the Negro girl. No, she wasn't in the mood. What a model she'd make.

And that left Miss Garland and old Mrs Handforth unaccounted for. Which of them would welcome his seventy-six-year-old lust to their bosom? Neither. Was it a crime then to get horny at this age? To remember what you used to feel like, and have that feeling return – for how long? *Let's smuggle it up to London, quickly, milord* . . . There was a little tramp working in Scully's Bar. But to pay money was always wrong. A girl, a girl on the couch there, a girl he knew as a human being, stretching out her arms . . .

He swore a violent Greek oath, and began to undress, throwing his clothes on a chair.

An interesting evening. But what did Mrs Handforth want? She had money, land, house, a special position in Monomoy. What did she *not* have, that the name of the park could give her?

'Ah . . . ah, so that's it,' he said softly, speaking aloud. 'So you are my sister under the skin. You too want to live for ever.'

Wearing only long johns, grey hair matted on his chest and the hair on his head disarranged when he pulled off his shirt, he advanced on the easel.

'Not for you, even without my signature,' he said angrily. 'There are plenty who would recognize my brushwork.' He tore the painting from the easel and began to break it up, banging the frame on the edge of the Franklin stove, ripping the canvas with a knife and thrusting the pieces, frame, canvas, and all, into the stove. Another smaller painting standing on the floor in the corner caught his eye, and he attacked that in the same manner as the first. The fire crackled, muffled and indignant, in the stove.

'That's better,' George Zanakis said.

All right. Some bad work is burned up. But where is the great work? Where would he find it, already seventy-six and nothing, nothing still living except *The Druggist*, immortal beyond his power to kill.

What sort of thing would the immortal subject be? When it came, would he recognize it? If he recognized it, would he be able to paint it? Would his eye see true, would his hand work true to the vision of his eye? When he had found the subject and the object, and brought hand and eye to them, and the work was done, would he recognize it? Would he burn it? *Had he burned it already?*

Late, Maria Damato appeared out of the kitchen. She was thin and dark of skin, her thick grey hair drawn back in a bun. She held a skillet in her hand, and scrubbed it energetically with a scouring pad as she talked. 'You better stop drinking, why you drinking alla time? You been drinking alla day.'

'For Chrissake speak properly,' Frank said, 'you sound like a goddam wop.' His own accent became more Italian when he was excited, he knew. Maria never made any attempt to hide hers.

'So what became of the Holy Name Society?' she said vigorously. 'Maybe you wanta wash out your mouth with soap, and say ten *Aves*. Cristoforo out drinking too, what do you expect?'

Maria said, '*Che forabutto!* He's a no-good liar, rotten rotten! Why you never come to Mass? Father asking me again, thissa morning, why don't Peabody go stand onna Green outside the other church, you're a Catholic.'

'I told you a hundred times,' Frank said. Was this the girl who had crooned like a wild animal under him the first time, in a field, thin, like she was now but her hair a dense black wave that he had to sweep back to kiss her?

The scourer made a harsh and realistic sound under her voice. 'You had enough, Francini, you better go to bed.'

They both heard the front door open. Maria turned her head, and Frank rose quickly. The boy who came in was sturdy, wide-eyed, well built. He could have been a football star, like Joe Bellino, but he was too small, only 5 foot 5. He made to go straight on down the passage toward the kitchen. 'Hey, Chris,' Frank cried, 'got nothing to say to your dad?'

'Yeah,' the boy said, unsmiling. 'Buzz, fuzz.' Maria let out with a backhanded slap that caught him on the cheek. '*Spacciato*,' she said venomously.

Frank cried, 'Don't hit the kid, Maria . . . What were you doing snooping along the dune this afternoon? Crable saw you.'

'Peddling goof balls,' the boy said, 'and planning to rob a bank.' He went on down the passage.

'He no joke,' Maria said, nodding her head vigorously. 'They sell goof balls, they jump on decent girls and women, they steal little things. Soon they steal big things, bank maybe, or store cashbox . . .'

'Maria, I don't think . . .'

'And pretty soon, our Cristoforo gonna kill someone, and go to the electric chair.'

'Maria.'

John Remington drove very carefully. On Sunday night the roads were liable to be full of crazy teenagers . . . Well, perhaps they weren't all bad, but one was enough, when he'd tanked up with booze he couldn't hold.

'Poor Nelson,' Alice Bryant said. 'Does he often do that?'

John was strongly aware of her perfume. It was a heavy animal perfume, and she used very little of it, but he recognized it. It was the same stuff Janet took to using, near the end. Janet used to slosh it on like water, until that guy taught her better.

He said, 'Sometimes, I believe.'

'I don't blame him,' Alice said '—having to live with *her*. That hair, those clothes! She always looks like a caricature of the dejected housewife.'

'They don't have much money,' John said defensively. Mary

Pryor did look a mess most of the time, but he liked her. Plenty of things mattered more, in a woman, than looking smart. He'd learned that the hard way.

'Money has nothing to do with it,' Alice said. 'She has no taste. Press the lighter for me, there's a dear.'

Her fingers, taking the glowing lighter from him, touched his briefly. The sweet smell of tobacco filled the car. Monomoy light shone straight at them down the road, momentarily cut out, and shone again.

'And what did you think of Avaloka from Alabama,' Alice said. 'It would make a great song title, wouldn't it?' She laughed cheerfully.

John said, 'You mean, you think she's a Negro?'

'Sure. High yaller, maybe. She could have some Indian or Javanese blood somewhere, more likely Chinese. Did you ever see the Chigroes in Jamaica? Some of them look very like that.'

John said, 'And he's going to marry her?'

'Why not?' Alice said negligently. 'She looks like a real good lay. That counts a lot with men, before they marry it. Afterwards, it's only, wait till I tell you what happened to me on the fourteenth green.'

She laughed again, and John thought, She's a very real person, all the way through. She really has money. She really knows what to do with it. She really is witty and sophisticated. She doesn't read *Vogue* to see what a smart woman should wear, the editors of *Vogue* come to her to find out.

But if Avaloka were a Negro, then the next Monomoy Handforth would be a mulatto. Negroes got a dirty deal all around. More than once he'd taken strong action to see that the United States Coast Guard wasn't slighted or insulted, in the person of Negroes who had the right to wear its uniform. But for a Negro to be the Handforth of Monomoy, that wasn't right. It didn't fit. People expected the Handforths to act in a certain way, to be a certain sort of person.

Alice said, 'Forget about them. Robert doesn't want to live here and try to steer the estate through what's coming. It's too much trouble, even if he was interested. Sure, some people will make it tough for them – the old families, society with a capital S. Why should he worry? They can live in Paris, London, Rome . . .'

John said, 'But that would mean there won't be another Handforth in Monomoy.'

'So what? They raise you right feudal in Wyoming, don't they?'

They reached the front of her house, and she said, 'Park her round the front.'

'The front?'

'Facing the bay. That's what *we* always call the front, not the side facing the Green . . . That's fine – here.'

She stayed seated until he came round and opened the car door for her. Then, as she stepped out, she straightened, stretched with a long, slow out-thrusting of her arms, and lowered the arms round his neck, her fingers clasped. She drew his face down. Her body pressed quietly to him. Her lips were soft and wet and parted.

After a time she moved her head. 'Yummm. I like hard men. Let's go in, and I'll put out the *drink*, and turn on the *music*, and get into something *com*fortable. That's the right phrase, isn't it?'

John thought of many things, all in the space of a second. The Monomoy light dipped, shone again. Hell, I'm in no mood to argue with myself, he thought. Take it the easy way, for a change. He followed her into the house.

Alice Bryant stretched her toes, and turned over to lie on her side, her head propped on one elbow. In this position she could see herself comfortably in the big mirror that hung, slightly downtilted, above the fireplace. It was a pity the couch was not wide enough for two, then they could still be lying here together, and she could admire his barrel chest and narrow hips, and the brown colour of him, as though he were made of dark oak wood, and the pattern of him against her own white skin and soft curves.

He had gone off to the bathroom, and she was alone. Perhaps he was one of those men who have a compulsion to wash their hands and faces, brush their hair, and maybe, their teeth, after making love to a woman. It always annoyed her slightly, as though she were unclean . . . He had been surprisingly voluptuous in his love-making, shy at first, then strong and sensual. She had given as good as she got. Maybe a bit better, she thought comfortably. It wasn't *her* who'd first cried hold, enough! Women had a big advantage there, of course, and, boy, did they need some advantage in this man's world!

She examined herself carefully. Thirty-six, and that's the truth, but I'll swear I don't look more than twenty-seven in that mirror: bosom high and firm even without the bra, waist good, hips under control, legs fine, complexion – well, a girl's complexion usually was nice and rosy after a good lay. Except maybe . . . she rolled to her feet, walked across the room, and peered intently into the mirror. God damn it, the lines were coming back around the eyes. Christ, next year – thirty-seven. Year after – thirty-eight.

He came back into the room, closing the door carefully behind him. He stopped and stared at her. 'Won't you get cold?'

He disapproved, rather. Well, the hell with him. He was a nice guy, but, in the end, what was he? A poor kid from the wild and woolly West, an enlisted man. He wasn't going to alter her way of life one damn little bit. Bill Decker had tried for five years, and found he couldn't. Lloyd Hartford Bryant the Third had known all along he couldn't change her. So he hadn't tried. So they were still married.

'You don't think I look nice without my clothes on?' she said, almost rudely.

He came forward then and took her in his arms. 'You're beautiful,' he said earnestly, 'really beautiful.'

She pressed against him, thinking, He means it, and it's true! He was back in his clothes, and his buttons were pressing into her bosom. She slipped out of his hold, picked up her wrap, and put it on. 'Now, bring me a drink, a big, dark, whisky and water, just like Nelson drinks. Only mine's Scotch.'

John Remington bent over the table to make the drinks. She must have mentioned Nelson from some Freudian compulsion, she thought. He had stood where John was standing . . . and then he'd poured himself a gigantic bourbon. Ever since, when they met, if he had a drink in his hand he looked at her with a special look, remembering, but not begging for a repeat. A nice man, with that awful wife like a millstone around his neck.

She patted the couch beside her. 'Sit down. Put your head back. Relax . . . Why didn't we do this earlier?'

'We nearly did, last summer,' he said. He coloured, and added quickly, 'Least I was thinking—'

'Oh, you needn't apologize. So was I. We'd been talking about your wife . . .'

'I'd had a couple more whiskies than I needed,' he said quickly. 'Would you like me to put on a record?'

'No. And don't change the subject . . . You were childhood sweethearts, weren't you?'

'Yes.' He spoke with his head averted, sullenly.

She put her hand on his arm. 'John, I'd like to know. We are at least friends – now – aren't we?'

Hell, did she really want to know? Did she want to assuage the unmistakable fear of women in him? Was it idle curiosity? Too late now, for he'd taken a big gulp from his glass, and turned to her, and begun to talk. She drew up her knee under her chin and listened.

'Janet and I were kid sweethearts. We didn't call it going steady in those days. She was the girl next door. Her father worked for a construction firm. He lost his job, too, like my dad. That was the depression, you know.'

'I've heard of it,' she said.

'It damned near killed *us*,' he said. 'It did kill Dad, in '38 – working at lifting logs, the only job he could get, when he knew he had a bum heart. I was eight then, and I remember him, thin, stooped, looking about ninety, catching my hand one time, when he came in dead beat from the job, and saying, Work for the government, Johnny, don't let this happen to your kids, do you hear me, Johnny, remember now. We didn't have the right kinds of friends. I couldn't get a nomination to any of the service academies when I grew up . . . maybe I wouldn't have passed the exams anyway . . . so I enlisted.'

He glowered at her, as though she had contradicted him, and she said, 'What has this to do with Janet?'

'Plenty,' he said. He jumped up, poured another drink, and came back to the couch. 'Plenty. I enlisted in the Coast Guard, but I didn't enlist for security, in spite of what Dad said. I saw everyone grubbing in the dirt for food, men standing cap in hand like goddam slaves, women running off ahead of their best friends to get the last job going at the new store, men lying, stealing. Fellows I know used to go out and set fire to the forests south there, along the Colorado line, so there'd be work for fire-fighters putting out the fires – 60 cents a day. Dad did that, too. All I could see was that money made people act like animals . . . '

'Lack of money, you should have said,' she interjected.

'Yes . . . no! Some people made a little money, and those were the ones who gouged and bit and kicked harder than any-one, to make more . . . It made me sick to my stomach, so I enlisted. That was in 1948. In '52 I married Janet. I was B.M.3 by then – Boatswain's Mate, 3rd class – and I felt rich. I felt rich to Janet, I felt rich to myself, then. Two hundred bucks a month and all found. Our first post together was San Diego, California. We were happy there. We were both discovering a lot of things . . . music, how to eat decently, white tablecloths, flowers on the table. John Junior was born there, in '53. So was Betty, in '55. Then I was posted to San Francisco.'

'Buy me another drink,' she said. 'Just like the last.'

He got up without a word. She felt comfortable. No ticking clock reminded her that time ground cruelly onward. John gave her a whisky, and began to talk, with the same half-eager, half-bitter animation.

'Things started to go wrong right after that. We got into debt, and I found out why. It wasn't anything special, just our ideas changing. And her ideas changed faster than mine. Everything was reasonable, when you took them one by one. It's false economy to use cheap grade oil in a better car. How can a man complain that his kids are getting heavy cream when they used to get the top off the Grade A? How many pairs of shoes is a woman supposed to own before it becomes extravagance? . . . I had to go to Seattle on temporary duty, and when I came back it had happened. She'd got friendly with a fellow . . . a contractor.'

'Like Elliott King?' Alice asked lazily.

'Well, he was a big guy, like Elliott, otherwise he was quite different. I liked him. He was a friend. He came to our house and took us out a lot. We went to good restaurants, better than I'd ever thought of going into, even if I'd been able to afford them. We ate things we'd never heard of, and drank wine out of old bottles with cobwebs on them . . . Janet moved faster than I did. She read books and I didn't have time to. She went to matinées, and I was on the station. Then one day she told me, she and this man, they were in love. Just like that she said it, very calm. I felt like she'd hit me between the eyes with a rock. Later we had a fight. I said it was his money she was in love with. She called me an animal. I went to see him, the man, and he just about cried on my shoulder. He hadn't wanted this to happen, but it had. Janet hated me. He told me, and it was true. She told me, too.'

'Of course she had to hate you,' Alice said, 'otherwise how could she not hate herself?'

'She left,' he said bitterly. 'She walked out, with the kids. She didn't ask for any money. I let her divorce me. I applied for transfer to the east coast. I can see the kids any time I want to, have them with me for a vacation, he'll pay the fares. They live in a big house on Nob Hill . . . Everything broken and spoiled, because of money. I don't know what's going to happen to this country, to the world, everyone grubbing for money worse than during the depression. Does anyone think about duty any more? About honour?'

He ended, and she did not speak. His wife had left him because she had seen another way of life, and he had not been able to give it to her; or, perhaps, not able to adjust his ideas quickly enough. He was a troubled man.

He spoke at last. 'Are you going to race *Delilah* again next season?'

'That's the idea,' she said.

'I'll beat you this time,' he said, smiling. 'I'm scraping *Viking's* bottom and repainting with a new fast paint that's my own invention. I'm going to take something off the centreboard. I'll beat you, two to one. Five bucks on it?'

She laughed. 'Done! Unless this storm silts up the bay and we don't get any racing at all. What's the latest? Will it be exciting? I love excitement.'

He looked at her oddly. 'It could be. It could be too exciting.'

She sat up quickly, clapping her hands, and the wrap fell apart from neck to knee, 'Goodie goodie gumdrops, then I shall stay! I shall stay and live through the Great Storm like a real Cape Codder, and you'll come and hold my hand when it thunders and lightnings, won't you?'

He drained his drink and stood up. 'Any time you need help, unless I'm on duty, of course. I'll be pretty darn busy up at the station . . . I'd better be going. A late report ought to be in, and I must see it. Don't get up, please.'

She made no attempt to hold him, but accepted his awkward kiss with a smile and a slithering caress of her hand over his shoulder. A minute later he was gone.

Why hadn't he stayed a bit longer? Here she was, on display from the snaggle to the zatch, and, not to be too goddam genteel about it, still horny as hell. The last man who'd left her in this state was that hulking, pipe-smoking, shaggy hero, Elliott King. My God, five years ago – no, six – anyway it was the summer after she married Lloyd. But Elliott King and John Remington were very different sorts of men. Elliott hadn't any duty to go to. He'd just gone. She remembered the way he looked at her and took deep breaths into his chest, and sort of grunted like a bull until she was ready to rip her clothes off right there on the beach, sand and all. She'd hardly managed to get up the slope, into the car, and home, and say, 'Won't-you-come-in-for-a-gin-and-tonic-Elliott?' Then she'd stood, ready, aye, ready, waiting, eyes closed, thinking he'll rip my skirt off and my pants off and throw me on to the floor and then, oh, boy, what's he going to feel like, that big battering ram of a man?

And then – nothing, good-bye, gone. Conscience, maybe? Fright? Thinking his wife would find out? What would he care if she did? Anyway, it wasn't conscience. She knew what a man's conscience looked like. It looked like a prick in reverse – big, hard prick, little flabby conscience; little flabby prick, big hard conscience.

The hell with them. She got up, poured herself a generous drink, and took it upstairs to bed.

CHAPTER FOUR

MONDAY

Nelson parked his car, switched off, and for a moment sat motionless. His head throbbed, his eyeballs ached, and he would have liked to rest his head on the wheel; but the cop on duty outside Town Hall was watching him, and there were people about. Old Nelson must have tied one on last night, he could almost hear them saying. Old drunken Nelson. Well, they still voted for him, didn't they? Though why they should want to do that for a no-good, inefficient, helpless bastard like him . . .

The wind blew strong and cold from the north-east, the sky was overcast. Between the houses of the Green, Longships Bay showed dirty grey streaked with dirty white. Soiled snow and sand whirled up into his eyes.

'Morning, Mr Pryor,' the cop said.

'Morning, Johnny,' Nelson said, and walked up into Town Hall.

They were waiting for him round the table in the small conference room. Walter and Jim; Flo Monsey, town clerk and treasurer; Bertha Robinson, clerk to the Selectmen; Fred Haggerty, assistant to the Selectmen; George Lathrop, surveyor of highways; Elliott King, chairman of the School Committee; Walter Kimmel, harbourmaster; Martin Fox, town counsel; Dr Henry Burroughs, chairman of the Board of Health; Merrill Crosby, fire chief and forest warden; Frank Damato, police chief; and the four prominent citizens invited for their special knowledge or position – Arthur Evans, chairman of the board of the First National Bank of Monomoy; Chief Boatswain's Mate John Remington, U.S. Coast Guard; Harold Morgan, contractor; and Mrs Elaine Handforth.

Nelson said, 'I'm sorry we had to phone you so early, but when Chief Remington called me with the latest Weather Bureau report, I knew we'd have to get together and decide what we ought to do. The report forecasts a whole gale will hit the Cape sometime tonight with snow or rain. Probably snow.'

There was a shuffling of feet and creak of chairs as all settled themselves more comfortably.

Nelson looked at his notes. 'Well, first, what about the fishing boats?'

The harbourmaster said, 'The gale warning's up. I wouldn't go, not with the wind in this quarter.'

Walter Crampton said, 'Except for the last few days, we've had bad weather, storms and fog, since Christmas. The fishermen can either go out to fish, or go on relief, or starve. Unless it gets a sight worse than it is now, there'll be plenty going out.'

Nelson said, 'In that March storm three years ago, a lot of the houses along Front Street were flooded. You know we've been thinking about building a sea wall, but we don't seem to have got around to it yet . . . so meantime, maybe the people along Front Street, and the lower houses on the cross streets – like yours, Walter – should move their valuables to the upper floors, and be prepared to go and live with relatives or friends. When's the next spring tide?'

'A week today,' the harbourmaster said, 'full moon. The storm'll be long gone by then.'

It ought to be, Nelson thought, but maybe it won't be. Everyone talked about the weather, no one did anything about it – and damn few even knew what they were talking about.

Elliott King said, 'What's the situation on that sea wall, Nelson? A committee was going to investigate and report to you, about now.'

'Yes,' Nelson said.

Elliott went on, 'I heard they recommended building a sea wall from Town Pond to . . .'

'Maybe they did, maybe they didn't,' Nelson said. God, how his eyeballs hurt.

Elliott cocked his heavy handsome head to one side. 'We'd sure be pleased to start building it, Nelson – Harold or I – or both of us together.'

Nelson snapped, 'That wall would cost over two hundred thousand dollars, with state and federal aid covering less than half. What's that going to do to the tax rate? Over and above what we're already committed to, for the extra police, for Town Pond, for the auditorium, a lot of road improvements . . .'

Frank Damato sounded anxious and hurt. 'We need the police, for sure. You know what happened on Saturday.'

'If we don't do something about Bayside Road . . .' Lathrop began.

Nelson Pryor banged his knuckles impatiently on the table.

107

'This meeting's about the storm. What needs to be done? What *can* be done? Chief Remington's been thinking about this for a long time. John, give us your opinion.'

Remington looked down at the notebook open on the table in front of him. He said, 'It's a big storm – two in one, actually. The Mississippi valley one joined the Florida one last night ... It's moving very slowly, and it could dump a great deal of snow. We expect very high tides on the outer beach, and in proportion, on Nantucket Sound and in Longships Bay . . . I don't think fishing boats should go out, but I can't order them not to. But any captain proposing to go out should ring the station, and tell us where he's going. And I'd like a list of boats already out, where they are, and when they're expected back.'

He paused, looking at Walter Kimmel. Kimmel said dubiously, 'I guess we can figure out who's at sea . . . not when they're expected back.'

Remington continued: 'I don't think we're going to be able to keep any but the most important roads open, after the first twenty-four hours of snowfall. But we'll be in a better position if we commandeer all the bulldozers and earthmovers on the peninsula. Mr Lathrop knows more about that than I do, though.'

The surveyor of highways was a short wiry man in his fifties, with a long nose, arched eyebrows, and a weather-beaten skin. He said, 'The country roads will be real bad, even though the Great Dune protects them from drifting too high – except on the Tongue. It could drift there, so bad the ploughs can't clear it. That happened in '54 and '27. Elliott, you have a couple of dozers in town, don't you?'

'Yep. Rented from Bigley Construction. They're on a job right now, working like crazy trying to get it done before the storm hits.'

'Right. We won't get any more down from the mainland, because everyone up there's going to be in the same boat. Unless we offer a heck of a lot of money, and right now.'

'That's out of the question,' Nelson interjected. Money, money, money, he hated the word.

Lathrop continued: 'If the snow keeps piling up, a lot of houses, some streets, are going to get blocked off, because after a couple of days we spend most of our time hauling the snow down to the bay, and dumping it.'

Nelson said, 'Thanks, George . . . Any more, Chief?'

Remington said, 'I think the fuel dealers should make sure

their tanks and trucks are full. Gas stations, too. The ploughs and sanders and spreaders will be going day and night, and they use a lot of gas. The power lines are likely to come down – then there'll be no light, and no cooking in a lot of houses. Fire's going to be a big danger, with the roads blocked. What about all firemen living in the firehouse? The police, too . . . If the roads are going to be blocked, one or two fishing boats should be rigged up for emergency work, like taking firemen and equipment across the bay, or to West Village, or even along the front here in town . . . taking out doctors and nurses, bringing in sick people. Rescue teams need to be organized, to work with the police. We're going to need snowshoes and skis. The grocery stores should stock up on canned goods, crackers, cookies. Skip frozen food or perishables. If the power fails, we won't be able to keep them, except out in the snow perhaps. I think anyone very sick, anyone who's going to have a baby in the next month, ought to be taken to Hyannis, to hospital, at once . . . Then there's the probable flooding that's been mentioned. How are those people going to live – in upstairs rooms? Without heat, cooking, light, drinking water, not able to use the johns? . . . There's a danger of looting, with stores left unattended for days on end.' He paused.

Quite a list, Nelson thought. The rest were looking down at the table, mostly. Did they think Remington was a scaremonger? Or had he impressed them?

Remington said, 'My opinion is that the town ought to centralize, right now. We ought to collect kids, old people, ill people, people from houses in danger of flooding, doctors, mechanics, nurses. Collect them in one central place. I think this is an emergency, and we should treat it that way. The civil defence director should take charge, right now. That's all.'

After a long silence Merrill Crosby, the fire chief, said, 'Sam Budden's in Florida.'

'Send him a cable,' Remington said briefly. 'He might be able to get back in time. Or have the deputy take over.'

The silence was brief this time, but more heavily charged. Nelson knew why. The deputy director of civil defence, a retired naval captain, was an alcoholic. The town believed he'd been given the honorary post because he was a part-time drinking pal of Nelson's.

Nelson said, 'Fred – send Sam a wire.'

The Selectmen's assistant said, 'I'll see to it, right after the meeting.'

Jim Carpenter said, 'The Weather Bureau report said the storm might veer away from land.'

Remington said shortly, 'Yes. It might. But we can't go wrong if we prepare for the worst.'

'Except that it'll cost us a lot of dough,' Elliott King said.

Carpenter said, 'Some of Chief Remington's recommendations won't cost anything. Fuel oil and gasoline, for instance, will be used up sooner or later. The same with canned goods. But everything else will cost money, and we must ask, who's going to pay? If the firemen gather in the firehouse as soon as snow begins to fall, they may lose two or three days' business, perhaps more. They've all got jobs or businesses. Fixing up a fishing boat is perhaps an excellent idea, but it will cost money. And the snowshoes . . .'

'What we need is trained polar bears,' Elliott King said. Laughter spread round the table.

John Remington flushed slightly, and said, 'We have the choice of spending money or risking lives. That's all.'

Elliott King said, 'Can I say something, Nelson?'

'Sure. Go ahead.'

Elliott spread his big hands on the table. 'I'm a stranger here,' he said. 'Only been here sixteen years, since I came back from Iwo.' He got his titter, and continued : 'But even I have seen a few nor'easters. Just like Chief Remington says, they're bad, and we don't want to get caught by one. And I think, sure, the oil suppliers ought to check their tanks and trucks, and the food stores ought to check canned goods and baby food, powdered milk, stuff like that. The rest of us – why, sure we ought to check our storm windows and snow shovels and rock salt – and the ladies ought to look over what's in the kitchen cupboard, just like we all have before. Each man looking after himself and his own. The American way. If someone thinks he can make a little dough fitting out a boat for rescue work, let him do it, then, if the town has to use his boat, he can charge for it and make a profit. If no one needs it, why, he's lost his bet, just the same as he might on the stock exchange. Chief Damato can decide whether he needs to move his police into the station. Chief Crosby can decide about the firemen. That's the way to do it. Leave it to the good sense of the people individually.'

Nelson looked down the table, peering over his glasses. 'Anyone else anything to say? Walter?'

Walter Crampton's voice was deep, strong, Cape Cod flat. 'I agree with Elliott King. Every man and woman in Monomoy has a responsibility, to himself, his family, and the rest of the town. Let him see that he don't fail.'

Nelson Pryor said, 'Anything else? . . . Well, that's about it. We know a storm's probably coming, and we're grateful to Mr Remington for his suggestions. I guess we all know what to do . . . and we're going to send a wire to Sam Budden to come up from Miami and help us do it.' A wire which will never reach Sam in time, John added privately.

He pushed back his chair and stood up. Elliott King said, 'I've got two cases of Old Crow in the cellar. That ought to see me and Dorothy through.'

They had all stood up. Some moved towards the door, others gathered in corners, talking animatedly. Nelson went over to John Remington and took him gently by the elbow. 'It'll be O.K., John,' he said. 'They're good people here. They've had good warning, and they know what to do.'

'Sure,' John said. He looked dispirited. What does he want me to do? Nelson thought. Issue detailed military-type orders? I couldn't do that. And if I could, I'd never be First Selectman of Monomoy, so I'd never have the right to issue them.

Jim Carpenter and Elliott King stood with heads close at the top of the table. Elliott was speaking: 'We've got to push a decision on this park deal before the summer people come down, Jim. There's enough of them that own property to make a difference in the voting, and they're mostly stinking rich. Meaning, we'll never get 'em on our side by promising more dough. It's amenities they want – old-fashioned, quiet Monomoy, that stuff. But if we do have to deal with them, I've got an idea. Listen to this . . .'

Jim Carpenter listened carefully, keeping his eyes on Elliott's face. Elliott was a strange guy, now crude, now almost femininely sensitive: but he had influence, and Elliott King's friendship could do a politician and lawyer no harm.

Elliott said, 'There's pressure for houses, factories, everything. We can't just close the door, or it'll be busted down. We've got to roll with the punch – this is the line to sell the summer people – and there are two ways of doing it. We can turn the southern half, the Handforth Tract, into a park, and let the extra houses and factories be built right here, where we all live now. The zoning law's weak, and in that case there won't be a hope in hell of getting a tougher one. But suppose we open the Handforth Tract for building – all kinds – and slap a tight zoning law

111

on this section, to keep it the way it is now. See what I mean?'

Jim Carpenter said, 'The summer people have always wanted a tougher zoning. Why don't you speak to Mrs Bryant about it? As a trial balloon, eh?'

Elliott said, 'Good idea! Great! . . . We're going to win, Jimmy boy, don't you have a doubt of it. We can't help it! Look at the people on the other side! Every damn crackpot in Massachusetts, foreigners even, and all the nuts in Washington, D.C.'

Jim Carpenter nodded. Elliott often reminded him that a young politician couldn't afford to be on the losing side. What Elliott said about the proponents of the park was also true. Why, then, did he feel vaguely unhappy, vaguely cheap?

Elliott said, 'O.K., be seein' ya!'

Jim Carpenter glanced at his watch. Better get to his office. Mrs Handforth, standing in the door, caught his eye. She was waiting for him. He walked round the table, thinking, How can anyone get away with clothes like that, clothes that would shame a dogcatcher? Well, a couple of million bucks and a name like Monomoy Handforth or Le Fevrier helped a lot.

Mrs Handforth said, 'I have not yet had an opportunity to tell you, Mr Carpenter, that I have not forgotten my promise, about dinner. We had a small party last night, but at very short notice, to let a few people meet my son's fiancée. She's from the Orient, a princess or some such, I believe. Avaloka. Isn't that a charming name? A charming girl, too . . . My son has decided to stay with us, in Monomoy, through this storm.'

Noblesse oblige, Jim thought. Or Mom, saying, Don't you dare run away! And the girl, was she staying too?

Mrs Handforth said, 'The very next dinner party. Do tell your wife.'

Jim mumbled thanks. *Do tell your wife.* Damned old bitch. She knew Barbara would go into transports of delight. Damned young idiot – Barbara – to set so much store by such crap. Damned fool – himself – not to break free. Free from what? No, free *for* what?

He watched, fascinated, as Mrs Handforth fumbled in the recesses of her coat, found a man's peaked red hunting cap, and perched it carelessly on her grey curls.

Walter Crampton stood on the steps, looking across the Green. Where had that elm blight come from? Some foreign

112

place, likely. And, once they found it and knew what kind of bug it was, why hadn't they been able to make something to get rid of the dirty brutes? Too darn busy putting men into tin pills and shooting them off into the air, the way a kid throws stones, not caring where it lands, or what it hits, and with no particular reason to do it in the first place, except it makes him feel good.

Dirty weather blowing up, real dirty. With the waves running three or four feet high inside Sachem Island, they'll be six or seven feet at the Outer Mark, and breaking clear across the deck of the *Pendleton*, on the ocean side.

Arthur Evans came down the steps, stopped beside him, dropped a hand on his shoulder. 'Walter . . . how's Daisy?'

'About the same,' Walter said.

'I'm sorry to hear it . . . You going home now?'

They walked in step, slowly, along North Commerce. Evans said, 'That Coast Guard fellow's an alarmist, I would say, wouldn't you, Walter?'

Walter said, 'No. He's in the service, that's all. Wants to do everything by the numbers. Hut-two-three-four! In the service a man can't blow his nose without he has three others to help him, an officer to give the order and a petty officer to yell it louder, in his ear. The Coast Guard's better than the Navy, at that. Remington's all right.'

'Glad to hear it . . . Did you get a chance to read that pamphlet I gave you last week?'

Walter grunted wordlessly. That candy manufacturer in Boston was right most of the time, warning about dirty socialism and communism being everywhere, creeping up on you, all set to grab everything you owned. Maybe he'd send him some money, so he could spread the fight, but he wouldn't join this Birch Society, or any other society, and he didn't think Mr Eisenhower was a Communist.

They stopped at the corner of Second. 'Come on down to the bank a minute, Walter,' Evans said, 'I'll give you a cup of good coffee, and we can chat a bit.'

Walter said, 'Still trying to take my money?'

The little banker said, 'Well . . . heck, Walter, yes. It's not for our sake. You know darn well your money isn't going to make any difference to us. It's for your own sake. You just shouldn't have that amount of money in your house. However much it is,' he added quickly. 'It doesn't make sense to sit on your dollars when they can be earning for you.'

'That's what you fellows were saying before '33, too.'

'But, Walter, it's different now. Banks can't close now, because—'

'—you got more government regulation. Banking ain't so different from the civil service now, to my reckoning.'

'Walter, you don't imagine . . .'

Walter Crampton permitted himself a small grin. 'Don't take it to heart, Arthur,' he said. He patted the small man on the back. 'I feel better looking after my own tackle, my own boat, my own money. I got a pistol, and I know how to use it.'

John Remington looked round Elliott King's 'den' with interest. It smelled of pipe tobacco, old leather, and gun oil. Guns and rifles stood in glass-fronted cabinets along the walls. Fishing rods in canvas or aluminium cases lay on racks above the guns. A moosehead thrust its great shovel antlers into the room over the fireplace. A Marine Corps steel helmet, still wearing its painted cloth cover and garnishing of skrim, hung rakishly from one antler. Three Japanese officers' swords dangled from pegs near the door.

It was an overpoweringly masculine room, but like a sporting goods store, not like a place where men actually worked. As a boy, he'd seen plenty of ranch tackle rooms and gun rooms and bunkhouses. They had smelled principally of sweat, horse sweat impregnating the saddle leather, men's sweat dried into the wranglers' woollen shirts. There were also smells of cheap soap, cold water, oiled steel, but you heard women's voices in them, and felt their presence welcomed, because women worked in those rooms, used the guns and rifles and saddles just as the men did. This was different . . .

Elliott took up stance by the fireplace, the blue shirt stretched over his big chest. He pointed his pipe at John. 'You're wondering why I asked you to come with me, eh? Well, it's because what I have to say is personal. And, like I said, it won't take long, then you can get back to your li'l ol' storm . . . Want to guess what I was doing last night?'

What am I supposed to say? John thought. 'Laying your wife?' 'Attempting to lay someone else's?' Or was this going to lead to some snide crack about Alice Bryant and what *he* was doing last night? His fists clenched slightly, and he shook his head, not speaking.

Elliott laughed heartily. 'Ha, ha! I was visiting with Harold Morgan. I offered to go partners with him – forty per cent to him, though my business is at least twice as big as his. He didn't

114

say yes right away, but he's going to. He doesn't have any choice. It's join me or go under . . . There'll only be one contractor in Monomoy. And you know who I'm going to offer a piece of this deal to? This is strictly confidential – Nelson Pryor. And we're going to have two, three thousand acres to work on, all by ourselves, because that park is going to get voted down. It's easy, when you know how. Split 'em. Take 'em one by one. Find out what each one *really* wants. Old Elaine Handforth doesn't give a hoot in hell for the park, except she wants it called the Handforth Park. So make sure it's called something else and you've got her against it, right? Alice Bryant doesn't give a hoot in hell for the park – she wants the riffraff kept away from her house. So tell her the park's going to bring more riffraff to town, and you've got her, and everyone else like her, right? Nelson Pryor's short of money, always has been since he bought that house. And he's overinsured, never been able to get out from under the premium payments. Well, anyone knows how to put the squeeze on a guy in *that* position. You needn't look down your nose, John. I'm not doing anything illegal. This is private enterprise, finding out what people want and then getting it for them. What did that guy call it? – enlightened self-interest . . . I like you, John. I like your style. I'm going to offer you a job, because you got a sense of duty. I was a major in the Marine Corps, and—'

'I know,' John said.

'I need a guy like you to be my exec. How about it?' Elliott gestured largely with the pipe. The scent of piny after-shave lotion hung around him. 'We'll go a long, long way. I got friends, John. You'd be surprised. Anything I want fixed, any little thing, they'll do it . . . Think it over. Resign from the Coast Guard. I'll pay you three times what you're getting, just to begin with.'

John got up from his chair. Elliott reminded him of a heavyweight in the moment of victory, unmarked, confident, the champion, holding out his fist in the big-hearted gesture: I've got 'em all, women worship me, the Selectmen are in my pocket, I own this and that, Senator Snooks is on my payroll . . . He ought to take the outstretched hand, receive the bear hug. Instead, he wanted to give the guy an almighty sock in the jaw.

The telephone rang. Elliott picked it up, listened, handed it to John. McGill, speaking from the station, sounded breathless. 'Boat job, Chief. They're launching the 36-footer right now . . . It's a Spanish freighter, S.S. *Goya*, 10,000 tons, broken in two,

115

seven miles north-east of Pollock Rip. Crew of twenty-one, two swept overboard and lost when she broke up. All our big cutters are on other jobs. Mr Helm is sending us and the Chatham boat.'

'Right. I'll take her out.' He put down the receiver. 'Run me to the station please, Mr King. I've got a boat job.'

As they passed Nun 6, opposite the short jetty of West Village, the radio began to squawk: 'CG 36500, CG 36614, this is Group, over.'

John Remington leaned over the radio set in the starboard corner behind the low windshield. Charlie Tyson stood wedged in the left corner. Bob Gardner had the wheel.

A voice blared, 'This is 500, I read you loud and clear, over.'

John said, '614, I read you loud and clear, over.'

Ahead, the blunt bow hurtled to starboard and Bob Gardner turned the wheel against it. A short sea broke steeply over the turtle deck forward. Chief Boatswain Helm's voice came on. 'We have picked up S.S. *Goya* on our radar, one blip only, repeat one blip only. She is now, from Pollock Rip Lightship, 6 point 1 miles, at 43 degrees true. Her estimated course, 241 degrees true, drift speed 1 point 4 knots. Coast Guard Monomoy, do you have radar identification of the target?'

John recognized McGill's voice. 'Not over, yet.'

'Acknowledged . . . 614 – we do not have you on radar yet. Have you put on radar tube? Report position, over.'

John glanced round. A long metal tube, like a map case, covered the bare flagstaff at the stern. The 36-footers, of all wood construction, had poor reflective qualities for radar signals. Whenever a 36-footer left port, this Rube Goldberg device had to be used to enable the radar sets on shore to pick her up. Even with the tube in place, she could seldom be tracked more than eight miles from the radar set.

John spoke into the mike: 'Radar tube O.K. We are coming up to Nun 4, leaving Longships Bay, over.'

'Acknowledged . . . 500, we have you approaching Chatham Bars, blip intermittent. Report sea conditions.'

'500 speaking, sea . . . sea . . .'

John gripped the handrail hard. That was Dick Roberts, his opposite number in Chatham. Dick was a quiet Maine man, who had to live and work in the masterful presence of the Group Commander, Helm. Dick had answered jerkily, and ended in a hiccup.

116

The voice came up again. 'Sea . . . very heavy . . . bar exposed . . . between seas . . . out'.

For a few minutes the radio gave out only an electronic crackle. Then the Chief Boatswain's gravelly tones broke through: 'O.K., Dick. You're the boss . . . Monomoy, do you have 614 on radar, over.'

'Monomoy here, affirmative. We have just picked up 500, too, over.'

His own boat lurched savagely to port and water surged over his seaboots, but John saw only the image that the radio messages had conjured up in his mind. Chatham Bars would normally be covered by about ten feet of water at this tide. Now the seas were running so big and steep that between the waves they dragged all water off the sandbar. Dick Roberts had to cross that bar to reach the ocean.

Dick's voice came on, blurred and faint: '500 here . . . struck bars, rolled over twice – trying again, over.'

His face set, John bent over the chart pinned on the small, flat space behind the windshield, which answered as a chart table. To work here, he had to jam himself against Bob Gardner, holding the wheel at his left. Spray and wind-blown water from the superstructure blew in his face and splashed the chart. The boat heeled and swung, dipped and rolled with rapidly increasing viciousness.

John took the small compass from his pocket, laid it on the chart, and pencilled in the latest position of S.S. *Goya*, the time, and the drift course. Along the line of the drift he marked the position the wreck should be at after each successive half hour. Now his own course . . . He paused, staring into the tossing, grey murk where sea and sky, water and air, mingled in a single element. He could make no sensible calculations until he knew what his speed would be once he came out from the comparative shelter of Diadem Cape into the open ocean. Meanwhile, it was enough to know that once he turned Diadem Cape his course would be almost the reciprocal of the drifting wreck . . . One blip only, they said. Was it the stern or the bow that had sunk? Probably the part that had the radio equipment or there would have been more messages from her. That would be, in a general cargo freighter, the section under the bridge, well forward of the centre line.

The radio came up: '500 here . . . bow smashed . . . all in crew injured . . . returning . . . sorry, Chief, over.'

'500, acknowledged. Well done, over.'

John sighed in relief. Bob Gardner said, 'They'll get back.'
John nodded. The rescue of the *Goya's* men was now entirely
up to him.

They plunged past Can 3. The sea was as bad as he had ever
seen it in these comparatively sheltered waters. They were out
of the complicated crosscurrents of Longships Bay, and the
waves ran evenly before the wind. The wind came straight out
of the north-east.

He nudged Gardner and took the wheel. The B.M.3 wedged
himself into his old position in the starboard front corner.
Charlie Tyson in the port front corner chewed bubble gum
with a loud smacking noise. The fourth member of the crew,
Engine-man Dave Lerroux, was in the survivors' compartment,
forward.

The tall black and white vertical stripes of the Outer Mark
bobbed wildly on top of a wave a mile and a half ahead, then
sank out of sight. The *Goya* would run ashore before he could
get to her, at this rate. John turned to Gardner, his mouth
forming a word. Before he could shout it, Gardner said, 'I think
she'll make it, Chief.'

John turned the wheel steadily to port. He had been about to
ask Bob Gardner whether it was safe to cut across the submerged sandbank that ran out from South Point to the Outer
Mark. Bob Gardner was a Monomoy man, born and bred,
descendant of generations of mooncussers. He was tall and thin
and lantern-jawed, his hair a thick thatch of pale, sun-bleached
straw. He was thirty-five, and Boatswain's Mate 3rd Class. He
would go no further and had reached even that level only after
a long struggle, for he could hardly sign his name; but he knew
the sea and small boats as no one else John had ever met. He
was the only man on the station of whom John asked advice in
moments of sea crisis. If the crisis had to do with accounts,
or administration, Bob Gardner was as helpful as a striped
bass.

The motion changed to a severe, quick roll. Charlie Tyson
stirred and hitched himself more firmly into his corner. John
remembered the last time he had brought the 36-footer out. It
was a falling tide again, and he was doing exactly what he had
told Charlie not to do. He turned, smiling, 'This is an emergency, Charlie. And the sea's much too rough for us to be
grounded permanently.'

Charlie snapped his bubble gum with a single explosive crack.

John's temper short-circuited. 'Get forward!' he blared. 'Get out of my sight!'

Charlie Tyson unhitched himself and went forward along the narrow catwalk on the port side, his hands in his pockets. As he made ready to jump down into the well between the engine housing and the survivors' compartment, Bob Gardner leaned round the windshield and yelled, 'Hold on, you crazy . . .'

Too late. The boat gave a sunfish buck, ending with a whip-lash smack into a wave. Charlie Tyson went overboard as though fired from a cannon. John swore fiercely, spun the wheel full circle, and throttled back. Bob Gardner scrambled forward to the well, one hand grasping the railing, the other a life ring. Charlie Tyson's life jacket showed like an orange stain to star-board. The boat lurched round in a tight, drunken circle, every wave surging up into Bob Gardner's face. Dave Lerroux peered out of the survivor's compartment hatch, saw Bob, and ran to join him. Each downward swoop ended in a short, jarring thud, as though the water below had been compressed into a dense inelastic solid. There couldn't be more than a couple of feet, anyway.

The orange life jacket lurched high, sank out of sight, re-appeared. Charlie's face was white, his eyes staring, his mouth open. He held his arms up, and the water slapped his face viciously. John eased the throttle to dead slow, and turned the bow across the sea. For a moment she drifted down upon the man in the water. In a heavy roll Bob Gardner threw the life ring. It went past Charlie, the line dropping neatly across his shoulder. He grabbed it and the two men on deck began to pull steadily. John edged the throttle up and turned the bows into the sea. A minute later they had him at the gunwale; a roll and they had him on deck. He knelt for a moment between them, water pouring from him, then stood up. He stared at John, and John stared grimly back. The kid's face was frightened still, the teeth clenched and the skin a dull blue. At last he half raised one hand, but it was impossible to say whether the gesture was of defiance or of thanks. Lerroux took him by the shoulder, and pushed him through the hatch. Bob Gardner came aft. 'He's O.K.,' he said, 'goddam fool.'

There were blankets forward there, but no spare clothes. Tyson would be very cold before this trip ended.

The radio boomed. 'Coast Guard 36614, this is Group. Have blip on radar that might be you, on mile north-west of South Point. Blip very faint. Is position correct?'

119

Bob Gardner took the mike off its hook. '614 – yeah, that's us Chief. Sea's real dirty. Tyson just fell overboard but we fished him out, over.'

Harrison F. Helm's voice growled, 'Why? . . . Resume listening watch.'

'614, you ought to be able to see *Goya* soon. It bears 45 degrees from you, about a quarter of a mile.'

'Can't see anything yet, out.'

It was near two o'clock in the afternoon and very dark. The Pollock Rip light shone out as though it had been midnight. Above the waist they had no shelter on the coxswain's flat now. The windshield superstructure went two minutes after they'd rounded Diadem Point. A monstrous black wave, fast moving and purposeful as a locomotive, swept the vessel clean as a shaved plank, taking the searchlight on the forward compartment roof, the bell on top of the engine housing, the wooden frame of the windshield, the windshield, and all. John had been making 4 knots when that wave hit, and had been able to maintain no more than 3 through the tortuous Pollock Rip channel. Every ten minutes Helm or someone else at Group came up on the radio to report the position of the drifting wreck. His own station radar, in Monomoy, also had him and the wreck on its screen, but kept silent, except, at Helm's order, to give a bearing, or a separation, which could not be detected from Chatham.

John held the boat to 2 knots. Anything less and he'd lose the momentum necessary to keep her on course against the buffeting waves. She had a steady motion now and was in no danger as long as the course stayed directly into the seas. The sheer size of the waves was frightening. Here there was none of the petulant toss and pitch of the Sound, no to-and-fro snapping and jerking. These were Atlantic rollers, with a fetch of a thousand miles behind them, evenly spaced, 500 feet apart, 25 feet from crest to trough. For two hours now he had been watching them in awe, as though lifted outside himself and outside the boat. The long crest lines surged forward, rippling with blown spray and white foam from horizon to short horizon. His small white boat climbed, endlessly climbed, then slid down, down into the dark-green lightless trough, shuddered as the bluff bow sank deep and the water embraced it, then the lift and lift, to the crest, and, ah, the sudden bite of the wind and the cold smash of the spray, and then the new long, gliding downward swoop.

120

They were all four jammed on the coxswain's seat now. The Pollock Rip lightship was broad on the starboard beam, about one mile. The light shone in Tyson's face and made his eyes gleam like a madman's when he turned to look at it.

Lerroux said suddenly, 'Port bow, Chief! There she is.'

Then John saw a long wall across the blackness, red below and blacker above. She lay parallel to the waves, 200 yards to windward of them.

'She's making a lee,' Bob said.

John nodded. Coming directly up on her from a lee, and her lying broadside the way she was, the waves came smoother to the 36-footer, coming like rolling grassland rather than jagged mountain ranges. The hulk ahead was the stern half, or two thirds, of the ship, lying canted 30 degrees to starboard. The great single screw slowly reared out of the water, and plunged again, as the waves moved the wreck. Several feet of her red bottom paint showed above the heaving, irregular waterline. She had broken cleanly just ahead of the single, tall, old-fashioned funnel.

614 rose and fell like a dizzy swallow now, turning slowly across the seas, as John held the engine to dead slow, circled in the lee, and considered what to do next. This was the best side from which to make a rescue attempt, because the ship made a lee; but this was the blind side. He could see no one along that high, exposed rail up there. He had to find out whether there was anyone alive. Salvage of the ship itself was out of the question.

He leaned toward the Third. 'Bob, I'm going round her stern. Get in the well and stand by to shoot a line. Tyson, you help. Dave, report to Group.'

Lerroux picked up the mike. '614 here, we're with the *Goya*'s stern section now. No sign of life yet. We're going to take a look round her, over.' Randall and Tyson scrambled forward with the line-firing gun.

John eased the throttle forward and turned the wheel. The 36-footer eased out from behind the bulk of the ship into the bite of the wind and the sting of the spray. He kept well away from the stern, with its huge propeller and the metallically screaming, half-unhinged rudder. The Pollock Rip's beam shone on the faded, flaked lettering. GOYA, BILBAO. Another minute and he could see the deck. It was a welter of white water, like a sloped beach facing a full gale. The tilted funnel leaned out over the sea, the waves breaking against its base. The davits on either side of the funnel were empty, and seemed to have been smashed by the sea. The deck cabins on the lower, starboard side were underwater most of the time, the tremendous waves continually pounding at door and portholes. Even as he stared, a sea tore a loose door from its hinges, sucked it into itself, and a few moments later sent it smashing down again, to shatter a porthole.

The radio growled. '614, *Goya* is two point two miles due west of Pollock Rip Lightship. At present course and speed of drift she will strike the north end of Bearse Shoals in about one hour, over.'

Lerroux answered, 'Acknowledged, out.'

On the *Goya* nothing moved but the sea. One hour and she would be aground, eh? Well, one thing at a time.

Bob Gardner's voice blew back to him on the wind. 'Man . . . by the funnel.'

John peered through smarting eyes. Yes, there was a man on the upper side of the tilted deck, one arm linked round a funnel stay and the other waving something in the air – a cloth perhaps, but it was too dirty to show up.

So there was at least one survivor. No good trying to get anyone off the ship on this, the exposed side. The line ought to come up from the other side. But would the man up there see it? Suppose he shot the line from this side, the man fastened it, then he tried to work it round the stern? No good; far too many things for it to catch on. And how many more survivors were there? Maybe he could work slowly round to the lee side again, keeping the man's attention and then shoot.

Lerroux suddenly yelled, 'Look at that!' He pointed. John saw the bright life jacket in the water.

'He didn't fall, he jumped,' Gardner yelled back. 'He grabbed the shot line and jumped.'

John saw that Gardner was paying out the thin shot line. Tyson had the other end of it, and was swimming toward the hulk. The giant waves rolled ceaselessly and the noise seemed to be increasing.

Crazy bastard, idiot, show-off! No use swearing. Bob had secured his end of the shot line to a messenger, in case Tyson made it. A hawser line lay ready. 'Go and help Bob,' John ordered Lerroux. Nothing else to do but hold the boat under control, keep her off the hulk, and hope for the best.

He held the 36-footer bows on to the sea, letting her fall very slowly astern toward the *Goya*. Now they saw Tyson high in a wave, now he disappeared, the line plunging into black water. Only luck, pure luck, would decide whether he got his head smashed or was washed safely up the deck when he reached the ship.

'Now!' he heard his own voice cry, as though the orange dot out there, now apparently dancing upright in a wave crest, could possibly hear or, heaving heard, obey. The figure slid down the wave, the wave dissolved into heavy white foam, and suddenly he was there, an orange and black fish near the base of the funnel. The fish became a man, Charlie Tyson, on his knees, grabbing a broken davit as the next wave swept up the deck. The Spanish sailor was there, hand outstretched to help. Tyson unfastened the line from his waist, and in the waist of the 36-footer Bob Gardner began to haul it in. John eased the bow quickly to port.

The radio came up. '614, hulk is heading to go aground on the Bearse Shoal in forty minutes. Report situation, over.'

John said, 'Tyson is on board *Goya*. At least one survivor. Will shoot line from lee of ship, over.'

'Acknowledged. Watch out for the Bearse, she may be breaking farther out than usual, in this sea, over.'

Bob Gardner yelled, 'Line in.'

John shouted,'Make ready to shoot again!' Bob raised his hand.

The wheel spinning and kicking in his hands, the boat plunging, rearing, slipping, climbing. John brought her under the *Goya*'s lee and partly exposed bottom. Now three heads showed on the high rail above, Tyson's in the centre. Bob Gardner raised the shoulder gun, and fired and the line snaked upward. As the line passed the high rail and came into the wind, it seemed to curve back and fall, but it was an optical illusion, for Tyson had it fast, one of the others was waving. More heads, more oilskins reflected the Rip's light. The messenger line had gone. Now the hawser . . . 'Ready!' Gardner called. John gave the signal to begin, then unhooked the mike. '614 here. We have a line to *Goya*. Rescue operations are beginning, out.' He felt, suddenly, very tired.

Dorothy King had looked miserable at the firehouse party. Mary Pryor thought, really miserable. But being married to such a handsome man, and with a roving eye, what could she expect? She was lucky to get him. Men like Elliott King didn't grow on trees.

They were sitting in the living-room, alone. Nelson was asleep,

123

and snoring quietly. The house shook under the blows of the wind outside and the surge of rock-'n'-roll inside, coming from Betty's room. Betty was home, and actually doing her homework . . . only because Charlie Tyson was at sea. Or was she sitting by the window, looking out into the darkness toward the ocean? She had an impulse to run up and comfort her . . . but that would mean acknowledging Charlie Tyson again.

Every time Nelson looked at Alice Bryant that silly sheep's eye look came over him. That woman, coming down here, pretending it was to look after her house . . . Sure, fix a few shutters, wearing tight blue jeans and a Saks Fifth Avenue sweater, just when Nelson was sure to be passing by. After inviting John Remington back last night.

Nelson sat up quietly, yawned, stretched, walked across the room, and poured himself a drink. He raised his glass. 'My first today! Elliott tried to make me have one, but I've learned my lesson.'

'Till next time,' Mary said sharply.

'Ah, quit nagging, honey. Everything's hunky-dory. I'm sober as a judge, and we're going to have a fine dinner.'

Mary leaped up and hurried to the kitchen. She turned off the oven, thinking, just in time.

Back in the living-room Nelson said, 'Birdbrain! It's a wonder we eat at all.'

Mary said: 'What did Elliott want to talk to you about?'

'Business,' Nelson said. Then suddenly, 'Hell, it wasn't just business. It never really is, with Elliott. He offered me a partnership—'

'What!' Mary exclaimed.

'—for nothing. Well, eventually I pay out my share of the profits. Of course I have to use my influence against the park.'

'What are you going to do?'

'I don't know . . . it's kind of soiling. But I'm soiled already, a little round the edges . . . . There's no way to stop a man like Elliott King in a small town. Maybe I could . . . if I didn't get falling-down drunk now and then.'

'Don't talk about it,' Mary said. It hurt inside her chest to remember.

'That's the trouble,' Nelson said angrily. 'I was drunk as a shunk, right? Why does everyone pretend I wasn't? Why didn't Mrs Handforth throw a bucket of water in my face and say, Beat it, you lush. Instead, everyone so polite, everyone looking the other way! Poor Mr Pryor's been taken ill, it must have

124

been something he ate. Poor Mrs Pryor. Dear Father, will you take him home and call a doctor, I *do* think he should see a doctor, don't you?'

'Hush, Nelson,' Mary said, 'Billy will hear you. He's working in his room.'

Nelson said, 'Drink! What else can a sensible man do when he looks around? I mean, *looks* . . . I wonder whether that 36-footer's back yet?'

He stalked out of the room, glass in one hand, spectacles swinging in the other. Mary looked at the liquor cabinet. She could do with a drink herself. After dinner, maybe, if she could get Nelson to sit down and be awake and talk to *her*, not about Elliott, or elections, or drains, or tax rates . . .

Nelson returned. 'They're O.K. They've turned Diadem Cape.' He drained his whisky. 'Dinner ready, honey? Let's eat, then.'

Lynn Garland considered the stacks of canned meats. It was seven o'clock, and the A & P was open late so the people could stock up against the expected storm. The warning had come on the air at 2 p.m. and again at 4, on station WCCD, in Hyannis. She didn't know what it was like on the rest of the Cape, but here in Monomoy people didn't seem to be taking it very seriously, for the A & P was almost empty. Perhaps the warnings had been too noncommittally worded, implying the citizens must prepare for disaster, but, at the same time, there was nothing to worry about.

Business must not be alarmed, she thought sourly. She stared at rows of Spam, corned beef, meat loaf, ham loaf, chopped ham . . . But was it morally right to stock up at all? Suppose you were very poor and couldn't afford to? Or were old and unable to look after yourself for the number of days that the food would last? There was something atavistic, squirrel-like, about people buying a stock of cans, taking them home, stashing them away in some safe, secret place. And what did you do with careless, thoughtless people – or merely forgetful ones – who didn't stock up? Were you supposed, when they came begging, to fire warning shots at them? To let them starve?

She took six cans of corned beef, and six of Spam. With powdered milk, canned vegetables, and crackers, she'd be all right. Better have another jar of instant coffee and perhaps some multivitamin tablets, to guard against scurvy.

A woman passed, behind a cart loaded high with detergents,

hair rinses, economy-size cornflake packets and 7-Up. An old man was buying ice-cream, a young woman was buying baby food.

The girl at the check-out counter was JoAnn Griffiths. She had dropped out of high school before Lynn came to Monomoy, but Lynn knew her well enough, by face and reputation. She was chewing gum, punching the cash register, and stacking a customer's purchases in a carton, all with withdrawn, impersonal efficiency. When Lynn's turn came, she felt impelled to explain the twelve cans of meat. 'I'm stocking up,' she said, smiling, 'just as the Selectmen told us to.'

JoAnn said, 'I heard about that. Not many doin' it.' She slammed two of the corned beef cans so hard into the paper bag that she burst the bag. She shook out another bag with pursed lips. 'Sorry, Miss Garland,' she said, 'I was thinking of the fellows out in the 36-footer. These cows don't care. Listen to them.'

Muzak filled the heated air with treacly music. Heavy, sweet perfume coagulated between the stacked aisles. Synthetic colours and invented brand names glittered under the powerful lights. Close by, the woman with the hair rinses and another were discussing a new TV serial. Of course, the wind had been blowing all day. Everyone had had plenty of time to make ready, if they intended to. The girl was being too hard on the ordinary, uncommitted . . . 'What did you say?' she said sharply. 'Did you say the 36-footer's out? The Coast Guard lifeboat?'

'Yeah, with four men. Dave Lerroux, Bob Gardner, Charlie Tyson, and Mr Remington. I know them all. Of course, I don't know them all the same.'

'You mean, that little boat's gone out, in this weather?'

'Yeah. There was a ship broke in half, a Spanish one.'

'I heard about the ship on the radio,' Lynn said, 'but they didn't say anything about the boat going out. I didn't know . . .'

'I found out,' JoAnn said. She looked hard at Lynn 'I shoulda thought *you* would.'

Lynn hardly heard. A woman was rattling her cart impatiently behind her, and she paid quickly. At the exit she buttoned her coat to the top, tied a scarf over her head, and went out into the wind, the two big paper bags heavy in her arms.

She walked slowly, her eyes unfocused. The lifeboat was at sea, and no one cared. If they cared, how could they buy and sell, sing, drink in taverns? Their own people were out in a cockleshell, amid huge waves, pierced by this wind that shrieked down every cross street, and sent sand stinging into men's cheeks, and coated the house fronts with salt.

Their own people? Hers, too. She could not shuffle off all the ignorance and egotism on to others. How was it that JoAnn Griffiths, town tramp, knew the lifeboat was out, while Lynn Garland, liberal humanist, did not? Why was nothing done? Men whose duty took them to sea on a night like this were entitled to lookouts in lonely towers, to women waiting in candlelit windows.

On a sudden decision she passed her own corner and hurried on to Boat Street, her cheeks smarting and her arms aching. She hurried up, crossed the parking lot – how the wind boomed here, through the Gap – climbed the steep steps toward the Coast Guard station. At the top the wind suddenly rammed cold air, compressed with sand, down her throat so hard that she could not breathe. She turned her back to it, and gulped in air, while the wind ripped at her coat and thrust her toward the sheer fall where the station stood on a concrete foundation wall ten feet high. She turned again, feeling that the weight of the canned goods helped to hold her down, and managed to struggle round the back of the station to the northwest corner. The light-house beam showed sea and sand, vanished, returned. Salt caked round her mouth and her eyes burned. Reality and imagination blurred together, of churning sand, black mountains of water, white banners on advancing crests, artillery fire, the dune trembling, the wall shaking, the wind pressing her down, down . . .

A strong light shone behind her and a voice called, 'Who's there?'

She half turned, the wind plucked her from the corner and sent her cannoning into the man in the open doorway. He grabbed her, and the meat cans fell and the paper bag burst inside the door with a great clatter.

With care and effort, leaning hard against it, he closed the door. He was a big man, red-faced, slow of speech. 'I thought I saw someone go past – Miss Garland, isn't it?'

She leaned against the wall, recovering her breath. She was in a broad entrance hall, a reception counter straight in front, a door marked 'Stores' on the left, and on the right another marked C.B.M. J. REMINGTON.

'That's the Chief's cabin,' the man said, following her glance. 'I'm McGill the exec. The Chief's out on a boat job.'

She paid taxes for the Coast Guard just as she did for the

Army and the Navy. As a taxpayer and a voter she held herself responsible for what the Army did. Therefore she was responsible for this. She, Lynn Garland, had ordered those men to sea.

'They're on their way back,' McGill said.

'Oh, good! . . . But how do you know?'

'Radar, and radio, miss. It's all in the operations and lookout room at the top of the station here.'

'Will you show me? Please! It would make me feel better.'

The man was embarrassed. He said, 'Well, miss, I wish I could let you, but ladies aren't allowed up there, except on a proper visit, you know what I mean.'

She said, 'Oh! . . . Wait! Isn't the wrecked ship Spanish? Then the crew will be Spanish? Do any of the men in the lifeboat speak Spanish?'

'Not unless the Chief does. I don't think he does.'

'Suppose the survivors want to say something, something important, when they're in the lifeboat? Perhaps I could help. Please.'

McGill gestured in the air, then said, 'O.K., miss. We'll call you the interpreter . . . But don't speak on the mike, or anything, unless I tell you. Mr Helm's listening up in Chatham. This way.'

She followed him up the stairs, intensely impatient now to make contact with those men at sea.

The Outer Mark beacon blinked faintly through the driving spray. A little after eight, tide about half, and making. John thought, I could save twenty minutes by cutting across the bar level with Nun 4, as we did on the outward trip. Twenty minutes less before he could sleep . . . He could not take any risks now, with thirteen rescued men aboard.

'Steady for the Outer Mark,' he muttered.

At the wheel, Bob Gardner answered, 'O.K., Chief.'

The bluff bow pounded steadily into the seas, the hull quaked to the smash of the waves, now running almost directly into them from ahead.

The Outer Mark came abeam, and Bob Gardner began the turn. The scattered land lights wheeled steadily past to port. The waves caught the 36-footer on her port bow, then broad on the beam, then on the quarter. She lurched and heaved, rolled and wallowed, but always moved on. The beacon fell back. Her stern lifted high, the dim white roar of the surf on the wavetop

128

came up from behind, drew level, then the boat slid long and far down the forward slope. The trough came, and Bob spun the wheel to hold her straight.

Lights glowed in Monomoy House to port, but West Village, to starboard, was no more than a patchwork of thicker darkness against the land. The channel buoys tossed and danced like mad ghosts, red to starboard, black to port.

John forced himself to speak. 'Tired, Bob? Want me to take her?'

Gardner said, 'Sure, I'm pooped, Chief, but not so bad as you.'

John mumbled wordlessly, tightened the grip of his hands on the engine housing, and let his head rest on his wrists. At once his eyes closed, and the next roll sent him cannoning into Bob Gardner at the wheel.

The lights of Monomoy town showed over Sachem Island now. The Monomoy light showed strong and clear. The Reverend Mr Day had turned on the light at the top of the spire of the Old Church. That was an old, old custom, to put a light there when the Monomoy lifeboat went to sea at night. The wind blew very hard across the bay, out of the northeast, knifing through his sodden foul-weather gear as though it were made of thin cotton. The chop was steep and confused here. He shivered, remembering moments of the day. At the entrance to the Pollock Rip channel, the seas had been 30 feet high and come racing out of the dark astern at 15 knots to his 9. When he'd tried to turn Diadem Cape, her first roll hit just on 90 degrees and put his head in the sea. He'd got thirteen Spaniards aboard, but there'd been fourteen on the *Goya*: he could see the man now, on the high rail, the slip, the high scream whipped away in the wind, the body whirling bump, bump, bang down the steel wall, into the sea, and vanishing for ever.

Bob Gardner eased the throttle forward, and the bow dipped more heavily into the water. Lights glittered along the Coast Guard pier, and he saw a couple of cars, and a school bus parked beside the boathouse. Forward, the door of the survivors' compartment opened, and Dave Lerroux and Charlie Tyson appeared. Now he recognized the men waiting on the pier – Randall, Knighton, Santos, half a dozen civilians. Bob Gardner had her lined up, the engine burbled in neutral, a touch of reverse, neutral again, and they slid alongside. Tyson threw the line to Santos.

John stepped across the narrow gap, instinctively grasping a proffered hand. The hand was firm and hard, and lifted him to the centre of the pier before letting go. It was Walter Crampton, his face deeply shadowed under the long bill of his cap.

'What shape are they in?'

'Not bad.'

'Hear ye had to go clear to Nantucket before you could turn.'

'Not quite . . . bottom end of the Handkerchief.'

The Spanish captain stepped ashore with a single long stride, followed, one by one, by his twelve men. Watching them in the bright pier lights, John thought again, as he had during the rescue, that they were not twelve different men, but twelve versions of one. They were all about 5 foot 5, dark, black-eyed, wiry. They had left the Coast Guard blankets on the boat and stood now in a silent group behind their captain. They wore thin blue shirts, thin blue trousers, faded and patched, and cheap shoes or sandals. They did not seem to feel the cold or the wind, but waited, expressionless.

Nelson Pryor came up fast, hand out. 'John, you son of a gun! You made it! We're proud of you . . . McGill asked for the school to put the Spaniards in, but I thought, heck, why don't we get a piece of the Longships Hotel, so we did that. In the morning we can fit them out with warmer clothes, and send them to Boston, or wherever they ought to go. There's a school bus here, and we've got blankets and hot stew at the Longships.'

John said, 'They don't speak English. Here, captain . . .' He beckoned with his finger, and pointed at the waiting school bus.

The Spanish captain made an old-fashioned bow, and moved toward the bus. A woman's voice, at John's ear, said, 'Mr Remington, I speak Spanish. Can I help?'

He stared dully at her. The schoolteacher. Spoke Spanish. Why not?

Nelson Pryor said, 'Please tell them . . .'

'I heard,' she said, and then she was speaking slowly and carefully to the Spanish captain. At the end, he inclined his head and they began to get into the bus. It was all of 200 yards to the Longships Hotel, he thought . . . Still, got to give foreigners the right impression. He grabbed Lynn Garland's arm as she was about to enter the bus. 'Names,' he said, 'we need their names, rating, home addresses, next of kin. So I can send it to the agents. Also, definite information on men missing, who saw who drown, get killed . . .'

'Are you all right?' She was holding his arm, and her hand looked small and smooth against his sleeve.

'Yeah,' he said, 'fine. If you get that information, I'll be down soon to collect it. Then . . . then . . .'

He forgot what he had been about to say. Her eyes were large on him, and bright blue, her hair falling down one side of her forehead. His belly contracted and he thought, Oh, Jesus, not again, when I've just made myself safe, and built a sturdy little wall, and patched up the holes.

'Go on!' he said, and pushed her roughly into the bus. She smiled at him, and called down. 'Take care of yourself.'

CHAPTER FIVE

TUESDAY

Lynn Garland found herself silently, inexplicably awake. She stared at the ceiling until she realized what it was, and knew she was not in her room. She turned her head and saw a dim fireplace, and a darker rectangle that was probably a painting, over the mantel. Her legs felt odd and, investigating, she found she was lying under many blankets in a strange bed, wearing only her slip.

The Longships Hotel! Getting the Spaniards settled, taking particulars, refusing John Remington's offer to drive her home . . . the Spaniards might need something in the night.

Everything was quiet. No sound at all. She slipped out of bed and went to the window and pulled back the curtains. The room faced east. The street lamps on South Commerce Street stood like blurred sentinels. Beyond, on South Hill, the lamps showed old houses standing in a close row, as though with arms linked to hold back the Great Dune. The hard line of the dunetop ran straight as a ruler across the horizon, dividing the night from the earth.

A white dot appeared on the windowpane in front of her nose. She stared at it, and tried to wipe it away. But it was on the outside. Another dot, larger, appeared on the pane farther up and to the right, then another, lower, then another directly in front of her eyes. Quickly the night filled with driving white dots. Their squadrons increased and became denser as she watched. Her heart began to thump. This is a flurry, Johnny, F-L-U-R-R-Y, as 'a flurry of activity on Wall Street,' a 'flurry of action in the bottom of the ninth inning.' Or, if there was no way of avoiding the word, you could say, 'a flurry of SNOW.'

She looked at her watch. Five o'clock. She'd never sleep now, and the sailors might be getting up any moment. She began to dress quickly. Breakfast . . . the Coast Guard had promised to send down breakfast at seven o'clock. She remembered the warmth of the station through the hours she had waited yesterday. Why not ask if she could come up and have a cup of coffee? Her hand reached out for the telephone on the bedside table before she remembered that the Longships exchange was disconnected. She'd have to walk.

132

Five minutes later she let herself out of the hotel's side door and hurried up the street. The wind had dropped a little, but so had the temperature. Already the street was white and slippery underfoot. Overhead the Monomoy light suffused the snow with a weird white glare, vanished, reappeared.

The station was a cave of light and warmth and the smell of coffee. The mess deck was empty and, after a hesitation, she began climbing the stairs to the observation and operations room. The door to it stood ajar and she saw John Remington at a table, and another man, standing beside him, reading from a paper in his hand. John held a cup of coffee in his hand. Both men had their backs to her.

The standing man read aloud:

'Barometer 29.32 and falling. Wind nor-east, 30. Pollock Rip Light reports seas breaking clear over the ship, and surf hitting the light, but she's O.K. – no drift. Weather Bureau reports the storm moving very slowly now, and getting slower, they expect it'll stop right here and blow its guts out. They don't say how long that'll take . . . No ships at sea in our area. Highland reported the light was getting clogged with snow, but they're clearing it . . . Oh, Mr Crampton rang a few minutes ago, said it had started to snow, I said thanks, he said he'd come by for a cup of coffee.'

'O.K.'

'Me, too,' Lynn said, and went forward, smiling.

The two men swung around. John Remington got up, frowning. 'I know I shouldn't be here,' she cut in quickly, 'but I wanted some coffee and I couldn't telephone, so . . .'

'You might have run into a couple of seamen going to the showers – stark-naked,' John said.

'Oh, I guess I'd survive,' she said lightly.

'Yeah, but would they?' the other man said. John Remington frowned at him, and said sharply, 'What about some coffee for Miss Garland, Ritchie?'

'Sure thing,' the young seaman said, and darted out of the room.

John Remington did not speak for some time. She waited, feeling warm and secure. 'You did a good job yesterday,' he said at last.

'So did you,' she said.

'I mean, getting all that information about the Spaniards,' he said. 'Are they all right down there?'

'I think so,' she said.

The Seaman Ritchie returned with the coffee, and John Remington tried to explain the wonders and mechanical marvels of the room, in much more detail than she could assimilate; and a steady step on the stairs brought Walter Crampton, coffee cup in hand—

'Morning, miss,' he said, then turned his back on her. 'Well, she's here, John. My guess is, she'll stay three, four days now.'

'Mine, too.'

'I was thinking about them Spaniards. If we don't get 'em out of Monomoy right away, we'll never get 'em out.'

John said, 'The shipping agents said their man would leave New York this morning, but he'll never make it now. We might get them to Chatham, but what's the use?'

The door opened again and Frank Damato burst in, powdered with snow. He grinned cheerfully, the snow incongruous against his swarthy skin and Mussolini face. 'Morning, Chief!' he cried. 'Morning, Walter . . . Morning, Miss Garland . . . Well, she's here, eh?'

'I reckon,' Walter said.

'I felt like a cup of coffee, someone to talk to . . . Maybe you'd like to know, the road to Chatham's going to be blocked for the next few hours. One of the Combine's fish trailers jack-knifed just short of the flat, under Monomoy Hill – you know where the road runs through that sand cut a couple of hundred feet north of the junction of Bayside and the Chatham Road. The driver broke an arm, otherwise no one hurt, but it's one of the big trailers, and it's all over the road, on its side, nothing can get by in either direction, least, nothing bigger than a motor-cycle.'

Walter said, 'That's that . . . I was thinking if the Spaniards have got to stay here, John, we'd best put someone to look after them. Cook and housekeeper, like.' His blue eyes turned to Lynn. 'And she'd better be able to speak their lingo. How about you, miss?'

'I'm a terrible cook,' she said quickly.

Even Bernard Kauffmann, who had thought it bourgeois to like good food, had complained. She had sometimes suspected that it was her cooking, not McCarthy or the FBI, that had eventually sent Bernard into hiding.

'Ain't nobody else speaks Spanish,' Walter said. 'Least, not that we can get at, and, being a woman . . .'

Being a woman . . . she could cook, obviously. It was a capacity women had, to compensate for their birdbrains. John

Remington was looking at her with a faint expression of surprise. Didn't she want to help the poor shipwrecked sailors? Of course, she did, but, oh, damn it . . .

'I'll try,' she said at last.

'I'll advance you money,' John Remington said, 'And put a truck and driver at your disposal temporarily. You'll want to do some marketing. And have the telephone connected.'

'I'd get the food as soon as you can, miss,' Chief Damato said. 'The snowploughs are out already, but they'll have a hard time keeping all the roads open.'

Walter Crampton rose to his feet. 'High tide in the bay at eleven o'clock, John. I think it's going to flood the lower houses, like I said. We'll know by ten, then Nelson will probably call another meeting. I'll be asking you to join us.'

'O.K.,' John Remington said. Damato and Crampton left. John turned to her. 'I'll drive you back.'

'I can walk,' she said, 'but, I've been thinking – the shops won't be open till nine, and by then there'll be such a rush, and the roads will be so bad . . . would it be possible for you to lend me stores for these men from your stocks? Then you could . . .'

'I'm sorry,' he said. 'Only in emergency. This isn't an emergency.'

'It was just an idea,' she said lamely. 'I didn't mean . . .'

'It's not just the regulations,' he said, almost angrily. 'I'll break the regulations if need be Those stores are to keep this Coast Guard station running and . . .'

'Neither snow, nor rain, nor heat, nor gloom of night . . .' she said, smiling. 'I understand.'

At seven o'clock, in the Coast Guard station, there was no real day, only a lightening of the atmosphere so that a man looking out the west windows, on the lee side, could distinguish between snow and air, and between the snow that was falling and the snow that was lying. The wind blew and the earth shook to the pounding of the sea, but all in a thick silence. John, settling at his office table with a good meal of bacon and eggs inside him, wished he could curl up and go back to sleep. By God, he'd been tired last night . . . and Lynn Garland had spent a couple of hours in the operations room. Because of him? Out of idle curiosity?

He lifted his head. 'Is that the fire alarm?'

Seaman Appel, typing at the other side of the table, cocked his head. 'I can't hear anything, Chief.'

135

John went to the front door, and out on the step. Yes, the alarm was going. Normally it would deafen you even with storm windows closed. Now it was a faint and choked wail in a minor key, like a child dying in a snowdrift.

His fatigue disappeared. Snow and fire made a dangerous partnership, and now here they were, threatening Monomoy – his Monomoy.

'I'm going to find out about the fire,' he told Appel. 'Tell McGill.'

He struggled into his foul-weather gear and hurried down the steps into Boat Street. The snow lay three inches deep in the open and had drifted to a foot against the sheltered side of walls, fences and buildings. One of the town's three combination firetrucks roared out of the firehouse as he reached it, and another had already gone. Inside, the assistant fire chief looked up from his desk and spoke before John had time to ask his question.

'One of those old houses at Seventh and North Hill,' he said. A voice was speaking unhurriedly on the radio, and John went out with a word of thanks.

A few pedestrians plodded along the sidewalks, heads bowed. A few cars ploughed slowly down the middle of the street. One, stalled at Second and North Commerce, had already begun to lose shape and identity under a thickening tarpaulin of snow. Frank Damato was there, talking to the driver of a Highway Department snowplough. People and vehicles seemed to pounce out of the swirl, loom gigantic for a second, and as suddenly vanish. They ought to stop all traffic except emergency vehicles, John thought. There's enough trouble without blocked. streets

Seventh Street, like all the numbered streets of Monomoy, ran east and west between the Great Dune and Longships Bay. In this area the town had grown in a particularly haphazard manner. The block bounded by Sixth and Seventh, North Hill and North Commerce, contained the Warren Mercer Company's furniture factory, a Shell gas station, half a dozen private houses, and two eighteenth-century rows. For no particular reason the row on 7th Street was occupied by labourers, fishermen and the like, while the very similar row on North Hill gave a desirable address to half a dozen business and professional men. The fire, as John saw when he reached the spot, was in the low-income row on 7th Street, actually in the end house.

Packed in with a hundred other spectators behind a police

136

line, he watched the smoke billowing from upper windows. Red fire burned behind the glass, as yet unbroken, at street level. The scarlet fire engines blocked 7th Street, and firemen on ladders, the hoses trailing down, directed columns of water into the smoke. Hoses writhed in the roadway, like snakes trying to get rid of the snow from their backs. The wind here, close under the Great Dune, blew dense and cold and snow-filled, sometimes from the north, swooping down over the houses on the north side of 7th Street, sometimes from the east, sighing directly down the long steep face of the dune.

'Everyone out of the houses?' John asked the man next to him. The man said, 'Dunno . . . They got 'em out of this one. That's the feller who lived there.' He pulled a hand out of his pocket and pointed. Beyond the engines, half obscured in the driving snow, John saw a man standing close to the fire chief, a man wearing a short lumber jacket, oatmeal-coloured longies, shoes, and nothing else. The man stared at the upper windows of the burning house, his mouth open.

'They got the wife and kids away. Took 'em to friends across town,' John's neighbour shouted.

John looked more closely about him. Nelson Pryor and Walter Crampton stood near the fire trucks, talking to Frank Damato and George Lathrop, the Highway Department chief. Dorothy King was here, close in front of him, her hand to her mouth. Joe Steele was here, with his sister and Chris Damato and Gene Begg and the Jenkins boy and Bill Vernon, Vernon's prognathous jaw hanging low in a deep grin. George Zanakis was here, alone, snow thick on his grey thatch, a sketch pad in his left hand, right hand busily at work, eyes darting from the fire to the pad and back to the fire.

The ground-floor windows of the burning house exploded outward with a sharp double crack. Long tongues of deep-red flame licked out into the street. The crowd swayed back, like trees in a wind, its sighing scream rising for a moment above the roar of the fire and the hiss of the hoses. The fire chief gave an order and the firemen on the ladders began to come down. John's neighbour said, 'They're giving this one up. Trying to save the others, see.'

A heavy hand pushed John to one side. He turned in anger as Elliott King thrust past. Elliott reached the policeman holding back the crowd, and pushed past him, too. John heard Elliott's shouting: 'Merrill, did you get Mrs Ingle out of there?'

The fire chief came running toward him. 'Mrs Ingle? They

137

told me she went to her sister's after we told her about her husband. They went back to bed, and—'

'She didn't,' Elliott bellowed. 'She changed her mind, came home, and took a sleeping pill . . .'

Flame poured through the windows, and leaked between the clapboards, streaking the front of the house with red and orange. The firemen directed their hoses on to the next house in the row. Heavy smoke turned the blizzard a dark grey. The crackling and roaring and hissing steadily increased.

Elliott King grabbed an axe from a fireman's hand and ran forward. The fire chief shouted after him, but he did not pause. Another fireman struggled up from the lower house, dragging the hose after him. Elliott reached the door and swung the axe with a running, hurling motion. The door burst open and Elliott ran in through a sunburst of flame. The fireman edged closer, his head turned away from the heat, and played the hose through the door. In the crowd every man and woman leaned forward in the churned snow, toward the burning house. Thirty seconds passed, and no one spoke.

The flames at the doorway puffed outward and Elliott appeared, a woman in his arms. The powerful water jet nearly knocked him down. Then men were running forward, and John found himself running with them, and they were taking the woman from his arms, supporting him, handling him gently. The woman wore a flannelette nightie, and kept screaming in a low, monotonous key.

The crowd began to cheer, a surging football roar of sound. John had a lump in his throat, and damp eyes. He wrung Elliott King's hand and shouted, 'Great! Great!' Elliott's arm was round his shoulder, and the strong fingers kneading and caressing.

'You crazy bastard, you crazy bastard,' the fire chief yelled happily.

Elliott shouted, 'Ingle used to work for me . . . before he went to the Combine. I knew they rented a back room here.'

'I would have searched the place, Elliott,' the fire chief said, 'but it was already dangerous, and the man swore everybody was out.'

John disengaged himself from Elliott King's grasp. The woman must be the wife of the truck driver who'd jack-knifed the trailer up by Monomoy Hill. Trouble enough for one family for one day; but there was more to come, for many more, to judge by the virulence of the flames.

138

A fireman hurried up 7th Street and spoke to his chief, 'I've been round the backs, like you told me, Merrill, and it looks bad.'

'I'll come,' the fire chief said. 'Nelson, you'll be here when I come back? About ten minutes, maybe less.'

Nelson Pryor nodded. Now John saw an old man, well dressed and plump, face mottled red-white with anxiety, tug at his arm. 'Nelson, if this spreads, the factory will go.'

'I know, Warren,' Nelson said patiently. 'Merrill's gone round the back to check up.'

'He doesn't need to do that,' the old man cried, 'I *know*! If the fire spreads to the row on North Hill we're done for. The last house has a common back wall with my old warehouse. It's spreading down this row, Nelson! Look at it. Why aren't there any more fire trucks here? I've been asking for half an hour to . . .'

'All ours are on the job,' Nelson said, 'and we can't get any from Chatham or Harwich – even if they could spare them – because the road's blocked.'

'Six per cent of the labour force in Monomoy!' the old man cried. 'Eleven per cent of the town's payroll, thirteen per cent of the town's taxes! You can't afford even to *risk* having my factory burn, Nelson!'

John listened, standing a little back from the knot that had gathered round the First Selectman. Fifty feet beyond, the crowd waited behind the police lines. Close on the right George Zanakis drew with frowning intensity. On the left, in a separate phalanx John recognized the twelve small Spaniards and their captain.

Merrill Crosby returned, snow mantling his helmet and shoulders, and went straight to Nelson Pryor. 'The first thing I got to do is empty the tanks in the gas station. That'll take one truck, and we'll pump the gas out down 7th Street into the bay. No, there's no other gas station I can take it to in the time.'

'O.K.,' Nelson said quietly.

The fire chief said, 'I've got to do that first, Nelson. If that gas station goes up, the whole town could go . . . But as soon as we're free, which ought to be in about fifteen minutes, we'll have to knock down the North Hill row.'

'Why?' Jim Carpenter asked. John remembered that Carpenter lived in the North Hill row himself, in two of the old houses combined into one.

The fire chief said, 'Like Mr Mercer said, Jim, they touch the factory.'

'My house means just as much . . .' Jim Carpenter began. He cut himself off short.

The fire chief said, 'There's thousands of gallons of paint in there, Jim – dry lumber, varnish, chemicals, glue. Gosh a'mighty, if the factory goes up, we'd have the makings of a fire storm, an' . . .'

'All right,' Jim Carpenter said, 'I understand.' He stepped aside from the group, his face set. Standing there, his eyes wandered over the group beside him, then at the distant crowd, then looked at John. He looked away again, but in a moment his glance returned. He began to walk toward John, his feet moving slowly, as though unwilling.

The fire chief was saying, 'Elliott, I got to have some dynamite, and a man to use it.'

'How much?'

'Don't know. We'll have to ask the expert . . .'

'Austin. I think we've got enough. I'll bring Austin and the dynamite, and detonators.'

Jim Carpenter reached John Remington's side. His voice was low and urgent. 'Chief! Will you come with me?'

'Sure.' John followed through the crowd, and down North Hill Street. In front of his own house, Jim Carpenter stopped. 'In a few minutes someone will think of organizing work gangs to help us clear our houses, before Merrill Crosby blows them up. I've got to clear my attic before that. I want you to help. I trust you . . . The attic is my studio,' Carpenter said, 'and it's full of paintings – nudes of my wife. If anyone sees them I'll never be voted into office again. Those who don't sneer will laugh. Will you help?'

'Sure,' John said. He didn't know whether he was about to laugh or cry.

Jim Carpenter opened the door and hurried in, calling, 'Barbara!'

His wife came out of the living-room, her eyes wild but her hair in perfect order. Jim snapped, 'Is Molly still here? Good. Tell her to take the kids and your jewels to her house. All of them have got to be out of here in five minutes. You stay here. Stay at the door. If anyone asks to come and help, tell 'em we don't want help.'

'But . . .'

'We're going to clear the attic. The house may be blown up – probably will – in about fifteen minutes. *Hurry!*'

140

John retained a vivid print of Barbara's face, turned suddenly a deep scarlet, as he raced up the stairs at Jim Carpenter's heels. On the second landing Jim dashed into a bedroom, and came out dragging three sheets. At the end of the passage he pulled down a counterweighted attic ladder, ran up it, took a key from a chain at his belt, unfastened a heavy padlock, and pushed up the trap door.

For a moment, in the big attic, the only light was a red flickering glow reflected down from the snow on the window. Then Jim Carpenter turned on the light.

The attic was narrow and long, the window facing east. An easel stood in the middle of the floor, and there was a chair, a table, a red-velvet covered divan, and a portable electric heater. Paintings, stretched but unframed, stood against the walls, and one on the easel. All were nudes, sometimes only face and breast, sometimes only the torso, sometimes a thigh, sometimes only the loins, but more often the whole explicit female body. The colours glowed brighter than life, and the drawing was not accurate, but to John there was no impression of amateurism. There were exaggerations and mistakes, but they seemed to have been done deliberately, to create some effect that the painter was not sure of. The model was always, and recognizably, Barbara Carpenter.

Jim grabbed a knife from the table and began to hack the canvas out of a heavy golden frame. John set to work on the paintings stacked round the walls. Only your hairdresser knows for sure, he thought – your hairdresser, your husband, and the moving man. He let out a sudden explosive chuckle. Jim said, 'I know . . . but, the hours I've put in . . . the only times I've been happy . . . I *won't* burn them.'

They cut and tore, pulled and stacked. John said, 'Start another pile. That's all we'll be able to carry in one roll.' They continued.

The trapdoor creaked, and Jim Carpenter spun round, teeth bared, knife in hand. His wife's head appeared in the trap. 'Frank Damato came, and asked whether we needed any help. I said No.'

Jim said, 'O.K. Come on up.'

John ripped and tugged . . . Twelve studies of the breast on a single canvas; the shoulder blade, twice life size; head and shoulders; Venus emerging from a too-blue sea, with long fingers holding up the breasts and Barbara's outraged modesty above.

The woman herself wailed, 'I don't know what you'll think of us, Mr Remington. He made me do it. (*Legs of a woman up to the crotch, anonymous, but he knew that small mole very high on the inside of the right thigh by now.*) He wouldn't even let me wear a bathing suit. (*Back view, a woman bending over, arm outstretched, foot pointed.*) I'll never be able to look anyone in the face again.'

Jim said, 'Shut up.'

A little later they finished. 'Three rolls,' John said. 'Anything else you want to get out of the house?'

'Yes. Legal papers, a few things. You and Barbara take the pictures between you. I'll clear out the other things I want, and go direct to Molly's with them.'

'O.K.'

They struggled down the narrow steps, Jim panting with urgency. The three fat rolls of canvas, swathed in sheets, lay like corpses on the landing. Barbara stood by, wringing her hands. On down the stairs, hoist the rolls on to the shoulders. Ready! Jim whispered, 'If anyone asks what they are, say they're valuable rugs, O.K.?' He opened the front door and closed it behind them. They were outside, breathing with difficulty in the blizzard. Men closed in all round, speaking, offering help. Barbara Carpenter's face had turned green in the streaky light. People did not press her in her sorrow. Soon they were free, plodding slowly down North Hill Street.

'Where are we going?' Barbara asked miserably.

'My house. Two blocks,' John said.

The sky was a dirty black sieve, painted with orange streaks from the fire, snow pouring from it.

Half a block from safety Barbara Carpenter slipped in the snow, her legs flew out from under her, and she fell. The sheeted roll burst open. 'Oh, oh, oh!' she cried.

'Shut up!' John cried furiously into her ear. He knelt quickly on the fluttering sheet and canvases. Under his knee Barbara, naked and golden tanned, stretched voluptuously on a red divan, one knee raised invitingly.

'Gee, that's a pretty picture.'

The woman's voice came from over his shoulder. John swung round, at the same time trying to turn the top canvas face down. Barbara Carpenter howled like a dog.

The woman was JoAnn Griffiths. She crouched beside him, turned the canvas right way up, and carefully wiped off the snow. She said, 'It's real pretty of you, Mrs Carpenter.'

Barbara Carpenter wailed, 'Oh, no!'

142

John came to a decision. 'We need your help, JoAnn. Help us carry these paintings to my house. But don't say anything about them, now or ever. We're pretending they're rugs.'

'O.K.,' the girl said. She swiftly rolled the canvases, and refastened the bundle with A & P expertise, talking as she worked. 'Half the shnooks in this town think there's something wrong in a girl taking off her clothes, even to go to bed.' She hoisted the roll on to her shoulder. 'Some of these dirty-minded old bastards would like for us to wear canvas long johns into the tub.' With her free hand she brushed snow off John's coat. 'Are you all right?'

'I'm fine,' John said. Then they came to his house and he put down his burden, sighing heavily with relief and exhaustion. 'Thank you,' he said to JoAnn. 'I'll carry them up. You run along, JoAnn. And don't say anything.'

'Course not,' she said. 'Not if *you* don't want me to.'

The blizzard swallowed her. Barbara muttered, 'Her, of all people! That slut! It'll be all over town in five minutes. I'm ruined.'

John said, 'She's a good girl, Mrs Carpenter . . . Let's get them upstairs and put away somewhere.'

Jim Carpenter worked rapidly, opening drawers, riffling through the contents of his filing cabinet the way a man riffles through a deck of cards, taking out what papers he wanted, and laying them neatly in one of the two suitcases open beside him. He felt exhilarated and, at the same time, in full, cold possession of his faculties. Any real crisis did this to him. If only life were a continual crisis, instead of a continual compromise! Boy, there'd be no stopping him. If he could have been in the war, for instance! But the war ended when he was sixteen, so instead of having wings and medals and stars he had a little brown briefcase.

Glancing out the window he saw a truck that had not been there a few minutes earlier. The firemen were playing hoses on houses up the block, nearer to the original fire. The crowd in North Hill seemed to be denser, as though they had been pushed back from 7th.

He returned to work. One thing at a time.

Man oh man, someone should have taken a photo of Barbara's face when she realized that Remington was going to see the paintings. It was a lousy thing to do, like ripping off her clothes slap in the middle of the Green and calling on everyone

143

to admire her – but what else could he do? *Yeah, but are you sure you didn't do it because you were desperate for someone else to see your work? Remember looking around for Zanakis, then deciding he was busy?* He was lucky to have got Remington. Remington was a solid, almost stolid sort of fellow, maybe not the brightest guy in the world, certainly not the best educated or best born, but you could trust him, and he gave you a good feeling because he was a man doing the job he wanted to do, without regrets or envy or secret yearnings.

Just about opposite to himself. That was Barbara's fault. Where was the mistake? Did the parochial schools in Baltimore give her a parochial outlook, in the bad sense? Or was it Vassar afterward, filling her with snobbish dismay over her own background? She sure as hell secretly despised *him* because he was an alumnus of Boston College. Not so secretly. Silly bitch . . . He slapped a file into a suitcase . . . But why blame her? Wasn't a man supposed to be able to teach his wife the way she should go? Didn't he love her, or why would her silliness bother him? And if he wanted to paint, if painting gave him the only real feelings of accomplishment he'd ever known, then why didn't he have the guts to *paint*? For the glory of being Third Selectman of Monomoy, Mass.?

The house echoed to a heavy rapping on the front door. Jim called, 'Coming,' snapped the suitcases shut, carried them down the hall and unlocked the front door. Frank Damato stood there in cap and winter coat, behind him falling snow and the flashing red lights of a fire truck.

Jim said, 'I'm ready, Frank. They can come in now.'

Frank said, 'Merrill's not sure they'll have to.'

Jim breathed out in a long whistling sigh. His legs felt weak and rubbery. He put down the suitcases and said, 'Come in.' They went into the study.

Frank said, 'They emptied the gas tanks at the Shell station, just in time. The garage and office buildings caught fire . . . The wind's been steady from the east, blowing flames and sparks over North Commerce, so they're putting the dynamite charges under that tenement block across from the gas station . . .'

'The block Elliott owns?'

'Until a couple of weeks ago. He sold it to some fellow from Providence . . .'

'Elliott is one hell of a lucky guy,' Jim said.

The police chief dripped water and snow on to the carpet, and fiddled with an unlighted cigar. He said, 'Well, they're

144

going to blow that block any moment now. Then they'll come here – but they don't have any more dynamite, and with the wind the way it is, and being able to spare more trucks for up here when the tenement's flat – you ought to be in the clear.'

Jim said slowly, 'Thank God for that. I never realized what this house meant to me until . . . you told me maybe I won't lose it. I need a drink.'

Damato said, 'I'm with you.'

Jim headed toward the kitchen, speaking over his shoulder. 'Have you told . . . ?'

Frank interrupted. 'What's that?' Jim stopped. They both heard rustling and scuffling from behind the kitchen door. 'Anyone else in the house?' Frank muttered.

'No.' Frank drew his pistol and Jim threw open the kitchen door. A blast of cold air, filled with snow, swirled round the room from the open window, now half blocked by a bulky shape. Jim dived forward and grabbed the man by the leg just as he tried to swing it out. Outside, dim in the snow, Jim saw more figures, running, rising like heavy birds into the air – ah, they were climbing the wall into the factory, they were gone.

The man in the window stopped struggling.

'You get smart an' I'll kill you dead,' Frank stuttered.

The man fell back into the room, 'Jeez, Chief,' he whined, 'we were trying to help Mr Carpenter.'

It was Bill Vernon, occasional labourer, occasional truck driver. His hair was a dirty blond, and his dull brown eyes were sunk deep under a sloped frontal bone. Now he licked slack lips, and the eyes shifted from Jim to Frank to the refrigerator to Jim.

'Get up,' Jim ordered.

'You – you were stealing,' Frank shouted. 'Worsa than that, you were looting! You know whata you get for looting, Vernon? You get *shot*!'

'Who was with you?' Jim interrupted.

'No one, honest, I didn't see anyone, Mr Carpenter. I was watching the fire and then I heard they was going to blow up these houses, and I didn't see you around so I thought jeez I'd better help Mr Carpenter save his stuff, so I tried the front door and it was locked, an' I came round the back . . .'

'Empty your pockets,' Jim said.

Vernon turned his pockets inside out. 'See!' There was nothing. Jim leaned out the window: nothing in the snow. He glanced round the kitchen. Nothing important or valuable seemed to be missing. A whisky bottle gone from the high shelf. Some food from the refrigerator, probably.

'Beat it,' he said, wearily.

Vernon struggled through the window. Jim closed it after him and the leaping curtains subsided. It was very quiet, and they watched the man climb the wall.

'No use charging him,' Jim said.

'The smart ones got away,' Frank said.

'Sure. The smart ones always do.'

'They're the worst,' Frank said viciously, 'leading innocent kids astray, then getting off free themselves, because . . .'

'Vernon isn't innocent,' Jim said, 'and I don't know but what he isn't worse than the smart ones like Joe Steele. There's something plain terrifying about Vernon. To raid a house with the police chief and the owner in it. To lie so obviously, without a chance of being believed. It makes you realize we're still very close to the apes.'

The house shook to a brief series of explosions. 'There go the tenements,' Frank said. 'I tell you, Nelson didn't raise any objection when Merill wanted to do *that*. Now that Elliott doesn't own them any more, no one objected . . . Well, I'd better get back to work.'

The small clock on the wall chimed a tinny eleven strokes. Nelson Pryor looked round the table, and said, 'Well, ladies and gentlemen, it looks like the hour has struck.' No one laughed, and Nelson took off his spectacles and began to polish them with his handkerchief. 'We'll have to go without Mrs Robinson,' he said. 'She seems to be snowed in. Will you take notes, Fred?'

'Sure.'

Nelson put on his spectacles. 'The storm's off to a good start, eh? . . . Jim and Walter and I reckoned we'd have executive meetings like this every day, while it lasts . . .'

They were sitting round the table. Most had dirty faces and soiled hands today, and big puddles of melting snow covered the floor.

Nelson said, 'Tell us about the roads, George.'

The surveyor of highways leaned forward. 'We're keeping them all clear in town, so far. I don't know how long we'll be able to keep up on Monroe and Hill. Close under the Great Dune there it's drifting something fierce. Out of town we're doing Bayside all the way, but not the Chatham Road.'

146

'West Village Road?'

Lathrop shook his head. 'Can't spare the ploughs, Nelson. They're O.K. out in West Village. Hell, they don't come into town but once a month, anyway.'

'Can you get through to Chatham yet?'

Lathrop hesitated. Frank Damato cut in: 'I got a patrol car up there. That trailer's in a real bad position. One of George's breakdown trucks couldn't move it, so we're trying two together.'

'No way of gettting round it?'

'No. And the snow's drifting bad there, in the cut. There was three, four feet on the lee side the trailer half an hour ago.'

'Can we get Chatham to help? They're nearer.'

Lathrop said, 'I spoke to Dennis Robinson. He said they're up to their ears themselves. Same with the whole Cape, I guess.'

Nelson fiddled with the pencil in his hand, drew a circle on the paper in front of him, then put a neat square inside the circle. He turned to Merrill Crosby. 'Fires under control?'

'Yes. The row on 7th has burned right out. The rubble from the tenement tried to catch fire a couple of times, but it was easy to put it out. I got a truck on watch down there. We're still keeping the row on North Hill wet, and the walls of the factory, close to the fires.'

Nelson drew a triangle inside the square. He looked at the harbourmaster. 'How's the harbour?'

'George didn't mention it, because I guess we all know. The bay's flooding. Front Street's under water two, three feet. It's in the ground floor of the bottom few houses on every cross street from First north.'

'High tide at eleven – now?' Nelson said. 'So it'll get better?'

'Until the next tide,' the harbourmaster said. 'Jimmy Runnel's boat started dragging but we ran her up on to the Fish Slip. The rest are riding it out O.K. It's not too bad inside Sachem Island – so far.'

Nelson said, 'Let's see, what else now? All schools closed, of course. Elliott's out on the roads somewhere, he couldn't come . . . First, any suggestions as to emergency action, anything we ought to do right away?'

'Yes,' Frank Damato said at once. 'Keep all private vehicles, cars and trucks, off the streets. They're slick, and you can't see half a block. It's murder.'

Nelson looked out the tall windows. He saw a dense grey blur, in which were reflected the electric lights in the conference room.

'It's a long way from north to south of town,' he said slowly. 'Not everyone's finished their shopping . . . People are going to want to find out whether Granny's O.K. What do you think, Walter?'

Walter Crampton said, 'They paid taxes for the roads, so they ought to be allowed to use them. WCCD'S full of announcements from every town on the Cape, about keeping off the roads. We could have them put out a message from us. But I reckon people are going to see what it's like and stay home, anyway, unless it's an emergency. If it's an emergency, it's our job to help them get through, not stop them.'

Nelson nodded, and Jim Carpenter said, 'I agree.'

Nelson noticed the tightening of John Remington's jaw muscles. Of course it would be more efficient to issue the order, but let one man be kept away from his business, let one woman slip and break her leg because she was walking instead of driving, let one old person have a heart attack carrying a heavy load . . . !

He said, 'There's one thing we can do. If cars stall or are abandoned, or parked on the street, you can tow them away.'

'Where to?' Frank Damato asked. 'Every parking lot's piling up with snow, and it means—'

Nelson interrupted him irritably. 'Somewhere, you can find somewhere, can't you? . . . It can't go on for long, at this rate.'

'But suppose it does,' George Lathrop said. 'The ploughs aren't going to be able to keep the streets clear, because there'll be no place to pile the snow. It's pretty deep on the sidewalks already. Another few hours of this and the roads outside of town will be like trenches. The sides will cave in as fast as we plough.'

Dr Burroughs, chairman of the Board of Health, said, 'How many families have had to leave their houses, so far?'

Frank Damato searched in his tunic pockets. 'I got a piece of paper here somewhere . . . here it is. Six families from 7th Street, because of the fire, twelve families out of that tenement block, nine so far out of the houses being flooded. That's all we've heard of.'

'There'll be more,' Walter Crampton said. 'Neap tides – so far. They'll get higher, even without the storm.'

'Where have these families gone?' Dr Burroughs asked. 'Who's taking care of them?'

'I don't know,' Frank Damato said. 'We asked them if they

148

had some place to go, and they said yes, or they'd find somewhere . . . We have plenty to do, doctor, every man in the department's been on his feet since five o'clock, and no . . .'

'Of course,' Nelson said soothingly.

If it had been only two or three familes, the local Red Cross would have looked after them. But with only two or three families, come to that no one would have had to bother, because there would have been so many places for them to go to. But it was twenty-seven families . . . already worse than any calamity in his memory; and this the first day. He felt a little cold across his shoulders.

He turned to John Remington. 'Any suggestions, John?'

Remington said slowly, 'We've had plenty of warning. Every recent weather report has emphasized that the way things are this storm could last a long time – four, five days, even a week.'

'Judas priest,' the harbourmaster muttered.

'It's snowing about an inch an hour. Twenty-four inches a day for seven days is close to fourteen feet, where it's *not* drifting. Houses are going to be buried in snowdrifts if only half that amount falls. With that kind of snowfall, how long can Mr Lathrop keep *any* roads or streets open? *Then* what will happen if there's a fire? Or if we get higher and higher flood tides in the bay, like Walter says.'

'Fourteen feet!' Nelson said. 'It's impossible, John. You're trying to scare us.' But some of his own fear left him. This was the kind of thing nobody said, yet it needed to be said. Once the words were out, you began to develop the right frame of mind to deal with the situation.

John Remington said, 'I told you we'd need snowshoes. There are only two pairs in town, that I know of, in Franklin's Sports Store, plus one pair I bought this morning for the station . . . The power lines are liable to go, also the telephone.'

Nelson said, 'What do you think we ought to do?'

Remington said, 'It won't be possible to take sick people to Hyannis Hospital. Pregnant women will have to have their babies at home, without help – or hot water. Old people who need to be visited every day won't be.'

Nelson said, 'What should we *do*?'

Remington said, 'Hole up. Fit out a place where pregnant women and old and sick people can go. And families who are liable to be flooded out. Anyone who might have difficulty surviving seven days in their own homes, without light or heat or

149

telephone. Put in doctors, cooks, nurses . . . Warn the town that that is the only place the fire department or the police can guarantee to look after. Hole up in it.'

Flo Monsey, the treasurer, said, 'But if the power goes, Mr Remington—'

Remington said, 'If the sick and babies are in one place, we could fix up auxiliary motors to make power for it, at least.'

'What about food?' Jim Carpenter asked.

'You'd have to commandeer it, empty the grocery stores.'

Walter Crampton shook his head without speaking.

John Remington went on remorselessly, 'If it's going to be done, it's got to be done now. Tomorrow will be too late.'

Round the table all sat silent. At length Jim Carpenter said, 'Could you order us to take such action, John? Military emergency, something of that kind?'

Smart boy, Nelson thought. A wise politician always stood ready to shuffle the responsibility on to someone else. Remington said flatly, 'No. You have to do it yourselves.'

Nelson thought, Suppose I telephone the Governor and ask him to proclaim a state of emergency in Monomoy, and declare martial law? It might be a dangerous step, unless other towns took the initiative, or the Governor made the order state-wide, which he would never do.

'We'd be the laughing stock of Massachusetts,' Walter Crampton said, 'putting all that stuff out on WCCD, so everyone will hear.'

John Remington turned on him. 'What do you suggest?'

Walter growled, 'Let everyone sit tight, keep his own and his family's head above water . . . You don't hear me complaining. My home's flooded. I carried Daisy in my arms up to Sachem's Tavern. They hired me a room.' His mouth closed with an almost audible clack, like a sprung trap.

John Remington said, 'Walter . . . I agree . . . but everyone isn't as strong as you are. Or as independent. What's going to happen to a pregnant woman whose husband happens to be away on a trip?' He spoke pleadingly. He admires Walter, Nelson thought; we all do, but to John Remington Walter means something special, related to the sea, to the craft of seamanship, to Cape Cod and an old, lost America.

Walter said, 'Lookee, Nelson, I can see you want to go ahead, like Chief Remington suggests. And, Jim, so do you. So I'm outvoted, two to one.'

Quite right, Nelson thought. So now the smart thing for

150

Walter to do is vote against, so that he'll be on record, if everything goes wrong. That's what Jim Carpenter would do. That's what he himself would do.

Walter Crampton said, 'Well, I'll vote with you, so we make it unanimous.'

Nelson quickly banged the table with his fist. 'Passed unanimously,' he said. 'Jim, you put it into words, what it is we passed . . . By God, I feel better already. And when it stops snowing, in the middle of the night, and we've spent five thousand bucks, then I'll feel great, just great.'

'It won't,' Walter said.

Nelson said, 'Where's this place going to be and who's going to be in charge? Those are the first questions.'

He'd like to have Remington in charge, but that was not possible. Elliott King would be an obvious choice, he had the push and the drive . . . but it ought to be one of the town's elected leaders. He himself shouldn't do it; Walter was no man to run a glorified refugee camp; that left Jim. He said, 'Jim, you're elected boss of the fortress, eh?'

Jim had obviously been thinking along the same lines for, although he made a grimace, he nodded and said, 'I guess so . . . I think the Selectmen will have to move in, wherever it is. We must be together, to make decisions. This place is going to be the nerve centre of the town, as soon as it's set up – and later, maybe, the only place with light, the only place with radio except for people with battery sets . . . Now, where's it going to be?'

Walter Crampton said, 'It's got to be the Longships.'

'I was thinking of the high school,' Nelson said.

The high school was under the School Committee, who could be cajoled into letting the town use it. The Longships Hotel belonged to a Boston corporation, which would not be easy to reach, but could make a lot of trouble later, if its property were damaged.

'The Longships,' Jim said. 'It's the only place with the beds, the linen, blankets, space for storage, cooking facilities. It's got everything. We'll have to get hold of that caretaker, Ernest something, right away.'

Nelson said, 'Ernest McElroy. He lives across the street. But remember the Spaniards are in there now, and Miss Garland . . . Well, we'll have to telephone the corporation in Boston and tell them what we're doing. Get their O.K., if possible. You do that, Fred.'

151

Walter said, 'You won't get anything out of them. They'll say, sure, you have the power to use it in emergency, but that don't mean they agree. They won't commit themselves. Makes more sense to ring Elaine Handforth. She owns quite a few shares in that corporation.'

'I'd forgotten. I'll speak to her . . . What are you writing, Jim?'

Jim Carpenter looked up. 'Some of the things that'll have to be taken care of right away. I'm going to be swamped. I've got to have a secretary, an assistant . . .'

'We'll see to that in a minute,' Nelson said. 'Pity Bertha isn't here . . . Who are we going to bring into the Longships? We'll have to word the announcement very carefully, before we try to get WCCD to put it on the air.'

'You do that,' Jim Carpenter said. 'I've got to go to the Longships. I can't take anyone till, say, three o'clock. O.K.?' He pushed back his chair and, with a brief wave, hurried out.

Flo Monsey said, 'Is this about what you want to say?' She pushed a sheet of paper across the table. Nelson read: 'The Selectmen of Monomoy announce that they have taken over the Longships Hotel as a refuge for the town. Reports indicate that the blizzard will last several days. Power and telephone lines are liable to be cut. Most roads will become impassable. All who do not feel confident, for any reason, that they can survive one week isolated in the homes, should prepare to enter the Longships Hotel. No food or bedding need be brought, but special items such as diapers, babies' bottles, special formulas, and one change of clothing will be required. This notice is particularly addressed to those in danger of flooding, to pregnant women, women with very young children, women living alone, and old people. The hotel will be open from 3 p.m. Telephone 213-2323 for inquiries, but only if urgent.'

Nelson said, 'Fine, Flo! Great. I'll call WCCD right away. You and Fred better stay by the phone for the time being, until we can get things worked out . . . Anyone hear the latest weather report?'

'Nine inches in Provincetown, eight in Chatham, nine in Hyannis,' Elliott King's voice boomed cheerfully behind him. 'Sorry, I couldn't get here earlier, Nelson. What have you guys been doing while I've been trying to get my caterpillar running?'

'Flo'll tell you,' Nelson said, 'or just hang around a few minutes. Turn on that transistor radio of yours, Fred – and

152

you'll probably hear it coming right over the air. I've got to make a phone call.

Immediately after broadcasting the Selectmen's message to Monomoy, the WCCD announcer gave a brief weather report. Still seated at the conference table, Walter Crampton listened gravely. Snow was falling all over Connecticut, Rhode Island and Massachusetts. Snow was beginning to fall in Vermont, New Hampshire, Maine. Heavy seas from Eastport to Cape Hatteras. The announcer began on another special message, this time from the Selectmen of Falmouth.

'We're all in the same boat,' Elliott King said.

'All in separate little boats,' Dr Burroughs said. 'Each of us isolated, unable to call for help – or give it.'

A good and just thing, too, Walter Crampton thought. Now each man would have to stand on his own legs, supported only by his own will and skill.

George Lathrop and Frank Damato stood up. 'If there's nothing else, Nelson . . .'

The door burst open and Alice Bryant stamped in. Her face was pale, snow mantled her bare head and short car coat, her eyes seemed large and her hands shook.

'What in hell does George Lathrop get his pay for?' she snapped. 'Roads blocked everywhere. Nearly pushed off the road by a crane . . .'

A burly man in work-stained clothes hurried in behind her. 'There you are!' he yelled. 'Damn bitch! Why didn't you stop when . . . ?'

Nelson banged the table violently with both fists. 'Be quiet!'

The burly man, whom Walter knew to be one of the Highway Department's part-time employees, would not be silenced. He turned to Lathrop. 'We'll never get the road cleared now, Mr Lathrop. This woman came tearing up, passed the crane on a curve, put herself into a skid – forced the crane off the road. It's on its side in the ditch now. No one hurt bad.' He turned to Alice. 'Not that you cared. You didn't stop, did you? There might be a couple of men lying crushed under that crane now, but you don't care. Chased her all the way back, I did, and . . .'

Alice spoke in a high quick voice: 'Oh balls, I could see perfectly clearly they weren't hurt. Besides, I didn't even know they'd gone off the road. I didn't know anything about it . . . Nelson, I have urgent business in New York, I must get off the peninsula. Frank, you'd better drive me out.'

Frank Damato mumbled, 'Mrs Bryant, the road's blocked, and . . .'

Hysterical, Walter thought. Lost control of herself. Lying and didn't even know it. But why?

The crane driver said. 'Coming back, she was slipping and skidding all over the road. It's a miracle . . .'

'The road's blocked,' Alice Bryant said tensely, 'I can't get out.'

'Didn't you see the notice by Town Pond?' George Lathrop said. 'There's a big notice, and flares by it.'

Alice ignored him. That sort ignored notices, too, when it suited them. Walter thought. She turned to John Remington. 'I *must* get out. You have a helicopter? You can get one?'

Remington said, 'I'm afraid not.'

'The 36-footer, then. To Wychmere or Allen Harbour. It wouldn't take long.' She spoke wheedlingly, looking up into the Coast Guardsman's face. She put up her hands and rested them on his shoulders.

A loose weak woman, Walter thought, with grim pleasure. Remington had committed adultery with her, no doubt, and now she meant to exact payment. But Remington, though he looked embarrassed and unhappy, would not be budged.

Nelson Pryor spoke gently. 'There's no need to be frightened, Alice. We're all going to be O.K.'

The woman's brittle control shattered. '*You've got to get me out!*' she screamed. 'I'm not going to stay!' She pounded her fists on Remington's chest. 'Exciting, you said it would be exciting. It's not, it's awful! We're going to be buried alive!'

Nelson said, 'We are not. But we all have to get through it together.'

'Thanks to you, Mrs Bryant,' George Lathrop said.

She stared at him, head high, blonde curls falling back from the ravaged face, mouth open and trembling. Slowly she sank into a chair and sat, staring. Water dripped from her coat to the floor. Elliott King watched her from across the table. Damato, Crosby, Lathrop, Dr Burroughs, and the burly Highway Department man slipped out of the room.

Fred Haggerty, the Selectmen's assistant, came in. 'The calls are flooding in, Nelson,' he said. 'Reverend Day wanted to know if he could come in to the Longships, and bring his collection of porcelain.'

Nelson laughed shortly. 'What did you tell him?'

'I told him O.K., but the porcelain would be safer in his

house . . . Mrs Handforth rang. She said we ought to have asked her first about using the Longships and I said we were sorry, we just didn't have time. She's not mad. Said she'd fix it with the corporation. And she's coming in to the Longships, with Robert, to help organize.'

Elliott King said, 'Boy, that's lucky. We peasants and tradespeople would make a mess of it by ourselves . . . and of course they'll be sort of wardens, seeing we don't damage their property too much.' He laughed loudly. Alice Bryant rose to her feet abruptly and walked out of the room. Fred Haggerty followed her. There was a moment of silence as they watched her go.

Nelson said, 'We'd better move to the Longships as soon as we can. We don't have enough telephones here . . . Jim's going to need men, lots of men, any minute now, for moving furniture, shovelling snow, carrying supplies. Where are we going to get men from?'

'The fish cannery,' Flo Monsey said. 'That's not working.'

'Good! Then, we're going to need schoolteachers, to look after the kids the mothers bring in . . . plumbers, electricians, cooks, carpenters. Jesus, do we have a lot to do!'

Yes, Walter thought, and not much time to do it in. Outside the windows the snow continued to fall exactly as it had been all the hours since first light, an opaque, swirling, slanting flood.

Fred Haggerty called the next room, 'Nelson! Mr Pryor! . . . It's a woman, sick, in West Village. She wants to come in. The road's not being ploughed.'

John Remington stood up. 'We'll get her,' he said. 'Tell them we'll be at the West Village pier in about three quarters of an hour. Then get me the station.' He too left the room.

Standing at the head of the table, Nelson Pryor said, 'What a hell of a position for a simple country boy like me to find himself in! If I'd known it was going to be like this, I'd never have taken up politics.'

Mrs Monsey shuffled her papers busily. 'I think one of you had better get settled in the Longships as soon as possible, and then we can close down here.'

'I'll go first,' Walter said. 'It won't take me long.'

He started out of the room. Nelson called, 'Hey, don't you want any help, Walter? The ambulance to move Daisy . . . ?'

'I don't need nothing,' Walter said. 'We'll be in the Longships in half an hour. You just tell Jim.'

He buttoned his coat and went out into the cold, snow-filled air. Get Daisy ready; pack the suitcases with the money and the

155

bonds and the pistol; pack a change of clothes; ring Hal's Taxi. Daisy wouldn't go in any ambulance, not while she had any life left in her.

Twelve noon. It looked to be a good storm, a real old-fashioned storm, the kind of storm that stripped a man down to what he really was, not what his pretences and the support of the goddam government made him look to be.

Captain Lacoma stood at one end of the Longships lobby, some of his crew at his side. He had not eaten for two days before the rescue and the food prepared by the schoolteacher here had been all but inedible. Nevertheless, he would like to know when those in charge proposed to serve him and his men the evening meal. Failing that, he would like to smoke. But it would not present at all a correct appearance for even a seaman to ask about food, and certainly not for the captain of the vessel. Nor would be proper to smoke when he had only seven cigarettes, for of course he must be able to offer cigarettes to gentlemen with whom his responsibilities would oblige him to meet . . . as, for example, the Mayor, and the Coast Guard officer.

His hand starting of its own volition to the pocket where his cigarette pack was, drew back under his stern reproach. It ached slightly, now. That was good. As a young man he had fought the manifold temptations of the flesh by willing a physical punishment of the offending member. After a few years of intense concentration, aided perhaps by the appropriate saints, he had been able to will a numbing pain into almost any part of his body. There was a philosophical question here, of course. In the case of a man desiring to smoke when it was not proper that he should, which member was guilty of the sin? The hand that reached for the cigarette pack? The mouth whose lust to receive it sent the message to the brain? The brain itself . . . ?

The hotel was in a great chaos. People ran to and fro like decapitated fowls. They were making more noise than was necessary, more than Americans usually made, much more than he would tolerate on his ship. But this was not a ship, it was a town. There was need of men with capacity for organization and a habit of command. It was for consideration that he should offer his services in some manner. He might let it be known that in fact he spoke and understood English well, having served a number of years on British tramp steamers. He was a man of experience in calamities, and could perhaps be useful. But he

156

was a guest, and it would be in appropriate to mention his qualifications. It was an American town, full of American people. If they wished his help or advice, they had only to ask him. Meantime, it would be proper to stand back, to observe, to listen, to study that most absurd and remarkable of God's creations – Man.

Ah, *there* was a point to emphasize. All these people were human, just as he was, just as his sailors were. Because these spoke Spanish, those English, one must particularly avoid the fallacy that they were therefore of separate species. The differences were so easy to detect – the words, the tastes, the manners and mannerisms; but they were unimportant in the eyes of God, even of the somewhat bigoted Church to which he belonged. He must in no case think of himself as Spaniard and of them as Americans. He must think of, and see, Man, and wonder, as so often before, to what purpose God had created Man, and wonder whether God was not now, perhaps, becoming a little weary, a little disillusioned . . .

John Remington walked out of the Coast Guard station at 5 p.m., leaving McGill in charge. Everything seemed to be under control. He had given three men time off to move their families from rented apartments into the Longships, but they would be back on the station before six. The 36-footer was back from West Village, high and dry in the boathouse. Randall had done that job quickly and well. He ought to have congratulated him, but somehow hadn't found time. Randall was a fellow who set a lot of store by the way you spoke to him.

Twelve inches of snow in Hyannis, and still falling. A huge fire out of control in downtown Worcester. New London, thirteen inches and falling fast. New York City, sixteen inches still falling. Ships on the approaches reporting heavy snow and high winds two hundred miles out to sea. The Nantucket Lightship reporting visibility of twenty feet, heavy seas, snow . . .

Plodding down Boat Street, he began to worry about the Diadem Cape beacon. Suppose it was getting clogged by snow? He ought to send someone to check it. But they weren't ploughing the road, and no one could reach the beacon except on snowshoes or by boat. So he could do nothing about it. The thought made him nervous and jumpy. He ought to report that he didn't know whether the beacon was working or not. A hell of a report to send to Harrison F. Helm . . . Up on the Great Dune you could *feel* the ocean pounding against the land. He

157

ought to send men to walk the beach, like in the old days. Suppose a shipwrecked sailor was lying there, half drowned, dragging back and forth at the edge of the waves, maybe only a hundred yards along the beach? The radar wouldn't pick him up. He'd just die. Maybe he should ring Dick Roberts at Chatham and suggest they each send out a pair, walking toward each other? They could rendezvous where the old wreck of the cutter stuck out of the sand above the high-tide mark. But suppose the storm had buried the cutter . . . ?

He turned on to South Commerce. The street was becoming a shallow trench, the sidewalks hidden under steep-sided snow walls four feet high. The streetlights glowed in the early dusk and car headlights illumined the falling, crowded snowflakes. People looked like bundles of old clothes rolling slowly ahead of the wind and snow. As he came abreast of one he saw that it was a woman carrying a baby under her coat. Another woman's shape showed advanced pregnancy. A man was leading her by the hand.

All the lights were on in the Longships Hotel, so that the building, clearly remembered as a huge, white-painted, black-shuttered colonial residence, now loomed like a factory, its dimensions unknown because the blurred rectangles of light that were windows disappeared upward, and in both directions to the side, to be lost in the snow. A snowplough was clearing the circle in front of the main entrance.

In the lobby John paused, filled with wonder. The roads outside had reminded him of pictures of war – any pictures, any war: the Germans retreating from Stalingrad in midwinter; Napoleon's retreat from Moscow; French refugees fleeing before Hitler's panzers . . . Inside it was like a mutiny in a prison. Men shouted, children cried, women screamed, boxes banged and bags thumped. Small boys clattered, whistled, raced, yelled, slid down banisters. People occupied all floor space – people moving, sitting, standing, people angry, people patient, people excited, people frightened.

Gradually, as his eyes became accustomed to the brightness and his ears to the noise, he realized that it was not quite as bad as it seemed. The chaos, like overlapping whirlpools, circled round two distinct epicentres of discipline and calm. At the reception desk two women worked at typewriters, and a third marked a chart on the wall behind. Standing among the women was Luke Elgin, head teller at the First National Bank, who seemed to be allotting rooms. The people inched slowly forward,

158

in rough lines, to that desk, and then to their rooms, carrying bottles and babies and bags, sometimes guided by a boy or girl of high school age.

At the other end of the lobby a group of men stood in a close, still formation, like police awaiting a riot. They were the Spaniards, the captain at one side and a foot apart from the others, the gap as emphatic as a quarter-deck rail. The sailors all wore the same neutral but alert expression. One or two were smoking cigarettes, the rest were doing nothing, only watching.

He noticed Lynn Garland moving through the crowd, tight-lipped, toward the Spaniards, pushing people out of her way as she went. She reached them and spoke briefly to the captain, who inclined his head gravely. Then she went back through the crowd, the Spaniards following. They passed through a door into the hotel's small dining-room, and out of sight.

John followed, working his way carefully among the people. The twelve sailors were settling round a long table, the captain already seated at the head, his aloofness from them only emphasized by his proximity. Lynn Garland set a great bowl on the table in front of him.

John went forward. 'How's it going?' he asked.

She pushed the heavy hair back from her face. 'Awful,' she said.

John sniffed cautiously. There was a strong, brown smell. The captain dipped his spoon into the stew, tasted a mouthful, and quietly put down his spoon.

John said, 'It smells burned.'

Lynn Garland burst into tears. 'I can't cook,' she cried, 'I told you I couldn't! There are a thousand women in Monomoy who can cook better than I can. Why did you pick on me? I did my best.' She sobbed miserably, head hanging, furious at her weakness.

The Spaniards, all spoons laid down beside the plates, ate bread with slow-champing jaws. The girl's dead-tired, John thought. 'Don't worry about it,' he said awkwardly, 'we'll get someone else. I'll speak to Jim Carpenter. I'd like you to ask the captain if they're all right . . . otherwise, I mean.'

'In a moment.'

Silently he gave her his handkerchief. She dried her eyes, blew her nose, and spoke to the captain in Spanish. He rose to his feet, said a few words, bowed, and sat down.

Lynn turned to John. 'He said, everything's fine and the food is excellent.' She laughed, her cheeks still damp. 'Damned liars!

Mr Carpenter's in the manager's office, just across the passage, through that door.'

'Thanks . . . I don't expect I'll be long. Where will I find you afterwards?'

'Oh, here, hereabouts . . . I'm in Room 142.'

Jim Carpenter called, 'Come in,' without looking up. I've got to have a receptionist on guard, he thought, otherwise we'll never get anything done in here. The clacking typewriter, momentarily silenced, began again, loud and hostile as a machine gun at his left hand. Sitting at the big, paper-littered desk, Jim saw from the corner of his eye that the newcomer was John Remington. He continued dictation to his wife, throwing the words at her in staccato fashion.

'—Silver, HH xx – Hawkins, H, x x – Ellman, x – Adams . . . – Ackerman, H – Warner H – Nolan – Frontino, H x – de Patto – James x x – Trusewicz, H, x, it doesn't matter now you spell it – Kimmel, H— That's all, so far. Now go and get Luke Elgin or one of the girls to fill in the room allotments for this list, and bring back the newest list of arrivals.'

Barbara Carpenter scurried out, head bent and face a light scarlet. What the heck? Jim thought. Then remembered that the visitor was John Remington. He lit a cigarette and pushed back his chair. 'What a day. Barbara's not much of a secretary, either. She types well enough, but I need more than a typist. Besides, she has the kids to look after. What's on your mind?'

John said, 'The Spaniards . . . Lynn Garland's no cook. I just found that out. Why don't you have the Spaniards eat with the rest, now that there are going to be cooks, and bring Miss Garland in here to help you?'

Walter Crampton, sitting bolt upright in a hard chair behind the desk, the telephone at his elbow, said, 'Miss Garland can't cook?'

John laughed. 'No. She told you so up at the station this morning. She made some stew for the Spaniards. It smelled so god-awful I thought there was a skunk in the room.'

'She ought to be able to cook,' Walter said sternly.

Damned old Yankee mule, Jim thought.

Walter said, 'She's in trouble with the School Committee. Elliot thinks she's a Commie. Told me she lived with some Jew Communist in New York, and all. We don't aim to have that sort of woman working with the Selectmen.'

Jim saw the Coast Guardman's knuckles turn white. Aha, he

160

thought, Salt Horse is not so impersonal as he would like people to believe.

Remington said quietly, 'I don't think she is a Commie, Walter. You aren't going to judge anyone on hearsay, are you? Elliott King's hearsay? Why don't you let Jim give her a chance? A chance to do a good job.'

Walter said grudgingly, 'Do a good job . . . That's what matters. Don't see, myself, how any Socialist can do a good job, seeing they believe the goddam government's going to do it for them.'

'Give her a chance,' John said.

Walter said, 'O.K. That's only fair.'

John turned to Jim, relief apparent in his face. 'How's it going? Is there anything we can do?'

Jim picked up a paper. 'About 150 people in here so far. We have 150 rooms, so space is no problem yet, and I don't think it will be. The ploughs are having a hard time keeping the roads open, but they're managing so far. As far as we know, all the old people who want to come, are in already – six men, eight women. We've got two doctors – Miller and Burroughs – and two R.N.'s – Mrs Lodge and Miss Gates. They're collecting volunteer nurses. There are a few in town with experience in the war or before they were married. I know Mrs Gee was a nurse in the first war. She's here. Mrs Rhodes has collected a kitchen staff. Father Bradford and Reverend Day are in. He brought Mrs Day instead of the porcelain. We have rooms set aside for nurseries, sickrooms, doctors' consulting rooms, serious wards, sick bays for minor cases – even one operating room, though neither of the doctors it at all anxious to operate.'

'A jail?' John asked.

Jim looked up, startled. 'You don't think we'll need that, do you?'

Walter Crampton said grimly, 'We sure will. This town's full of punks.'

Jim remembered Bill Vernon and the raiders in his kitchen. He said, 'I'll try and find something suitable. If we have a jail, and everyone knows it, we're likely to need it.'

'A judge?' John asked.

Jim said, 'Yes. Judge Mooney's here, because Mrs Mooney is bedridden. I suppose we'd better allot a courtroom for him. Police, we have. We have a laundry staff and should get the laundry going early tomorrow . . .'

The door opened suddenly and Charlotte Quimby came in.

She breathed deeply, her face red from exertion, and snow dappled her abundant, henna-edged hair.

Jim said coldly, 'All questions should be—'

She interrupted: 'It's Harold . . . Mr Morgan. He's disappeared.'

Walter Crampton stood up. 'What do you mean? Calm yourself, ma'am. Speak slowly.'

She was recovering her breath, the generous mouth regaining control of itself. She said, 'When I heard the announcement over WCCD I put on my coat and boots and went to Mr Morgan's house. I wanted to know whether he meant to come here or stay in his house. I felt that whatever he did I should do.'

'Naturally,' Jim said.

'I am his secretary,' she said. 'I rang three or four times at the front door, and knocked, but there was no answer. So I was going round the side of the house, in the snow, to look in the side windows and try the back door, when his car passed me, slipping and sliding. I didn't see or hear it until it was right on me, because of the snow. He leaned out and shouted something about Boston, and business, then he'd gone. He didn't look – well.'

'Here, ma'am, sit down,' Walter said.

She sat down wearily. 'I knew the road was blocked up by Monomoy Hill so I waited. He'd left the back door open, and I went in, and waited, and waited. He didn't come back. He never reached the roadblock while the police were there. They don't know anything. I've called his friends, thinking he might have gone to someone's house when he found he couldn't get through.'

Walter said, 'We'll take care of it. Are you moving in here?'

She hesitated, 'I don't know. I was waiting to see what Mr Morgan wanted.'

Walter said, 'You should stay, now you're here. Jim, here's another secretary for you.'

Excellent, Jim thought. Mrs Quimby was a very efficient woman, Harold said, even though she terrified him. Perhaps that was why she terrified him. I'll put you in with Miss Garland, who will also be working for me. Room 142. Tell Mr Elgin at the desk. Report back to me here as soon as you've settled in.'

'We'll find him,' Walter said, 'don't you fret.'

The door closed behind her, and Jim broke into a chuckle.

'Harold saw her coming and ran away. Otherwise, he could see that he was going to be shut up in that house with her for a week.'

Walter said, 'Maybe so, but he never thought the roads would be this bad so soon. If he knew the road was blocked at Monomoy Hill, he must have meant to leave his car there and walk to Chatham. Reckon he'd report to the Chatham police when he got there?'

'No.' Jim said.

'I'd best try 'em, all the same.' Walter picked up the telephone and dialled.

Jim waited, leaning back in his chair. Walter spoke briefly, and put down the instrument. 'No report. They don't think anyone could have made it after about eleven this morning. Their ploughs tried to come south to the wrecked trailer before that, and had to turn back at the town line, on the flats there – drifts six feet deep, couldn't see the road or the markers, air full of foam and sand as well as snow.'

They sat in silence. Then Walter said, 'Guess I'd better talk to Frank. John, you want to see Daisy a minute? She likes to have you visit with her. Don't know why, except maybe you're young and handsome. Women don't change, however old they get. Room 205.'

He left. Jim began to ask Remington whether he had any ideas on how best to find Harold Morgan, but before he even had time to formulate the question, Nelson Pryor came in, followed by Robert Handforth and the Princess Avaloka. Nelson threw his hat on top of a high filing cabinet and flopped on to the couch that stood against the back wall. 'I feel older than an elephant . . . Where's Walter going?'

Jim told him. Nelson laughed. 'We'll find him. Wonder where he's holed up? . . . Please sit down, miss. Jim, Robert here's got an idea. Sounds interesting. But of course it's up to you.'

Robert Handforth did not seem to be standing as stooped as usual. The girl lit a cigarette, a half smile on her wide, wide lips.

Robert said, 'Most of the people in here will have nothing to do. You have women to cook, teachers, married women, doctors, police. You have pregnant women, old people. What are all their husbands and wives going to do? Have you had time to think what you're going to do with all those people?'

Jim said, 'No. I guess they'll just have to sit and be quiet till they can go home again.'

'They'll go crazy, Jim, shut up in here. You'll have fights, quarrels, feuds. I think we must engage their emotions before they start to run wild.'

Jim waited. Did Handforth mean they should organize bridge tournaments? Indoor athletics?

Robert Handforth said, 'I think we should produce a play. I want to involve everyone who isn't otherwise engaged . . . as actors, costume makers, stage hands, electricians, scene painters. Even as spectators, because spectators are part of a play. You have that huge balloon here, and nothing you can do with it except perhaps hold concerts or prayer meetings, and we wouldn't interfere with those. There's the small dining-room next to it, which we could use for dressing rooms and so on . . . we would do *everything* in public. It's the best way to *engage* these people, give them a sense of interdependence, of creativity, rather than of just passing the time. All their hostilities and frustrations – and fears – at being forced to come here will be released in the play, instead of in real life.'

Jim looked at Nelson. Nelson said, 'It's an idea, you know. Of course, there could be problems . . .'

There certainly could, Jim thought. And all the problems would come to him for final settlement. He needed a buffer between himself, as administrator of the Longships Hotel Refuge (or whatever title was appropriate), and such schemes as this – for there would be others. There would be bridge players, enough young people to make organized dancing a necessity. A solution appeared to him.

He said, 'I'm for it. But I think there ought to be an Entertainment or Recretion Committee, responsible for the play, and dancing, and whatever else might be suggested.'

Nelson said, 'Hey, that's it! Elliott King as chairman, and the two reverends – Mr Day and Father Bradford, eh? I'll fix that . . . What play do you want to do?'

The girl spoke for the first time. '*The Iceman Cometh.*'

John Remington said, 'Eugene O'Neill.'

They all looked at him, surprise obvious on the girl's face. Remington said, 'My wife, and a friend, took me to see it in a kind of attic in San Francisco.'

'I've never heard of it,' Nelson said.

Jim had heard of it, but he had not thought about it since English 104 in sophomore year at B.C. He said cautiously, 'It's very long, isn't it? And do you have enough copies? I'd have thought it would be easier to put on *Macbeth*, or *Julius Caesar*, or something like that. They must have hundreds of copies of them up at the high school. People know them, too.'

'That's the point,' Robert said eagerly. 'We must challenge their minds with something new. I brought my copy over. We can type out more copies, or the individual parts, from that.'

Jim said, 'Well, you'll have to fix it with the Recreation Committee, when Nelson's got around to telling them they've volunteered.'

'I'll do it now,' Nelson said, heaving himself upright. 'What room have you allotted as the Selectmen's office, Jim?'

'Seven. It's the small meeting and reception room down this passage, on the left.'

There was a knock on the door and he called, 'Come in.'

Frank Damato entered, uniform cap under his arm. 'I've sent a rescue team out to look for Harold Morgan,' he said. 'If we find his car, we'll find him, I reckon . . . Joe Steele's come into the Longships. And his sister. And the Vernons. And Pete Worrell, Henry Howard, Pat Roney, Gene Begg, and Stan Jenkins. The lot.'

The whole Steele Band, except for Chris Damato, Jim thought. And Chris was here with the family.

Damato burst out, 'Can't we keep those jerks out? Whatta they want in here? Just make trouble, steal from the rooms, hold up old people in the halls . . .'

Jim said, 'I'm afraid we can't keep out anyone who wants to come in, Frank.'

'Bunch of lousy vultures!' Damato muttered.

Nelson said, his cheerfulness obviously forced, 'You keep a close eye on them, Frank, and if they make any trouble, we'll throw them in the cooler quicker than you can say Jack Robinson.'

The police chief left, shaking his head. In quick succession the others followed. When he was finally alone, Jim Carpenter lit a cigarette, sighed, and began to make notes on things that still had to be done.

When John Remington left Carpenter's office, the corridor was quieter, the turmoil in the lobby considerably lessened. He went up the main staircase and walked slowly along the second-storey corridor. Women stood in groups outside opened doors, and in every room he saw a mess of coats, shoes, and snow boots. A few old men were standing round a radiator, chewing dead cigars. Television sets were switched on in all the rooms, but the picture seemed to be distorted and fleeting.

He found Room 205 near the end of the passage, on the landward side of the building, and knocked gently. A tiny voice answered, 'Come in.'

Daisy Crampton sat propped up in the bed, three pillows behind her shoulders and a shawl around them. Her face was so wasted, the hand on the cover so clawlike, that he did not understand through what tissue blood could pass. A smile touched her face and eyes, and passed. The hand patted the bed. He sat down carefully.

'Can't see a thing, out,' the small voice whispered.

'There's just snow,' he said, 'it's still falling.'

'No people in the street?'

'A few are still finding their way here, I suppose . . . Soon there'll be something more exciting than people on the street for you to watch. Robert Handforth's going to put on a play. You can watch everything.'

The eyes turned toward him. 'A play, here? And we can see the rehearsing and all?'

'Yes.'

'When?'

'I don't know. I suppose they'll start as soon as possible. Tomorrow, maybe. I suppose they'll want to have it ready by the end of the week.'

'The summer,' Daisy said, 'let them act it in the summer, on the Green.'

'Yes,' he said, trying not to sound uncomfortable.

'I'll watch,' the faint voice said. 'Walter can take me down . . . . don't weigh much . . . watch everything, so that I shall know, in the summer, how it was done.'

The eyes closed, opened, closed. The voice, a thousand miles away, whispered, 'Thank you . . .'

John waited, but the eyes did not open. With anxiety he reached out to finger her pulse. As he touched the dry crackling skin, she moved her hand and for a second grasped his finger in her hand with a tight, strong grip. The grip relaxed, and he went out.

JoAnn Griffiths sat on a high stool in Doug's Diner, drinking her second cup of coffee. You couldn't see a thing out – the street lights like balls of white fur or something – headlights coming up slow, flashing in the window a moment, then gone –

snowploughs flashing red, roar and clatter, then gone. They were pushing the snow into the bay now, off the Coast Guard pier, some fellow said. Nowhere else to put it.

Doug said, 'He ain't coming, JoAnn.'

She said, 'Who ain't?'

'Him. Whoever the guy is you're waiting for. You ain't waiting to meet your *mother*, are you? Besides, I'm closing, going home before they bury me alive.'

JoAnn finished her coffee and got up. Doug said admiringly, 'I don't know why your can ain't square. Jesus, you been sitting here three hours, just today, but it's not square at all, no, sir.' JoAnn put on her coat, picked up her pocketbook, and went out.

She saw him almost as soon as she entered the Longships. He was walking quickly across the lobby, glancing at his watch, coming straight at her.

'Hullo,' she said.

He looked up, surprised, and stopped. 'Oh, hullo, JoAnn.'

'I been waiting for you in Doug's Diner,' she said aggrievedly.

'Waiting for me? But I didn't say I was going to be there, did I?'

'No, we didn't have no date, but Doug said you often dropped in for a cup of coffee. It makes a change from Coast Guard coffee, he said you said.'

'Oh, yeah. Sure.'

He was looking flushed and very handsome. She said, 'I wanted to tell you, I'm glad you got back O.K., yesterday, from the boat job. I didn't get a chance to tell you this morning. You know, on the street.'

That was when he and Mrs Carpenter were carrying all the naked paintings of Mrs Carpenter. She was too thin, really. A man liked something he could get a hold of.

She shifted her weight comfortably from one leg to the other. 'I was thinking, you'd want a cook, with so much to do.'

He said, 'I'm living in the station, until this is over.'

She said, 'I could cook there, for all the men.'

'You know we have a cook,' he said sharply. Then he smiled and put his hand on her arm. 'Look, JoAnn, they need dishwashers, kitchen help, here in the Longships.'

Over his shoulder she saw Lynn Garland coming toward them. When the schoolmistress saw the two of them together, she hesitated, then turned back and disappeared. Mr Remington hadn't seen her. JoAnn said, 'Did she come to the pier last night?'

167

'Who do you mean?'

'Her. Miss Garland . . . in the evening, she didn't even know you was out.'

'Yes, she did,' he snapped. 'She was up at the station.'

'After I told her,' JoAnn said. He was mad at her now. What the hell. What could a girl do? She said, 'She's here. She went into that room, there.'

He turned eagerly. JoAnn rubbed her sleeve wearily across her eyes, and walked toward the reception desk.

Noah's Ark, Jim Carpenter thought, smoking a last cigarette in the lobby, long after midnight. A patrolman dozed in an easy chair, and one of the reception ladies was asleep on a sofa, a blanket wrapped round her.

Some he'd seen come and some the grapevine had told him about, and now they were here: George Zanakis, with a box and a roll of canvas; Alice Bryant, with whisky and pills; Walter Crampton, with those heavy, heavy suitcases; Avaloka, with a huge hatbox; the Vernon family, empty-handed, obsequiously aggressive; Joe Steele and his sister, eyes hooded above the debauched below; Mary Pryor, clucking over her children; his own wife, loaded down with cosmetics, hair set, and curlers.

He stubbed his cigarette out carefully in the sand-filled receptacle and went upstairs, yawning mightily.

CHAPTER SIX

WEDNESDAY

Lynn Garland awoke slowly out of a dream. In the dream she was wading an icy river, snow falling and the far bank and the landscape beyond white with snow. At first the view was clear, then her legs became cold, the fog thickened, and she could not see across.

The telephone jangled. Charlotte Quimby cried out in the dark, 'Oh! . . . Have they found him?'

Lynn switched on the light and picked up the phone. A man's voice said, 'Sorry to bother you, miss . . . this is Luke Elgin at the desk. We don't seem to be getting any heat. I've had two or three women down, about how the babies are crying. It *is* cold. Mr Carpenter told me to put all calls through you, until six o'clock.'

Oh, he did, Lynn thought, and stifled a shivering yawn. 'You just ring Mr Carpenter,' she said. 'Heating's one thing I don't know anything about.' It *was* cold, bitter, creeping cold.

Charlotte Quimby sat up in bed, her hair in curlers, her eyes big and strained, the blanket pulled round her shoulders. She said, 'I was having a nightmare . . .'

'So was I.'

'I was dreaming of Mr Morgan . . . The rescue team aren't back yet, are they?'

'No one's told me,' Lynn said. There was no reason why they should; or tell Charlotte, for that matter. But they probably would, as her desire to be Mrs Morgan seemed to be a good joke among the men.

The phone rang. The high school girl's voice was shivery. 'Miss Garland? . . . Gee, it's cold, Miss Garland.'

'Is that you, Fay? Still on duty?'

'Yes, Miss Garland. There've been so many people asking, I wondered.'

'That's all right. I just told Mr Carpenter.' Lynn hung up, smiling. The kids were good, really. Give a modern kid a job, and a sense of responsibility, and he lost all the evil traits which seemed to set him apart from earlier generations. That Fay was

169

a real smart little thing, with an excellent brain . . . born to wash dishes for some lout, most likely. And, most likely, happy to do it.

Charlotte said, 'I suppose they might have had to take shelter in a house, after they'd found him.'

The phone rang. Jim Carpenter's voice was sharp. 'I've spoken to Vernon. He says the furnace is not working. I've told him to come to the office right away. I've told the operator to tell anyone who asks, that we're working on it. So you shouldn't be disturbed any more.'

'I'll dress,' she said, but he had hung up. She began to put on slacks, a heavy wool shirt, and wool socks. It was no good trying to go back to sleep now. About half past four. There'd have to be a system of duty secretaries, same as a duty roster on the hotel telephone exchange. She couldn't work all day and answer questions all night.

'Leave the light on,' Charlotte said, 'I can't go to sleep either. I wish there was something to do.'

Lynn found Jim Carpenter already in the manager's office when she reached it. He was fully dressed, and his smooth face seemed to have aged in the past twenty-four hours. The horn-rimmed glasses flashed in the light as he said, 'No need for you to bother, but as you're here . . .'

Bill Vernon shambled in, without knocking. 'Morning, Mr Carpenter,' he said. His eyes shifted from Lynn to the ceiling, to the wall, back to the ceiling. His big hands moved, sometimes touching each other, then rubbing down the seams of his trousers, wiping, kneading, never still. The undershot jaw hung loose, and the mouth was slack.

Jim said, 'You've been sleeping in the furnace room?'

'That's right.'

'When did the furnace go out?'

'I couldn't rightly say. She's full of fuel.'

'For God's sake, man! You were sleeping right beside it. A furnace that size makes a terrible racket. When did you last inspect the furnace, then?'

'An hour ago, hour and a half. She weren't working. Out of order. She's full of fuel.'

'An hour and a half ago! Why didn't you tell someone? Did you try to fix it?'

The heavy head shook, and the dull brown eyes passed blankly over Lynn's face. 'I looked. Couldn't do nothing. She's jammed up, good. She's full of fuel . . . '

'You said that twice, three times. Why didn't you tell anyone?'

Bill Vernon hung his head. 'No one couldn't do nothing about it.'

'How do you know? We've got plumbers in this place.'

'Ain't no use,' Bill Vernon said. 'She's jammed up, good.'

'Come on.' Jim Carpenter grabbed up a flashlight off the desk and hurried into the passage. Vernon followed slowly, and Lynn followed the two of them. It was dark at the foot of the narrow, curving stairs to the basement, and there was a sound of music. Lynn recognized a Brahms piano concerto. She didn't recall the number. Jim Carpenter flashed his light round the walls until the beam found the switches on the wall. 'Where's that music coming from?' he asked.

'My radio,' Vernon said. 'My little radio. That's Bach, that is.' He pronounced it Back. 'I like Bach, and them.'

Jim flicked the switches and lights came on. The furnace occupied most of the room. To the right, a door led to a huge, empty storage room. The ceiling and walls were dense with pipes in dropsical white asbestos casings. Gauges and dials studded the wall-like front of the furnace. 'I listen all the time,' Vernon said, 'I can't remember any of the names, Symphony number something, and Fugue, names like that. It makes me feel queer.'

Jim Carpenter opened the furnace door and peered in, flashing the beam. 'Where's the fuel nozzle?' he snapped.

'Only this funny stuff, not the other stuff, like they have in juke boxes.'

Jim Carpenter looked at a dial and put his hand round the back. 'Wire disconnected,' he said, 'and the point's stuck at *Full*.' His eyes glittered. 'There's no fuel. The tank's empty. That's the truth, isn't it?'

'She's full,' Vernon said. 'She was filled yesterday morning ... yesterday afternnoon, right after Mr Pryor called and said to do it ... I wish someone would tell me about music, then—'

'Shut up! Where are the tanks?'

Vernon said, 'Through that wall, ten feet out, buried, that's where they are. Buried under six feet of snow, too.'

Jim Carpenter said, 'You mean, you think no one can check to see whether they're empty or full?'

'That's right,' Vernon said.

Jim Carpenter picked up a heavy wrench and stepped close to Vernon. 'The tanks are empty,' he said. 'Come on, God damn you, who did it?'

'I don't know . . . What you trying to do to me, mister? I ain't done nothing wrong, just doing my best, volunteering to come in here and look after the furnace.' The voice was whining and cajoling.

'Like you volunteered to save my belongings from the fire, eh? Come to the office.' He stalked out, the wrench swinging in his hand, and up the stairs. In the upper passage, where all the lights blazed, he said, 'Miss Garland, please call Mr Pryor and Mr Crampton. Ask them to come to the office right away.'

She made the call from the telephone on the secretary's desk in the corner. While she spoke, Jim Carpenter sat down, carefully placing the wrench in the centre of the blotter in front of him. To Vernon he said shortly, 'Stand up. There.'

She eyed Vernon as she spoke. He was a sort of ape, in something like human form, and wearing a man's clothing. He was repulsive, horrible. Yet, when you really examined him, he was natural, animal-natural. Now he was an animal that has done something forbidden, but doesn't know why it's forbidden.

It was not one of the Selectmen who appeared first in the office, but Mrs Handforth. She was wearing gardening trousers and a chinchilla coat. 'It's so cold,' she said. 'I think the heat must have failed.'

'It has,' Jim Carpenter said. 'We're just going to look into it.'

Mrs Handforth nodded and said, 'Good.' She sank on to the couch. Lynn caught Jim Carpenter's eye. He gave an almost imperceptible shrug. If Mrs Monomoy Handforth chose to sit in, they couldn't stop her.

The other Selectmen arrived. Jim Carpenter said, 'There's no fuel oil in the tanks. Vernon says the furnace is shot, too, and he ought to know. He's taken off the nozzle bolt and probably thrown it away . . . *Shut up!* . . . What I'm afraid of is that if there's no fuel oil in the tanks here, there's likely to be none in the tanks at Monomoy Fuel. Vernon was their driver.'

Nelson Pryor sat down so suddenly that Lynn rose in alarm, and Walter Crampton caught his arm. Nelson looked up, his face grey. He spoke to Vernon. 'I got you the job, Bill, Mr Byrne didn't want to employ you . . . You filled the tanks here, didn't you?' A small, rising inflection of hope was in his voice.

'*I* didn't fill 'em,' Vernon said.

'You told the caretaker you did,' Jim Carpenter snapped. 'He says he has the book, with your signature.'

Bill Vernon looked past them all. 'That's not right, Mr

172

Carpenter. I went home . . . Rose wanted me . . . Jerry Grimes drove. He said he'd do it for me.'

'Jerry Grimes left town two days ago,' Walter Crampton said.

Bill Vernon said quickly, 'No, it was Joe Steele.'

Jim Carpenter said, 'You're lying, Vernon. Nelson, we must ring Mr Bryne and have him check his tanks right away . . . he's here, in the hotel. He's eighty-four, isn't he?' He wheeled on Vernon. 'How long have you been stealing oil?'

''Bout six months,' Vernon said. 'Hey, I didn't say . . .'

'How much oil is left in the company's tanks?'

'Ain't none,' Vernon said.

'Old Mr Bryne relied on you, that's it, eh? Now, who fixed the books? You couldn't do them, could you?'

'Joe Steele. Joe Steele and Chris Damato, they told me what to do. It warn't my idea.'

Nelson Pryor sat hunched and silent. 'Get the caretaker to see what he can do with the furnace. I don't suppose he'll be able to do anything. Tell old Byrne. See if we can't get this man arraigned before Judge Mooney. And the others, if there's any evidence against them. I bet there isn't . . . Did Steele tell you to short-deliver the oil to the Longships here, when we ordered it yesterday?'

Vernon said, 'No. He was mad. Kicked me like a dog when I told him. But we was going to go away tomorrow, an' I thought . . .'

'It never struck you that the shortage was certain to be discovered? Or that now you couldn't get away? Take him out before I hit him.'

'Beat it,' Jim Carpenter said. 'Your family's here, right? Go to your room and stay there.'

As Vernon shuffled out, a loose grin on his face, Lynn saw that a crowd had gathered in the passage. There were thirty or forty people out there, including some Spanish sailors. A low buzz and murmur of talk died away as the door opened. Mary Pryor hurried in, closing the door. It was quiet again.

Mary's hair was awry, her eyes clogged with sleep. She had a blanket wrapped loosely round her, and her feet, in street shoes, stuck out underneath. 'What's happening, Nelson?' she said. 'All sorts of rumours are flying about . . .'

Nelson said slowly, 'Bill Vernon – and others – have been embezzling fuel oil. There's none here, or in the town. It's my fault.'

173

'Oh, no, Nelson,' she said.

'My fault,' he repeated, 'just for a few lousy votes.'

His wife went to him, and touched him. 'You couldn't know, Nelson.'

Lynn felt her eyes smarting. Nelson Pryor should have known. The promised votes hinged on jobs for the boys. It didn't seem to matter now.

'I've got to tell them,' Nelson said, looking at the door.

'There's no need,' Walter Crampton said roughly. 'I'll tell 'em Vernon stole the oil, and that's that.'

Mrs Handforth said, 'I think that will be sufficient, Nelson.'

Lynn could hear the murmuring of the crowd in the passage now. They didn't sound like a cageful of wild animals demanding that a martyr be thrown to them, but Nelson obviously thought so. Yet he disengaged himself from his wife's hold, and said, 'Thank you, but this is my job.'

He went to the door and opened it. Mary took a couple of paces and stopped. The people at the front of the crowd eased back as though Nelson might strike them. Seeing only his back, Lynn could not know what was his expression, but the people there seemed awed and a little frightened.

Nelson said, 'There's no oil in the tank here, and maybe none in the town. We'll find out, and we'll see that there is heat, somehow. I want everyone to know this affair is my fault, so don't go blaming anyone else.'

No one spoke, there was not even the shuffling of a foot or the cry of a child. Lynn saw, among the crowd, George Zanakis and JoAnn Griffiths, and Stan Jenkins of the Steele Band, and Father Bradford in his cassock, and the Reverend Day in pyjamas and overcoat. Abruptly Nelson turned on his heel and re-entered the office.

'I'm resigning as First Selectman,' Nelson said. 'After this—'

Walter Crampton interrupted. 'We don't accept it. None of us is going to run away from anything, now.'

Nelson stared at them in turn. 'I guess you're right,' he said, 'Well, the first thing is to make sure Monomoy's Fuel tanks *are* empty. I'll send a man to do that.'

Mrs Handforth said, 'Could we pump fuel out of houses which the people have left?'

'Some,' Jim Carpenter said, 'but the filling plugs will be mostly hidden under feet of snow. It will take a long time to get even a few gallons.'

'I'll look into it, though,' Nelson said.

174

Walter Crampton said, 'This is an old hotel. There's a fireplace in every room, and big ones in the ballroom, dining-room, and the rest. Suppose we collect coal . . .'

'Very little soft coal in Monomoy,' Jim said. 'One or two firms use anthracite, but everyone else is gas or electricity, or wood for home fireplaces.'

'We got to collect wood then,' Walter said. 'There's stacks in Morgan's lumberyard, and . . .'

There was a brief knocking on the door. Jim groaned, 'We've got to set up a receptionist outside . . . Come in!'

The young man who clumped in was white from head to foot, his face grey with exhaustion. His huge ski boots thumped heavily on the floor. 'Patrolman Juzek,' he said, 'from the rescue team that went out to look for Mr Morgan. We got him.'

'What? Here?'

'Yeah. In the lobby. Mr Elgin told us to ask you where to take him.'

'Call Dr Burroughs—' Jim Carpenter began, but Lynn already had the receiver off the hook.

'How is he?' Nelson asked.

'Exhausted . . . some frost bite, but I don't think it's too bad . . . we found him in a house . . . the last one on Bayside Road . . . he was out, on the floor . . .'

Dr Burroughs came on the line and Lynn told him the situation. 'Take him to Room 20. I'll be right down,' he ordered.

'We lit a fire,' the young cop said, 'burned chairs, beds . . . He came round, told us he'd abandoned his car, tried to walk to Chatham . . . couldn't make it, passed out in the snow, came round, managed to reach the house, and break in . . . We started back about one o'clock, three of us, on skis, towing him on a refrigerator door we broke off . . . Came down the old railroad bed . . .'

'Looks like you did O.K.,' Walter said.

'Thank you, Mr Crampton.'

Lynn said, 'Dr Burroughs says, take him to Room 20. I'll just go and tell Mrs Quimby.' She hurried out and along the passage.

In her room the light burned, and Charlotte Quimby was sitting up in bed, her knees to her chin.

'They've found him,' Lynn said, 'he's in the lobby, he's all right.'

Charlotte lifted out of bed in a single motion, her nightgown flying, 'My coat, my shoes . . . the poor man . . . poor Mr Morgan . . .'

In a moment they were hurrying back along the passage. Harold Morgan lay on a sofa in the lobby, the other men of the rescue team around him, melting snow spattering the floor, the inevitable crowd watching.

Charlotte Quimby burst through them and knelt beside the couch. 'Mr Morgan, you're all right now! Everything's going to be all right.'

Harold Morgan's eyes opened. He stared at the woman bending over him. His eyes closed and a long faint moan fluttered from his lips. Charlotte Quimby crooned, 'Special nursing, that's what you need, just a room to yourself, and proper care, and rest . . .'

The clock showed a few minutes past ten. Lynn remembered having breakfast, but otherwise did not recall moving from her seat since before dawn. During those hours a floating population of the town's leading citizens had occupied the chairs or leaned against the wall, with Jim Carpenter at his desk as the focus and only permanent fixture. For the rest, it was Frank Damato and George Lathrop, or Dr Burroughs and Mr Byrne, or Elliott King, or Mr Kimmel, or Martin Fox, or Fred Haggerty.

At this moment it was Nelson Pryor and Father Bradford. Nelson said, 'Do you want to try that telephone again, Miss Garland?'

Lynn picked up the telephone and at once the high school girl's voice came on. 'I was just going to call you, Miss Garland . . . the exchange says the line's gone between here and Chatham. They can get West Village, but nowhere off the peninsula.'

'Thank you, Lou.' She turned to Nelson. 'The line to Chatham's gone.'

Nelson slowly stretched out his hands, and then the fingers on them. 'All right. We're on our own.'

Father Bradford said, 'We could send out urgent messages on the Coast Guard radio.'

Jim Carpenter said, 'Yes, Father. But who to? I mean, things are as bad off the peninsula as on.'

Nelson said, 'Did I tell you, George Lathrop says he can't keep all the streets clear any longer? I told him to make sure of the really vital ones – Boat, Fifth, Nickerson, and of course all three north-south ones . . . except that Front Street's under water most of the time now. How's the fuel situation here, Jim?'

'We collected about a thousand gallons from various places.

176

The caretaker's got the nozzle working. He says he can keep the hotel at 60 by day and 50 by night for maybe four days with that amount. Elliott King's collecting firewood for after that.'

Nelson asked suddenly, 'Did you get the fuel out of the churches?'

Jim said, 'Yes. Reverend Day and Father Bradford here both reminded me they had fuel, and to go ahead and take it. But it wasn't much . . .'

'What are you cooking on here, by the way?'

'Bottled gas – industrial-size tanks. We have enough to last two weeks.'

The lights went out. Lynn found herself sitting in a dull murk, as though submerged in a deep, polluted sea.

Jim Carpenter swore. 'Get me the electrician, please, Miss Garland.'

Lynn picked up the phone. It was quite dead.

Nelson said, 'If the hotel exchange isn't working it probably means the power's gone. Well, this is one thing we did prepare for. We've got a couple of generators, on trucks, standing by. We ought to have light pretty soon.'

Jim said, 'How's the town off for gasoline?'

Nelson said, 'Harry Amoco has 3,000 gallons. Shell was pumped dry yesterday morning, remember? Cities Service on Front Street's under water. Esso and Mobil have 4,000 gallons each. The ploughs are using about 50 gallons an hour, between them, that's 1,200 a day. We ought to be O.K.'

Lynn could see more clearly now. Jim Carpenter was on his feet. 'Snow's halfway up the windows. I'm going to see about the power. If anything urgent crops up, I'll be in the basement garage.'

He went out, and Lynn saw a corridor dark as at twilight with two or three shadowy shapes waiting.

Nelson said, 'I'm beginning to feel like Job . . . except, listen to those radiators clank and talk! Someone must have got the furnace started, at least . . . I'm going to the Selectmen's office.'

Soon she was alone, for the first time all day. She yawned, and rested her head in her hands, her elbows on the table.

'Go to bed. Send Mrs Quimby along. Let the nurses look after Harold for a while.'

She jerked her head upright. Jim Carpenter's hand gripped

177

her shoulder gently. She felt wide awake. 'I've had half an hour,' she said, looking at the clock, 'I feel much better.'

Jim slumped behind the desk. 'We've got the generators working. But before we put the current into the system we must cut down the number of bulbs. And put out a notice about not using irons, hair curlers, toasters . . .'

'They'll need bright lights for the play,' she said.

'They can't have them,' Jim snapped.

Walter Crampton entered. 'Better not let Daisy hear you say that. She's bound and determined she's going to see that play, all the way. And Robert was right, everyone's interested. Must be twenty people have asked me about it.'

Jim said, 'Well, O.K., I'll see what we can do . . . Walter, I think we ought to send a team out along the power line to see whether they can find the break and fix it.'

Walter said, 'Yes. We'd look darned silly if we sat on our hands and the break was only a hundred yards past Town Pond. Have we got any linemen who can use skis?'

'I don't know,' Jim said. 'But if not, a rescue team can go out, find the break, then come back and maybe pull a couple of linemen out on a sleigh. Meantime, I think we should take a line up to the Coast Guard station, so that we can cut in on their power in case of emergency. I know they have an auxiliary. I guess they're using it now. Will you go up and talk to Remington?'

Walter Crampton shook his head. 'Nope, I'm taking a look at the houses at the bottom of Fourth and Fifth, and along Front, to see how the tide's hitting them.'

Jim looked at the clock and groaned. 'I'm ten minutes late to meet Mrs Rhodes in the kitchen already. After that, storeroom, furnace, money conference.'

Walter said, 'Why don't you send Miss Garland?'

'Alone? In this weather?' Jim began dubiously; but Lynn was on her feet.

'The streets are cleared – it's very close,' she said. 'Besides, I need some fresh air.'

'O.K.,' Jim Carpenter said. 'And listen, you needn't come back till five o'clock. Just ask Mrs Quimby to come along right away.'

A few minutes later Lynn snuggled her neck deeper into her collar, opened the side door of the Longships, and went out into the blizzard. The aspect of the town had changed again. When she last saw it, Commerce Street was a wide avenue running between banks of snow about a man's height. It had reminded her of an illustration in a childhood Bible, showing Moses turning back the waves of the Red Sea. Now, the light still that unearthly shade of dirty green, the snow still slashing down in endless, slanting torrents, the street had become narrower and the walls higher. It was not the Red Sea, but a railroad cutting, with hardly room for two tracks. A pair of snowploughs and a yellow bulldozer were working at the intersection of Boat and Commerce. The dozer panted as it sliced in the mountain of snow in a corner, and pushed a chunk into the street. The ploughs took it and pushed it toward the bay. A muffled policeman beat his gloved hands together, and stamped his feet, and looked at her out of snow-rimmed eyes.

'You O.K.?' he called. 'Where are you going? Want me to go with you?'

She shook her head, smiling, and went up Boat Street, across the parking lot, up the steps – two seamen were working on them with shovels – and into the station.

John Remington met her in the entrance hall, smiling, clean-scrubbed, his uniform pressed, a faint smell of after-shave lotion hanging around him. She felt a stir of resentment. Everyone else had had their lives disrupted, the wretched civilian leaders of the community grappled with problems far worse than his, and he seemed to be enjoying the blizzard.

'Come into the office,' he said cheerfully. 'What about a cup of coffee?'

'No, thanks,' she said shortly. 'We have coffee at the Longships . . . but we don't have any power.'

He nodded. 'It went out at' – he glanced at a pad on his desk – '10 : 13.'

'We're sending a ski team to find the break.'

He said, 'That's a waste of time. Monomoy's power comes from the substation outside Hyannis, and the break's near there.'

'How do you know?' she asked.

'The Highland, Chatham, Nauset, and Race Point stations all lost power at the same time,' he said cheerfully. 'I checked on the radio. Has the ski team left yet?'

'I don't think so,' she said sullenly.

He pressed a buzzer on his desk and a man came in. 'Send a man down to the Longships, tell Mr Carpenter the power lines are down near Hyannis.'

When the man had gone she said, 'I have a message from the

Selectmen. They're sorry they can't call on you in person, but they're all busy. They don't have men waiting at their beck and call just to run errands . . . They want to bring a line up here, so that we can tap into your power in case of emergency.'

John Remington shook his head decisively. 'I'm afraid not. Our engine has to run the Monomoy Light, and the Diadem Cape beacon – also our fuel pump, radio and radar sets, ordinary lights . . . we couldn't afford to lose any juice.'

'You have lights everywhere here,' she said. 'Two, three bulbs in this room alone. The mess deck's ablaze . . . lights on in the New Boat House. If you economized, the way we're having to . . .'

He said, 'It wouldn't help. The point is, if the Longships cut in on our generator, they'd take so much power that it would affect the working of our radar and radios. The lights are on in the boathouse because we're working on the 36-footer.'

'What on earth for?' she said angrily. 'I know the lifeboat was double-checked yesterday. Why don't you turn the beacons off? What good are they when no one can see them through the blizzard? And there are no ships at sea.'

His face was growing red. She felt a glow of pleasure because she had angered him. His uniform was too neat, his expression too calm and competent. He said, 'You ought to know better than that. This is the United States Coast Guard. We can't give up on our job just because the town didn't prepare properly for what it knew was coming . . . There *are* ships at sea, beyond the storm, which can run into it or get into trouble and drift. There may be people trying to make land in open boats. The lights have got to be where they're supposed to be, and working properly. We have our duty to do, and we're going to do it.'

'I bet you're glad the opportunity came,' she said, 'like soldiers wanting a war. There's no danger of a mechanical failure in these military systems – only of human failure.'

He said, 'Is there any other message from the Selectmen?'

She saw that she had hurt him, and now wanted to cry because the hurt seemed to be as bad in herself.

'Mr Carpenter mentioned fuel to me, earlier,' she said miserably.

'We have no spare fuel oil,' he said curtly. 'You may know how long this storm is going to last. I don't. I have fuel to heat the station at 10 degrees below normal, day and night, for three weeks. And diesel fuel to run the charging engine for three weeks. And to run the diesel in the 36-footer for 60 hours. I intend to keep all of it . . . I can spare about ten men, at any given moment, for work at the Longships. Does Jim want them?'

She said, 'I don't know. I don't suppose so. We have a good many able-bodied men . . .'

The telephone rang and Remington picked it up. He listened briefly. 'O.K. I'll be right up.' He turned to her. 'Excuse me now,' he said with an odd, abrupt tone.

He started away and up the stairs. She ran after him, calling, 'John . . . I'm sorry . . . I've been terribly tired.'

He had stopped on the third stair, and now put out his arm so that it went around her shoulder, and squeezed hurriedly.

'What was the message?' she asked.

'Our radar has picked up a ship, close in and coming straight at us. I think it must be the stern half of the *Goya*, come off the shoal she's been stuck on. Want to look? Come on then. It's O.K. for the Selectmen's personal representative to go where a woman can't.'

In the operations room she sat in the same chair that Mr McGill had drawn up for her the night of the rescue. The radar screen, shimmering and speckled with stray dots of light, looked quite different. The pencil of light, anchored in the centre, swept endlessly round and round as it had that night, still dragging a thin, dying luminescence along its trailing edge. But the familiar, recurring blob of light at about half past one on the dial, and halfway to the edge, was not there. 'Where's the *Pendleton*?' she asked.

'Can't detect that far,' John said. 'The snow's too thick – bounces the signals back and makes this blur. Here's the new blip.' He pointed with the tip of a pencil. Lynn saw a blurred, large area of light, also at half past one, but much closer to the centre.

'Half a mile,' John muttered. 'Stand-by a beach cart crew.'

'O.K., Chief.' She recognized McGill's voice, but was too absorbed in the radar screen to look up.

'I'm sure it's the *Goya*, but we can't take a chance . . . she's coming straight at us. High tide an hour ago. She'll run halfway up the Great Dune.'

'She's making near eight knots,' a technician at her elbow muttered.

'She must be standing pretty high.'

'She sure is. Look at that blip.'

John said, 'O.K. Time to go down.'

'Can I come too?' she asked.

'Sure, if you don't mind snow in your shoes.'

I don't care, she thought, hurrying down the stairs. I ought to be back at the Longships, with Nelson Pryor and Jim Carpenter and the rest of them, harried by crying children, sick old women, failing power, and complaints about the arrangements for drying diapers. That's where the real struggle was. The fit, hard young men here were like little boys hunting imaginary lions in a hospital corridor. So it was ridiculous that her heart pounded with excitement and the blood pounded in her veins and she felt ready to shout . . .

A seaman was waiting on the ground floor, just inside the door. 'Handcart's standing by in the Old Boat House, Chief,' he said.

John nodded. 'O.K. You come with us.'

They went out, heads bent, and ran down the steps to the parking lot. The wind blew in a steady hissing roar through the Gap, shaking the Old Boat House and sending a vicious stream of snow and sand particles into the eyes of anyone trying to head into it. More slowly, bodies inclined forward, they worked down the steep, broad flight of steps which gave access to the ocean-side beach.

Lynn found her hand held firmly in Remington's. She kept pace with him till the stone steps ended, and with him jumped off into the snow. The seaman landed at her side, and they stood together, looking out to sea.

The waves ran at them out of the north-east, and smashed down very close with a continuous thunder. The black water, laced and fretted with white, lurched up the steep sand, failed, and hissed back dragging new snow with it, so that there was a thin strip of clean sand between the sea water and the snowy dune. The sand stung her face and she began to edge behind John Remington for protection. 'Hurts, doesn't it?' he shouted, smiling. She gave up the struggle and cowered directly behind him, peering past his shoulder occasionally.

'Here she comes!' the seaman cried. 'A little left, Chief.'

She stared hard, forcing herself to keep her eyes open against the tingling sand. Her lips were cold and cracked and there was a taste of salt in her mouth. Ahead, a wall materialized, quickly created by magic from snow and air and water. Colour began to suffuse it, black above and red below. It grew gigantic, and came on fast, straight at them. It would strike on top of them and then what hope would they have?

The seaman said, 'She'll hit a little south.'

It was almost broadside and less than three hundred feet away. She became aware of another figure at her side. Turning, she saw it was the Spanish captain. Behind, on the steps, stood his men. The captain was wearing his blue coat, a brown shirt and black tie, and his captain's cap. The sailors were wearing their thin blue shirts and patched blue trousers.

The right end of the broken vessel struck bottom, and she felt the dune shudder under her feet. The left end, the curved stern, swung round, and kept on swinging. High above her the letters gleamed dimly: G-O-Y-A. Fifty feet farther down, it struck and again the sand quaked.

John shouted, 'Ask the captain, is there a possibility of anyone else being aboard, alive? Anything that must be salvaged . . . if possible?'

She translated, shouting in the captain's ear, and he said politely, '*No, señorita, nadie. Nada.*'

They stood a while longer, staring. The great waves struck full at the ship now, striking first near the front end and running fast along the side, finally rushing farther up the beach than they had before. She thought the ship was still responding to the water, rolling slightly under the waves, each time heaving a little farther up the slope and at the same time inching down into the sand.

'Dismiss the beach cart crew,' John said. The seaman nodded and began to work back up the steps. The Spaniards followed, none looking back. Lynn stared at the ship, at the rough red paint and the great flakes of rust. She heard the ship groan and mutter, a wailing and a muted calling. John said, 'That's the soul of the ship, Lynn, making ready to leave her . . . there's nothing we can do for her.'

He took her arm and guided her up the steps and away.

When Lynn heard the one firm tap on the door, a few minutes before nine o'clock, she knew who it was.

'Come in,' she called, not turning her head. The door opened behind her, and she went on typing. 'Just a moment, please,' she said, throwing the words over her shoulder. *Cans of corned beef hash, 12 oz. – 120. Bottles of tomato ketchup – 100. Packets of cereal, large – 640* . . . These must be put into alphabetical order. As it was, they were listed just as the team counting the stores had come across them. *Sugar, pounds – 80.* That wasn't very much. She saw that she had typed 90, and with pursed lips made the correction.

She turned, and found an expression of surprise. 'Oh, hullo.'

John Remington smiled at her. 'I dropped by to see how you were after getting so cold this morning.'

'I'm fine. Thanks.'

'Everyone's in the ballroom,' he said. 'I just looked in. I've never seen such a crowd. Come along and take a look. It's worth a dollar a minute.'

She pretended to hesitate, picking up a file, glancing inside, and putting it down again. 'All right,' she said at last. 'I don't think there's anything else I can do tonight.'

The grand ballroom occupied the south end of the main floor. It was a relic – like the hotel itself – of spacious Edwardian times, when the three or four hundred guests from New York and Boston, and their friends from the leading families of the Cape, filled the ballroom three nights a week, in white tie and tail coat and long tulle dress and mountainous hair coiffure, and twelve Viennese musicians fiddled waltzes and polkas and lancers until three in the morning.

Now chairs filled the body of the great room – chairs of all types and sizes: overstuffed chairs dragged from sitting-rooms and card rooms, sofas brought from the lounge, straight-backed chairs from the dining-room. Light poured like broken water from the thousand glass points of the chandeliers. The heavy draperies, of faded crimson velvet with tarnished gold tassels, hung in sculpted Grecian lines from the ornate valances. Between the windows light brackets spaced the wall, the lights dim under crimson shades. Through all this faded splendour Lynn's eye was drawn inexorably to the far end of the room, not by spotlights or any guiding quality of the perspective, but by the human content of the room: everyone was looking in the same direction, and so must she.

A low dais, which had once been the musicians' stand, occupied the far end of the room. People were grouped on the dais, some standing, some sitting. Robert Monomoy Handforth was there, long and thin and stooped, a book in his hand. Elliott King was there, puffing a pipe. The tall girl, Avaloka, was there. Alice Bryant – Father Bradford – George Zanakis – two or three others.

At John's side, Lynn went slowly up the broad, makeshift aisle. 'Everyone's here,' John Remington muttered. 'Even kids who should have been asleep hours ago. Look at that!'

Lynn said, 'Mrs Handforth's waving to us. We'd better go.'

'I don't know why . . .' John began; then ended, 'O.K.'

'Sit here,' Mrs Handforth said, patting the sofa beside her. 'This has been going on for nearly three hours already. I am so surprised.'

'What's happening?' Lynn asked. 'I thought Mr Handforth – Robert – was just going to meet anyone interested in the play, and decide what to do next.'

'That was the plan,' Mrs Handforth said. 'But everyone came – look! So Avaloka suggested they turn it into a workshop – I think that's what she called it – with everyone taking part in everything, right from the beginning. So Robert first explained what the play is about – *The Iceman Cometh* – and I can't say *I* understand even now, and then he started listing what kind of people are needed besides actors – like designers, carpenters, costume designers, electricians, and so on – and now he's been explaining the characters in the play. I think he has all the male parts allotted now.'

Lynn turned her head toward the dais. Robert Handforth came a step or two downstage and raised his hand, the book open in it. The talking and whispering died down, the clack of knitting needles stopped, and a woman murmured, 'Hush! Shhh!' to a whimpering infant.

Robert Handforth said, 'Now we come to the ladies. There are only three. They are called Pearl, Margie, and Cora. O'Neill's description of them is, ah, brief and precise. They are streetwalkers.'

Sound returned to the huge room in the scrape of moving chairs, the exhalation of breath, the renewed click of the needles.

Mrs Handforth said, 'One couldn't have mentioned a word like that in Monomoy forty years ago. The people here were so narrow-minded.'

Robert's high voice continued: 'Both Reverend Day and Father Bradford support my view that these women are necessary to carry out O'Neill's purpose. Now, who can I have to act the parts? The women are coarse, underprivileged, and uneducated. The accent O'Neill has given them is Brooklynese, but any strong local accent would do . . .'

No one spoke. All around, Lynn saw people glancing at each other in silence. He'll never get anyone, in a community like this, she thought.

A woman rose from a chair close in front of her. 'I'll do one of them, if I'm good enough,' she said in a low voice.

'Well, I declare,' Mrs Handforth said, 'that's Dorothy King.'

On the dais, simultaneously, Robert Handforth said, 'Thank you, Mrs King,' and Elliott King cried, 'Dorothy!'

Dorothy King was up to him then, calmly stepping up on to the dais. Everyone in the room heard Elliott. 'You're not going to act the part of a – of a loose woman, Dorothy. I forbid it.'

'I'd like to try,' she answered. Her voice was almost a mumble, and Lynn caught the look exchanged between Robert Handforth and Avaloka: with that voice, she'd never do. Perhaps Elliott King caught the look, too, because he said heartily, 'All right! Go ahead! Have an audition. That's the word, isn't it?' He laughed.

Robert Handforth flipped quickly through the book. 'Here,' he said, 'read this. Begin here: *No, dis round's on me.* Imagine we are all in a tavern. You know us all. You're telling how you robbed a drunken sailor.'

Dorothy King took the book from his hands, and read silently for a minute, head bowed. Then she looked up. Her head went back, her eyes opened, her small breasts thrust out.

'*No, dis round's on me. I run into luck.*'

Her voice came out strong and harsh. Lynn sat up with a jerk, and all talk and noise around died with an almost audible suddenness. Dorothy King might never make Broadway, Lynn thought, because there were women with the same intensity, a more tractable and wider-ranging voice – but here, in this ball-room, she was stunning. She throbbed with commercialized sexuality. She used little variation of tone or gesture, but simply spoke, and moved, and was a whore.

She ended. Clapping broke out, increased to a storm, and died away. Slowly, under the chandeliers, the hands returned to the shuttling needles. Several women picked up small children and took them out.

Robert Handforth said, 'You've got the part!'

Avaloka stared at the little woman with something like fear in her slanting, kohl-shaded eyes. 'That . . . that was wonderful!'

Elliott King said, 'That's no part for you, my girl.'

His wife murmured, 'I wish to play it, Elliott.'

Elliott gestured decisively with his pipe-filled fist. 'I forbid it.'

She raised her head then and looked at him. 'Forbid away as much as you like. I'm going to play Cora.' It was the whore speaking, her stance cocky and unafraid.

Elliott blinked, and fiddled with his pipe. Everyone started talking. Many turned aside in embarrassment. Lynn stared,

186

fascinated and astounded. Elliott seemed to be speaking to his wife, though Lynn could not hear a word.

Elaine Handforth said, 'You – can't – do this, Dot, you're – making – an exhibition – of yourself . . . Lip reading. I'm a little deaf, like most old women. What he means is, she's making an exhibition of him.'

Dorothy King's voice rang out harsh and clear. 'I am not going to design costumes. I am going to play Cora.'

'It's awful,' Lynn murmured, 'it's like seeing a teacher hounded out of his class by his pupils.'

Elliott King spoke up loud and hearty. 'Fine, fine! Robert, you've got yourself a new star. Sure you can play it, honey. I just wanted to make sure you knew what you were letting yourself in for. Kissing and cuddling on the stage, and like that.'

'There's none of that,' Robert Handforth said.

Elliott said, 'Well . . . go ahead. Give it all you've got.'

Lynn thought, Dorothy might at least say Thank you, Elliott. She might at least allow him to pretend that he had, in the end, given his permission. She said nothing.

Elliott waved his pipe. 'You'll give me the dimensions of the stage first thing in the morning, Robert? Right. I have a few things to see to.' He stepped lithely off the dais and went quickly out of the ballroom, waving a hand at friends here and there, the smile big and easy on his face.

George Zanakis paced up and down the basement storage room. From the furnace room came the low roar of the blower. The light was on in there and the door open. He could see the caretaker asleep on a mattress on the floor.

Midnight. Too early for an old man to go to sleep.

So ended the second day . . . Why did everyone involve themselves so thoroughly with the production of the play? Was it to escape the reality of the storm? . . . Four o'clock in the afternoon, hearing about the wreck coming ashore, he'd hurried out with sketch pad and pen. Black, rusty, towering wall. Waves racing along the side. Snow, spindrift, sand, fog. The ship cut in half like a lizard or a snake, this half near death but still living. Soon it would die, and then there'd be the burial waves . . . What a scene. Tragedy. Ambition thwarted. Nature versus Man. Five sketches made and not the beginning of greatness among them . . .

'Hey? What? Who's there?' His own words broke him out of his reverie. An army of faces were framed in the door. No.

187

One of those Renaissance painter's tricks to make five men look like fifty. Joe Steele, in front, by himself. Young Damato, Jenkins, Pete Worrell, someone else.

'What do you want?' he asked testily.

Steele did not answer. None of them answered. Goddam TV gangsters, saying nothing, just looking around, cold, fishy. Humphrey Bogart.

They went away. 'Go to hell!' he said aloud. 'Why do you have to come here? Why don't you stand out in the snow and freeze to death?'

'Eh? What?' Now it was the caretaker awake.

'Nothing,' George said. 'Go back to sleep.'

He sat down in the kitchen chair in front of the big rough-hewn table. Quite a studio. Plenty of room anyway. If he got the designs done tonight, the carpenters ought to be able to start work around noon, and the women the same time. 'Back room of a tavern on the lower West Side, and part of the bar. Early summer, 1912.' Robert wanted a proscenium arch, masking wings and a back wall of flats, painted to suggest the bar-room.

He began to sketch rapidly.

He looked up, for there had been a change in the light. Jim Carpenter was standing beside him, looking at the sketches with open admiration.

'They're great,' Jim said. 'You've done all that since – when?'

George looked at his watch. Jesus. Two o'clock.

'Midnight,' he said. 'I just wrote in the colours. And they'll depend more on what we got than on what we need, eh?' He yawned. 'What are you doing up?'

'Just looking around, before I go to bed,' Carpenter said. 'Looking for the Steele Band . . . someone said they were wandering about.'

'Yeah. They came in here. About midnight.'

'Damn punks.'

'Everybody hates them. Maybe that's why they're like they are.'

'Maybe it's the other way round . . . What's this going to be for?'

'Front curtain,' George said. He was pleased with that. That'd make them sit up. The design was simple enough – a giant horse-shoe crab, crawling diagonally down and across the curtain, its round head bottom left, its spike tail upper right; and, riding on its back, a woman and a man, both naked, the woman in

188

front holding on to the crab's armoured eye patches for support, the man holding the woman round the waist.

'Some people are going to be mad, aren't they?' Jim said. 'You getting at them when they can't hit back, like this.'

George said, 'No one's mad here. They're frightened . . . I'll paint that tomorrow night, if I can get a big enough piece of cloth, and a model. For the girl, at any rate. Never paint a man or a woman from memory.'

'By God, no!' Jim Carpenter said with energy. What? What? The man meant what he said. He painted, then. Painted nudes?

George said, 'Do you know where I can get a model? A nice fat girl's what I want. I'll ask Robert to call for volunteers, eh? . . . By God, it's getting cold in here.'

'The heat's been down to night level for hours,' Jim said. 'I could murder that son of a bitch Vernon when I think . . .'

George picked up his pencil and altered the perspective on the upstage flats. 'You can't blame Vernon,' he said. 'He's an animal. Like maybe a warthog, or a coyote.'

'He came damn near ruining us,' Jim said grimly. 'If this storm goes on long enough, he might do it yet.'

'That kind of person, I mean like a coyote, isn't the only bad one,' George said, his pencil sweeping round in a long curve. 'There's the lapdog sort, too. Like Mrs Bryant. She cut this town off. It wasn't the snow, not at first. It was her, thinking only of herself, her rights, where she'd be safe. And there's worse still – those African adjutant birds – stand everyone in line, *hup*, two, three, like that Coast Guard feller, Remington. And the ostrich guys – like Nelson Pryor . . .'

He glanced up. Young Carpenter looked uncomfortable. Well, where the shoe fit, let 'em wear it.

George said, 'That's that.' He closed the sketchbook. 'Time to go to bed.'

Jim Carpenter said, 'Mr Zanakis . . . George . . .' His voice dropped. 'I've done some painting – of nudes.' He had turned quite pale.

'Good for you,' George said, and waited.

'Can I come, when you paint that front curtain, to learn?'

'Sure.'

'But . . . can you specially ask me to come, to help? Otherwise, people might think . . .'

George felt old and impatient. 'No, God damn it,' he said. 'You saw Mrs. King. You heard her. She stood up and said she

189

wanted to be a whore, in the play. If you want to paint naked women, why, stand up and say so. You'll never paint worth a damn until you do.' He stumped out and up the stairs, going toward his room.

In the great ballroom all the lights were out except a standard lamp in one corner of the dais. The windows rattled and the heavy curtains shivered.

Standing in the pool of light Louise Lincoln stretched out her arms and said throatily, 'Alone at last!'

Robert Handforth, slumped in a chair, muttered, 'I thought the Spanish sailors would never go.'

'They don't want to miss anything,' Louise said. 'I get a feeling they think it's their duty to be on hand. They never raise a finger, though – just watch. And the sick lady – she didn't go till about half past one, all wrapped up and such a terrible colour.'

'Daisy Crampton,' Robert said.

'Just laying there, watching you and me talk, not close enough to hear what we were saying most of the time . . . and your mother.'

'Mother doesn't like to miss anything either,' Robert said. He changed the subject. 'This has been a wonderful day for me. Now I *know* I'm doing the right thing, to go into the theatre. It's the first time I've felt that any job I had was worthwhile. Just making money never seemed to be.'

'It would if you'd never had any,' she said.

'I always have,' he said simply. 'Someone, or something was always pushing me. It wasn't really Father, I see that now, though it was easiest to pin everything on him at the time.'

'What would you have done if we'd met before he died?' she asked. 'Five or six years ago, say.' She watched him closely.

The light flashed from his glasses. He looked frightened. 'I don't think I could have done anything,' he said. 'You don't understand how strong it was. All the freedom in the world, in theory . . . but impossible to *be* anything but what was there. Like choosing a suit – but when you get to the store, there's only one, for *you*.'

She said, 'Are you sure you don't feel good about this play because these are your people? Your feudal serfs. Do you think it would be the same on Broadway, working with the unions, self-centred stars, backbiting fairies, crooked producers, nervous

190

angels? This is a kind of amateurs' heaven, isn't it? Or a one-shot special case.'

He was very earnest and seemed to have forgotten his fatigue. 'Of course, there's some of that,' he said, 'but it's not the driving force . . . I spent thirty years on strings – a puppet among real people. Now I see that everyone's on a string. The theatre, to me, is a place where we discover reality, inside and outside ourselves – and take it back to the so-called "real" world. I mean, tonight, look at Mrs King. I was amazed to see how much better she was than Alice Bryant – though it looks as if we're stuck with Alice for Margie.'

That Bryant babe'll never be an actress, Louise thought. An actress has to have communication with the real world. The world's a blizzard, people dying of frostbite, people starving somewhere, people afraid of being burned, of suffocating when the roof caves in. Alice Bryant won't acknowledge any of that. She really wanted to pull *The Iceman*, like a blanket, over her head.

Robert said, 'The Bryants have no background. She was a Potter. Her mother tried to get into the "sewing circle," Mother told me, about 1919, but she wasn't accepted.'

Louise felt a familiar tightening of the muscles round her mouth. She said, 'But it would have been all right if the mother had called herself a princess?'

Robert said seriously, 'No, I don't think so. It's a question of . . .' The dark eyes turned up suddenly to her, the prominent Adam's apple bobbed up and down. He said, 'Darling . . . I'm not responsible for that.'

I love him, she thought, and yet felt her skin trembling, like dry leaves in a wind. I love him, and not because I am sorry for him. I have never given him the breast nor held him curled in my arms, rather he has held me and I have found comfort and strength. Where it lies, I don't know. I only know that for me, it is there. But then comes this shaking of leaves and whispering of voices. Is it really the voices of the Niger, as Gramma used to say – Great-Gramma, black on the stoop of the tenement, black, black, crooning to herself, while Louise nestled into the lap and peeped now and then at the wrinkled, scarred face, loving and terrified, exhilarated and appalled.

Her skin ached and her mouth hurt. She said, 'You went along with the gag. Who do you think you're fooling?'

'It's for her sake,' he said, anguished. 'She's old, she's led a certain kind of life. She's really wonderful, darling. She's afraid of nothing.'

191

'Except being unimportant,' Louise said.

'It's not that. She's the guardian of something she thinks is valuable . . . has value. The house, the land, Monomoy, the name.'

Louise said, 'I wouldn't mind so much if she knew she was pretending. She did, at first – but only for an hour or two. Since then, since the end of that ghastly lunch the first day – it's been real. I *am* the Princess Avaloka, from India, or Java, or Annam – notice how she can never remember? – romantic, aristocratic and a long way away.' She took his hand and forced her long nails into it. 'And you've been trying hard to believe it, too.'

His eyebrows were high on the high, thin forehead and his mouth an inverted V of misery. 'Darling, I . . .'

'Do you realize, since that lunch, you have never once called me Louise? Always darling, or honey, or dearest. My name is Louise Lincoln.'

Blood welled slowly from the nail marks on his right hand. 'For her sake, darling, please . . . let's go along with it. I just don't know what will happen to her, inside, if we force her to face the truth. It'll be different in New York, in the theatre. This is her country, her life. For me, please, just while we're here . . .'

The rustling stilled and she felt tired. She laid her head on his shoulder and one of his hands came round her waist. She tried to close her eyes in a weariness of surrender, but something moved, out there in the darkness of the enormous room and she stared, wondering, while Robert kissed her shoulder. At last she realized it was the Spanish captain, sitting upright in his blue coat on one chair in the darkness, and playing solitaire on the seat of another chair. He could hardly have seen the cards, but his hands moved with steady, precise speed. She wondered if she should tell Robert, and decided, No. It didn't matter. It was almost proper that the Spanish captain should be present.

Robert found her mouth and she let her lips part softly under his. His breath came deep and short. The mating respiration of men, she thought. If you loved them it took physical possession of you, as definite as an embrace.

He said, 'Where can we go?'

She said, 'I'm alone in a tiny single room. I moved out of the other, because my room-mate found it too constricting to be sharing a room with a princess. She dressed under the bedclothes this morning, so that I wouldn't see her old grey girdle . . .'

He reached out his hand and flicked off the light. The room sank suddenly into darkness. She thought of the captain playing solitaire. Well, if he wanted light, he could switch it on again. Her head resting on Robert's shoulder, she guided him to her room.

CHAPTER SEVEN

THURSDAY

John Remington glanced at the clock. Three minutes past eight. Two whole minutes since he'd looked at it last. The sound of voices, droning in bored argument, floated up from the mess deck. The men were getting bored, and so was he. Snow over New England; no movement; no orders, except to keep alive, keep watch, report emergency, though no one could do anything about it. The wind much less – 16 mph, north-east. The snow-flakes floated separate in the sky and visibility was six, maybe seven hundred yards.

He went to the west windows. The town looked like a paint-ing, the sort of painting you saw in the windows of modern art stores – white, with black lines here and there, and shapes that made you wonder, Now what's that supposed to be? The Long-ships Hotel was the extreme limit of visibility to the south-west. You could only see it because of the regular pattern of black lines, and after a long time you realized they were the shutters, the white walls you couldn't see at all. To the west – black lines, broad, a sharp nearer edge, blurring beyond – that was the edge of the bay, with cutouts for the houses on the Green. Something yellow moving, two of them, one behind the other, then closing, like mating horseshoe crabs. Jesus, they were taking over, just like George Zanakis had warned . . . it was a bulldozer and a snowplough, working at the foot of Boat Street.

He walked across to the east windows. What could he find for the men to do? Maybe tomorrow he'd put reveille back to ten o'clock. That would shorten the day. And shoot the system. They had regulations to obey, duty to do. If they couldn't take it just because they were bored, how would they take it when it got really rough? . . . Much better, probably, because that's the way men were.

The view this side was like the old-fashioned sort of painting. The Great Beach ran away north and south, a thin wet ribbon at the edge of the waves. The snow was white, pure and perfect along the dune. Southward the long wall of the *Goya* stood out like a giant breakwater from the land. Already the waves, pounding along it, had begun to eat into the shore line at the point where the stern rested. That could alter the shape of Monomoy, John thought; could even cut through the dune. A big piece of driftwood caught his eye as it rolled up the beach, paused, and rolled back again. He took the telescope from its stand and put it to his eye.

He put the telescope down. 'Wallace, there's a man washed up on the beach. I'm sure he's dead, but get me Knighton and four. Usual gear. Tell the Selectmen. Ask them to have Captain Lacoma come, in case he can identify the body.'

When he reached the top of the beach steps, the crew behind him, he paused in surprise. A man in dark clothes was bending over the body, pulling and tugging it up the short, steep beach.

John went fast down the steps, jumped into the final snow slope, and waded toward the couple at the water's edge. The dark man was kneeling now. The two were in profile, the dark kneeling figure above and the white corpse below. The dark figure's hand moved slowly, and gold flashed momentarily in it. John recognized Father Bradford, holding out the crucifix from his neck. The other, naked, lay on his back, in the position of one crucified. His skin was the colour of a halibut's underside, and, like that, faintly wrinkled and pimpled. The shield of black hair at the groin stood out like an armorial blazon, and the patches of hair under his arms were like misplaced stigmata. His eyes were blue and wide open, his mouth open and full of sand. The snow fell quietly on his eyeballs.

The priest muttered, half chanting: '*Inclina, Domine, aurem tuam ad preces nostras, quibus misericordiam tuam supplices deprecamur: at animam famuli . . .*'

The Coast Guardsmen took off caps and hats and bowed their heads.

'. . . *in pacis ac lucis regione constituas, et Sanctorum . . .*'

A sense of presence made John turn his head. Three men stood close, Frank Damato, Arthur Day, and the Spanish captain. Damato dropped to his knees and crossed himself.

'*Per Dominum,*' Father Bradford said, and stood up.

'*Amen,*' Damato muttered, and remained kneeling.

John turned to the captain. 'Was this man one of your crew? He . . . yours?' He pointed from the corpse to the captain. The captain shook his head.

'How do you know he was a Roman Catholic?' The Reverend Mr Day's voice came out high-pitched and stuttery.

'I don't,' Father Bradford said politely.

'How did you get here? Before any of us? Before Chief Remington even?'

'I was standing in the shelter of the Old Boat House,' Father Bradford said, 'Wondering whether the storm was going to end. Then I saw – him.'

'Hail, Mary, full of Grace, blessed art thou among women and blessed be the fruit of thy womb, Jesus,' Frank Damato intoned, kneeling in the snow.

Mr Day said, 'How many deathbed conversions have you made in the last year? Ten, is it? Eleven?' His face was red as a beet, drops of water streamed from his nose, his eyes were suffused with tears. Snow mottled Father Bradford's neck like the plague of a new disease.

John Remington barked, 'Knighton, take his arms. In the stretcher. Blanket. Lift.'

Mr Day said, 'Take him to the crypt of my church, the Old Church.'

'Will he . . . ?' Frank Damato began. 'I mean, how long . . . ?

'As long as the storm lasts,' Mr Day said. 'There's no heat in the church.' He turned and shuffled away through the snow and slowly up the bank, and carefully up the steps. The Coast Guardsmen lifted the stretcher and followed. Father Bradford, Frank Damato, and the Spanish captain walked behind, not speaking. The hull of the *Goya* reverberated with a deep, bell-like booming as the procession of the waves pounded along it to the shore.

Elliott King pulled up a chair to the bed. He stretched out his hand to squeeze Harold's shoulder but, just in time, saw the other wincing away, and, instead, cuffed him lightly on the cheek. 'How's the boy?' he asked.

'A little better, thank you, Elliott.'

The voice was weak but controlled. Old Harold always spoke so prim and precise.

Elliott said, 'You're damn lucky to be lying safe in a warm bed, doing the damn fool thing you did. By all odds you ought to be a stiff now, like the one they just found on the beach.'

'Oh, Mr King, I was hoping we could keep that from him. He's not strong yet, and . . . '

The woman's voice was reproachful. It was Charlotte Quimby, fiddling in the chest of drawers.

Harold said irritably, 'I am quite well enough to hear news.

I am not a child. Please leave us now. We have some business to discuss.'

The woman began, 'Dr Burroughs said . . .'

Harold closed his eyes and spoke at the ceiling. 'I don't care what the doctor said, Charlotte. Please leave us.'

'Only for fifteen minutes, then,' the woman said and went out.

So it's 'Charlotte' now, Elliott thought. Poor old Harold was in a bad way. Once let a woman get her claws into you, and they never let go . . . bloodsuckers, every one of them.

Harold said, 'Now I can go to the john. Won't be long.' He climbed out of bed, went into the bathroom, and closed the door.

Elliott thought about the corpse. About 6 foot 2, black hair, white skin, beautiful. The skin looked strange, having been in the water so long, but really only emphasized the perfection of the fellow's build – long thigh muscles springing from the groin, flat stomach, deep flat chest, a *man's* chest, all the lines curving down and up to the crotch and, boy, what a piece of . . .

Harold Morgan came back and sat on the edge of the bed. 'Is there any way out of Monomoy now, Elliott? Any way at all?' he asked.

Elliott grinned heartily. 'What's the matter? That dame? You're frightened of her? Just tell her to blow, take off, scram, drop dead.'

The blue eyes were big and watery behind the lenses. 'I can't,' Harold muttered. 'You can do what you like with women, but it's just the opposite with me. They can do what they like with *me*. Always have, one way or another . . . Every time she stoops she fills her dress, and I find myself imagining what's under. Every time she bends over me, I'm looking down between her breasts, and she's well endowed, Elliott!'

'She's doing it on purpose,' Elliott said. 'That's the way women are, everyone of them, from the prissiest little bluestocking to the lousiest six-bit hooker.'

Harold hardly seemed to hear. 'One day,' he muttered, 'I'll reach out my hand, and I'll . . . I'll . . .'

'Get a dirty hand,' Elliott said, laughing loudly. And wash it, wash it, wash it, he thought, wash off the stinking gunk. 'Hey, I didn't come here to talk smut,' he said. 'I just wanted to tell my future partner in Morgan and King, Incorporated, that the board of directors proposes to send him to Miami for a good vacation, as soon as this goddam snow stops. On the firm, of course.'

Harold said, 'I'd want to do my share of work. I don't want to be a passenger.'

'Sure, sure,' Elliott said, 'but there's more than one way of working. I do the pushing and shoving. You take it easy, go fishing three, four days a week. Keep a rein on me because I'm as like to put my foot in my mouth as any place else. How about it? You with me, boy?'

Harold said, 'I suppose we could work out something satisfactory.'

Elliott dug his finger into Harold's ribs. 'You bet your life – and we'd only need one secretary . . . mine.'

Harold said, 'Eh? Oh, I see . . . How's Dorothy?'

Elliott stood up, and the legs of his chair caught in the carpet. The chair crashed to the floor. 'Fine, fine!' he said.

He laughed heartily. 'Women! You can never understand them, so what's the use of trying? . . . Know what she's doing? Acting a whore in this play Robert Handforth's getting up. Dotty – a whore! Ha ha ha! Some people thought she shouldn't do it, and I discussed it with her, but, hell, she's got the acting bug, so of course I said, Go ahead, baby . . . I'll be running along, kiddo . . . We've got to become partners, Harold, remember, and the first thing we got to do is torpedo this park thing. If we don't, we'll just stay small-town carpenters the rest of our lives . . . If we do, we're in the clear for a couple of million bucks, *each* – without trying, Just work on anyone who comes to see you, eh? You know the lines – free enterprise, more money all around, only crackpots on the other side . . . Take it easy.'

'I don't know as I want two million bucks . . .' Harold began, but Elliott had gone.

Jim Carpenter leaned back so that his chair was supported on two legs only. Lynn Garland was making a rapid and purposeful clack-clack with the typewriter. The light was dirty grey. Had he remembered to get a gang of men out clearing the snow from the lower windows, so that there would be more light? . . . Yes about an hour ago. They'd have to work from the inside at first, pushing the snow away, then crawling out the windows and heaving it up on top of the drift.

The snow seemed to be lighter today, falling more thinly from higher cloud, with little wind. God Almighty, it couldn't go on for ever the way it had been the first forty-eight hours. Or could it? This morning at breakfast someone with a transistor set had picked up a station in Illinois. It was the damnedest thing hearing about a place that didn't have snow. Damned terrifying, too. 'Mrs Thelma F. Bigwash has been elected to the school board, in a close vote. State Senator Peter P. Pepper yesterday attended a $20-a-plate fund-raising dinner. The J.C.s' campaign to reroute Maple Street has won the approval of Mayor George X. Lasagna.' Way, way later, lines tossed away before a station break; 'The snowstorm continues over New England, with many areas now isolated.' Brother, that's all!

Here were maybe ten million people in six states just vanished, put back into some prehistoric time when men couldn't move far or speak to each other, and across the river and behind the hill no one knew what was happening. Didn't know and didn't care.

He recognized the careful one-two-three knock, and swung forward in the chair before the door opened. Elaine Handforth came in. 'Good morning, Jim. Good morning, Lynn.' She sat down carefully and precisely, pulled a handkerchief from her pocketbook, blew her nose, and replaced the handkerchief.

She said, 'I have been speaking to Lester Pease.'

Jim wrote the name on his note pad. Mr and Mrs Pease were the aged couple who, in return for rent-free accommodation in the Charter House, acted as official guardians of the Charter, showed it to visitors, and collected the 25-cent fee on behalf of the town.

Elaine Handforth said, 'They're worried about the roof of the Charter House with this weight of snow.'

Jim looked away. The old lady's eyes were not accusing, but they were cool and direct. The Selectmen had refused, again, last year to allot funds to strengthen the roof beams of the Charter House.

Elaine said, 'They told me they received permission from Nelson to come in to the hotel.'

'I believe so,' Jim said. 'They couldn't have stayed there alone anyway.'

'No. Nelson said it would be all right to leave the Charter, and the Peases felt no alarm – until now. When they woke up this morning, and looked out, they began to worry, even though it isn't snowing so hard at this moment. The Charter House has a very flat pitch, you know.'

'Yes,' Jim said. That was the reason Elaine and the garden club set had pressed for new beams. But it was going to cost $15,000, and the ordinary people were dead against it.

'The Charter table is directly under the peak of the roof,'

Elaine said. 'A collapse would break the table and crush and tear the Charter.'

Jim wrote, 'Charter – save? How?'

Mrs Handforth rose. 'I think it should be seen to. When the family gave the Charter to the town, the town undertook to preserve it for all time.' She nodded, and swept out.

'Phew!' Jim exclaimed. 'How the heck am I supposed to do that? The Charter's in a big wood and glass case, screwed to the table. The road's not ploughed . . .'

The door opened abruptly and Nelson Pryor strode in, grey of face, followed by Walter Crampton. Nelson said, 'Jim, we got no water, anywhere in Monomoy.'

Jim said, 'Miss Garland, get Frank Damato at once, tell him to put a policeman on the water tank in the attic. Tell the caretaker to shut off all supply from the tank. After that, no one's to touch it. No, go yourself, and tell them not to talk about it. We'll make an announcement as soon as we can.'

The girl slipped out and he turned back. 'Where's the break?'

Walter said, 'No reason for snow to break a buried pipe. So it's got to be either the pumping station at Harwich gone out or the sea's broke through the Tongue. If it's the pumping station, maybe we get water back any moment. If it's the Tongue – we don't.'

Jim thought, We'll have to presume the pipe's broken. A few outlying houses had their own wells, but most of Monomoy received its water from artesian wells and spring-fed lakes in Harwich Township, on the Cape proper. The water company's works, purifying tanks, and pumping station were there, and from there the water was pumped in a large, buried pipe to the Monomoy water tower, near Town Pond on the northern outskirts of town.

'The tower held 400,000 gallons,' Nelson said with a groan. 'Christ, if we'd only known earlier we could have shut off the supply, and had all that to use. Those guys at the pumping station must have noticed the way the water was pouring out toward Monomoy. Why didn't they tell us?'

Walter said, 'The station's a mile from the nearest house. The telephone's not working. The snow's drifted six feet deep, and still falling, and there's only one man on watch. What can he do?'

'The question is, what can we do?' Nelson Pryor said.

Jim said, 'The people in the houses can melt snow . . . if they

200

have enough fuel. For the Longships, we'll have to get water from Town Pond. Are the roads ploughed that far?'

'No,' Walter said. 'About two hundred yards short.'

'Will you tell George Lathrop right away? As soon as he's through, get the fire trucks on to bringing water here, and pumping it up into our tank.'

'If there's a fire in the town now . . .' Nelson said.

Walter got up. 'I'll tell George.' He went out. Jim scribbled on his pad: 'Water – purify? Burroughs.' Hell, he should have reminded Walter that the firemen would have to cut through the ice on Town Pond, and keep the hole open. Walter would remember.

Nelson said, 'O.K. I'll survive.' He looked older, sadder and, in spite of his fears and troubles, stronger. He wasn't drinking either, no more than a shot in the evening, here in the office. He kept his bottle in the corner cupboard, on top of paper and carbons.

Nelson said, 'Let's work out that we're going to do, when I'll make an announcement . . . I guess we'll have to cut off most of the taps. Or all of them except at certain times of day?'

'That's the best way,' Jim said. 'And tell 'em to go easy with the johns, because they'll only get to flush them at those times, and then only once each.'

'Are they going to like that?' Nelson said. 'Living with the john full of shit half the day!'

'In town the johns are going to be full of shit *all* day,' Jim said. 'We can't allow baths or showers, except under medical orders. Put 'em all on the honour system.'

'O.K.,' Nelson said, 'I'll fix it.' He went out.

Jim looked at his note pad. Power gone, fuel going, telephone gone, water gone. No future, and the glorious past about to be buried under a collapsed roof.

Under his pencil a reverse curve appeared on the pad. Lousy. He tried again. And again. Still lousy. Again, very slow this time. Worse. It was awful. Anything else, you could get it by taking pains, by working at it. You could be an amateur artist that way too. But to be a real one, after you'd done all your study and practice, the pencil had to be an extension of your eye, and the line had to come fast, economical, right. A woman's neck, shoulder and arm, seen from behind, if she was leaning away from that arm, would look something like this – but not quite.

Why hadn't he gone to George Zanakis' summer classes, along with the fat women in flowered prints and the thin old ladies in picture hats, who wanted to record Monomoy's famous hydrangeas and roses, and the silvered grey of Cape shingles worn by sand and sea wind? George sometimes ran a life class, when he could get a model. People sniggered about that – with reason, unfortunately. The students in *that* class were all dirty old men or college sophomores. The model, imported from Provincetown, always looked like a female Paul Bunyan. One of the students had told him about it, adding, 'I thought we were going to see one of those *models*, you know what I mean?'

The sniggering had got under his skin. That stuff didn't do a selectman, or a lawyer, any good.

Yeah? Well, suppose he went to George Zanakis and said, I'm going to help paint the stage curtain, because I like painting nudes – just like that? Suppose he let Barbara wail and sulk, and went right ahead, doing what he wanted to do? By God, what he *needed* to do?

In the mess deck of the Coast Guard station Charlie Tyson fumbled awkwardly with the ends of rope on the table in front of him. Knots, for Christ's sake. Boy Scout games with knots. Double sheet bend, this one was called. He looked at Colonna across the table, but Colonna's head was bent over his work, his fingers weaving. At the other tables it was the same. Chicken-shit! Were the fellows all bucking for B.M.?

'Half hitch, clove hitch, and sheepshank,' McGill called. 'Tyson, haven't you done that double sheet bend yet?'

Charlie held up his knot, aggrieved. 'Sure, I done it.'

'What the hell is that, Tyson? I said a double sheet bend. Do it again, and then the other knots.'

Sulkily Charlie yanked out the knot he had made. Stupid bastards. Colonna was giving him a funny look. Like it was *him* who was the stupid bastard. But Colonna was an O.K. guy. So maybe this knot tying wasn't all that bad, at that, when there wasn't anything else to do. So why did he just naturally come out glaring and frowning against it, and either not do it at all or do it wrong? Not just the knots, everything. Everything as long as it was ordered by guys like McGill and Remington. And Mom. The longer he stayed away from home the less Mom weighted on his mind, the more she seemed almost human. It must be the hell of a thing to have to make up your mind, have to say yes or no to so many crazy questions, half of them

202

you *couldn't* know the answer to, no one could – but you'd have to say yes or no anyway.

Like marrying Betty. Should he, shouldn't he? She let him make out whenever he wanted, so he didn't need to marry her for that. But he loved her. How would it be, having *babies* around, yelling in the middle of the night? Who could he ask? The other guys here would laugh at him, and as for all the old bastards . . . except Father Bradford. He wouldn't laugh, and him an Irish quarterback, too . . .

It was getting creepy, being shut inside here all the time, knowing that if you went out you were only going from like one jail cell into a bigger one, because Monomoy was cut off, too . . . Why didn't they send a plane with skis, paramedics, radios, food? She'd come in low down the dune to get under the cloud base, and then circle and *whee*, flaps down, *krrr*, more flap, *krrr*, nose a little up, the snow flattening out. Himself there in the seat, on the left, '260' he says, quiet but sharp, and the co-pilot raps '260, sir!' – '60 degrees flap!' – '60 degrees flap, sir!' . . .

Chief Remington came in, glowering, and said, 'McGill, here a minute, please. You fellows get on with splicing.'

The Chief and McGill moved to Charlies' end of the room and sat down at an empty table. The Chief said, 'The water's gone, at the main.'

McGill said, 'Why, I was washing my hands only ten minutes ago.'

'Yeah. Well, our tank's nearly empty. I just had a look.'

The B.M. said, 'We'll have to melt snow.'

'Or borrow water from the town. They're going to use the fire trucks to bring in from Town Pond to the Longships.'

McGill whistled in admiration. 'Hey, that's a good idea.'

Old Salt Horse growled, 'Sure it is. So now the United States Coast Guard has to go beg water from the civilians. I've been saying for years that every station ought to have its own well. But all they think of is money. Saving pennies, not doing the job.'

McGill said, 'Maybe it'll make the civilians feel good, Chief, if they have to save the Coast Guard.'

The Chief said, 'It doesn't make me feel good . . . begging for water. It sticks in my craw.'

McGill said, 'They know we'd do the same for them if they were in trouble. I think it'll make us more popular down there. It shows we're all in the same boat, see?'

203

Charlie found himself staring straight into the Chief's eyes. The Chief said, 'Some guys can splice without looking, Tyson. You can't.' Charlie dropped his eyes hurriedly to his task. He heard the Chief say, 'Go and beg for me, Mac . . . no, damn it, I must eat the humble pie myself. I'll try to get five gallons a man a day . . . Tyson!'

Charlie look up quickly. 'Chief?'

'Do you feel like you're in jail or something?'

Charlie said, 'Yes . . . sort of.'

The Chief said, 'I'm going to look at the Diadem Cape Beacon. On foot. You and Siska come with me. Start from here after I've been to the Longships. Half an hour.'

Charlie said, 'O.K.'

'And, Mac, you take two more to Monomoy Hill and the Tongue. Report whether the sea's broken through.'

'Aye, aye, Chief.'

McGill called, 'O.K.! Dismiss from rope class!'

Charlie stood up, stretching. Son of a bitch! *Walking!* Why in hell didn't he send for a copter and fly down the beach, *whiooosh*, the chopper pounding away overhead. You could do the whole thing in twenty minutes, less. Still . . .

Remington was talking to McGill. 'We've got to use this clear spell while it lasts. The Weather Bureau says the heavy snow and wind will be back tonight. Leave Gardner in charge here. Send Randall to take the 36-footer out and inspect all the buoys to the Outer Mark. Take a look round the fishing fleet and the yacht club pier and see they're all O.K. to seaward.'

'Aye, aye, Chief.'

Feeling strangely cheerful, Charlie went off to get into his foul-weather gear.

JoAnn Griffiths shifted her position slightly.

'You uncomfortable?' the old guy Zanakis asked quickly.

'No,' she said, 'only I could sure do with some gum. I ran out, and no one's got any left. Or they ain't saying. Do you have any?'

'No!' the old guy said. 'No gum.' It would spoil the shape of the mouth.

JoAnn dismissed the thought of gum. Soon a pleasant blankness came, like lying in warm air on a summer afternoon, with sort of things floating slowly past, which you knew were thoughts, if you bothered to reach out and catch them. She didn't bother.

She was sitting naked astride the back of a sofa, and the old guy had made her let down her hair, so it floated on her shoulders and down her back.

'Wouldn't you like a book to read? We could put it on a table in front of you, and you could turn the pages without upsetting the pose.' That was Mr Carpenter, who was doing the painting.

She said, 'I don't read.'

Mr Carpenter sure liked to paint naked women. She was glad it was her he was painting now. It was kind of creepy thinking about a guy painting his wife over and over, as though maybe that's all there *was* to do with her.

'She's a natural model,' the old guy said, 'just takes the pose and fills it. Perfect. She doesn't feel cold or heat, but she's not like wood. Plastic! Wonderful! She likes sitting there naked, proud of herself and her body. Proud.'

Proud . . . it sounded like she stood looking at herself, stroking her boobies, the way that Mrs Bryant did, for sure. It was how the men looked at you that made you proud. With her they looked kind of religious, like going into a church. When she stepped out of her clothes just now Mr Carpenter looked like he was listening to an angel . . . and the old guy grunted like and started jumpin' around getting paints and stuff.

A long time, silence. The old guy pushing his hand through his grey hair, working on something at a little table, coming back to look at Mr Carpenter, kneeling on the floor, painting on a big sheet of canvas. A ship's sail, it was, rolled along the edge. 'Good, Jim, that's good,' he'd say, 'but watch the proportions. You're not ready to distort – not yet . . . Good, good . . . no, colour is in the shadows, Jim, form in highlights . . .'

Silence for a long time. She thought briefly of gum. Those Spanish sailors ought to see her now. Maybe they had women a different shape over there. They sure as hell kept themselves to themselves.

'The public image clashes with the private wish . . . private fulfilment, really. Imagine trying to make the grade in Boston politics, and the house full of these, and models. What do you think I should do?'

'Paint out that line, to begin with. Look at the girl again. *Look!* You have the line where you *think* it ought to be, not where it is . . . I can't tell you what to do, Jim.'

'Barbara will leave me.'

No one spoke. Maybe she would, at that, JoAnn thought. She

was a woman who'd feel kind of dirty without her clothes on, instead of cleaner. That showed in her face and little chicken's-ass mouth.

Someone knocked at the door. 'Jim, are you in there?' She recognized Elliott King's voice. 'I want to speak to you about that charging engine in the yard.'

Mr Carpenter put down his brush. 'Hold on, I'll be right out.'

'Let him come in,' she said.

'You don't mind?'

'Me? No, course not.'

Mr Carpenter opened the door a crack, and Elliott King sidled in. He looked lousy, she thought. The way Mrs King treated him last night, right up there at the dais, would be enough to make a man go hide in a hole. That, or smack her a couple of good ones. That's what she needed.

Mr King looked at her, sneakily, and turned away. He had a funny expression on his face, like he was upset. Mr Carpenter was talking, fast. 'George is letting me paint the curtain. There's his design for it.'

Mr King examined the design. 'Who's going to be the guy sitting behind her, holding her . . . ?' He slapped Mr Carpenter on the back.

Old Mr Zanakis said, 'Why not you, Elliott?'

It would look good, JoAnn thought. Ought to feel O.K., too. He was a big, strong guy. A little old, but that didn't matter.

'Why not?' Mr Zanakis said.

Elliott King looked at her, his eyes hurrying all over, and away. 'Hell, why not?' he said. 'If Dotty can be a whore, I can be a . . . a . . .'

'Man riding a horseshoe crab,' the old guy said.

She moved herself, hitching her body into a more comfortable position, spreading her thighs and bringing them together again. Elliott King kind of coughed, and said, 'O.K.! What time?'

Mr Carpenter said, 'About eight tonight.'

'I'll be here,' Elliott King said. 'In my shorts, holding JoAnn, you have to let a guy wear shorts.' He gave her a quick, false leer. She nodded vaguely. Elliott King was a big, strong, important guy, but he was beginning to give her the creeps.

Mary Pryor thought, Really, it's amazing what people can do if they put their minds to it. In a single night and day the ball-room had become a theatre – a theatre still under construction,

206

with carpenters waving folding rules and electricians uncoiling electric cable. There had been talk of raising the dais, but they must have decided against it. A heavy curtain line crossed the room, a couple of feet behind the forward edge of the dais. The curtain hung from a row of poles and crossbeams. Only the centre section was designed to be drawn. At the sides it hid what would become dressing rooms, property rooms, and the lighting panel.

Bill Vernon was there, carrying heavy pieces of furniture up the side aisle and into the curtained-off area. Trying to work his way out of the doghouse, she thought.

Elliott King was there, talking to two men in blue jeans. Ah, one of the men wasn't a man at all, it was her son Billy. Elliott pointed at the floor, and now she heard him quite clearly, 'We've got to anchor the posts somehow. Go ahead and screw in the angle irons. I'll make it as good as new afterwards.'

He was a good boy, her Billy. Better with his hands than his head, to tell the truth. It had taken Miss Garland to find that out – or, at least, actually to flunk him. Up to then he'd managed to scrape through. And why shouldn't he, if others did who were certainly no smarter but just didn't happen to study English at Monomoy High under Miss Garland?

Billy left the room and she continued her survey. They'd marked off proper aisles now, and a fireman was always on duty – now it was Hugh Towle, the assistant chief. There were always three or four high school girl usherettes to help the mothers with babies; and a patrolman came in and looked around now and then, mainly to keep an eye on the Steele Band. Kids were so easily led astray.

Where was Betty? Not here. Not out anywhere, for sure. Holed up with a bunch of other silly giggling girls in one of the rooms somewhere. Suppose it wasn't a bunch of girls, but only her and a boy. That Charlie Tyson . . .

A clock struck eight.

Daisy Crampton's couch – *her* couch, everyone called it already – was there near the front row, toward the right side, but empty. Walter said, about four o'clock, she'd been taken worse. No, she didn't want a doctor. She was fighting and didn't need no interruption to take her mind off it. He went back upstairs to her. Four hours ago. Suppose Walter came into the ballroom now? Would she know, from his face, whether the end had come yet? It was not easy to read Walter's face.

Robert Handforth and a lot of others were standing on the

dais. Robert held a book, the others unwieldly piles of paper, from which sheets kept coming loose, to float to the floor. They'd put some of the stage furniture in position – a long bench, two or three chairs, three tables put together to look something like a bar. The girl Avaloka, sat on the corner of the bar, long dancer's legs outthrust, in pink stretch pants, to rest on one of the chairs.

They had been reading aloud, and now began again. Dotty King said, '*You can see dey're pretty, can't yuh, yuh big dummy?*' She spoke in that creepy, coarse, deep voice. Then Mr Rowan, one of the permanent summer firemen, said, '*Yeah, Baby, sure. If yuh like 'em, dey're aw right wid me.*'

It was funny the way gentlemen like Robert Handforth went for stuff like that. Bill Vernon now, standing there at the side of the stage gaping at Dorothy King – this would be just his mark. Was Dorothy smiling back at him? It couldn't be!

Mrs Bryant said, '*When do we light de candles, Rocky?*'

Mary Pryor pursed her lips. Couldn't act at all. La-di-dah New York accent thick as butter . . . And there was Nelson, just come in through one of the side doors, gawking at her like a schoolboy.

She *must* get her hair done. Surely someone in the Longships could do hair?

Nelson looked worn, but the extreme fatigue she had noticed earlier had now left his face. Even from here she could see the slight upward curve at the corners of his mouth. Men! What could he see in the woman, knowing now what a selfish, heartless, silly *bitch* she was?

The tall dark girl swung off the bar and went to whisper in Robert's ear, her head rested catlike on his shoulder. Physical, love was so obvious that Mary felt suddenly deserted. And they not married yet! Well, it was no business of hers.

Nelson sank into the chair beside her. 'Enjoying yourself, honey?'

'Very much. Have you finished for the night yet?'

'Yeah. The tank's filling up now, and all the dishwashing and baby-washing's done. We'll be O.K., unless the fire trucks go on the fritz.'

'You seemed to enjoy watching Alice Bryant just now,' she said.

'Mmm,' he said. She saw he was asleep. In half an hour he'd begin to snore, and she'd have to wake him. Then he'd go back to the office for an hour or two.

208

She leaned over and eased the cushion under his head, so that he could sleep more comfortably.

Nelson Pryor watched the dais through half-closed eyes. He didn't often sleep in chairs, but it did no harm to let Mary think he did. A guy got more rest, not having to answer questions . . . Dotty King was making the old eye at Bill Vernon. No doubt about it, no possible doubt. Jeez-us H. Christ. Vernon, standing at the edge of the dais, a chair hanging from his great ham of a hand, blinking down at her. Her, smiling up at him, those tiny bubs stuck out. The hell with them. He closed his eyes.

Dollar signs and zeroes floating round in his head like goddam seagulls, and the beat of pumping engines. Elliott R. King, big wheel of Morgan and King, contractors – the *only* contractors on Monomoy, don't forget that – hereby offer you ten (10) per cent (%) of the partnership, plus a salary of ten thousand (10,000) dollars ($) per annum as Treasurer. In return for what? Why, heck, nothing, Nelson.

I could do it, too. (The total would come to maybe forty or fifty thousand a year.) I could do it, and feel dirty the rest of my life, the way I was feeling before this goddam blizzard hit and turned the world upside down. (Or right way up?) Being shut in here by the snow is making me think different. What I feel now is, suppose I crap in the corner, there's no way of just walking away from it. So don't crap in the corner, heh? How's that for an idea? Do what I think's right, turn down Elliott's cozy little offer, and live like a happy Boy Scout. Might even go on being elected for ever, that way. And never make any real dough. And stay in debt for ever. And look every son of a bitch straight in the eye. And have Elliott turn nasty and start playing real dirty at the next elections?

On stage Dotty King said, '*Hickey ain' overlookin' no bets, is he? He's even give Hugo de woiks.*' Bill Vernon stood close, mouth open. Jeez-us . . .

Let's see now. Mrs Handforth against the park because it wasn't to be called the Handforth Park. Robert, only this afternoon, coming out for it, because he doesn't want any more money coming into Monomoy. He's seen what it does to people and places. He ought to know. He only has a couple of million himself. Another doomsday message from George Zanakis, smeared with paint, taking a moment off from painting scenery down in the basement to point his brush at Nelson's face and say, 'I warned you, didn't I! Another two weeks of this, and the

209

horseshoe crabs and the birds, which you decided to get rid of, will be eating us.' The old bastard had chuckled nastily. It was hard to know whether some guys were geniuses or nuts. Maybe both.

Walter – against. No compromise. No socialized bird care. Look after yourself. Take nothing, give nothing.

Nearby, he heard Lynn Garland say, 'I hear you have no water either? So you're in the same boat with the civilians, after all.'

That would be Chief Remington she was talking to. Women were crazy.

'Why do you keep needling me?' the Chief said, aggrieved.

Because she's falling for you, man. That's the way they are.

'Wake up, Nelson. You're snoring. And I'm going to bed.'

'O.K., O.K.' He yawned. 'Well, I'll go take a last look around, then I'll come up.'

Walter Crampton walked across the lobby at a steady, un-hurried pace. It was a fair piece from the room to the front door in this here hotel, but if a man's been stepping outside to look at the sky before going to bed, for a matter of forty years, he doesn't quit doing it just because it's a different door. And it wasn't just a habit – he needed to do it the way a religious man needed to say his prayers. At home, in good weather he'd walk to the top of the street. In foul, he'd go a few steps out into the rain or the snow, and have it fall on his skin. That way, you could hold counsel with sun and wind, the way you held counsel with your boat.

He went out. The snowbanks on either side of the ploughed drive were higher than automobiles. The snow was falling harder than it had during the day. The wind had backed a point or two. The glass was likely falling again. His cheeks felt rough and cold and his ears tingled.

He went back inside the hotel, carefully brushing the snow-flakes off his bare head. Now he could sleep.

He glanced in at the open main door of the ballroom as he passed. Maybe fifty people still in the audience, and all the actors on the stage. Play-acting was something his dad had been dead set against; but he himself couldn't see the harm in it. Couldn't see much sense, neither, but if you encouraged Daisy and the rest of them to work their fool fingers to the bone sewing old-fashioned dresses for the Fourth of July or the Ter-centenary of the Charter you didn't have the right to point the finger at Robert Handforth and his iceman.

210

The durn strange thing in this hotel was, you began to think there was no life, no world, no people outside. As you moved away from the front door, the sound of the wind hushed and you couldn't see the snow falling. It wasn't warm, but no one was freezing, either. Right now the cloud and snow hid the beam of the lighthouse. At home the sweeping light made the opposite roof white, like clockwork, and you could look out the back and see the lights at the fish pier and the cannery. In the hotel you could grab a man and ask him, Is there anyone else alive in the world, and he'd think a bit and say, Sure, my cousin at home and the fellow on the radio, and so on . . . but until you asked the question, there was no one, nothing.

He reached the second floor and paused. No light. Maybe the generator had quit . . . but that would kill all the lights in the place. There'd been light downstairs. A fuse must have gone. That shouldn't take long to fix.

He walked at his deliberate pace in the dark, down the centre of the passage, and laid his hand on the knob of the fourth door on the left. He stopped, waiting for the accumulation of will-power and moral strength. It was she who had sent him out, whispering, 'Go out . . . tell me.' She was better, at that, to be able to put the words together, and, almost, to raise her head. But it had become necessary to escape from thinking of her for a few minutes, every few hours. Sometimes the opportunity did not come, and then he'd feel his heart and mind stretching, stretching like thin wires trying to hold a battleship . . .

He was ready. He opened the door and went in, speaking quietly. 'It's me, Daisy. The lights are off for a while. Fuse gone, I reckon.'

She did not answer. He paused. 'Daisy, are you asleep?'

From the darkness of the room, in the lesser dark outside, he could see the heavy whirling flakes of the snow, circling in air like wolves trying to enter the room. He went forward and tripped over something hard. Stumbling, he recovered himself by grabbing the edge of Daisy's bed.

'Daisy! . . . Daisy!' He heard his own voice rising, cracked and high. The light came on.

She was lying across the bed, the bedclothes covering her but disarranged, and her head hanging over the side. Her pillow lay on the floor. At Walter's feet, upside down, was the thing that had tripped him up in the dark – the suitcase. The money suitcase. The life-savings suitcase. He turned it over, his hand stiff and without feeling. Empty. His other hand crept out, reaching

211

for hers, that dangled there over the edge of the bed. The tips of his fingers touched her; still no feeling. He hitched toward her and held her by the wrist. Now he could feel. Her wrist was warmer than his. A hot steel band tightened in his chest. A shock of intense pain travelled like a tidal wave to the farthest extremities of his body. The light became red. Her wrist quivered in his and the light went out.

Dorothy King crossed her legs extravagantly and leaned back on the bed. It's not difficult to act a . . . a loose woman,' she said. 'We all are . . . or can be.'

He must be able to see all the way up. He must be thinking, Is she doing it on purpose? If Bill Vernon had any power to think. He didn't have to think. He just had to be . . . What was the word they used? She'd heard it once or twice, and pushed it deep. Now it was up, huge and bright, and indescribably sexy. That's what he was thinking of. And there was another word. Horny. She trembled with a steady throbbing rhythm. That was the word for the cattle that milled in the tight, hot pen of her dreams, bulls and cows pushing, smelling, rearing up.

Bill Vernon sat on the edge of the chair, his mouth dropping open, the dull brown eyes blinking occasionally. His big hands rested on his knees. Big, coarse hands, dirty fingernails. His mouth twitched occasionally. He smelled of stale sweat and stale alcohol. The smell revolted her, and gripped her loins so that she felt on the instant red-hot and creepy, and her breath came fast and shallow.

'Mr King ain't coming?' he said at last.

'No. No.'

'This ain't his room? He don't live here . . . with you?'

'No,' she said. Of course Elliott shared the room, but what would that matter to this animal? She shivered, her knees shook, and his hands grew bigger every moment.

She slid off the bed, stood over him, and took his hand off his knee. She thrust it up under her skirt. He held her, where she had put him. He licked his lips and his eyes shifted quickly to the door.

'It doesn't matter,' she whispered furiously. 'Don't you understand? He won't do anything, even if he walks in now! I'll tell him to go to *hell*. And he will! Don't you understand?'

She heard the creak of the door a fraction of a second before it opened, and instantly bent her head to kiss Vernon's hair. The hair was dry and coarse under her lips and she felt exultantly ready to vomit. Now let Elliott pretend any more! Her moans of sexual passion were real, they and the disgust part of each other, caused by each other. She looked up, ready to laugh in her husband's face, but it was one of the Spanish sailors. Vernon's hand froze on her crotch. The sailor bowed, and said, '*Perdón, señor*.' He went out.

'You didn't lock the door,' Vernon said, aggrieved. He got up and went to it, and locked it.

She lay back on the bed, exulting. Even with animals, a time came when fear was suppressed. 'Leave the light on,' she said.

He came at her, half running, his eyes flat and dark, like old wood. 'Ah. Oh. Ow,' she cried, 'you're wonderful.' She raised her voice and thrust herself up against his heaving bulk.

Elliott was knocking at the door. 'Honey, it's me. Elliott. Let me in.'

'Go away,' she called. 'Oh! Ah!'

'Are you all right, Dot?'

'Go away. I'm rehearsing!'

How do you like that, Elliott?

Waves of ecstatic disgust sent her head back, and she heard herself yelling with laughter. Her head snapped forward and she buried her teeth in Vernon's shirt and chest. She went into a long, shaking orgiastic trance.

The light swam back, at first deep red and drowned a hundred fathoms in pain and a leaden exhaustion. The red gradually faded to a dull, mottled grey.

The carpet was an inch below his eye. He was lying on the floor. He was Walter Crampton of Monomoy, Massachusetts, a fisherman, Second Selectman, married to . . . There had been a pain. It was still in him, centred in his chest, but much less than before he keeled over. He had been trying to reach Daisy's hand, to know whether she'd died at last. But there was a suitcase with his savings, and he'd . . . fainted.

Walter Crampton's the name, by God, and he hadn't fainted, he'd had a heart attack. He must get up and see Daisy. A man could only die once.

He moved his head, and then heard the small voice: 'Walter.'

He raised himself slowly, first holding to the edge of the bed, then pulling himself upright, by stages reaching his stature as a man, and finally standing tall, one hand on the bedpost.

She whispered, 'Lights went out . . . pillow on my face . . .'

Walter held her wrist. Her pulse was faint, but when had it

been strong? She had no colour, and not sufficient strength even to cry out loud enough for people to hear outside. No one would come in unless they were asked, because that was the way they both wanted it. He'd told the doctors, Keep out, when we want you we'll ask.

He found the old fob watch in his pocket and looked at it carefully. One o'clock. He'd been unconscious three hours then. Daisy . . . maybe only a few minutes, and after that, lying helpless athwart the bed the way she was now.

Carefully he straightened her, until it was all shipshape again, and the bedclothes tucked close under her chin. She lay with eyes closed and a faint smile on her face.

Now – nothing for it – he'd got to look at the suitcase.

It lay at his feet, gaping a large empty grin. It had been his father's once, and was more like a small leather trunk than a suitcase. It was lined with sheets from the Monomoy *Gazette*, June 16, 1933 . . . They'd put a pillow over Daisy's face. But not held it down so she'd die. Just put it there, in the dark, careless, not giving a damn whether she lived or died. They ought to care. If they'd held it down, just a minute or two, she'd be out of pain now. No more doctors' bills. No more fighting with the doctors when they tried to tell you there was no charge. No more worrying about that new operation they could get in France, that he'd read about. He hadn't slept well for a month, thinking, Should I take her to France? I've got the money, I can do it . . . but *should* I? Now, he still had the doubt, but not the money.

She had not seen the empty suitcase. She did not know why the lights had gone out and, in the dark, someone had put a pillow over her face.

Look after yourself and your own. That's what his father taught him. That was the New England way, before the Jews and dagos came and because they didn't have anything started shouting what I have is yours and what you have is mine. It wasn't so, and never would be.

Now, who'd done this? Vernon maybe? That Dillon fellow, who once got two years for robbery in Pawtucket, Rhode Island? No, he'd left town last fall. Steele? Steele and Jenkins and Begg and young Chris Damato . . . ?

Whoever'd done it would be smart enough to take the cash out of the hotel and hide it, quick. He'd never get it back. Unless maybe he got Steele alone and put the gun to his belly . . . and when he'd got his money back, pull the trigger anyway.

He felt weak in the knees, and had to grip hard on the bed-post to prevent himself collapsing. Helpless. After so many years. Helpless, like a baby . . . he'd forgotten what it was like. By God, it took away your manhood, your self-respect.

Daisy's eyes were open, looking up at him, and she was not smiling.

He went to the chest of drawers, opened the second drawer, and felt under his shirts. The pistol was there. He took it out, and slipped it into the big side pocket of his coat.

He returned to the bed. 'You want to see Dr Burroughs now, Daisy?' he asked her softly. 'You're looking a bit peaked.'

She muttered, 'No . . . sleep now . . . you're back . . .'

'Don't tell no one what happened,' he said.

'No.'

Her eyes closed. Funny, the way she didn't ask him why he'd been lying there, three hours, on the floor. Of course she'd seen him, and she'd seen the empty suitcase, and now, perhaps, she'd seen him get the pistol. She was playing an old game – that she only knew what he told her. It was a good game, in bad times. She had fallen asleep and her breathing came stronger. He turned out the light and lay down on his back, fully clothed, on the other bed.

Live and let live. To each his own. Am I my brother's keeper? He'd kept the rule, but *they* hadn't. So now what? Go begging? Tell them he'd lost his savings and needed help? The cackling of their laughter shrieked like gulls inside his head. They were dancing in the snow, pointing at him and yelling, 'That's Walter Crampton, the wise guy, the man who looked after himself and his own! That's him, with his cap in his hand.'

He tasted blood on his tongue and slowly relaxed his clamped jaws, but lay in a rigor of shame and fear, sweating heavily.

CHAPTER EIGHT

FRIDAY

Nelson Pryor pulled forward his chair and prepared for business. Ten o'clock in the morning and dark, grey dark, the snow high up the windows. 'What's the Weather Bureau say?' he asked Remington.

Remington said, 'That other low-pressure system over the Atlantic's holding ours in position. And there's more snow in her now than when she arrived.'

'Christ,' Nelson said.

Elaine Handforth cleared her throat. 'You said something about gasoline, Nelson.'

Nelson collected his thoughts. 'Yes. We're using a heck of a lot of it, for dozers, ploughs, fire trucks, pumping water, generators, police patrols . . . I'm getting nervous. I think we ought to order rationing, but who can we cut down? We got to plough. We got to have water. We got to have light and power and telephones inside here . . .'

No one spoke for a minute. Nelson looked from one to another of them round the table: Crampton and Carpenter, Selectmen; Flo Monsey, town clerk and treasurer; John Remington, Chief Boatswain's Mate; Elaine Handforth, Lady of the Manor.

Walter Crampton said, 'Plough less.'

Nelson said, 'Well . . . where, less?'

'Nothing south of Harry's Amoco. Nothing north of Seventh. No cross streets.'

He's looking very grey today, Nelson thought, badger grey, old, and dangerous. Was the goddam storm *ever* going to end?

Chief Remington said, 'You're not going to plough Boat Street?'

'No.'

'How am I going to get boat crews down to the pier?'

'Plough it yourself. You've got a plough blade, and a truck with chains, and gasoline.'

'That gasoline . . .' the Chief began.

216

Walter interrupted him. 'If you want to use Boat Street, you plough it.'

Nelson thought about having a drink. Before the storm, when it got bad – in politics, in town problems, if Mary was difficult, any time he didn't know what he was doing or why he was doing it, whenever the world turned this dull, grey colour . . . why, then a couple of drinks made all the difference. A little colour came into the light, and the funny thing was that often the problems got solved, somehow. There was a fifth of bourbon there in the cupboard behind Flo. Well, later. As soon as he got a chance.

Walter said, 'We've got to tell everyone what we're doing. The police can take a loudspeaker around town. You'd better expect more people in the hotel, Jim.'

Jim Carpenter said, 'We have room for about twenty more families.'

Walter said, 'Right . . . Now?'

Elaine Handforth said, 'I am worried about the birds, Nelson. At this time of year there are usually hundreds of thousands of wildfowl on Monomoy, or resting on the sea off the Diadem Cape. We cannot save them from freezing, but we might save some from dying of starvation.'

'How?' Walter Crampton said.

Well, could we not dispatch a radio message to Mr Kennedy, and we would instruct the Fish and Wildlife Service to take action.'

'The message could go through Coast Guard channels,' Nelson said. He kept his face straight. Oh, boy, she was a honey, a real honey.

Chief Remington wrote in his notebook. 'O.K.,' he said. 'The message ought to come from the F. & W. L. administrator here, but I don't mind sending it as from you, Mrs Handforth.' He glanced at Nelson, his left eyelid flickering.

Nelson said, 'Next?'

Jim Carpenter said, 'I think we have to talk about the Kings. I'm running this hotel, and I can't just pretend nothing's happening, because it is, and it could lead to violence.'

Flo Monsey said, 'I couldn't agree with you more. That Dorothy King! I would *never* have believed it. I can hardly believe it now . . . like a . . . a *tramp*, there's no other word for it.'

Nelson said, 'Elliott slept in the ballroom last night. On one of the sofas. The patrolman saw him at five o'clock.'

Flo Monsey kept on talking: '. . . on the stage yesterday. Like a farmyard. Dorothy *King*! I can't get over it.'

Jim Carpenter said, 'There must have been ten people in the passage last night when Elliott was trying to get into the room. Everyone in the hotel seems to have known by breakfast.'

'Bill Vernon! What has Elliott ever done to deserve this? If she had to – kick up her heels, though, mind, married to a man like *Elliott*, I don't *understand* . . .'

Elaine Handforth said, 'We are none of us able to judge the true causes of this unfortunate situation. Mr King may be a different person to his wife than he appears to the rest of the world.'

'Men!'

'. . . as it is clear that Mrs King is different from what she appeared to be.'

Chief Remngton said, hesitantly, 'This isn't really my business, but I think Mrs Handforth's right. You never know the truth. I've learned that much, from making inquiries into family troubles in the service. Discipline is all we – you – can concern yourself with.'

'There's no Articles of War here,' Walter said.

Jim Carpenter said, 'No, but suppose Elliott ups and shoots Vernon. Then . . .'

'He won't,' Remington said briefly.

'*Disgraceful* . . . right there, behind a locked door, noises like . . . well, I can *tell* you . . .'

Elaine Handforth said, 'If you will accept my advice, Nelson, you will take no official notice at all. Some of Dorothy King's friends are bound to speak to her. As for Elliott, I agree with Mr Remington. If he damages anyone, it will only be himself.'

'Very well,' Nelson said after a pause. 'You agree, Jim?'

'I suppose . . . Yes. I do. After all, what could I actually say to either of them? What could I do, short of putting them in jail . . . . which I can't. Can't even get Vernon into jail. Adultery doesn't count as bail jumping. . . O.K. . . . . We've got a heating problem, here in the Longships. The fuel's being used faster than we calculated. We're O.K. for now, but when I look out and see the snow, still falling . . . we need a reserve. Not fuel oil, there isn't any. Wood.'

Nelson nodded. 'Every room has a fireplace, right? They don't heat well, and we'll use a heck of a lot of wood, but I guess it's our only choice.'

Walter said, 'There ought to be some driftwood along the beach.'

'We can help there,' John Remington said. 'I'll put some men onto walking the beach. We'll deliver to . . . where?'

Jim said, 'It'll have to be on the south side. The ploughs'll have to clear a space.'

'Right,' Walter said.

Jim said, 'That's very generous of you, John, but driftwood won't be enough.'

They waited. Nelson said, a little impatiently, 'So?'

'Do you mind if I have the Reverend Day come in? He spoke to me earlier. He's waiting outside.'

'Sure,' Nelson said.

Jim went out and returned in a moment, holding the door open for the minister. Around the table the men rose. 'Good morning, Reverend.'

Arthur Day looked ready to burst into tears. He'd got thinner, his collar was two sizes too big for him and he looked more than ever like a sad and nervous bloodhound. His Adam's apple worked convulsively. 'I heard we were short of fuel . . . Jim come to me . . .'

'Reverend Day came to me,' Jim said. 'It was his idea.'

'Oh. Yes. Well . . . we're going to have to burn fires in the fireplaces, and there isn't any wood, or coal.'

'Not enough, Reverend.'

'Well . . .' The Adam's apple bobbed and the harassed brown eyes suddenly gleamed. 'Burn the pews in the church.'

They sat in dead silence, all staring at the minister, except Jim Carpenter. Jim, head bent, examined his folded hands.

Mr Day spoke fast. 'There are enough pews to seat nearly a thousand people, you know how the congregation has dwindled since the whaling days . . . And then there are the foot rests . . . more than two hundred more benches in the crypt . . . keep them for church bazaars and the harvest service, the outdoor one, you know. And more benches in the Sunday School . . . forty desks, I think . . .'

'Why, that's . . . that's very generous,' Nelson said slowly. The old guy was in a state. Why did everyone think of him as old? He couldn't be more than fifty-five, fifty-six.

The minister spoke more slowly: 'It's not the outer shell that imparts grace to a church – or to a man. It is the presence of the spirit, the Holy Ghost.' He spoke the last words so low that Nelson could hardly hear them.

Jim Carpenter said, 'I think we're going to have to accept the reverend's offer, Nelson. What else can we burn, to keep people warm? We can't burn houses. Stores, perhaps, but how do we get at them, and what do they have to burn nowadays? The Old Church is close . . .'

'And in the circumstances, I'm sure Father Bradford would permit us to burn the pews in St Peter's, too,' Nelson said.

'The Old Church was built in 1720,' Walter Crampton said, his voice suddenly stern. 'She was built right, from meadow oak and ship timbers. You can see the spire from south of the Diadem Shoals and east of Pollock Rip. Those pews were gifted by sailors and whalers and fishermen.'

'Not for the glory of God,' the minister stuttered, 'for the glory of Monomoy . . . and of self. The name of the donor is carefully marked on each one. I'm s-s-sorry, Walter, but it's true!'

'I'll send men later,' Jim Carpenter said. 'With saws and axes. And a truck.'

'Thank you,' the minister said. His head bowed and shoulders shrunk, he left the room.

As the door closed behind him, Walter Crampton spoke to Mrs Handforth. 'I reckoned you'd have been more concerned, ma'am, being a deaconess.'

Mrs Handforth said, 'I am, Walter. And Mr Day does seem to be in quite a hurry to burn his church. But perhaps he is right. Have we not, so far, been consistently late with our measures? . . . I shall be sorry to see the pews go, but he is also right in saying they are not important. No material thing is, only the intangible things – spirit, name, breed, history.'

A large bank account does no harm, Nelson added silently. Aloud he said, 'I think we must all agree with Mrs Handforth. . . . Next problem?'

Walter Crampton said, 'The snow's wet today. Real wet and heavy. It's going to lie real heavy on the roofs.'

Nelson sat bolt upright. 'You mean the roof's in danger? Here?'

'No. We got a good pitch and it's a new roof, new beams, put in in 1936, after that fire. But any house that's got a flat pitch, or weak beams, is liable to cave in.'

Nelson felt very uneasy. For days now his mind had been attuned to the particular danger of fire, but all the time he had been wondering what other unforeseen peril was creeping up on him from behind. Maybe this was it – houses collapsing, people

220

buried alive, no one knowing, or able to help if they did. He said, 'Do you think we should have that put out on the radio? Only people with portables are going to hear by now . . . but they can shout to each other, across the streets.'

Walter said, 'We've got to tell everyone about the ploughing. Warn them about the wet snow at the same time.'

Nelson said, 'All right. Anyone heard anything special on the radio, by the way?'

Chief Remington said, 'Yes. I heard the news on a station in West Virginia. Miss Laura McQueen's broken the women's airspeed record from Dallas to Los Angeles by one minute six seconds. Elizabeth Taylor had dinner with Richard Burton.'

Mrs Handforth said, 'The Charter House . . .'

Oh God, Nelson thought, that's it. She reminded us yesterday. 'I'm afraid it'll just have to take its chance,' he said. 'We racked our brains – didn't we, Jim? – but couldn't think of a way. The road's not ploughed. We couldn't send the rescue team on skis or snowshoes, for a bit of paper, when they might be needed, any moment, to rescue people—'

John Remington interrupted, 'What are the chances of the Charter House roof caving in, Walter?' His brows were bent and his jaw outthrust.

Walter said, 'Two beams cracked and dry rot in the others. I reckon she might go with today's snow.'

Nelson said, 'So what? The Charter's got to take its chance, like the rest of us.'

John Remington stood up. 'That's not right,' he said. 'I'll go and get it. It's in a teak cabinet with a glass top, and the cabinet is screwed to the table, right?'

'It's airtight,' Nelson said. 'If air gets in, the Charter will turn to dust . . . You're going to go by boat, for the Charter?'

'You bet,' John Remington said.

'It's real nasty out in the bay now,' Walter said. 'Wind's not too strong, but she's blowing straight down the channel, waves six or seven feet, I reckon, out there, and there's no dock. Tide's about half and rising. What are you going to take?'

Remington said, 'The DUKW. Can't run anything else ashore there.' He picked up his cap and left the room.

After a long time Nelson said, 'Well . . . hell . . . next?'

John Remington strode angrily down the passage toward the front door. Bunch of goddam tightwads! If you wouldn't spend a few thousand dollars to preserve the documents of your own history, the title deeds to the land you lived by, what *would* you spend it for?

He had been to the Charter House only once, and he'd gone in winter, and alone. Old Mrs Pease showed him the Charter room, and, after hovering a few moments, left him. He had stood a long time in front of it, mesmerized by the curlicue writing and the old-fashioned language. It was the original deed of purchase between Robert Handforth and Quasatuit, chief of the Monomoy Indians. The printed version, laid on the table at the side, made the details clear – purchase, the price, the declaration of the Indian's perpetual right to hunt the land and fish all the seas and lakes of the peninsula . . .

He heard her feet hurrying after him but did not pause or slow. She caught up with him in the lobby, among the usual crowd of old men, children, and pregnant women. Three of the Spanish sailors were there, smoking a single cigarette which they handed round between them.

'Are you really going – for the Charter?' she said breathlessly. 'I just heard.'

'I said I would,' he said. 'You don't believe me?'

'But it's crazy! You'd risk your life for a bit of paper?' she said.

'It's more than a bit of paper. It's the Monomoy Charter.'

She gestured violently. '*When* will you understand? Everything real, everything valuable, is in the heart and the mind. It isn't the courthouse building that has to be preserved in an emergency, but the people's respect for law. It isn't the paper of a treaty, or charter, that matters, but the fact that people agreed, and are keeping the agreements . . . You're calling for volunteers, I hope?'

'No,' he snapped, 'I'm ordering out a crew.'

'It'll look good in the papers,' she said. 'Perhaps you'll get a medal.'

She stood close, face and body outthrust in aggression, daring him to strike her. He had never hit a woman and she could not force him to do so now. The Spanish sailors watched, passing the cigarette.

He said, 'I'm sorry you feel like that,' and turned away and walked on.

He heard her begin to follow. He heard her drawing in her breath. To say what? To call out, I'm sorry? To throw more anger after him? He would not turn to see and went out the front door without looking back.

222

He walked fast down the drive. Suppose she was right about the Charter not being important. And he got someone drowned. Someone with a wife and kids, who would look at him accusingly the rest of his life. And him wearing the medal, perhaps.

He walked more slowly. What was right? She had put him into doubt, so that he wasn't sure. He liked being sure. It was hard to be a petty officer in the Coast Guard if you weren't sure. He ought to kick her out of his life and his thoughts. JoAnn would never say a thing like that. She'd know it wasn't right to put worries into a man's head when he had a job to do. Janet would never have said a thing like that.

Yeah. Well, JoAnn didn't *have* any such ideas, and as for Janet – at first she was too much of a kid to understand that anyone had problems, and later she just didn't give a damn. Lynn Garland was different. And better. No use trying to pretend she wasn't. She was more of a person – that hardly needed proving. She was more of a woman, too; at least, that was his personal opinion; some might not agree.

It was a funny experience, having a woman throw questions of duty and responsibility at you. It cut into the idea of separate men and women's worlds. A woman like that would give more, but she'd expect more, too. You'd really have to share your life, not just bits of it. And you'd have to be sure of yourself and what you were doing, because you'd have to justify it. It was easier to have a woman who'd say, I don't know anything about that, that's man's work. Easier, yes, but better . . . ?

He stopped in the middle of the street. No good trying to avoid it. She'd put doubt into his mind and he must face it, and deal with it . . . The Charter was in danger. Was it right to risk men's lives to rescue it? It would certainly be right to save an original copy of the Declaration of Independence, wouldn't it, in spite of what Lynn said? Sure, it would! And Lincoln's original notes for the Gettysburg speech, if they survived? Sure! To him and people in Monomoy, the Charter was nearly as important. Therefore he ought to go and save it. He might ask who wanted to go along with him, instead of ordering out a crew. Calling for volunteers was a bad thing, as a general rule but maybe, this time, it wouldn't do any harm.

John braced himself more firmly, tightened his grip on the wheel, and, huddling his neck deeper into the collar of his foul-weather coat, made the starboard turn round Can 13. The DUKW's heaving roll converted on the instant into a deep, sluggish pitch. Heavy, greenish-white water pushed out from the curve of the bow. A hundred gallons of it, half solid, half foam, came over the windshield and struck him full in the face. Beside him, McGill shook his head dismally. Carstairs, sitting beside the engine hatch, swore obscenely.

John shouted, 'Mind your language there, Harry!' He felt lighthearted and lightheaded. Chief Boatswain Helm would have his liver for breakfast when he learned he'd taken his exec and his station engineer and the DUKW to rescue a piece of paper, which might not be in danger anyway. And cynical, don't-give-a-damn Harry Carstairs had actually volunteered, pretending it was a goddam bore, a drag, a crock.

He kept the DUKW pushing into a moving, driving curtain of snow and sea. Behind, the town had already vanished. The waves ran about six feet high, and hardly more than that apart in the shallow bay. The DUKW wallowed about like a desperate hippo, burying itself every few seconds and then miraculously coming up, its engine roaring and its propellers whining whenever they were lifted out of the water by a crest. 'A bitch of a sea,' McGill had muttered, before they left the pier. The water came back steadily into his face now, like rhythmic icy punches.

McGill yelled, 'Buoy, starboard bow, close . . . Black!'

Black 11. He gave the wheel a turn to port. Work across to Red 10 now, and when he reached the edge of the surf, turn and head in. The Charter House was about fifty yards east of Red 10, and the buoy about a hundred yards off the beach.

In 1962 the Monomoy Charter was rescued from imminent loss by Chief Boatswain's Mate John Remington . . . These damn Yankees didn't realize what the Charter meant. Was it third or fourth grade when he'd first learned about it? He remembered looking out the schoolroom window, over the sun-baked plain, dry and yellow-gold in the late spring sun. Two Indians rode by with twenty horses, and he knew they'd be taking them up the road out of Laramie, over the Togwotee in the last of the snow, to graze them in the Hole. Then, looking back into the schoolroom, there were the coloured pictures in a big book the teacher had. He remembered white houses and blue sea – he'd never seen the sea, of course; and two black-coated Pilgrims stepping ashore from the *Mayflower,* muskets in hand; and, on the next page, a copy of the Charter . . .

McGill raised an arm and at the same moment John saw the wildly leaping red buoy, Number 10, throttled back, and spun the wheel to port. The first roll brought a torrent of water in

224

over the side, and a furious yell from Carstairs. Then she slowly rolled, and in a few moments mushed in to the line of breaking surf.

A cliff-fronted comber reared up at the stern, and suddenly to port and starboard it was roaring white water. The bow rose, the stern dipped, and a wave crashed over them, washing Carstairs up against John's legs. The stern rose again with the next wave, the front wheels hit the sand, and as another wave crashed over them they began to climb out of the surf on to the narrow rim of exposed beach. John roared up into the snow and as he brought her to a halt, started pumping out the water they had taken on.

'Get going,' John shouted.

McGill jumped ashore with an axe and a shovel. Carstairs followed, carrying two pairs of snowshoes. They tied on the snowshoes and waddled slowly off toward the half-seen triangle of the Charter House.

As the level of the water sank, John carefully manoeuvred the DUKW around on the narrow beach until she was again facing the sea. Jesus, the waves looked terrifying! The falling snow had begun to erase the snowshoe tracks.

He peered at his watch. Five minutes to get there, five minutes to unscrew the Charter, five minutes back. They ought to be here by now. He shut off the bilge pump and kept the engine idling.

They came awkwardly through the snow, side by side, carrying the Charter case between them. They reached him and handed up the case. 'We had to dig *down* to reach the top of the window,' Carstairs said. 'The roof is holding, but it won't for long. A couple of beams are split and the others are bent like a bow . . . Well, here's your goddam Early American toilet paper.'

'Let's go,' John said.

They scrambled aboard, and stowed the heavy case up in the forward compartment, under the square bow deck, wedging it securely with spare life preservers.

'All set?'

'O.K.'

John waited for a wave to crash on the beach, then drove forward into the sea, wheels and propeller both spinning. The next wave flung the bow high and the men held on hard to keep from tumbling backward into the surf. As she slapped down again the propeller whined in the air and then they were up

225

again in the next wave. Two more waves stood them almost on end and then she gained headway. After two desperate minutes they passed the white water and John swung her to starboard, heading for home.

Carstairs clasped both hands above his head in a boxer's signal of triumph. John turned to him, shouting, 'Get the medicinal brandy! We'll have a—'

McGill's high startled yell brought his head snapping round on his shoulders. 'Boat ahead!'

By God, there it was, dim in the snow, riding up, suddenly seen, vanishing in snow and spray, then again a blur of something darker in the dark-green troughs. It was a rowboat, steeplechasing eastward over the waves, an old dory, no more, painted black. The man at the oars was bundled in a heavy coat and wore sea boots and a red woollen cap. The oars chopped steeply into the water, came out after a short sea-stroke, chopped in again. The bow rose, the boat seemed to hang over the wave, like a pinned ant, then it zipped over and out of sight . . . in a moment to appear again, the rower pulling hard and steady, holding his course by expert rowing. He seemed to have no fear of the towering waves.

'He isn't going to make it,' Carstairs said suddenly. 'He's six inches down already . . . and can't stop to bail.'

John saw that the dory was not lifting as it should. For all the rower's skill, some water had been slapping in at each wave, and the dory was beginning to lose its buoyancy. The rower must know, but could do nothing except keep the boat moving, bow headed into the waves.

There was no need for orders. McGill and Carstairs moved to the waist of the DUKW. John eased back the throttle and came up alongside. Just as the DUKW's flank touched the rower's port oar, the man in the boat cried 'Hup!' A soggy black dog scrambled out of the dory and leaped toward the DUKW's gunwale. As Carstairs sank his fingers into its coat, the rower dropped oars, stood up, and jumped. McGill had him, and in a moment dog and man were aboard. The dory was already awash and wallowing helpless. John opened the DUKW's throttle once more.

Carstairs and the rescued rower came forward, while the dog shook itself. Carstairs was grinning fiendishly. 'Chief, permit me to introduce your shipwrecked mariner – Mrs Ibbotson of West Village, and Blackie.'

Then John saw the iron-grey hair under the red cap. Her face was blue with cold, her hands a dull purple. 'Where were you going?' John asked. 'What's the trouble?'

Her voice was flat, Cape Cod to the ultimate. 'Nothing in the house for my dag to eat, cap'n. Won't eat our food . . . I was going to town to get dag biscuits.'

John stared, speechless. The waves lessened, and Number 11 came abeam.

The woman said, 'Clem will sure be mad, 'bout the dory. He said, let the dag stavv, but I couldn't do that.' She moved aft, hands in pockets, rolling easily to the still-violent motion. The dog followed.

Carstairs was laughing with a silent, passionate intensity. 'What's the joke?' John asked sourly.

'Clem and Harriet Ibbotson, they been fighting nearly thirty-five years now. Every time Harriet wants to buy curtains, or a dress maybe, Clem says the dory needs a coat of paint, or oar-locks, or an anchor, so they can't afford it, and Harriet, she's been saying, thirty years, I'll sink your goddam dory one of these days, Clem Ibbotson, you wait. Now she's done it!'

He burst into open laughter. He was a Harwich man, John knew, so all this was part of his background, something he grew up with. To him, this was a laugh. A Cape Cod joke, see? There's this old woman and a dog nearly drown, and this guy loses his boat and can't afford another, see . . . John began to laugh. Carstairs, wiping his eyes with sodden, snow-covered gloves, shouted, 'Oh boy, wait till Bob Gardner hears about this!'

They were past Black 13 and in the lee of the land. John re-laxed his grip on the wheel and pushed the throttle wider. Ought to be home in five, six minutes.

Jim Carpenter put down the telephone and turned to Lynn Garland. 'Someone on the top floor says the DUKW's passing our jetty right now, Lynn. Do you want to come down with me?'

She made a pretence of shuffling the papers on her desk. 'I think I'm in the clear,' she said. 'I'd love to.'

It was only a few hundred feet from the Longships to the Coast Guard pier along the waterfront, but deep snow blocked that route and they had to go out the ploughed driveway and up Nickerson Street. A number of people seemed to have heard the news and decided to go out. She saw the Spanish captain, Elliott King, Father Bradford, and several others.

As they turned on to South Commerce Street she thought it was amazing how quickly the wall of snow had grown across it just past Harry's Amoco, where they had stopped ploughing. South Commerce was a canyon, houses hardly visible. The snow rushed on down in senseless, aimless abandon.

The DUKW eased alongside and Walter Crampton said, 'That's Mrs Ibbotson, and Blackie. Reckon she musta run out of dog biscuits!' Everyone laughed. The two other men in the DUKW handed up the Charter, Walter and Jim Carpenter took it and everyone cheered.

John was at the wheel, giving orders. He was always giving orders. The man he was speaking to nodded. He stepped ashore. She noticed she was suddenly alone, and standing just where he set foot on the pier.

'So you made it,' she said.

He didn't seem to recognize her for a moment, and when he did, she thought he would snap at her. She prayed he would not be angry, because she would have to respond with anger, and what she truly felt was an idiotic, inane warmth.

'Yes, we made it,' he said. 'The United States Coast Guard rescued one piece of paper, and ferried one woman and her dog to market . . . Your hair's white. Now I know what you'll look like when you're an old lady.'

She laughed and held his arm. 'You're soaked,' she accused him. 'Yes.'

'You ought to change into dry clothes at once.'

'I will. As soon as I get to the station.'

'Then come to the Longships, and tell me all about it. Was it bad out there?'

'No. Well, sometimes. I'll come down as soon as I've changed and had something to eat.' He grinned at her, and left. Smiling, she watched him walking up Boat Street till the snow hid him.

George Zanakis fumbled in his pocket for a cigarette, found none, and swore. He stopped his pacing and cocked his head to examine the huge 'canvas' on a makeshift stretcher on the floor. Jim Carpenter, on his knees at one side, worked carefully with a long-handled brush.

Not bad, George thought. Jim had no idea of the relation of the parts to the whole, but how could he be expected to, working for the first time on a canvas this size? He had talent, all right. Talent, ambition, and a silly wife, all pulling in different directions.

Elliott King began to talk again. 'I know how you feel, George, and I respect your feelings, believe me. But you've got to think how other people feel, too. Right? I don't have a thing against horseshoe crabs, but the fishermen have, see? The crabs eat the clams, right?'

Goerge did not answer. These days Elliott talked to hear the sound of his own voice.

'The clams are the fishermen's livelihood, shoes for the kiddies, bread, gasoline . . .' He was sitting astride the sofa behind JoAnn, his hands resting lightly on her naked waist.

'Hold her tighter,' Jim Carpenter ordered suddenly. 'Your hand looks limp.'

Elliott gripped tighter. JoAnn shifted her position slightly, returned to the pose, and was again still and calm, her big breasts riding proud as round-bowed vessels ahead of her. She chewed steadily. Where does she get the stuff, George wondered crossly. I can't get cigarettes.

'Same with the park,' Elliott went on. 'There are birds out there, I know that. Nice birds, pretty birds . . . but in Massachusetts there are people, people living in slums . . .'

'Hmmm,' George said.

'These hands are god-awful,' Jim muttered.

George said, 'Hands always are. That's supposed to be the mark of an artist, well, a draughtsman anyway, to be able to draw hands . . . Look at the proportion of the hand's length to its width. Go and measure it.'

Elliott King giggled, an extraordinary sound, as Jim bent, frowning intently, to stare at the hand that clutched JoAnn's flank.

George Zanakis returned to his pacing. Four o'clock, the fourth day, and snowing. Suppose it never did stop? Suppose he never did get back to his studio, and the canvases there? Suppose his time was up, not next year, or the year after, but now.

Christ, not now! It was there, inside, somewhere. After fifty years, it must be! It only needed the right flash, the right combination of event and emotion, of character and circumstance, and then it would come out on to the canvas and simply BE, for eternity, with his signature in the corner in big black letters: ZANAKIS.

For a moment he considered taking the brush from Jim Carpenter's hand and painting the big canvas himself. It might be the last one . . . But this was not his subject. It was all right for

229

a . . . for an advertisement, God damn it, an advertisement for a bunch of conservationist crackpots. Then where was *the* subject? Every time he thought he'd found it, and set to work in a fury of inspiration – most recently, at the fire – he soon realized that he had painted another nothing.

Then *were* *was* the subject that would erase *The Druggist* from the world's memory? Surely God had not allowed him to sacrifice his health, all normal life, the happiness of four wives, and the stability of half a dozen children – all long since gone, run away, vanished – to no purpose?

The stuttering whine of the power saw set the Reverend Arthur Day's teeth on edge and his nerves to a responsive, spasmodic vibration. Yet there came with it a gradually strengthening sense of accomplishment. It was like having a tooth drilled at the dentist's – every moment a stab of pain, and every stab another step toward completion and release.

Zzzzzzip, there went the back of another. Zzzzzzip, and another. In a corner by the door two men stacked metal remnants. Under the pulpit another wielded a long handled axe. A steady procession of men and boys passed down the aisle, carrying wood to the truck waiting outside.

Mr Day went up to the axe swinger and called, 'That's the spirit, Rod.' He added, 'It is God's work. Don't be afraid.'

The work had started very slowly. The men had approached the pews as though their task was to preserve them instead of to destroy them. He had had to attack a pew himself, puffing and grunting under the weight of the big axe, before they would really get to work.

It was getting dark. They'd have to stop soon. Well, it would be finished by tomorrow. Already the aisle, as such, had almost vanished. The church looked like an empty barn.

He saw a man with an axe, standing, looking around for something to do. 'Start on the pulpit,' he cried.

'The pulpit?'

'Yes, yes. Nothing material matters in the worship of God!'

'Not even the altar?'

Arthur Day swung round. Father Bradford stood close, glaring at him with eyes that were positively, yes, positively glowing with hate.

Arthur Day clapped his hands. 'Ah, Father, is this not the very first time we've had the pleasure of showing you our church?'

'I've been in,' the priest said, 'before my . . . before I went to Harvard. My great-grandfather gave the font.'

'Ah, yes,' Arthur Day crowed, 'the font. Of course. Of course.'

'This is appalling,' the priest said. His voice trembled. 'It is hardly more than a shell . . .'

Arthur Day smiled widely. 'Terrible, terrible! But the people must come first . . . in our faith, that is.'

A painful, bitter thought came to him, and his smile became a grimace. Was he stripping the Old Church so that Bradford could move in with his black scarecrows and censer-swinging eunuchs and gobbled Latin mumbo-jumbo? Why didn't God strike him dead, if He cared – or existed?

A man came up, white-faced in the gloom. 'Sir, Reverend,' he stammered, 'there's a corpse down there . . . downstairs.'

Arthur Day tried to concentrate. 'Oh, you were going to start on the benches stored in the crypt, weren't you? That's the sailor who was found on the beach yesterday . . . Move him into the corner out of the way.'

'If it's all right,' the man said doubtfully.

'Certainly.'

The man backed off. Father Bradford's voice was low: 'I asked you about the altar.'

'Oak,' Arthur Day said. 'Meadow-grown oak, fit for a clipper. A gift from the Handforth family, oh, about a century and a half ago.'

The priest said, 'Don't touch it! Don't dare touch that altar.'

Arthur Day felt ill and old. Bradford knew. Why else had he come in just at this moment? If he were alone now he could have taken the axe himself, and cut the altar in pieces with his own hands. Everyone would commiserate on the lengths to which the people's need had driven him. Then, when the storm was over, broken by what he had had to do, he could retire gracefully.

He muttered, 'I will preserve the altar as long as possible.'

The young priest said, 'You must not touch it!'

'For as long as possible,' Arthur Day cried out, raising his hands, 'don't you understand, for as long as possible.'

Walter Crampton's hands tightened their grip on the arms of the straight-backed chair. He stared at the people on the dais, but now saw nothing.

Suppose he should die before Daisy? Years ago it had seemed perfectly possible, of course. But not since her illness. Not until now. A man who's had one heart attack could expect another. Then what would happen to her?

She was asleep on the couch beside him. Or she was resting, her eyes closed. Nowadays there wasn't much difference between sleep and rest with her, or between either and death. Sometimes her eyes would open, and she'd look at the dais for a few minutes; then they'd close again.

Up on the dias they'd made it like a bar-room and the people were beginning to pretend they were bums and whores, but they were still reading from sheets of paper. Jim had the hotel heat cut off from all public rooms after eight o'clock. Now it was nine, and cold, in spite of the fires burning in the three big old-fashioned fireplaces. Burning pews from the Old Church to warm people making a play about bums and whores. Maybe the snow should keep right on falling. Then it wouldn't matter about Daisy being left to charity. Then the men who'd stolen his life's savings would smother too, and reap no harvest.

Elliott King stopped beside his chair, and spoke softly. 'Hi, Walter. How's . . . ?' He indicated Daisy with a motion of his head.

Walter said, 'The same.'

'I heard you had a hard time getting the doctors to let her come down here.'

'They didn't.' Walter said.

He'd had a very hard time. Doc Burroughs kept looking at him and asking. Anything the matter with *you*? Are you sure? And then he'd insisted on having a look at Daisy, and said, when they were alone afterwards, Well, it beats me, but she's still here, just keep her lying down. And then they'd gone back to Daisy and she'd whispered, 'Going to see the play,' and Doc Burroughs exploded, and swore he washed his hands of all responsibility. So here she was, and he with her.

'I've been talking to George Zanakis about the park,' Elliott said. 'I think, with a little axle grease we could swing him to our side. Form a Fine Arts Commission and put him in charge – something like that. He'd influence the other artists, and they'd have a big effect on public opinion off the Cape.'

Walter said, 'Hmmmph.' Why did some men lie when there was no need? Did Elliott think that he, Walter Crampton, needed reassuring that he was on the winning side? Elliott didn't know it, but what had happened in the past couple of days was making him think maybe the town would be better off buried, like Sodom and Gomorrah. If the snow didn't bury it or the sea sweep it away, then perhaps turning it into a park would be the next best thing. Not just the Handforth Tract but the whole Monomoy peninsula. Drive the Steeles and Worrells and Vernons to the ends of the earth, let them have no place to lay their heads . . .

Elliott said, 'Well, I'll be getting along . . . I was looking for Dorothy, as a matter of fact . . . wondered if she'd come by here.'

'Isn't she rehearsing, up there?'

'No. She's not in this scene, Robert told me. Well . . . be seeing you.'

'Sure thing.'

Elliott drifted away, greeting and being greeted. Walter watched him go. It took a storm to bring out the sailors, and Elliott seemed hell-bent on proving he was a landlubber. He ought to go find her and whale the living daylights out of her. But if he could do that, he wouldn't be wandering round advertising that his wife was being laid endways and sideways by the dirtiest son of a bitch in town.

Daisy whispered, 'Has he gone?' Her eyes were closed.

'Yes.'

'He sounds . . . almost real . . . at last.'

Walter took her hand and held it gently on his own. Let the rest of the world go about its business. He had his own decision to make.

Harold Morgan stared, mesmerized, at the plump forearm so close to him. The white, firm skin was covered with a sort of reddish down that glowed in the lamplight. The fingers were short and round, the nails well kept and with no trace of that disgusting red gunk women put on. She read on steadily. She had a pleasant voice, he had to give her that. He had no idea what the book was about, but if she wanted to read to him, heck, it passed the time.

She smelled of something. Not the musty stuff she was wearing when she backed him into the corner by the file cupboard, nor the other stuff she had on the day she locked herself in the toilet. She smelled clean and pretty good, like flowers and eau de cologne. He was sitting in bed, propped up by four pillows. She sat in a chair, and their heads were close together. He could not lean farther away without getting a crick in his neck. He knew, because he had tried.

The perfume seemed to be working on him like a dangerous

233

gas. The light grew brighter, dimmer, brighter. Her bosom receded, surged forward and hung in front of him, suddenly double, round, white-fleshed and rosy-tipped, without covering. Her thighs under the jersey skirt were round and plump. The silk stockings were stretched and rounded over the knees peeping out from under the skirt. A drop of sweat formed above his right eyebrow, and his left hand, near her, began to tremble, ever so slightly.

She read on placidly.

He could hardly breathe. 'I want to go and see the play rehearsal,' he said urgently. 'Leave me, Charlotte. I must dress and . . .'

'Oh, Mr M,' she said reproachfully. 'You know what Dr Burroughs said!'

There was a knock on the door. Harold jerked the blankets up to his chin. 'Who's there?' he called.

'Elliott . . . Hi! Hi, Mrs Quimby. How are you, boy? You look fine . . . Say, have you seen Dorothy around since dinner? Has she come in here?'

'No. She dropped by this morning to say hello, but not since.'

'Oh. Well. Thanks. Good night.'

The door closed behind him. Harold stared at it with a puzzled frown. 'That's strange,' he said, 'Dorothy's always hung on his coat tails, like a kid, or something.'

'Don't you worry your head about *them*,' Charlotte Quimby said firmly. 'Now, do you want me to read to you some more, or shall I tuck you up properly, and then you must go to sleep?'

'It's early,' Harold said. At the thought of her going, he felt lonely. It would be dark and cold, with no light coming through the frosted glass, and the wind rattling the shutters. And how could he sleep, with thoughts of the merger and of that bosom chasing each other round his head and up his spine. If only he could have got away that first day, by God, he'd have worked it off on a comfortable old whore in Boston and he wouldn't be trapped like this, horny as a goat and nervous as a kitten.

'I think you'd better go to sleep,' she said. She removed the extra pillows, plumping the one he was to have – bang bang bang bang, thump. She pulled the covers up under his chin and tucked them in, then said, 'Before I go . . . it's not my place to interfere, Mr M, but I have only your interests at heart. I don't think you should go through with the merger with Mr King.'

'Why not?' he asked. If only she could give him a sound reason! The thought of the merger had terrified him ever since

234

Elliott had first mentioned it, but he couldn't find the will-power to say no.

'You would lose your independence,' she said. 'Also, Mr King's business methods are not yours. I don't say he breaks the law, but he does do things you would not care to do. And I believe his business will fall off considerably after this storm.'

'Why?' he asked.

'He has not shown himself in a good light,' she said evasively. Harold felt warm and pleased. She was right. She had put into words all his own doubts and fears. 'How can I get out of it?' he said.

She said, 'Tell him you have thought it over and you have changed your mind. He won't raise any objections, after this.'

'After what?'

'This . . . this time in the Longships.'

'What do you mean? What happened? How has he shown himself in a bad light?'

'I'd really rather not talk about it, Mr M. I hate gossip, and . . .'

'I want to know, darn it all. If I'm even thinking of forming a partnership with him, I *need* to know.'

'Well,' she said, 'in that case.' She pulled the chair up close. 'It's like this . . .'

John Remington noted that it was half past ten. Time to go back to the station soon. It was warmer there too. And he'd said half an hour ago that he ought to get to bed. And on the dais the actors were only talking to Robert Handforth, asking questions rather than acting their parts.

'Penny for them,' Lynn Garland said quietly.

'Hm? Oh, just looking around. Recognizing people . . . A lot of them seem to look different than they did, and I'm not sure whether it's because I'm seeing them close-to or because the storm's changed them.'

'You are a strange man,' she said. 'Sometimes I think you have no imagination at all, and then . . . Well, for one thing, you go and rescue the Charter.'

He said, 'Hey, I forgot to tell you, old Mrs Osgood told me she's going to see that I get an award from the D.A.R. for that.'

Lynn laughed shortly, 'Great! Will you still speak to us after that?'

He said, 'I don't know why you think it's funny. I think it's an honour.'

235

'To get a medal from that bunch of old female reactionaries?'

'I don't have anything against them,' he said.

He couldn't understand her attitude toward the institutions that seemed to him to hold the country together and give it a disciplined shape: the Army and Navy, Coast Guard and Air Force, police and Marines, the D.A.R. and the Republican party and General Motors. Hell, you could laugh at any of them, but if you seriously started to question their good intentions, or worth, where did you stop?

She spoke softly, resting her hand lightly on his arm. 'I'm sorry. John. I didn't mean that. I'm proud of you. We all are. I wish we could have hours and hours to talk about these things. Then I could tell you why I distrust the D.A.R., and you could show me, perhaps, why I'm wrong, and I could try and explain what the liberal's view of military service is, and you would see, I think, that people are not automatically Communists or anarchists just because they question certain theories which the services hold as sacred . . .'

A shadow fell across them and John looked up. The tall figure of Father Bradford was leaning over the back of his chair. 'Excuse me, Miss Garland . . . Chief, could you drop by my room to have a word with me before you go back to the station?'

John rose to his feet. 'I was on my way. Father. I'll come now.' Lynn was looking anxiously up at him. He said, 'We'll talk about all those things after the storm. Then we'll have all the time in the world. Good night, Lynn.'

'Good night, John.'

He moved away with the priest. 'A most attractive and intelligent woman,' Father Bradford said.

'She sure is.'

The corridor was empty and Father Bradford slowed his pace. John walked at his side toward the lobby. 'It's about Charlie Tyson,' the priest said. 'He wants to get married.'

'Charlie?' John exclaimed. 'But he's not . . .'

Father Bradford smiled faintly, 'He's not a Catholic, at the moment. No. Nor is the girl he wants to marry – Betty Pryor.'

John spoke his thought aloud. 'They've been going steady, except for—' He cut himself short.

'Except for JoAnn . . . quite. Charlie tells me he is sure that Nelson will object to him marrying Betty. He's not so sure about Mary, but he guesses she will, too. They'll all be against him, in his phrase . . . Charlie came to me for help and advice. I'd like to know what sort of a man he is, from your point of view.'

236

They turned at the entrance to the lobby, and walked back side by side, heads bent. John said slowly, 'He's not a man yet, in some ways. Always daydreaming, about winning drags, knocking out Floyd Patterson, pitching for the Yankees, flying F-104s, rescuing the President from the sea . . . He sulks if you correct him, because it spoils the dream, I guess. Test pilot-heroes don't get told to wash their necks . . . He seems awful young to get married.'

Father Bradford said, 'Perhaps marriage is the only thing that will give him maturity. Then there'll be at least one person who has to treat him like a man instead of a boy. And, in nine months or so, another, probably.'

'I could have him transferred . . . to Puerto Rico,' John said, speaking his thoughts aloud.

Father Bradford said, 'Yes, but should you? They are both willing to become Catholics. With the parents' consent, I can marry them.'

John said, 'That will settle Charlie's idea of going to the Academy.'

'So I understand. But I do not think, myself, that he is officer material. Don't you agree?'

'Yes.'

'Then I'll speak to Nelson at the first opportunity. But, until it is made public, I'd be grateful if you would say nothing to anyone.'

'All right,' John said.

Smiling his good nights, Father Bradford turned back towards the ballroom. John walked on slowly. Charlie Tyson, husband and father. He couldn't see it. Yet perhaps Father Bradford was right. Certainly other kids had got married, even younger. The average didn't seem to run any better, or worse, whatever age people got married. You could make the same mistake at eighteen, thirty-eight, or fifty-eight. But how could the kid have the nerve to take on a wife and home and kids when he couldn't be trusted with a pair of oars and a dory? There ought to be some kind of rating system, and until you made the rating – no marriage. But who would do the grading? It was difficult. He'd like to talk to Lynn about it.

CHAPTER NINE

SATURDAY

John Remington sat up quickly: 4:22 a.m. The rumbling continued. Earlier there had been a distinct explosive crack, but dull. He picked up the telephone and dialled the operations room. 'Watch! Watch! What was that?'

'I don't know. Some kind of explosion.'

'You can't see anything? What direction did it come from?'

'I don't know. It was just a kind of bang and then a rumbling . . . It's snowing worse than ever, and blowing up a full gale.'

'From what quarter?'

'Nor'east.'

John hung up irritably, and lay back. Explosions and rumblings in the night and no way of finding out what they were. An aircraft might have crashed a few hundred feet out of town, and men be dying in it. A ship might have run ashore and blown up. No one could do a goddam thing. No one knew a goddam thing, except it was snowing. That they'd always know, because it wasn't going to stop. No, sir, not ever.

Lynn Garland and Charlotte Quimby awoke simultaneously in their room, and together cried, 'What was that?' Neither answered, and then Lynn switched on the light. Charlotte was sitting up, wide eyed, her hair full of curlers, wearing a woollen dressing gown over a sweater over pyjamas. The windows stopped a long rattling and shaking. Without a word Lynn switched off the light. The two of them lay back, but did not return to sleep.

Walter Crampton lay rigid. He had heard it all. The wind had been veering steadily all night, starting several points west of north, until now it was in the north-east. From many nights at sea he knew it was near twenty past four. A single heavy crash shook the Longships and the sandy soil on which it stood. The windows rattled violently, and then there was a noise that continued for several seconds, like someone pouring stones out of a bucket, a long way off. Most likely it came from the north, downwind, or the sound wouldn't have been as loud compared to the earth shock. The Russians started a war maybe, choosing

238

a time when Cape Cod was helpless? But a big bomb would make more noise than that, and who would go dropping small ones?

More likely something fell down. It would have to be big. The Coast Guard station . . . the cannery . . . the Catholic church . . . even the water tower . . . Who would ever know, or care?

He stared at the dark ceiling, holding his breath. Daisy's breathing continued, very faint but steady and firm in its weakness. Walter's fist closed again over the money in the pocket of the coat he was wearing in bed: two dollars, seventeen cents. After that, nothing. Nothing to pay Dr Burroughs with, or the telephone bills and the fuel bills that would be waiting. Nothing to pay for a decent funeral, neither for him nor for her . . .

All the people were awakened, and some cried, It's the end of the world, hallelujah; and some, My God, what was that?; and some, The Russians are coming; and some, Don't tell me about it, I don't want to know. But all noticed that the snow was still falling, rushing down more densely and with a greater fury than before.

At 7:30 John Remington was standing in the operations room, his hands deep in his pockets. Outside temperature 23 and falling. Barometer, 29.79, and falling. Wind, north-east, 33 knots and rising. Inside – cold, nervous, bad-tempered. The world was dull grey and full of a deep, senseless noise. The sweeping beam from the light made the falling snow almost white, but above it was grey and below it was grey.

He picked a pair of binoculars and focused them where the monotonous waves raced along the *Goya's* side. He spoke, without lowering the binoculars. 'When's high tide today?'

'Thirteen oh two,' the duty seaman replied.

'So now it's just after low tide?'

'About half an hour.'

John put down the binoculars. 'Call McGill.'

A minute later the exec appeared in the doorway. John handed him the binoculars. 'Take a look at the *Goya*. At the beach.'

McGill said, 'It's low tide, isn't it?'

'Yes.'

'I can't believe it.'

'Well, it is. We'll go down.'

The two men put on foul-weather gear and went out. After crossing the parking lot they took shelter in the lee of the Old

239

Boat House, and looked down at the beach. They were standing in the Gap, normally thirty feet above mean sea level. To right and left the Great Dune rose again to its average height of sixty feet. On the left the Coast Guard Station crowned the lip of the slope down towards the Gap. On the right the dune rose bare and white.

Below, the *Goya* lay almost at right angles to the line of the beach, the long steel wall of its hull guiding a broad front of waves to concentrate their energy on to one point of the beach. At that point – just south of the Gap – they had scored thirty feet into the dune. The concrete steps that used to lead down toward the beach had caved in, adding several tons of concrete to the wall formed by the *Goya*.

The two men watched for a time without speaking. Then John said, 'I reckon the waves are hitting the beach about ten feet above normal, on the weather side of the hulk.'

McGill said, 'Maybe a bit more.'

John said, 'You go back to the station. I'm going to warn the Selectmen.'

They were jammed tight in the Selectmen's office. It wasn't big enough to hold them in comfort, but Nelson Pryor had been anxious not to cause alarm by having the conference in a public room, so the chief elected and appointed officials and the principal private citizens had gathered here during the past twenty minutes, as inconspicuously as possible. They stood packed against the walls, only the two women and two of the Selectmen seated, Carpenter sitting on the edge of the table. It was a few minutes after 9 a.m.

John Remington finished his explanation of the situation, and Nelson said, 'Well, there is it. What do we do about it?'

Walter Crampton said, 'Couldn't be much worse. Outside there, the tide sets southward on the flood, five or six knots sometimes. All that's piling up against the wreck too. And you get the current out of the Sound, coming round Diadem Cape and backing up the tide along the outside.'

He sounded almost cheerful, John thought. His attitude was not merely, nothing can be done, but – nothing can be done, and a good thing, too.

Kimmel the harbourmaster said, 'I took a look just now. At this rate, I don't think it will cut through the Gap for another five, six days, and then only if the wind and sea stay in the north-east, at a full gale.'

'That's impossible!' Elliott King interjected, but no one else opened his mouth. Everyone else now considers it *is* possible, John thought grimly; in fact they think it's likely.

Arthur Evans said, 'Might it come over the top?'

'That's what Chief Remington has just been telling us – yes,' Nelson said.

George Lathrop said, 'Can we try to move the *Goya*?'

'She won't move,' Walter Crampton said abruptly. 'She's there till she breaks up.'

'Why can we not break the ship up ourselves?' Mrs Handforth said. 'That would allow free flow for the waves and current, would it not?'

That's right, John thought. That was about the only thing that would make any substantial difference to the situation.

'No dynamite in town,' the fire chief said. 'We used up what there was in the fire the first day. At least, according to my records, we did. You or Harold don't have any, do you?'

Elliott King said, 'No . . . but surely we can do *something*!'

Nelson said, 'We can try. Elliott, I'm going to ask you to take charge of removing that wreck. Do whatever you can. Talk to Chief Remington. Any explosives at the station?'

'No.'

'I thought not . . . Report to us, the Selectmen . . . All right. There are two jobs – see if we can break up, or move, the hulk, and see if we can build up the Gap.'

'I think we ought to warn everyone,' John Remington said.

'Me, too,' Jim Carpenter said.

Nelson spoke slowly, but with emphasis, and conviction. 'It's about 18 above zero, blowing a blizzard of snow. Already there's snow six, ten, twenty feet deep everywhere. Chief Remington can get a message to WCCD, and they'll put it on the air. What do we say? We tell everyone that the tide is coming so high it *might* – just might – come through the Gap. Everyone knows what that means. The ocean comes in, washes the town into the bay, every house, except a few up along North Hill and Monroe, maybe . . . What are the people going to do when they hear that? they're going to get out – but where? Are they going to come here? The Longships is smack in the path of the ocean. Half an hour after it breaks through the Gap, waves twelve and fourteen feet high are coming through here like goddam express trains. This hotel's going to be pulverized and swept clean away. So where can they go? And we? Up on the Great Dune. They'll be safe, but there's nothing there, nothing at all, just the snow and the bent grass sticking through where the wind keeps the snow from lying. They're going to get exhausted and lost in the snowdrifts just trying to get up there. They're going to freeze to death in a couple of hours if they do get up there. In a day or two they'll be dying of thirst . . . I don't want to make any announcement. I want us to be prepared. Before the ocean can come through the Gap, there's going to be worse flooding on the inside, to warn us, isn't there? I mean, we can't have a 30-foot rise on the outside and nothing on the inside, can we?'

John Remington said, 'It isn't as big as that, Nelson. The record high tide at the Gap was 15.2 feet above mean low water two years ago, and that didn't produce any flooding in the bay, because the same wind and sea conditions that pile the water up on the outside will be apt to blow it out of Longships Bay into Nantucket Sound . . . Another fifteen feet on top of that record, and the ocean will be up to the Gap. I reckon the *Goya's* added about eight or nine feet by itself. This storm could easily build up the other six or seven . . . even if the waves don't bring the Gap lower.'

'O.K.,' Nelson Pryor said. 'Then we've got to be ready. And we've got to try to reinforce the Gap. It's all part of the same problem. So get going, Elliott. I want at least two hours' warning before the sea reaches the Gap. Someone on watch there twenty-four hours a day . . .'

'I'll provide that,' John said.

'Right. The rest of us . . . we've got to think. Think what you will need if the town has to move up on to the Great Dune and live there for . . . until the storm stops and help can reach us.'

'It won't,' Walter Crampton said. 'Everyone's in the same boat – the state, the country, everybody!'

Robert Handforth tapped the table with his pencil. 'No, no, Mr White. Look at O'Neill's direction, at the head of the speech: *Hickey bursts into resentful exasperation.* You've spent hours – years – trying to make these dead-beats realize the truth about themselves, and, just when you thought you had succeeded, they are backsliding into dreams of self-respect, of a glorious future which you *know*, and have tried to make them acknowledge, can never come true . . . Now, try it again.'

He leaned forward in his place at the end of the bar. Hickey was being played by Ted White, the school principal. White was young and said to be imaginative, but it had been hard to make him feel who Hickey was, and what was his motivating force.

... you've done all that you needed to do! By rights you should be contented now, without a single damned hope or lying dream left to torment you! But here you are, acting like a lot of stiffs cheating the undertaker! I can't figure it – unless it's just your damned pig-headed stubbornness! Hell, you oughtn't to act this way with me! You're my old pals, the only friends I've got. You know the one thing I want is to see you all happy before I go – And there's damned little time left now. I've made a date for two o'clock. We've got to get busy right away and find out what's wrong. Can't you appreciate what you've got, for God's sake? Don't you know you're free now to be yourselves, without having to feel remorse or guilt, or lie to yourselves about reforming tomorrow? Can't you see there is no tomorrow now? You're rid of it for ever! You've killed it! You don't have to care a damn about anything any more? You've finally got the game of life licked, don't you see that? Then why the hell don't you get pie-eyed and celebrate? Why don't you laugh and sing 'Sweet Adeline'? The only reason I can think of is, you're putting on this rotten half-dead act just to get back at me! Because you hate my guts! God, don't do that...

Much better, Avaloka, beside him, had dropped her hand on his arm. He stole a look at her, and saw that the play wholly absorbed her. She stood, leaning a little forward, eyes wide and lips parted.

Aw, put a bag over it! To hell wid Evelyn! What...

'Good,' he said ten minutes later. 'Break. Start again after dinner.'

'But it's only four o'clock,' Alice Bryant cried, pouting. God knows how she'd make out when O'Neill's world was taken away from her and she had to return to this one.

'What's on your mind?' Avaloka asked him when the rest had gone. 'You look as if you're a thousand miles away.'

'Do I?' he said. 'Perhaps I am. Something Hickey said just got to me. I'm trying to work out why *I* don't get pie-eyed and celebrate. If there's no tomorrow, as seems quite likely – or, at least, no day after tomorrow – why don't *I* laugh and sing "Sweet Adeline"?'

Nelson Pryor watched the snow on Elliott King's coat. It was hardly melting. That showed better than anything how cold it was in the hotel: and, perhaps, how they had become used to the cold.

He was in the Selectmen's office. Elliott, George Lathrop the surveyor of highways and Chief Remington were standing round him. Their faces were drawn, their clothes covered in snow and sand, their heavy boots rimmed with salt and fouled with oil and grit.

Elliott spoke: 'It's dark now, Nelson. We can't do any more. We've been at it all day. We've tried men with shovels. They can hardly get through the snow in time, before more snow piles up. We've tried the dozers, but there are only two, and it's damned heavy work. The ploughs can't get up on top of the dune, and even if they could, they couldn't push sand off the top and down into the Gap – only snow, and that's not going to help.'

Nelson said, 'How high did the one-o'clock tide come?'

'About four feet short,' Remington answered briefly. 'We didn't bother to tell you.'

'Full moon on Tuesday,' Lathrop said.

'Four feet short, yes,' Elliott said, 'But these waves were chewing hell out of the Gap, on the underside.'

Remington said, 'We've got to get some dynamite, or gun-cotton – any cutting explosive – to break up that hulk. I'm going to put it to Mr Helm and Boston, top priority.'

'O.K. But how can they deliver it?'

'There was a jet overhead about noon. Went over from north to south, twice . . .'

'I heard him. What was he doing?'

'I don't know. But with radar and these new bomb sights, maybe one could drop dynamite to us.'

'Don't forget detonators and fuse.'

'O.K. Try it. Anything else?'

'Nothing, Nelson. The Chief here's got two men on permanent watch in the Old Boat House. They'll keep good watch all right! The goddam waves are practically washing in under their feet. Next high tide's due 1 :34 in the morning.'

'Any likelihood of . . .?'

'I don't think so. We marked the level, at each hour before high tide, this time, so we have a guide to tell us how any future tide relates to this one . . . which was four feet short.'

'Good for you.'

'Mind if I, beat it now, Nelson? I want to take a bath and a nap before the gals start pulling me out on the dance floor.'

'Dance floor?'

'Father Bradford's record hop for young and old.'

Elliott dug Chief Remington in the ribs. 'And you've got a heavy date, eh, Chief? That dame can twist, I can tell you. The kids taught her . . . And I'll be there, too, with bells on! Eat, drink, and be merry . . .'

'And sing "Sweet Adeline," ' Nelson said.

'Eh? I never liked that song.'

'Nor did I. Just something they were talking about in the play.'

'Oh. The play, Well . . . be seeing you.'

Avaloka stood at Robert's side, watching the dancers. A few old people, and the Spaniards, and one or two young women in advanced pregnancy also watched from the walls. Everyone else in the hotel seemed to be dancing.

'Everyone's enjoying themselves . . . or pretending to,' Robert muttered. 'Even the Steele Band. Look at them: Worrell dancing with Mrs Merchant, Steele with that nice high school kid who's on the telephone exchange most of the time.'

'Are they so bad?' Avaloka asked. 'Or is it just that they are excluded, usually? When they're accepted, and treated like ordinary decent people, then they act like ordinary decent people.'

Robert said, 'I wish I could believe it. But it's bad seed.'

'There's no such thing,' she said vigorously. 'Bad environment and upbringing, that's all.'

'Seed has something to do with it,' Robert said.

Music blared from a radio set tuned to a rock'n'roll station and turned up full volume. Legs and arms pumped in contra-rhythm, like a hundred steam locomotives. The kids danced in silence, eyes turned down, or staring glazed at a point six inches above their partner's head. The older people looked at each other, and laughed and spoke together as they danced. There was Lynn Garland, laughing, her long torso twisting, her bosom jerking into prominence with each pumping step. John Remington's feet slid left and right, but he was not leaning back properly, his face wore an expression of determination, and Lynn was laughing at him. There was Charlotte Quimby, teaching Mr Morgan; Charlie Tyson with Betty Pryor; Nelson and Mary; Elliott King and JoAnn Griffiths; the Carpenters together . . .

'Ah, come on,' she said, tugging at Robert's sleeve. 'This music's making my feet burn.'

Robert smiled affectionately. 'My dear, I physically cannot dance. My feet become crossed over and I fall down . . .'

245

'O.K., O.K.,' she said. Bad seed, crap! Nor could she erase from her mind the vision of gigantic waves, far above her head, battering a thin wall of sand. Her belly felt lean and hollow.

A gangling Negro boy passed, again. Every time he passed, their eyes met. He was dancing with a very plain Negro girl, her hair drawn back in a severe bun, with big feet and outjutting heels. Both boy and girl were very dark. The Negro families were gathered down there by the fourth big window. Whenever she looked that way, she always caught one pair of eyes just turning away from examining her.

She said, 'Well, here goes nothin', Robert,' and walked out on to the floor. She tapped the Negro girl on the shoulder. 'Mind if I take over, honey?' she asked, smiling. 'I'll give him back, in good condition.'

The girl mumbled, 'Oh . . . ah, sure, ma'am . . . princess.' She was not smiling.

'Call me Louise,' she said, 'Louise Lincoln.' She faced the boy, her thighs beginning to move in the smooth counter-motion of the twist. 'I'm a dancer, a man, and you look as if you are. What's your name? Henry, isn't it?'

They had begun to dance together now. 'Yes, ma'am,' the boy said, 'Henry Gage . . . That's my elder brother, Ray, acting with you. He's Joe.'

'Sure.' Joe was the only Negro part in *The Iceman*. Ray Gage was a heavier edition of this boy, a few years older, several degrees surlier.

She smiled into his eyes. He was half a head taller than she: sixteen, maybe seventeen. 'Let's show 'em how *we* do it,' she whispered. 'O.K. Fire, man. Cut out. Let's go!'

The boy was still not sure. There was suspicion in his eyes, and he had not answered her smile. 'You know the Mashed Potato, ma'am?' he asked cautiously,

'*Louise* . . . Sure.'

He began then. She had seen him about the hotel. Sometimes he danced a little jig, or slid from a regular walk into an exaggerated buck and wing, when he thought no one was looking. She had been angered. Did the kid *have* to conform so fully to the convention of the clap-hands nigger? But the truth was, he loved to dance.

She bent far, far back, exaggerating even the exaggeration of the step. The boy leaned far toward her, wilder, wilder. She had been looking at white faces too long. She had even found herself watching his family and thinking. They're very black.

246

The kid was noble because of his blackness, nobler than she because blacker. The surrounding white faces blurred into eye-less, mouthless balloons. Only the boy existed, real, strong, black.

The ofays were edging back, giving them more room. Some-one was clapping, someone yelling. Twist it, sister! So here she was again, performing for them! Was there ever to be anything else? Were they always to dance and fight, and throw and wrestle and jump, always in the centre of the cleared arena? The boy was with her some of the way, but not all. He was young, they were nice people here, and he hadn't come of his brother's sullenness. He was proud, but for the moment only proud of what he could do better than any of the other kids. Why don't you force me to the floor and screw me in the good old African tribal ritual? That's what they half expect, and I'm ready, believe me, boy, I'm ready for anything with you, because you're black.

The music stopped. The boy stood, breathing deep and easy. 'Gee,' he said, 'gee . . . gee whiz, Louise!'

The dark aura around him dissolved. She gave his arm a big squeeze. 'Thanks, Henry. You're pretty damn good yourself.'

She walked toward Robert, and everyone was clapping. The Carpenters passed, and Barbara cried, 'Princess, where in earth did you learn to do the twist like that? You were . . . fantastic!'

She smiled brightly. 'I learned in Harlem, Mrs. Carpenter, where I come from. I've known Chubby Checkers since way back . . .'

Old Mrs Handforth wasn't there to hear her; but twenty others were, and that was enough.

Robert was standing alone when she reached him.

'Well,' she said.

'Come outside.'

She followed him out, past the people, into the hall. He stopped in a deserted corner of the lobby. She could hear the music faint from the ballroom. A cop dozed on a hard chair near the door.

She flared suddenly. 'Well, I've done it now, haven't I? Now I've revealed the ghastly skeleton in my cupboard, that I was keeping secret, hoping to marry your millions. Now you can break it off, and everyone will understand, and sympathize. Except they'll think you were a fool not to know all the time. Well, you are a fool, so that's no injustice.'

He said, 'Are you saying this because you can't bear the idea

247

of marrying a white man, Louise? Because of what we have done, and are doing, to your people? If that's it, I won't say any more. I can only repeat, I love you.'

She began to shiver. He took her hand, and it shook in his. He said, 'Ever since that noise woke us all this morning, I've been wrestling, too. I made up my mind just now . . . about the same time you did . . . I'm not going to New York, or into the theatre. This is our town, and there's work here for me, work which is my duty, and, to tell the truth, my pleasure. I intend to stay here – if you will marry me.'

Now he made her afraid. She had imagined herself as Louise Lincoln, the actress, *who is, in private life, of course, the wife of the well-known producer* . . . Broadway, Sardi's, the Village, Bergdorf Goodman, *Show* magazine, all these had places in the future. But, Mrs Robert Monomoy Handforth, *in Monomoy:* the mother of the next Robert Monomoy Handforth, *in* Monomoy?

'If I dare,' he said softly, 'surely you dare.'

The trembling stopped. She said, 'Very well, Robert.' He kissed her on the lips. My God, she thought. What am I doing?

The little radio on the dresser continued its tale of woe. Fires, raging beyond control in snow-buried Boston, had taken hundreds of lives – how many hundreds, no one knew. The last surface link between Providence, Rhode Island, and the outside world had been cut with the abandonment of the long effort to keep the New Haven tracks ploughed. A woman in Vincennes, Indiana, was suing for divorce on the ground that her husband kept his favourite riding pony in the living-room. On the other hand, Mlle. Danielle Lavreux, in a souped-up Mystère fighter, had recaptured the women's air-speed record, from Dallas to Los Angeles.

'She's terribly chic, too,' Charlotte Quimby murmured.

Lynn Garland stifled a yawn. They were sitting on their respective beds, and it was half past eleven. John had to leave early – he didn't explain why – and Charlotte had sent Mr Morgan to bed soon after that.

She switched off the radio. Now, with the door ajar, they could hear the music from the ballroom. She yawned again. 'Quite a day.'

Charlotte said, 'Goodness me, yes! What with Avaloka, I mean Louise Lincoln . . . you should have *seen* Mrs Handforth's face afterward, when she'd heard, or overheard, people talking about it. Like granite, and just the same colour, too! And that

248

awful explosion this morning. Has anyone found out what it was, yet?'

'I don't think so. Mr Crampton thinks, probably the water tower.'

'And Mr King knocking that man down when he said that Mrs King was acting like a whore.'

'Who said I'm acting like a whore?'

The women looked up quickly.

Dorothy King, her hair drawn back tight from her forehead, dark circles prominent under her eyes and her lips swollen, stood in the door. 'May I come in?' she asked quietly. 'I'm tired.'

'Of course.' Charlotte hurriedly pulled out a chair. Lynn closed the door.

Dorothy King said, 'The man was right . . . Where's Elliott now? Do please tell me the truth. It's a little late for anything else, isn't it?'

Charlotte Quimby said, 'Well . . . he went off with JoAnn Griffiths. I don't know where to.'

'Not to our room,' Dorothy said. 'I looked in there just now. I've been with Bill Vernon, of course . . . but it's finished and I feel ready to talk to Elliott. You don't understand, do you?'

'It's not *our* business,' Charlotte said. 'When you get to my age, you know that there's more than meets the eye in most things . . . but Mr King did seem so attentive, and so . . . masculine. People are surprised.'

'The Marine Corps hero,' Dorothy said, 'big, handsome. But, Mrs Quimby . . . Lynn, I won't be able to tell anyone else – he doesn't like women! He hates them, physically. He's hardly touched me, as a woman, in fifteen years, and then with such disgust, nearly ready to throw up . . . ugh. It makes *me* feel sick again to remember it.'

Charlotte Quimby said, 'How awful! But, Mrs King, don't you think he might be different with other women? It does happen.'

Lynn looked at her room-mate with grudging respect. Charlotte Quimby was a very practical woman. One forgot, in her girlish mannerisms, that she had raised a child alone, for twenty years, and seen her married.

Dorothy King said, 'At first I was afraid of that. Soon, I came to wish it were true. If it *were* true, then his whole personality wouldn't have been a big lie – as it is – as it has always been. I feel sorry for JoAnn.'

'I don't think you need feel sorry for *her*!' Charlotte said.

Dorothy King said, 'I feel as though I've got rid of a growth. I'm sorry for the scandal, but it's over now . . . Thank you for listening to me. Good night.'

She went out, pale and spent, closing the door carefully behind her.

'Seventeen times in three days,' Charlotte Quimby said, nodding her head emphatically, 'and she *looks* it!'

'How on earth do you know that?' Lynn asked, fascinated.

'Vernon told his friends, and they talked. Of course, he may have been boasting, the way men do. Well, it only goes to show, doesn't it? . . . You and that handsome Mr Remington dance very well together, don't you?'

'Oh, after a fashion.'

Charlotte said, 'No, no, *I* saw. It's only a question of following properly, and when you have to lead, doing it so they won't notice. That's the God's truth, dear, all the time, with them – but how many women don't believe it, or fight against it, and finish up sour old spinsters? Serves 'em right, *I* think.'

Jim Carpenter watched his wife working on her nails at the dressing table. Her hair looked as though it had just had a permanent. That's what she must have been doing all day.

She talked, petulantly but without emphasis, as she worked. 'How am I supposed to know what to do? Get my nails straight, or pack to live on the Great Dune? Am I supposed to be thinking about just tomorrow, or a week? . . . This horrible storm upsetting everything . . . Since you've been painting that awful girl, of course she's told everyone about the others, the ones of me. Old Mr Evans leered at me today.'

'Why not?' Jim said. 'You're pretty enough to leer at . . . but I don't think JoAnn would break a promise.'

Barbara sniffed. She was wearing her heavy muskrat coat and her blonde hair shone prettily.

He said, 'Listen. Suppose we give up any idea of leaving Monomoy. Of my becoming a big corporation lawyer or a U.S. senator. Suppose we live our lives here, thinking about each day just as if it were for ever, not a stepping-stone to some other, better time.'

'You promised,' she said, her voice full of resentment. 'You promised I wouldn't have to live in this place for long. I can't wear any decent clothes. The richer the people are here the less they seem to care about food or clothes, or, or *anything* sensible.

. . . Why don't you paint landscapes or those modern paintings that don't look like anything?'

He got up, went through to the adjoining room and for a moment stood quiet in the dark, listening to the children's even breathing. Then he went back, undressed, and climbed quickly into his bed. He closed his eyes. Soon, behind his eyelids, he saw bright colours on a palette. He stared at them, thinking – for the shadows under the chin, he should use a deeper blue than he had been. A reddish tinge should come through the flesh.

He opened his eyes, saw his wife dipping into a pot of cream to apply a mask to her face, her hair already under a net. He said, 'Don't put any of that damned stuff on your face, and come here – into my bed.'

She cried, 'Oh! I forgot it was Saturday.'

'So did I,' he said. 'And from now on I'm not going to care either. And in the future no curlers in your hair at night. It's like making love to a porcupine. And as soon as we get home we're going to get a double bed.'

'A double bed! What will people think?'

'I don't give a damn. Hurry up, honey. It's cold in here without you.'

George Zanakis could not sleep. Sometimes the windows shook, and the faint, distant throb of dance music filtered clearly into the dark, cold room. The unheard wind and the silent break and crash of the sea on the outer beach filled George's mind.

Mr Jackson, his room-mate, an old retired grocer, snored with a thin, whistling sound. An old man's snore, George thought with disgust. Just because I'm seventy-six, why do they want to put me in with an old crock of . . .? Hell, about seventy-six. Not much longer to live, for either of them. What chance did 70-year-olds have on the Great Dune in the worst blizzard of the century, perhaps of all time?

They should pay more attention to artists here. Not Monomoy – the world. *Ars longa, vita brevis.* He wished he could regain Jim Carpenter's simple, virginal ecstasy in painting nudes. Later, he would realize that he must paint the nude either 'through the keyhole' or as a commentator . . . But what about Rubens? Perhaps it was possible to hold, for life, a dedicated enthusiasm for flesh, tone, texture, and human beauty.

The horseshoe crabs would come into their own *now*, all right, all right! *Now* they'd see who was going to get the last, big laugh! A few hundred human beings huddled on the Great Dune, cold,

251

starving, one by one dying from exposure, frostbite, starvation
. . . and, under the sea, those goddam horseshoe crabs, like tanks,
smug, armoured, safe. More than safe. Happy! Happy, while the
sea ate into the sand, and thousands drowned. All these people –
the nude flesh tones, the human beauty, the eye to see, the hand
to make – all food for goddam, prehistoric *things*.

'I don't want to hand over to the crabs!'

'Eh? Ah! Mm?' Mr Jackson half awoke, cried out, and returned to his snoring.

Maybe they'd all have to get out tomorrow. Where were his
paints, his chalks, charcoal, the big sketch pad? All downstairs.
Suppose the tide came up into the Longships basement right
now? Hell, got to try to get some sleep, and stop worrying.

JoAnn Griffiths moved her pelvis and asked, 'There, is that
better?' He didn't answer, but kept on pushing, groaning like a
whale. He weighed a ton and he was making her sore. Two hours
now, for heaven's sake. The electric flashlight on the dressing
table cast a thin light on his clothes stacked neatly over the
back of one chair, on hers thrown anyhow over another, on a
sort of glow in the mirror; on the key shining in the lock; and,
right above her, on his big face and popping eyes.

The poor guy would never make it while his thing was like a
little shrivelled-up beanpod. You'd think a fellow would have
found out *that* much by the time he was twenty, but they never
seemed to, especially when they'd had too much to drink, but
kept swearing and grunting and making excuses and trying to
order the thing to stand up and fight. But anyone knew you
couldn't order that thing to stand up and you couldn't order it
to lie down.

He rolled to one side and lay panting. After a time she heard
a low choking noise close to her ear. The poor bastard was crying.
She put her arm round him, and said, 'Don't worry. I don't
mind.'

He pushed her away and got out of bed. She watched him
dress, then fumble in his trouser pocket, find a pack of cigarettes.
'I'd like one, too,' she said reproachfully, 'unless you have any
gum.'

'Sorry,' he said, and gave her a cigarette. She curled up her
feet and legs. It was goddam cold in bed tonight, without a man.

'You don't really like it, do you?' she asked suddenly.

He sat up jerkily. 'Like it! I love it . . . forty, fifty women . . .'
In the vague light she saw his shoulders slump. 'No, I don't.'

'Maybe you're queer, and don't know it,' she said equably. 'I've heard . . .'

He was up from the chair, leaning over the bed. 'Shut up!' he snarled. 'You accuse me of that and . . . I'll strangle you!'

'I was only saying . . .' she began, aggrieved.

'Shut up! I hate them. Damn filthy, degenerate . . . mincing up and down Commercial Street in Provincetown just as though they were ordinary people . . . manicured hands . . . I saw one with painted toenails once . . . perfumed . . . wiggling their asses . . . the way they speak. They make me sick to my stomach . . . I tell you, in summer I go up to Provincetown two, three nights a week, and sit in bars and sweat, and sweat, thinking what I'd do if could get my hands on one of them . . . Jesus, I'd . . . I'd . . . One day I will, I know it, and then . . .'

John Remington pushed down the heavy glove and peered again at the watch dial: 1 : 35. Officially, high tide had passed a minute ago. It was hard to tell just what the level had been, but it had definitely been above the daytime high – a foot or eighteen inches higher. The sea made a continuous roar, reverberating inside his head. The hulk of the *Goya* gave out its metallic bass rumble under the impact of the waves.

He was standing in the old Boat House, peering down at the ocean through the small back window. The two sentries huddled together on a bench close by, one holding a heavy flashlight. John thought they had taken advantage of his long visit to go to sleep . . .

They ought to have had more old-fashioned dances, the kind where you held your girl close. She was a wonderful dancer. You forgot the wind and the cold, remembering. It was a long, long time since he'd felt like that – not since the early days with Janet, and for a short time after they were married. It made him think of her breasts, and then of his children. He had the photos of them in his wallet, and used to look at them every day. Not once since this storm came. They were safer where they were . . . The twist was plain indecent, and Lynn loved it, laughing at him all the time, her eyes sparkling, thrusting out her body. There'd only been one waltz, and in that suddenly she was demure, almost shy. When his arm tightened and his hand moved slowly across her back, she hung her head just as though no man had ever touched her before.

The side door opened and two men burst in on a flurry of

253

wind and snow. 'Here we are,' one cried. 'Come to watch the sea for Old Salt Horse.'

Their flashlight played along the wall. The two dozing sentries started up. The flashlight found John's face. 'Who . . .? It's the Chief!' the voice cried. 'I didn't know you were here.'

'I guess not,' John said. That was Walsh, one of the enginemen, and E 4. He would have expected Charlie Tyson, the other new sentry, to be in that mood, but Walsh was usually pleasant, reliable, and good-tempered. Well, the storm had gone on long enough to fray anyone's nerves.

Behind the two outgoing sentries he walked up to the station. As soon as they pushed open the door, John heard the angry voices from the mess deck: 'Jesus, you took two, not three . . .' 'You said . . .' 'I saw . . .' 'You didn't . . .' A chair scraped. 'You lying son of a bitch!'

John closed the outer door carefully, and waited, listening for McGill or Randall or Croce or Carstairs to use his authority.

'I'll beat your fucking brains out!' That was Santos.

'You try it, just you try it!' That was Carswell. Neither of them was normally a troublemaker.

John started up the stairs with an even, heavy tread. By the time he reached the mess-deck Carswell and Santos were standing apart, breathing deeply, but no one had thrown a punch. Three or four other seamen were there, and cards covered the table. Randall, the B.M. 2, was present but had done nothing to calm or control the men.

He paused at the end of the room, in a complete silence, and said, 'You're making too much noise. Keep it down.'

He went on up the stairs. 'Oh, Chief!' Randall called after him, but he answered, 'I'll be back in a minute,' and kept going. Perhaps it had been a mistake to cancel Lights Out, and keep the mess deck open twenty-four hours a day; but in these conditions, with so many men coming on and off duty at all hours what else could he do? Two men on watch at the Old Boat House, one in the operations room here, a snow-shovelling squad every four hours, day and night, or the steps would become hopelessly buried . . .

Seaman Carroll, in the ops room, was slumped in a chair, his head on the table. 'Wake up!' John said angrily. 'Do you want to be court-martialled?' The man stood up, bleary-eyed, and began to follow John around.

'Anything to report?' John asked.

The man hesitated. 'No, Chief.'

254

John looked at the barograph: 29·20 and steady. The anemometer: 31 knots, NNE, steady. He moved over to the radar screen.

He turned to the watch and spoke sharply, 'Here, the scanner's not turning.'

The watchman said, 'She was just now.'

John glowered at him. Carroll was a young, Tyson-like fellow. Now he wouldn't meet his eye. John said, 'How long has this scanner been on the blink? Come on – the truth.'

'Nearly two hours,' Carroll raised his head. 'I reported it just after I came on watch.'

'Who to, the First?'

'No, the Second.'

That was Randall. What the hell was going on here? Why should the kid not tell the truth straight out?

John went downstairs. As he entered the mess deck Randall was speaking: 'O.K., let's get going, and fix that radar, now the wind's died a bit.'

Seaman Harrington said distinctly, 'Like shit, we will.'

John forced himself to walk steadily and speak calmly. 'Have you given Harrington an order to go with you, Randall?'

'Well, not exactly, Chief, I mean, I was . . .'

'Give him the order now. Him and Carswell.'

The cards still littered the table, and the room smelled of sweat and something else, something sharp and aromatic.

Harrington said, 'What the fuck's the use of putting the fucking thing right? There isn't a fucking ship at sea within two hundred fucking miles.'

'Give him the order, Randall,' John said.

Harrington's voice rose. 'You think I'm going out to climb that fucking ladder, in this? The scanner's clogged with snow. Unclogging it's no fucking use, it'll just clog again.'

John could name the smell now. Whisky. Harrington was an unstable man at the best of times, and really dangerous when he was drunk. Better not let him climb that ladder in this state.

Harrington thrust his face across the table, 'Go fuck yourself!'

John reached out with his left hand, grabbed Harrington by the collar and pulled viciously, simultaneously punching hard with his right. Blood burst over the table from Harrington's shattered nose. John drew back his right fist again, and smashed it to the point of Harrington's jaw.

A man muttered, 'Jesus, Chief, you'll kill him.'

255

John released his grip and Harrington crashed heavily across the spattered table.

Randall muttered, 'I've been trying to get them to go out for two hours, Chief . . . didn't want to wake McGill . . . they've been in a bad mood . . . the storm's getting them down.'

'Don't make excuses,' John blared. 'What in hell do you think you have that B.M. 2 rating for? You're no damned good! I'll see that you get busted right back where you belong . . . This man's drunk. Lock him in his room. I'll deal with him when he's sober. Find his whisky. Pour it down the sink. Signal Group that our radar's been out since, whenever the time was, reason – disciplinary breakdown, the matter is being dealt with . . . Santos!'

'Chief?'

'Carswell!'

'Yes, Chief.'

'Wake Dropp. All put on foul-weather gear, and we'll go and fix that radar.'

'Aye, aye, Chief.'

He stared round the room. He had won, but suddenly he could not recognize in these men his comrades of the United States Coast Guard. If they were obeying, it was because he had struck down Harrington, not because they understood and agreed with the reasons for his actions, still less through any devotion to ideals of duty.

Captain Lacoma lay on his bed, on his back, his hands folded on his stomach. If he were to die in bed, in his sleep, which would be the best gift any human being could ask from God, then they would find him like this any morning, and there would be little for the women to do in arranging his body.

He was perhaps over-occupied with death. It was a national vice, foreigners had told him. Vice or virtue? When one encountered a man such as Millan Astray crying out *Viva la muerte!* one was certainly in the presence of an abnormality; but a recognition of death as an inevitable and climactic experience, therefore to be met with all possible grace and awareness – that surely was not a failing in a people or in an individual? The Americans, for instance . . .

One must keep constantly aware that such phrases were to be used with great caution. There were people in this place as aware of death as any Spaniard; and Spaniards as eager for a hedonistic life as any American . . . It had been interesting to detect

256

them, of each kind; to observe and learn; to study motives showing like stones under the torrent of events. It was particularly interesting, now, to wonder whether the people here realized, as a mass, that death was very close for them and for their town. The state of the tide, the extreme severity of the winds, and the geographical formation of the peninsula made it probable that the ocean would overwhelm Monomoy, as it had overwhelmed others of these North American sandspits – in the great hurricane of 1938, for example. Yet no one mentioned the possibility and certainly there was no overt preparing of souls for doom. Their behaviour might be a concerted plan, an agreement to defy death to the end by refusing to grant its existence. Perhaps – but he did not think so. It was, more probably, an ostrich-like refusal to contemplate the unpleasant. He would like to debate the subject with the Mayor, the intellectual yet attractive schoolteacher, and perhaps the Coast Guard Captain. Those three would have different opinions. He would like to put to them a question which had always been much in his own mind, and in the minds of philosophers. It was a question which under normal circumstances had to be theoretical, in that no one had the power to enforce whatever decision was reached. But here and now that was not the case. For himself, at least, the question could suddenly become practical.

The question was: Supposing you could save humanity from destruction, would you do it? That, in turn, obviously reduced to the question, Is mankind worth saving? Or, in religious terms, What has mankind done to earn salvation, grace, mercy? Equally obviously, the question here applied only to Monomoy, not to mankind. Yet, to those living here, and trapped here, Monomoy was mankind. Certainly one could consider the two as equivalent when debating the problem.

Personal inclination and personal involvement should not be considered. Any suggestion that Man should be saved because *I* am man, and I am frightened – that would be degrading. Man could know little enough of God, in spite of the Church's trumpeted certainties, but it was inconceivable that God should be an opportunist, that He should encourage a lack of dignity in his ultimate creation, the only being to whom He had given the power to comprehend Himself.

It would be a most interesting and instructive discussion. A pity, indeed, that were it to end with a negative verdict, which really seemed the more proper one on brief study (how much

257

jealousy, greed, strife, covetousness!) . . . there would be no one to read the record, no one to profit from the lesson.

Outside the basement door the generator truck throbbed steadily. A fire truck stood idle beside it, waiting for dawn and its next stint of pumping water up to the roof tank. The snow whirled around them both, and after listening a moment longer, Nelson Pryor turned back inside the building and closed the door.

Just inside the door, the fireman in charge of the generator slept on a pallet, and that set up on blocks of wood eighteen inches above the floor. A big shovel lay beside the pallet, so that he could dig out to the generator if need be. Beside the shovel there was a pair of rubber boots, for the basement was flooded to a depth of six inches.

Nelson splashed across the room, shining his flashlight right and left. They'd raised Jim Carpenter's huge painting out of danger, also all the pots, brushes and other materials. The furnace was out – perhaps for ever now. The caretaker snored on a couch at the head of the stairs.

Three thirty – just about high tide here on the Longships Bay side: two hours after high tide on the ocean side. No word from Remington, so it must have passed without special danger.

The next high tide, on the outside, would be a little after two o'clock in the afternoon. As soon as it was light he'd go up with Walter and take a look; and then he'd have to make up his mind. He, Nelson Pryor. Well, Jim and Walter would take their share of the load, and you couldn't have said that of Jim once. As for Walter . . . Walter gave his opinion, and that was that. Walter didn't hold with the idea that the Selectmen were, or ever could be, a collective body. They were just three separate men.

Damn it, this was the day he should have met the chairman of the Nantucket Selectmen, at four o'clock, to discuss the oyster war. And he remembered making a note, after that near riot at the Mercer Company, to ask old Warren Mercer just what he had against Gazza's union. And Lynn Garland's bunch had scheduled an organization meeting at the high school today, to get some kind of Pro-Park Association off the ground. It should have been a busy, useful day. Instead, what do we get? The end of the world.

That would be a bad time, when John Remington reported

how the tide was coming and they sat down to make up their minds. He must keep a good grip on his common sense . . . Suppose the word was definitely no danger this tide – then, O.K., no action. Suppose it was definitely yes, the sea's coming over – then, O.K., everybody up on the Great Dune. Now suppose it's only maybe – maybe yes, maybe no. Suppose the Selectmen guess wrong. An optimistic bad guess gets everyone swept away to death; a pessimistic bad guess makes the people spend a bad two or three hours on the dune. Looked at that way, there was no real choice. If in doubt – up on the dune. Several people would die up there. Daisy Crampton, for instance. Old Mr Sandhaus. The new Adams baby, born yesterday, that weighed hardly three pounds and was very weak. Two or three more, for sure. So, sending them up on the dune when he wasn't absolutely *sure* was like taking Daisy and the baby and the rest and shooting them in the back of the head . . .

Headlights swept into his eyes and swung away. He found he had reached the lobby, and a snowplough was circling the driveway. The ploughed area grew smaller every day. The huge, roaring plough made no sound that could penetrate the hotel.

What he needed, by God, was a drink, and, by God, he knew where to find one. Monomoy slept, the caretaker on his couch, the fireman on his pallet, the duty patrolman in an overstuffed chair here in the lobby. The snowplough operators were awake because it kept snowing, and he was awake because he was the First Selectman . . . poking his nose into everything . . . helping the caretaker to rescue Jim's naked gal . . . she didn't look much like JoAnn in the face, maybe as accurate as hell in the bubs and down in the crotch, but he wouldn't know. Perhaps he should, as First Selectman. The First Selectman should see everything.

Well, he'd seen plenty, just tonight . . . Like Frank Damato at the end of an upstairs passage, pleading with that punk of a son, the son sullen, contemptuous . . . The Reverend Day coming in out of the night after a walk, he said, covered with snow, and Florence Day anxiously waiting, why *so* anxious? . . . Elliott King alone in front of a fire in the small empty card room, with red eyes. Had clapped him on the back and told him to go to bed: 'Man, you deserve a rest. You've done marvels.' He had, too, working like a horse all day out there in the Gap with the Coast Guardsmen and George Lathrop's fellows . . . The Spanish captain, just walking around, the same as himself – and he'd felt quite put out, as though anyone else had the right to walk the quarterdeck. But that's what the captain had been doing, only he stood aside, with a deep, polite bow as Nelson passed. He was a captain, but in Monomoy Nelson was the admiral, and the captain acknowledged it; a nutty admiral, of course . . . Would have liked to find Seaman Apprentice Charles Tyson, and talk sensibly with him, man to man, but Tyson was up at the station. Mary tearful . . .

They had all gone long since, leaving him alone on the deck of his vessel. He needed a drink, and now felt fully entitled to one. Two short, sharp snorts and then to bed, with the alarm set for six o'clock.

He stopped outside the Selectmen's office, slipped his key into the lock, and walked in, flashing the light.

He saw the dark shape a moment before he realized that it was a man's back, and a full second before he realized, as the man turned round, what he was doing. The wall safe gaped open and the man's hand was inside, but coming out. It kept coming, a wad of bills clenched tight in it, and the head kept turning to face the beam of the flashlight.

'Walter,' Nelson said, 'Walter . . .'

An intense cold hurt his chest, and the gall rose vomitlike in his throat. He reached for the light switch. But the light would show, and someone might see it, and come in. He pushed the door shut behind him.

The rigid beam made a pale bull's-eye of Walter's right eye. 'Turn that thing off,' he said.

Nelson clicked the switch. It was dark, no light coming in from anywhere, the moon obscured and snow high above the windows.

Nelson recovered his equilibrium. 'You were checking the cash, eh, Walter?'

'No. I was taking money. Stealing money.'

'But . . . Walter . . .' The words choked him again, so that he could not bring anything out for a long space. Then, 'I don't believe it. I just don't believe it.'

The iron voice was rusty and thin, 'She doesn't die, Nelson. She goes on and on and on . . . I had a heart attack.'

'But . . .'

'Suppose I go first.' In the dark the big hand suddenly took Nelson's by the wrist, and held, the skin of the palm hard as ship's oak, abrasive as dry rope. 'I spent hours thinking. I should have let the pillow lie where they put it. Or I should put it there myself. Then she'd go quietly, no more hurt, and I shall be going soon, too. If she ever knew, she'd understand. Any time these forty years, she'd rather I stabbed her than see me begging.

Nelson put his hand over the other's. 'Walter, what do you mean, begging? You've saved plenty. It's not my business, and you've never spoken . . . but, well, I know. There was once a question of money, to save me, and Daisy let it slip that you had several thousand.'

Walter said, 'Two, three nights ago, I can't remember, they robbed me. No, don't talk about it. I don't aim to tell Damato nor no one else. They took everything. I been near out of my mind since.'

Nelson said carefully, 'Suppose we put on the light now, and have a drink, eh? You'd like a drink?'

'All right.'

'Let me put this money back first, and close the safe door . . . and then find my bottle . . . and a couple of glasses . . . There! Down the hatch, Walter. I'd say all we have to do is find some income-producing work for you, right?'

'I have to look after Daisy. Can't take no job.'

'Work inside the house you could, eh? You're a great carpenter, The Gift Shop sells a lot of wooden dory models, rope knick-knacks . . .'

'I'd never earn enough to pay for what Daisy has to have.'

'Well, that's as may be. No, no, the doctor will charge you his regular fee, but suppose Elliott or Harold, or even the bank, was to lend you . . .'

'I've never owed a penny in my life. Not a red cent.' The voice was old and hoarse and tired, obstinate now rather than determined.

'What about Daisy? She had an account at the store, and sometimes had to let it run, sometimes for two or three months. That's the same as borrowing. Let Daisy borrow the money . . .'

He took a small drink of the whisky. This was going to be a long course, and he'd have to run it with painful care, and very slowly, or the old skipper would turn his face to the wall. It was bad to lose absolute trust in anyone, or anything. When it was yourself . . . well, Walter might make up his mind to die. He was an old-line Yankee, and stubborn enough to be able to do it.

So here you are, Nelson Pryor, four o'clock in the morning, trying to help a guy who's a better man than you are, and always has been; and trying to control the fate of all the people on this sandpit thrust out from the land into the sea and the night. You don't know any answers. If there's a good thing and a bad thing to be done, you do the bad one. Your head's full of cottonwool or whisky, sometimes both. Why in hell don't you just lie down and quit? Or dance and sing 'Sweet Adeline'?

'Walter . . . listen, we're with you. All of us. We've all had bad times ourselves, and . . .'

CHAPTER TEN

SUNDAY

Judica me, Deus, et discerne causam meam de gente non sancta: ab homine iniquo, et doloso erue me.

Father Bradford's voice was high and thin, and, to Frank Damato, always sounded artificial – and never more so than when speaking Latin.

He read the translation in his prayer book: *Judge me, O God, and distinquish my cause from the nation that is not holy.*

What nation? Or did it mean non-Catholic people? Like Protestants, Jews, and heathens? Father Bradford sounded funnier than ever this morning celebrating the Holy Mass in the great ballroom, where there were no holy images for Frank to fix his eyes and toughts on. Maria and the four girls were with him, every one of them a distraction of his attention from Jesus.

. . . mea culpa, mea culpa, mea maxima culpa. Ideo precor beatam Mariam . . .

What had made that noise in the night? When would they be able to bury the poor man lying so stiff in the crypt of the Old Church, and smelling of the sea? Nelson Pryor looked bad when Father Bradford told him, late last night, about Betty and young Tyson. The Father should have waited. Maybe he should have sent the kids to Reverend Day. If Nelson got mad against Catholics, he could easily turn him, Frank, out of his job.

Aufer a nobis, quaesumus, Domine, iniquitates nostras: ut ad Sancta sanctorum puris mereamur mentibus introire . . .

Why couldn't everyone live in peace and never quarrel? Why wasn't his son, his only son, Chris, kneeling at his side?

Humilium Deus protector et amator, qui famulam tuam Mariam Bernardom Immaculatae Virginis Mariae apparitione . . .

St Marie Bernadette . . . So the world hadn't come to an end just yet. The days of the holy saints kept coming round, storm or no storm. But tomorrow?

Derelinquat impius viam suam . . .

The dance last night had been so popular there was talk of doing it again tonight. Better put two or three extra patrolmen on duty. Everyone was on edge. The punks were getting restless.

263

Jesus, he'd like to beat their brains out, stand them against a wall and give them half an hour with a rubber club. *Forgive me, Holy Name, forgive me! And Christ!* that coloured girl was trying to marry Robert Handforth.

Father Bradford looked tired. He'd be a cardinal before he was through. Then Frank Damato could go and see him in Boston and say, 'Hi, Your Eminence,' and kneel and kiss his ring. A priest called Bradford couldn't help becoming a cardinal . . . Half a dozen more families had come into the Longships about midnight, driven out of houses along the bay side of Commerce Street by the tide coming into their downstairs rooms. They were cold, and exhausted from struggling through snowdrifts ten feet deep just to reach Commerce Street. Only twenty yards they'd had to go, or thirty at the most, but some of them said they'd hardly made it. Perhaps some others hadn't. Who would ever know?

Munda cor meum ac labia mea, omnipotens Deus . . .

Harold Morgan looked disgustedly at the food on his plate. Canned ravioli, for breakfast. At his age! Things must be bad.

'What's it like downstairs?' he asked. 'Is everyone nervous? Any panic?'

'It's low tide,' Charlotte said. 'They'll start getting nervous again in two or three hours. *I'm* going to start packing your suitcase right after breakfast, in case . . . We don't want to leave behind any of our pills or that list of your bonds and securities.'

Ravioli for breakfast! Thank God the bread was real old-fashioned bread, not compressed cottonwool. Mrs Handforth's bread, baked under her personal supervision. What the heck was the matter with women nowadays, that no one except the old lady seemed to know how to make bread? TV dinners, and everything quick frozen, dehydrated, and prepacked.

'Can you bake bread?' he asked Charlotte suddenly.

'Why, Harold, of course! And beaten bread, corn muffins, French rolls, croissants, everything. I think it's a woman's duty to learn how to cook properly.'

She moved gracefully about the room, reaching up to dust the top of the wardrobe, bending down to rearrange a chair cushion. She made him feel hungry. He *was* hungry, anyway, for good food, and warmth, and proper light, but looking at her transformed the need so that he wanted to gaze on her bosom.

'Finished?' she asked, bending over him.

He nodded, speechless.

She put the tray on top of the dressing table, and sighed. 'That's the last meal I'll be serving you, here in your room.'

'Yes,' he said. 'And I could have eaten downstairs yesterday and the day before. I'm quite fit again . . . thanks to you . . . your care . . .' He finished mumbling indistinctly.

Her eyes gleamed large and wet. 'It's a privilege.'

He swung his feet out of the bed. His legs looked lousy, thin and white where the pants legs of the pyjamas rode up. Well, a man couldn't be young all his life. He sat down in the chair beside the bed while she began to tug at the sheets. There was her fanny, pink wool stretched tight across it, looking like a ripe peach.

He closed his eyes, and reasoned with himself. *Now* she said, Oh, Harold, and Yes, Harold, but soon enough it would be Do this, and Clean that, and Where have you been? and You are not to drink with those dreadful men at the tavern. They never let you be. A MAN IS ENTITLED TO WEAR A PAIR OF OLD SNEAKERS ROUND HIS OWN HOUSE ANY TIME HE CHOOSES TO.

It was amazing that she had not heard. He opened his eyes. She was leaning far over the bed, her back to him. He felt his legs jerk, and he was up. In a couple of steps he was beside her, his arm around her, one hand cupping her breast, the other under her chin, turning her face.

'Why, Harold,' she said softly.

The breast sent mounting tremors of lust down his body. With a quick heave he tried to turn her on to her back on the bed. She allowed him to succeed, and there she lay, on her back, legs spread, but her hands held him off.

She said, 'Harold . . . please! I'm not that kind of a woman . . . I don't think you held so low an opinion of me.' The tears were forming again in her eyes. 'I . . . respected you . . . I . . .'

His lust collapsed. He slipped slowly to his knees. 'Charlotte . . . will . . . will . . .' Three times he tried to stop the words coming out, but they would not be stayed, 'Charlotte,' he said at last, 'will you marry me?'

She sprang off the bed, pulling him to his feet. 'Harold! Darling! I didn't dare to hope. I've loved you since the first time I saw you . . .'

'Will you? For God's sake,' he cried, 'will you?'

'Oh, yes, yes! As soon as the storm's over!'

She held out her arms. 'Kiss me, Harold . . . then I must fly and tell . . . oh, everyone. I'm so happy, I can't *tell* you, with someone to look after again, someone I love and respect!' Her

265

lips were warm and wet, and full of promise. Harold thought, Well, it won't be long now; just as soon as the ring's on her finger and the words have been spoken. He could wait; if he were given the chance.

John Remington tapped the charge sheet with the end of his pencil. 'You've heard the evidence. Do you have anything to say?'

Seaman Harrington stood bolt upright in dress blues, staring woodenly at the back wall above John's head. Boatswain's Mate McGill stood, as rigid, at Harrington's side. Harrington's eyes were bloodshot and his nose a deep, sullen purple. 'No, Chief,' he said.

John said, 'You know this charge could easily have been a different one, that could have put you away for seven years?'

'Yes, Chief . . . I appreciate it.'

He was a good man except when he drank; and that was too often. Where had he got the whisky? What was the use of keeping a man in the service who couldn't hold his liquor? But what did he want for the Coast Guard, then – a bunch of angels?

Harrington was eager to be given his punishment and get out of there.

John said, 'Stand easy! Listen . . .' The two men relaxed their stiff pose. Harrington's gaze wandered for a moment to John's face, then drifted away again.

John said, 'I know the storm has got you down. I know it feels bad, shut up inside here for days on end. I know the ordinary routines get to seem stupid when there are no ships at sea, no fishermen on the banks, nothing happening that concerns the Coast Guard. But the same applies to the civilians. They are shut up inside the hotel, or their houses, just as we are inside the station here. They are cooped up, too, wondering when it's going to end, seeing the same faces hour after hour, day after day, with no respite and no change. They have nothing to do either, and they can do just that if they want to. They can let everything go to hell, if they want to. We can't because those civilians pay our wages, and in return they rely on us for certain things . . . to do our job even when it's dangerous . . . even when it's boring. Do you understand, Harrington?'

'Yes, Chief,' the seaman mumbled. He couldn't speak clearly because of his swollen lips.

'What it boils down to is that the civilians *rely* on us. Period. Come hell or high water, the Coast Guard up there is doing its job and will go on doing it. Come hell or high water, eh? Those aren't just words any more, eh, they mean exactly what they say now. Do you understand?'

'Yes, Chief,' Harrington mumbled again, his discomfort by now obvious. He was a man who suffered far more from words than blows.

John said, 'You did your best, last night, to destroy that image of reliability. Suppose there was a ship out there, drifting down wind, sinking. Suppose there were men, drowning, we might have got to. We would have betrayed the trust put in us. We would have betrayed our uniform.'

'Jesus, Chief, I didn't mean . . . I just got drunk.'

'Right. And a drunken man is not reliable. Particularly you. Will you remember? Attention! Thirty days loss of privileges, thirty days extra duties, fined fifty dollars. Dismiss . . . Wait here, McGill.'

After the door had closed behind the seaman, John said, 'Now I'm going to tell Randall that I'm recommending he be broken back to seaman. He was the real cause of the trouble last night. If he hadn't been there, some of the other men might have acted.'

McGill said, 'He came and woke me up, you know. The same stuff, about everyone being down on him, never been given a chance, never given credit for his good work.'

'Damn snivelling bastard. Send for him and I'll give him the works.'

When Dorothy King returned to her room after breakfast, she found her husband sitting on the edge of his bed. He had not been in all night. He was dressed, but unshaven. With his burly shoulders slumped, the big hands resting limp on his knees, his skin dark with the blue tinge of the uncut beard, he looked like a lumberjack resting after a night on the town.

She closed the door carefully. 'I've been looking for you,' she said. 'I think it's time we talked.'

'I heard,' he said. 'I was in the card room all night. Wondering.'

'What, Elliott?'

'Whether I ought to do away with myself.'

Dorothy considered. It would be a solution, yes, but to what problem? She had a problem herself. For instance, that man who had made love to her so often – what was his name? – he was not a solution to anything, only a statement of the problem, or part of it; yet she did not feel like committing suicide.

She said, 'We might go away. Start again, somewhere else.'

He said, 'That wouldn't help . . . I can't be what I was, any more, and I don't know what I am, who I am . . . well, I suppose I know, but I can't take it. I can't take it here, and I couldn't take it anywhere else.'

'What is it, Elliott?'

'I can't tell you . . . JoAnn knows. I tried to make love to her but couldn't. Same as with you.'

He was so changed in manner that, except for the clothes, she would hardly have recognized him. The man sitting on the edge of the bed was real, for the first time since she had met him. If you spoke to him, *he* answered.

She said, 'I see.' She saw nothing, except that the root of Elliot's trouble was sexual, which she had known from the beginning.

He said, 'It's was the worst time I've ever had.'

She wondered if the sexual need which had overwhelmed her a week ago would ever return upon her. It was a dark place in her memory, moist, red, hairy, and smelling of feral heat. It was, at this moment, repulsive and terrifying. Surely it was not physical, but mental, need that had driven her to that place? Surely she had needed only to force the reality of her marriage into the open, for both herself and others to see and accept?

She said carefully, 'I don't think I'll ever do . . . what I did, again, Elliott. I can't promise, but I don't think so . . . Do you think you could go to a doctor now?

He had refused, years ago, when she had asked him to go. He had refused with a blistering, febrile anger that had not left him for weeks, and for years had provided him with an excuse to avoid sexual relations with her.

'Not an ordinary doctor,' he said. 'It would have to be a psychiatrist . . . You can have a divorce.'

She said, 'Well, not now, thank you . . . Elliott, we might as well be newly met, you know, because we're different people. I think we'd better wait and see. After all, we've got to keep trying with what we've got, what we are.'

He stood up slowly, and went to the mirror and began to fasten his tie. 'All right,' he said, 'all right . . . Help me with this tie, Dotty. My hands are trembling.'

Mrs Handforth, standing in the bare vault of that Old Church, recited the responses without hearing what she or the Reverend Mr Day were saying. The congregation, thirty strong, were huddled round the foot of the altar steps. The cold wind howled through invisable cracks and Mr Day had urged the men to keep on their hats.

Now they were singing: *Eternal Father, strong to save, whose arm hath stilled the restless wave* . . .

It would not, but suppose it did. Then that girl might survive, and be Mrs Monomoy Handfórth, and give birth to children who would also be Handforths.

At noon Lynn Garland pinned up notices on the main notice board and in each main corridor. The notices read:

> *This afternoon's high tide (due at 2:08 p.m.) is not expected to breach the Gap. Everyone should, however, remain ready to evacuate the Longships Hotel at five minutes' notice.*
>
> *There will be a special Town Meeting at 3:00 p.m. in the Grand Ballroom.*
>
> (*sd*)
> *J. Carpenter*

The police undertook to pass the message through the town, as best they could. In the hotel there was some singing, shouting, and fist fights, which soon died away.

Jim Carpenter added the column of figures once more, and put down his pencil: 109 male, 117 female – correct. He picked up his notebook and checked carefully down the long list of notes. Each one had been ticked off, except the last. He turned his head. 'Lynn, has George Lathrop sent any message about the new road to the top of the dune?'

'Not yet,' she answered. 'He didn't think he'd know until four or five o'clock.'

Jim left the notebook on his table, face up. If the sea came through the Gap, it would pour first down Boat Street. It was therefore necessary to try to clear another path to the dune-top. Whether there would be time to use it, for those not already on the dune when the sea breached through, that was another question.

Not *when* the sea breaches, Jim corrected himself obstinately – *if*.

Frank Damato came in, after a punctilious knock. 'I think we got everybody told,' he said. 'What with going down the streets

269

on skis, and people yelling to each other out of windows . . .
But jeez, Jim, we can't do that at night.'

'Sure, sure,' Jim said, 'we know. There'll be an announcement
about the night tide at the Town Meeting.'

Frank Damato lit a cigar. 'Heard about Harold Morgan and
Mrs Quimby?'

'Who hasn't!'

Damato said, 'What's the town going to do with Monomoy
House, when they get it?'

'Monomoy House? What are you talking about?'

'Haven't you heard? I guess Nelson's been too busy to
tell you. Mrs Handforth told him, after church. She's going
to leave Monomoy House and the land on North Point to the
town.'

Jim said impatiently, 'It must be a rumour. She can't do that.
She only has the lifetime use of it, unless Robert predeceases
her. You must have heard wrong or she's gone crazy.'

Frank looked aggrieved. 'Nelson told me. Said she was pale –
but she was making perfect sense. Pete Worrell knocked Jimmy
Watson cold in a fight this morning. Watson won't make a
charge, because he's frightened that Worrell's pals will beat
him up. It's going to get out of hand unless—'

'O.K., O.K.,' Jim said irritably. 'We're doing our best.'

The five men stood in the lee of the Old Boat House. A Coast
Guardsman inside the building peered out at them through the
small side window, the distortion of the old glass twisting his
face into a look of surprise and horror. The snow whirled thick
and endless around them.

John Remington shouted in Nelson Pryor's ear, 'Ten past
two, Nelson.'

The First Selectman nodded. 'About a foot below the
top.'

The shape of the beach had changed drastically in the past
two days. There used to be a steep slope. Now there was the
long wall of the *Goya*'s hull on the south, and running down
along it a shallow slope of sand. Only the last five feet was steep.
The guided seas swept to this final slope, and reached out, and
dug sand from under it. The rhythmically spaced bigger waves
lapped the edge of the parking lot, where they stood.

Elliott King pointed south. 'Look along there. The blacktop's
underminded a couple of feet down there. Probably here,
too.

Nelson turned to Lathrop. 'Can we mix concrete up here and try to bind the Gap, George?'

"Fraid not, Nelson. The cement won't mix in this weather, in the open, and it would never get a chance to dry . . . even if we could get a cement mixer up here in time, and the cement.'

'The nearest mixer's under twenty feet of snow at the back of my yard,' Elliott said.

The five stared seaward. The snow poured down in coarse heavy flakes. The grey waves pounded on the sand beneath their feet. The air was full of the deep bell tone of the *Goya*. Sheets of spindrift blew diagonally across and up the beach. The whole outer wall of the Old Boat House was visible now. Spray and foam had washed away the snow which only yesterday had lain five feet deep on this side.

'We've got to move that ship,' Walter Crampton said.

'For Christ's sake, how?' Nelson cried in exasperation. 'We don't have any dynamite in town. We don't have a crane or anything else that can begin to make a dent in it, in time.'

'What's in her cargo?' George Lathrop asked.

'Mixed,' John Remington said. 'The captain saved his manifest, and showed me. Some printing machinery, chemicals, bananas, sugar, a bottling plant . . .'

Nelson said, 'How would it be if we tore down this Old Boat House, George, and used the timbers as a breastwork?'

George Lathrop said, 'It's on a cement base . . . solidly constructed . . . I reckon not, Nelson. If we leave it here, we have a 25-foot wall, well made, footed into cement across part of the Gap.'

'I've got to get back,' Nelson said. 'Elliott, you keep trying to put something solid in here, fill in the rest of the Gap and bind it, eh?'

'We'll do our best,' Elliott said.

The group split up and went their ways, John Remington up to his station, Nelson and Walter down Boat Street, Lathrop and King to a small group of men standing round a plough and a bulldozer at the far side of the parking lot.

Charlie Tyson sat on the edge of a table in the mess deck, his legs dangling. Everyone was here, every man on the station, except Harrington on watch in the operations room. Old Salt Horse was sounding off, speaking tough, like he was on *Wagon Train* or *Rifleman*.

271

'We don't know yet whether tonight's high tide is going to come over the top or not. But these past two or three days the closer the wind has been to north the higher the tide, with the winds the same speed. That's because of the *Goya*, I guess. The wind is north-east, veering toward east-nor'east, and my guess is we're going to be O.K. until tomorrow . . . This station stands on the edge of the Gap, and is certain to be undermined if the ocean breaks through. We have to think of that first . . . McGill, see that our secret files and code books are loaded on the 36-footer by five o'clock today. Also payrolls, personal history sheets, anything that is important to a man's future and is not duplicated in Boston or Washington.'

'Aye, aye, Chief,' the exec said. He looked grey and worried. McGill was a real square.

Salt Horse continued: 'Gardner, you're in charge of the 36-footer. See that she is ready for instant launching, from five o'clock. The crew to remain within hailing distance from then on, till further notice. Your job is to get the 36-footer afloat on my order, or as soon as it appears to you that the ocean is going to come through the Gap. Your task after that is to rescue people found floating, or in danger of drowning in houses, and to put them ashore here on the Great Dune.'

'O.K.,' Gardner said.

'I think the Selectman will have some fishing boats on the same job. They will be under your orders, of course, if you need to give them any. Your crew will be Ritchie, Tyson, and Lerroux.'

Me, Charlie thought with a start. His pulse began to beat faster. How would the ocean come through the Gap? In a goddam huge wave, fifty feet high, people like ants or mice whirling over and over in it . . . ?

Remington said, 'What's the report on the DUKW, Carstairs?'

Carstairs said, 'The head's cracked. No, we can't fix it here, and we don't have a spare engine to put in her.'

'O.K. . . . Bob, make her real tight, tarpaulin-covered, give her plenty of hawser and extra anchor chain and anchor her, for and aft, between the north end of Sachem Island and the fish pier. Do that as soon as we're through here.'

'O.K.,' Gardner said.

Remington went on yakking . . . about McGill's job, about food, water, reserve fuel for the 36-footer . . . about dragging the 22-footer up on the dune right away . . . about a kind of Coast Guard camp to be prepared five hundred feet north of the light, Randall in charge, Appel, Knighton, and Colonna to go out right now, start digging and put up a canvas roof.

Charlie's hand felt chilly. Where was Betty going to be in all this? There were married men here. What was Salt House going to do about their wives and kids?

The Chief said, 'As to Coast Guard dependents . . . you fellows are going to be on duty if the rush comes and won't be able to look after your wives and children. Dependents now in the Longships Hotel are to stay there, and I will see that the town provides some able-bodied men to help them move out if they are ordered to do so. Any other dependents now in houses in Monomoy may move into the station any time from now on. McGill, you'll arrange accommodation and food . . .'

Now he's going through most of it again. Charlie thought soberly, McGill in charge of the station, Gardner the 36-footer, and Randall the camp. The Chief's next words cut into his consciousness like a knife: 'Randall will transfer all arms and ammunition to the dune camp when the station is ordered evacuated . . . we may need them.'

It figures, Charlie thought. I thought once that handing out pistols would be real exciting; but now it's come and I sure as hell don't like it.

John Remington came last to Nelson Pryor's conference, a minute late. Lynn Garland, sitting at her desk in the corner, caught his eye and smiled. He nodded briefly, and she saw that he was very tired.

Nelson looked around, and Flo Monsey said, 'Everyone's here, Nelson.' Mrs Handforth's eyes seemed to be out of focus. She was wearing a large diamond brooch on the outside of her heavy coat. 'Nowhere else to put it,' she said vaguely.

Nelson Pryor tapped the table. 'Ladies and gentlemen . . . Chief, how's this tide going to be?'

John said, 'It doesn't start to make for another hour, so we still don't know. But if the wind stays toward the east my guess is that we'll be O.K. this time.'

Nelson said, 'The first question is, do we get everyone up on the dune now – tonight – or not? Anyone want to give us his advice?'

It was silent in the crowded room.

Nelson turned to Walter. 'Walter, then?'

Walter said, 'I say, no.'

273

'Jim?'

'I agree with Walter. Stay put, but have everything ready for an emergency move if conditions change. You have reliable men on watch, Chief?'

'Yes,' John answered shortly. Lynn smiled to herself. That was the sort of remark guaranteed to get under John's skin.

Nelson said, 'That's settled. I'll announce it at the Town Meeting . . . Any other points?'

Dr Burroughs said, 'Is there any chance of the Coast Guard evacuating a few severely ill cases, or people who have little chance of surviving on the dune, to the mainland?'

'No,' John said at once. 'The 36-footer might make the Vineyard, running straight before the sea, but I guess she'd be turned over half a dozen times on the way. Only very fit people, who are used to it and trained for it, would survive the battering and the throwing around. In any case, I'm keeping her here to pick up survivors and put them on the dune.'

Again, the tomblike silence descended. For Lynn the crowded, chilly room vanished. Grey waves drove like giant, moving walls out of the blizzard, the sea swirled, the sand was eaten away under her in great gulps. She stood, screaming, knee-deep, waist-deep. John Remington at her side tried to hold her upright, but the ocean was too strong even for him . . .

Walter said, 'I reckon we ought to put half a dozen of the best fishing boats on the same job. The crews should get aboard now. When the time comes, they can run for shelter behind Sachem Island, and then come back, looking.'

Again a long silence.

John said, 'Can some able-bodied men, or bigger teen-agers, be allotted to help Coast Guard dependents?'

Jim Carpenter said, 'We ought to prepare a message telling everyone to head for the dune at once, ready to send it to WCCD.'

Merrill Crosby said, 'We ought to send it to WCCD right now, and tell them to put it on the air when we say to. Or at a certain time, anyway, in case the radio breaks down, or they don't hear from us for any other reason.'

Lynn closed her eyes tight, and reopened them. *Or they don't hear from us.* She had written the words down on her note pad. Merrill Crosby, fire chief of Monomoy, husband and father and occasional beer drinker, had spoken them.

Mrs Handforth said, 'The Charter should be taken to a place of safety at once, lest it be overlooked in the rush later.'

Nelson tapped the table. 'One at a time, and we'll get everything settled. Or, at least, arranged. Chief, you first.'

As the special Town Meeting opened in the ballroom, Mary Pryor was sitting in the front row, twisting a handkerchief in her hands, Billy on her right and Betty on her left. The Selectmen sat on three hard, straight-backed chairs in the bar-room set for *The Iceman Cometh*. The big painting of a man and woman riding nude on a horseshoe crab hung askew on a side wall. The room was jammed.

As Nelson began to speak, Mary clutched her daughter's hand. Nelson looked stern and suddenly dignified, so that for the first time she felt in awe of him.

'Citizens of Monomoy . . . First, allow me to make a personal announcement. Mary and I are very happy to announce the engagement of our daughter Betty to Charlie Tyson, of the Coast Guard. They will be married as soon as this . . . this emergency is over. I can't ask the happy couple to stand up and take a bow, because Charlie is on duty, but—'

He motioned Betty to stand. Tears burned in Mary's eyes, and she began to weep wholeheartedly. Betty was waving like a newly elected beauty queen.

Nelson said 'Another couple, not quite so young, have an announcement to make, too, but Harold asked me to say he'd make it after the storm ends.' A roar of laughter and applause half drowned Nelson's last words. 'Meantime, we can all wish Harold and Charlotte good luck.' The laughter increased, then rapidly died away.

Nelson said, 'Now, to more serious matters . . .'

Mary wiped her eyes. Nelson was talking about the wind, the tide, the snow. Something about real danger. She ought to be listening, but she could only think of Betty. Nelson would tell her what to do, afterwards; but how could she have missed that knowingness about the corners of Betty's mouth? She had lost her innocence. It wasn't a child's face any more. She, her mother, ought to have noticed. And then what? Warned her against being a woman, against growing up? Hadn't the same change come to her mouth, after the evenings in the parked roadster with that boy, whom she hadn't told Nelson about, even yet?

Nelson finished his explanations and announcements and said, 'That's all . . . except, I think it would be proper to say a prayer, that we and our beloved town may be spared . . . Reverend Day, perhaps you'd come up and lead us all?'

275

Mary twisted her head to watch, as Arthur Day rose slowly to his feet, moved down the narrow space between the last chairs and the outer wall, edged past the Spanish sailors, past George Zanakis . . . carefully climbed on to the dais. His black suit was wrinkled and stained, and his thin hair stood on end. He raised his right hand and Mary saw that he was wearing grey mittens. The people bowed their heads in anticipation.

The minister's voice came out astonishingly strong. 'This is no time to pray!' it blared. 'What is the good of praying to a God who means to destroy us . . . if He exists at all?'

Heads jerked up. The minister pointed down at them with rigid arm and stabbing finger. 'It is a time for work, not prayer! Prayer won't save us, work might!'

She saw Father Bradford working unobtrusively forward. The people hummed and buzzed, feet shuffled, voices murmured and muttered. Father Bradford reached the dais as Mr Day sat down, head bent, lips moving. Father Bradford turned and raised his hand, his face shining with faith and confidence.

'Despise not thy people, O Almighty God, when they cry out in their affliction, but graciously succour them in their tribulation, for the glory of Thy name. Through our Lord . . . Let us pray a minute together, each after his own belief, kneeling in silence.'

He knelt, and, awkwardly, behind him Nelson knelt and Jim Carpenter knelt. Walter Crampton only bowed his head a few inches, and perhaps closed his eyes, though Mary thought not. Most of the people in the room were kneeling. The Spanish captain was not, nor the Reverend Mr Day. They were both standing, both staring at Father Bradford, the one with a clinical interest, the other with hate and bitterness.

A minute later, following Father Bradford's lead, the people rose to their feet with a great shuffling and scraping. Nelson spoke up. 'Wait, please . . . Jim Carpenter will now call the roll. We must know exactly who is in the Longships and, since there have been rooms changed without notification, and at least one birth, we must know exactly *where* everyone is. Miss Garland, come up here and make notes please.'

Then Nelson stepped down from the dais and came toward her, and she stood to receive him, the tears again welling into her eyes.

The ballroom was by no means empty, but most of the people had gone – to their rooms to make preparations, to the passages

276

to discuss the Reverend Mr Day's outburst. Louise Lincoln, talking to Robert Handforth at the foot of the dais, felt that they were meeting in complete privacy.

'Where did Mother go,' Robert asked, 'after the roll call? I keep trying to find her, to check that she's all packed up and ready, but she's never where I expect . . .'

Louise said, 'Well, when you do find her, tell her I don't *want* to live in that great house. I'd rather we had a smaller place right in town here and . . .'

'What are you talking about?'

'Haven't *you* heard? She's going to leave Monomoy House and its land to the town. Presumably so it'll never have a Negress giving orders in it.'

Robert shook his head vaguely. 'She can't do that. I mean she *can't* . . .'

Alice Bryant burst upon them. She must have come all the way down the room, in full view, but Louise had not observed. The effect was of a sudden eruption, as though Alice had stuck her head through a small window, close by her ear, and screamed, 'What's this, about no rehearsal this evening?'

Robert said, 'Yes . . . I announced it after the roll call just now.'

'I wasn't here,' Alice said. 'I wasn't going to come to listen to a lot of scare rumours.' She was wearing her full stage make-up.

'The danger's real enough,' Robert said. 'Nelson says that . . .'

'I don't care *what* he says. Don't tell me! . . . We ought to keep rehearsing. The show must go on! You said yourself, at the beginning, it was necessary to take people's minds off . . . off the outside. You said that the play's just as real as . . . outside. I think it's *more* real. So why don't we stop thinking about the stupid snow and the tide and rehearse the play?'

'The situation's changed,' Robert answered. The woman was on the edge of hysterics, Louise saw. Robert spoke very gently: 'We will continue the rehearsals just as soon as we can. And I am determined to put this play on . . . here, in Monomoy. Perhaps as a memorial to the great storm. Perhaps every year, like *The Lost Colony*, a festival sort of thing, and you could have your part as long as you want to come here and play it.'

Alice said, 'We aren't going to rehearse?'

'Not just now. Not today.'

Alice's brittle, made-up face fell apart, the stage paint seeming to crack, the eyes to sink back into their sockets. She seized Robert's arm in both hands and shook him strongly. 'Where

277

can we go?' she whispered urgently. 'There must be some way! We have all the money anyone could want, between us, to take us somewhere.'

Louise grabbed her elbow and spun her round. 'There is nowhere,' she said. 'Take off your make-up, Mrs Bryant. The play's in abeyance, for all of us. Even you!'

'*I'm* going to rehearse,' Alice said, her voice suddenly brassy and cheerful. 'The show must go on!' She stepped up on to the dais. '*I've* learned my part, at least! Listen to this . . . *Imagine Cora a bride! Dat's a hot one! Jees, Cora, if all de guys you've stayed wid was side by side, yuh could walk on 'em from here to Texas!*'

Louise muttered, 'Go and find Dr Miller, darling. I'll keep an eye on her.'

The woman on the dais stamped her heel into the floor. Her eyes flashed and her hands came up, the nails like claws. There was no audience now, except Louise and one of the Spanish sailors, a small man standing against the wall, watching with silent concentration and smoking one of the cigarettes that smelled like burning toilet paper.

'*I'll show yuh who's a whore!*' Alice screamed.

Walter Crampton sat at his wife's side, her thin, cold hand holding his. Her eyes were open, staring straight up, and the hand was trying to grip him, but there was no strength. She whispered, 'When it comes, Walter, take me to the dune . . .'

'Are you sure you wouldn't like it better on a fishing boat?' Walter said. 'It won't be too rough in the lee of Sachem, until the Gap breaks. After that, they'd come into the lee of the dune. You could keep a little warm.'

'The dune,' she muttered, 'the dune, with everyone.'

'What's the use?' he cried fretfully. 'You ain't in no condition for the dune, Daisy, not even ten minutes . . .'

He gave up. He'd talk to Dr Burroughs, but what was the use? She'd made up her mind.

'It hurts inside again,' she muttered. 'Ooh, it hurts, Walter.'

'Do you want to take one of the doctor's pills, Daisy?'

'No . . . no . . . I'm going to see the play. And the roses, come summer. And hydrangeas. You take me to the dune, Walter!'

George Zanakis stood at the back of a small crowd in the lobby, listening to the radio. It was nearly half past nine, when WCCD had a news broadcast. Most of the people gathered round the radio were old, but there was a scattering of kids, and two or three pregnant young women.

A fine time that one will have on the dune, he thought, watching one of the latter. a plump girl with a pale, blotched complexion, who perpetually shifted her ungainly weight from one leg to the other. She looked about ready to have the baby here and now. She had a stupid piglike face. She would have voted for killing the horseshoe crabs, if she'd bothered to come to Town Meeting at all. Now she was finding out what it was like to be the victim of a destructive force which you could not understand and could not communicate with. You only knew that it was bent on erasing you from the earth. There would be more justice if the calamity were God's punishment or some acknowledged sin. But that was what the churches liked to say, and it was better, more real, like this – to be annihilated without reason, or for reasons beyond comprehension, just as the horseshoe crabs could not be expected to understand that eating oysters and clams had suddenly, after several million years, become a crime . . .

Most of Provincetown under water, the people leaving their houses and going to a refuge camp on the high dunes round Race Point, the radio announced. That was a pity. A lot of good work would be lost in Provincetown, together with junk turned out for tourists by pseudo artists . . . Woods Hole flooded, some loss of life feared. In Nantucket, Siasconset evacuated, feared washed away, and the sea broken through into Head of the Harbour. Orleans flooding. Nauset Light undermined and fallen into the ocean. The Highland Light in danger of doing the same. . . . In Boston, Worcester, Portland, Providence, New London, Littleton, Bangor, Brewster. Great Barrington – *snow*.

He turned away. His little shack down by the Fish Pier was probably under water already, and with it a few paintings. Just the few he'd kept over the past fifty years, believing that these, at least, might have real, lasting worth. Good or not, they'd gone now. Now there was nothing left but that goddam *Druggist*, and a few pictures in private hands, all of them the same kind of facile, expert crap as *The Druggist*.

If only he'd been a sculptor, something might have survived. Someone digging in the sand, it didn't matter how much later – a thousand years would be better than next week – would find the perfect head, the torso that made you gasp, the vision in stone . . .

But the end of time allotted to him to create immortality

was set for tomorrow. He must paint, as best he could, with what he had. Paint what? The Negro girl, perhaps. There was something mournful about her. and she had tragic, experienced eyes, but pointed, proud breasts like a young virgin . . . No, that wasn't the great subject . . . Birth, maybe. That sow girl there, close to delivering a human child in the snow, on the Great Dune, with the world it was being born into on the point of dissolution by the waves?

Dear merciful God, it is foolish of me to expect that the inspiration I have been seeking for fifty years, and not finding, will now suddenly leap upon me . . . but I do expect it, and I do expect you to give it to me, damn you, damn you, damn you!

Why didn't that priest pray for *me*? Why don't they understand what I have to have – not a few more years, but immortality?

JoAnn Griffiths stared out the window. Some dope had come by, not long back, and asked her what she was staring *at*? The window, like all the others in the lobby, and on the rest of the ground floor, was under snow. The guy didn't understand you could look at a wall, and see through it if you wanted to.

It was getting cold, though. A different kind of cold. You'd swear from the winds blowing about the place that the windows must be broken, and doors left open. She tucked her hands deeper under her armpits. It would be colder up on the dune. She'd been up there once, a couple of years back, about this time – eleven o'clock, February – with a Coast Guard fellow. *They'd* kept warm, all right! But, heck, people had to eat, and sleep, and lots of women didn't even like doing it . . .

'JoAnn, have you seen Robert anywhere? In the last couple of hours?'

JoAnn turned her head slowly. It was Louise Lincoln, the big brown girl. 'No,' she said, 'I didn't have no date with him, miss.'

'Oh, I didn't mean that, but . . . Well, I did have a date. He was to come to my room an hour ago. He didn't. I've been searching. His room-mate doesn't know where he is.'

JoAnn said, 'Mrs Handforth would likely know where he is and what he's doing. She always went around with him, everywhere.'

'Not any more,' Louise said with sudden emphasis.

Well, you'll have a fight on your hands, JoAnn thought. Old

280

Mrs Handforth didn't take anything lying down, even though she did speak la-di-da and wandered around like she wasn't sure where she was going or where she'd been.

The brown girl wasn't saying any more, which meant she hadn't asked Mrs Handforth and didn't mean to. So now what? They should tell it all to the cop on duty, maybe? This girl tell a Yankee flatfoot how she is planning to get laid, and where in hell is the guy because she's got to have it *now*?

Jim Carpenter appeared in the lobby and JoAnn said, 'We'd better ask him.' While the other girl was still hesitating, JoAnn called, 'Oh, Mr. Carpenter . . . we can't find Mr Handforth.'

The response was the same as her own had been. 'Have you asked his mother?' But then Mr Carpenter's face changed and he said, '*Have* you?'

Louise cut in. 'No. There's no light under her door.'

Mr Carpenter said, 'Let's go!'

Louise asked. 'Why, what do you think?' and she sounded frightened; but now Mr Carpenter was hurrying along the passage and up the stairs so fast, Louise keeping right up with him, that JoAnn had to run.

'Her room's 344,' Louise said.

'I know. A single . . . here . . . now, you and JoAnn wait here . . .'

The bulb at the stairhead threw Mr Carpenter's shadow a long way down the passage. There was no answer when he knocked, so he knocked again. Then he put his head close to the door and said, 'Jim Carpenter here. Mrs Handforth. I'm sorry to bother you, but the electrician reports a continuous short circuit, and he's traced it to this room . . .'

JoAnn muttered, 'Gee, what a liar!' and shook her head in admiration. That was the kind of story that would terrify any woman, and she wouldn't know whether it was true or not.

Mr Carpenter said '. . . danger of fire, I must come in and fix it, I'm afraid. No, only me. The electrician is busy downstairs. 'He's told me what to do.'

After a while a key turned in the lock, and then the door opened a crack and Mr Carpenter went in. The door closed.

The tall brown girl beside her was trembling. Right after the door closed, she muttered, 'I should have known! When she told someone she was leaving Monomoy House to the town, and Robert said she couldn't . . . *unless he died first.*'

JoAnn thought slowly. 'You mean, you think Mrs Handforth . . .?'

The door of No. 344 opened and closed. Jim Carpenter said, 'What room is directly below this, on the ground floor? The numbers aren't regular . . . Come on. Hurry!'

They were running down the stairs again. JoAnn said, 'It's the third room from the stairs.'

Louise cried, 'What did you see?'

Jim Carpenter said, 'Snow on the floor by the window. His copy of *The Iceman* nearby. She hasn't tried to hide anything . . . JoAnn, get the cop on duty.'

They turned left along the ground-floor corridor, and JoAnn turned right. A minute later she returned with a yawning Patrolman Coyne. The third room from the stairs was Number 32. The door was open and flashlights flicking around inside.

Jim Carpenter came out. 'Coyne, get a rope. There's one on the nearest fire stanchion.'

'O.K. . . . Sergeant Barnes is on his way.'

The room was shared by two pregnant women, and a child in a cot in the corner. One of the women asked again and again, 'Is the tide coming over? I got all my clothes on. I'm ready.'

Jim said, 'No. A man may have fallen out of a window above. You haven't heard anything?'

'No . . . It isn't the tide?'

'Stay in bed, please.'

Patrolman Coyne hurried in with the rope. Jim Carpenter began to fasten one end round his waist. Police Sergeant Barnes appeared in the doorway, his flashlight joining the others in a moving tracery of light around the walls and ceiling.

Jim forced up the window. The snow stood like a slice of a huge white cake, reaching to the top of the window. A piece broke off and fell into the room, then Jim dug his arms into it and pulled chunks of it down to the floor. Then he wriggled out into it. Snow came flying back into the room, and one of the women in bed cried, 'Hey, look at our floor!'

The rope began to jerk. 'Easy now,' Sergeant Barnes said. 'Haul in, easy.' Jim Carpenter appeared in the open window space, crusted and thick-basted with snow so that he was a foot bigger in every dimension. He was dragging a big white sack, and then JoAnn saw that it was a man. The two fell into the room, one after the other.

Jim Carpenter spat out snow. 'Get a doctor.'

Louise was on her knees beside the body on the floor.

'Is he dead?' Sergeant Barnes asked.

'He's breathing!' Louise cried. 'Oh God, he's cold . . . Robert!
Robert . . .'

John Remington sat on the edge of his cot and stifled a yawn.
Tomorrow, unless the wind died away, the ocean would come
through the Gap. He ought to be thinking what he wanted to
try to save from his house. The house was in a good position,
right under the dune and well north of the Gap. The water
might not damage it too much. So, afterwards, he would own
a desirable sea-front residence. Sitting in the front window he
could watch the sea pounding to pieces whatever houses had
not been destroyed in the first breakthrough

'Chief . . . McGill here. May I come in?'

John stiffened. The First's voice sounded nervous – very
nervous. 'Come in.'

McGill was white, and moved stiffly, like a badly managed
puppet. 'Chief,' he began, 'Chief . . .'

John was on his feet. 'Speak up, man! What is it? Is the tide
coming high? Wind backed?'

'Randall's gone. With all the small arms.'

John said, 'Is that all?'

McGill's startled face showed he thought the remark was
meant to be funny; but it wasn't. 'How do you know he's
gone?'

'No one has seen him for two hours. Twenty minutes ago I
examined the armoury. Five pistols and two service rifles are
missing. Since Randall was in charge of preparing the camp on
the dune, I thought he might have taken the arms along there.
So I proceeded, with Engineman Carstairs and Seaman Jobell,
to the camp. I did not find the arms or Randall.'

McGill was standing at attention. John gestured wearily,
'Easy, Jimmy. That leaves us my pistol, right?'

McGill nodded. John went to the chest of drawers, pulled out
his pistol belt, complete with holster, pistol, and cartridges, and
put it on. 'Where do you think Randall's gone? Where *can* he
have gone? No one else is missing?'

'No.'

John drew the pistol and stared at it. Fred Randall, Boatswain's Mate 2. From Portland, Maine. A family that used to
have more money than it did when Randall was growing up.
Good education, which had moved him up fast in the service . . .
for a time. Then they'd found out about the instability. As of last
night, he'd started on the way down.

283

'I'll have to go and tell Nelson Pryor,' John said. 'And Frank Damato . . . Call all hands, Jimmy. Tell them what's happened. Randall is to be arrested on sight. I don't want anyone to take suicidal chances, but the guy's our responsibility. I'm going to the Longships . . . But, in the name of God, what's gotten into Randall? Do you think he's gone nuts? Is he holed up somewhere waiting for daylight, ready to shoot at anyone who comes into his sights?'

McGill said, 'I asked around. Some of the fellows think, well, that Randall may be thinking this is going to chalk up a strike against you, in Mr Helm's book.'

'So that Mr Helm will bust me before I get around to asking him to bust Randall?'

McGill said 'I know it's crazy, Chief, but when a guy's mad and frightened he doesn't always think straight.'

'You're right there,' John said wearily.

Now he would have to go and tell the civilians that their sure, disciplined shield had crumbled to nothing: worse, that it now threatened them.

He struggled into his coat and jammed on his hat, 'Get going,' he said.

'Aye, aye, Chief!'

They sat alone in the manager's office, Lynn and John. He had come to her room half an hour ago, and knocked. She had been long asleep, and even after she got up, struggled into her overcoat, and went out into the passage, she had not really understood what he was telling her. It had taken some time to convince her that the call had nothing to do with the danger to the Gap.

Finally, when she did understand, she had wondered why he was telling *her*. What could she do about it? But she waited, shivering, in the manager's office, while he went to tell Nelson Pryor and Frank Damato, and about half past one he came back. He closed the door carefully, and sat down.

His face was lined beyond his age and he looked ill. 'If only I could think where he is,' he muttered, 'I'd go get him.'

'You mustn't worry about it too much,' she said. 'He's not the only one. You heard what happened here?'

He shook his head in silence. She told him about the discovery of Robert Handforth.

'Poor old lady,' he said, after a long while. 'What are they doing to her?'

'Nothing. What can they do, yet? Robert's conscious, but asleep.'

'There's nothing wrong with the service,' John said. 'I thought there was, for a minute, last night. We had trouble then, too. I kept it private.'

'You knocked a man out,' she said. 'Oh, you had no choice. The men are all very proud of you. People *do* talk, you know.'

He said, 'You must be feeling pretty good. This is what you said once, remember? About human failure making all our discipline and planning and experience worthless . . .'

She said, 'I might have felt good, once. Not now . . . I'm sorry . . . sorry for the man. Really, it's not his fault that he can't take this special sort of strain.'

'And me?' he said. 'You don't feel sorry for me? My career probably ruined, everything I believe in falling to pieces around me?'

He spoke gravely, but with an intent to be answered. His head had come up and he was looking straight at her.

She said, 'No. No, I'm not sorry for you. For one thing, I don't think your career is ruined. Mr Helm and your other superiors must realize what you've been through. They're not fools. They'll all be going through this – and worse – themselves. We've all got to remember, all the time, that Monomoy is not anything special, or particular. The people here are people everywhere, what happens here happens everywhere . . . No, I don't feel sorry for you. Just the opposite. I've learned a lot about what you call "the service" during this storm, John. About your people's dedication, unselfishness, absolute honesty. I think you've learned something, too . . . Oh, that a chain's only as strong as its weakest link, if you like. That "the service," whatever it is, cannot simply be trusted and left alone. Suppose there were no Amendments, and private citizens weren't allowed to bear arms. Then where would we be, with this man having all the arms?'

'There are the police,' he said, 'but I never thought I'd hear *you* say thank God for the fuzz . . . Lynn, will you marry me?'

She opened her mouth, and after a long time sneezed violently. 'It's cold in here,' he said, 'you ought to get back to bed.'

'I will.'

'Which?'

'Both.'

'Of course, I'm going to stay in the service.'

285

'Of course. And I want to teach . . . at least some of the time. I'm a teacher.'

'I know.' He came round the desk and she stood up. He put his arms around her, and his face was cold as he kissed her. She pressed her body against him trying to give him warmth.

'Good night, Lynn,' he whispered, 'Good night, and keep warm.'

CHAPTER ELEVEN

MONDAY

John Remington said, 'With high tide at 3.16 this afternoon, it's about dead low now, at nine in the morning. Look at it.'

Harold Morgan looked, his hands deep in his pockets. The sea was some way from the Gap, but it was considerably above the low tide of yesterday.

Remington continued, 'The wind's backed into the north. Unless it veers way off, and drops, this is going to be it.'

Nelson Pryor said nothing. Walter Crampton said nothing. The snow kept falling, though in intermittent flurries rather than a steady downdrift. The four of them were standing by the Old Boat House. Up on the Great Dune to the southward, above the lip of the Gap, blurred figures made the ritual shovelling motions of stoop and straighten, stoop and straighten. A bulldozer coughed and stuttered somewhere out of sight behind the Coast Guard station.

Nelson Pryor said, 'We've got to get explosives, and quick.'

Remington said, 'I sent the message, way back. It was relayed to Washington, but there's no way of getting the stuff to us.'

Nelson said, 'Send another message. Tell them we expect the Air Force to bring whatever we need to blow that hulk apart, even if they risk losing aeroplanes and men to do it. What do we pay taxes for? Tell them that. If they don't bring it, thousands of people will get killed here, and a town will be destroyed. Tell them that. Tell them now.'

'O.K. Nelson.'

The Chief left them. Harold watched Elliott King, working like a madman up there on the dune. One of the dozer engines didn't sound too healthy. They should get a new one.

The trouble was, everyone else had the same troubles. You got into the habit of thinking you were different, you were special, that what was happening to you, good or bad, couldn't be happening to anyone else. When everybody's in trouble, where does help come from? From inside, of course. Inside each person, by the same logic.

Walter said, 'I reckon they've raised the level of the Gap about two feet.'

Nelson said, 'Yes. Just sand, though . . . We've got to go. You staying here, Harold?'

'Yes. I'm Elliott's executive officer and communications centre.'

The two Selectmen left him, plodding away through a thin snow flurry. Harold Morgan sniffed the air. He smelled burning varnish. They were burning Town hall chairs in a small fire at the south-west corner of the parking lot. Half a dozen men, snow-covered, warmed their hands and stamped their feet in front of it. Charlotte was there, with a big kettle supported on a complicated arrangement of tyre jacks and iron bars. She saw him watching, and began to pour out coffee from the kettle.

She brought him a paper cup full of steaming black coffee. He sipped slowly, blew, and sipped again, eyeing her as she returned to the fire and poured coffee for the other men. She hooked me, he thought, hooked me fair and square. Fair, he couldn't deny that. A fine-looking woman. If it had to happen, he was lucky to get her. Maybe it did have to happen, or there'd be no more people: no more horseshoe crabs, come to that.

Dozing uncomfortably in the armchair, blankets wrapped around her and her head set uncomfortably on a pillow propped into the back of her neck, Louise Lincoln awoke suddenly to a sense of lateness. It was nine o'clock. Nine o'clock in the morning. That was late. Late for what?

'What time is it?'

She dropped her blankets and stooped over the bed, feeling for his hand, 'Nine o'clock, darling. How do you feel?'

His voice was a little hoarse, otherwise he sounded normal. 'O.K.,' he said. 'Who found me?'

'I did,' she said, 'Jim Carpenter, JoAnn, and I . . . Dr Miller made me promise to keep you quiet when you woke up.'

'It was Mother,' he said.

'Don't talk,' she muttered.

'I went to her room, to see how she was . . . She talked very sensibly, about *The Iceman*. Then she went to the window and opened it wide . . . with a jerk. The snow roared in, and the wind. Papers blew all over the place. I ran to the window . . . I remembered saying, "Mother, what on earth . . .?" as I got my hands on the sash, to pull it down. She slipped behind me and gave me a tremendous push . . . all her strength . . . more than her strength.'

Louise slowly stroked his hand.

'I could have saved myself, I suppose. I was holding on to the sash still, and had only to bend my back against her . . . But you know what it's like when you suddenly realize someone means to hurt you? I didn't want to. As I went out, I half turned, enough to look into her eyes. She didn't say anything, just pushed, her teeth clenched. I went out.'

After a time, when he did not speak, she said, 'I'd better go back to New York . . . when this is over.'

'Oh, no,' he said, his voice as matter-of-fact as ever. 'We'll go through with our plans.'

Louise said, 'Suppose she tries again. Not immediately. Perhaps not against you. Against me. Or our baby. Don't you think she should be . . . put away?'

Robert said, 'We'll say nothing.'

'But, Robert . . .' she began.

'We can't send her to jail or an asylum, Louise. We just have to live with it, the way other people have to live with blindness or polio . . . I don't remember falling, only waking, very cold, deep in snow. No bones broken, but no strength. I thought of you and tried to struggle, but it was no good. Then I felt sleepy . . .'

Dr Miller bustled in rubbing his hands. 'Aha! Awake! Hum! And how's our patient today? Much better, I hope. He'd better be. The wind's changed, and we may have to get out today. Now if you will, ah, wait outside, Miss Lincoln, we will, ah, examine the patient.'

'Kiss me first, Louise . . . there . . . perhaps this is going to provide the only acceptable answer to the future of the Handforth Tract – submerge it all under ten feet of water.'

Dorothy King wandered aimlessly along the second-floor corridor of the Longships. She felt she ought to be doing something but did not know what. It was about nine o'clock, and she'd heard rumours that the tide was very bad. The corridor was full of other people, all drifting. Most of them were women, most had children at their heels, as though they no longer dared to let them out of their sight, even for a moment. The men were out in the Gap, working.

On the whole people didn't look frightened, or act frightened, though it had been a bad night, full of movement, and crying, and whispers. And old Mrs Handforth trying to kill her son. It had taken a lot of telling before people believed that. Some still didn't. That was the truth about the tide and the danger – people didn't believe it.

'Mrs King . . . Mrs King . . .' A hand plucked at her sleeve, but she didn't recognize the whining voice, and she didn't remember meeting the woman before. It was a small, plump woman, the eyes tired and the mouth pinched; sallow skinned, a dirty baby in her arm and three more at her skirts, one hardly able to walk; pregnant; smelling as though she had never washed.

'I'm Rose Vernon,' the woman said.

'Oh . . . how do you do?' Dorothy said. She felt numb, waiting for the attack.

The woman looked up the corridor. They were standing near the big window at the south end and there was no one very near. The woman said, 'You done wrong, Mrs King. You and my Bill.'

'I'm sorry,' Dorothy said. The feral matings with Vernon were a million years ago.

The woman said, 'You was led astray, wasn't you? Or was you, are you trying to take my Bill away from me? You, a rich woman with a lovely home.'

Dorothy closed her eyes and stood fast against the window to prevent herself falling. Out of the darkness she said, 'I apologize, Mrs Vernon. It won't happen again. It was I who led your husband into wickedness. I am not . . . I will not try to take him from you.'

The woman said, 'They're all the same, aren't they? . . . I was jealous, God knows he's given me enough cause. But he's a big man, see, the women throw themselves at him. It's not his fault. . . . I love him, see?'

'I know. I know.'

'Well, if you didn't mean any harm . . . though you shouldn'ta done it . . . Good-bye, Mrs King.'

'Good-bye.'

The woman went away, her face lighter under the dirt. The children, who had been silent witnesses, broke into caterwauls and whining.

Elliott King, standing over the fire with a cup of coffee in his hand, heard a distant sound as of an engine being raced. It stopped. 'That's the dozer!' he said, dropped the cup and ran up the southern slope. He pushed himself at full speed up the sand and snow . . . What chance of a heart attack? Damn little, unfortunately. He was a fit man. From the beginning the goddam Provincetown fairies had always turned their queer, shining eyes on him in admiration, they'd always primped and simpered when he had to talk to them . . .

He reached the top of the dune, through thinly falling snow saw two men two hundred feet farther south. The two men were peering over the east, the ocean, face of the dune. There was no sign of the bulldozer. Elliott ran to the men.

One turned, his face like putty. 'The dozer went over the edge.'

Elliott said, 'Who was driving? Tom?'

'He's O.K. He jumped, and rolled down the dune, but off to one side. He got wet.'

'Christ. We got to try to get this one back. The main bearing's seized up on the other one,' Elliott cried. He slid down the precipitous face of the dune. The dozer was resting upright in the edge of the sea, about fifty feet on the lee side of the *Goya*, where the waves were much smaller. Back scouring had hollowed a deep trough close to the ship's steel wall, but the dozer was in only about three feet of water. Waves broke regularly over it. The operator, Tom, stood at the edge of the ocean, soaking wet, covered in snow and sand, and shivering violently.

Elliott began to swear at him, then saw that he was a young man, tired and frightened. He cut off the explanations. 'Forget it!' and waded out towards the dozer.

Jesus, the sea was cold. The waves hit harder than you expected. The dozer looked like a prehistoric yellow monster, emerging from the sea to conquer the land. A yellow horseshoe crab, maybe.

He scrambled up into the driver's seat and pressed the starter. The engine spat, coughed, and roared. 'Here we come!' he bellowed at the top of his lungs. The dozer moved forward, slewing sharply to the right.

Thrown a tread, he thought, swearing aloud. But the dozer stood sideways to the sea now, and a big wave nearly knocked him out of the seat. The motor coughed, coughed again, and died. He cupped his hands and yelled, 'Get a strong rope, or we'll lose this tread!' The grey waves, cold as moving icebergs, struck heavily at him with the rhythm of a flagellation. Now John Remington was there at the sea's edge, and Harold Morgan, and a dozen other guys. Elliott waded ashore, bracing himself against the waves that tried to push him on to his face. He reached the sand and yelled, 'It's a winch job! God damn it, I had her started!'

Remington said, 'We'll manhandle a winch down here right away. And get another set up on top.'

Elliott clapped him on the shoulder. 'You do that, boy!'

'You better get changed, Elliott,' Harold said.

Elliott shouted, 'I'm fine!' It was the truth. He felt fine. As long as he could run and dig, fight and push, he felt fine. Don't stop, don't think, just keep going.

JoAnn Griffiths stood in the dormer of the little attic room she shared with another girl. She stood with her weight on her left leg. her left hip out-thrust, staring out.

Snow everywhere, and the top of the dune sort of dirty white so it was hard to tell from the sea behind. There were a lot of people near the Gap. Down below you could look into the back yards of the houses on South Hill Street. There were six of them in the block, and for days now it had been hard to tell that they *were* houses, there was so much snow on them. Something had changed during the night. There was a kind of trench running alongside one of the houses, from South Hill toward South Commerce. Someone must have worked hard to dig that in the night. And now men were walking down it, one behind the other. Now they were climbing slowly over the high snowbank on South Commerce. Now some were turning right, towards Boat Street, and some were coming on towards the hotel. They all disappeared from her view.

It was funny, up here, how the snow sometimes seemed to be falling upward. She'd meant to ask Mr Remington about that, how could snow gó upward, but she's forgotten. She was getting a crick in her neck from stooping in this window. This was where they put the maids when the hotel was open in summer. In the old days there'd be four or five in each of these little rooms, some girl had told her. Slave drivers, that's what they were. Think of being shut up in this pen for three months with three other women!

The snow was falling straight down today, but not all the time. She wondered vaguely what time it was. About half an hour since the breakfast washing-up got finished. One of the other women had kept yelling, 'Last dishes we'll *ever* wash, positively the *last* dishes,' until Mrs Tucker shut her up. The woman was nuts. She was a woman, so she'd be washing dishes in the Pearly Gates Eatery, right?

Now, she must have come up to the room for some good reason, before staring out the window got her, the way it always did. What was it? Room-mate not here to ask; anyway what did that dumb dish know about *anything*? Ah, pick up clothes and get ready to leave the hotel, in case someone said to. How about going up to the dune and finding a good place near Mr Remington and the Coast Guard fellows? Or Mr King . . . A frown creased the smooth white skin of her forehead as she thought of Elliott King. It was a wonder Mrs K. wasn't nuttier than she was. It gave you a real jolt, to think you might marry a guy like that, without knowing. Well, JoAnn Griffiths would know, you bet your sweet life! But there must be something wrong with her, the way she didn't really want to get married. She spent hours, sometimes, imagining a ring on her finger and a guy cooing, Wifey, come here a minute. It never gave her a charge. No, it would always be about the same, sometimes Mr. Carpenter painting her, and fellows like Charlie Tyson, all different and all the same; and a few real men like Mr Remington, and about half a step behind them some woman running up to claim him, as though he was a piece of lost baggage and she'd arrived just in time to catch her sneaking off with him . . .

The door opened and she turned round. Chris Damato and Bill Vernon came in. She said, 'Don't you fellows ever knock before . . .?'

'Shut up!' Chris snarled. She saw then that he was carrying a gun. 'You got anything valuable? Rings, jewels, anything – and money.'

Bill Vernon had a big sack. He was jerking open the drawers in the chest even as Chris spoke. He found her pocketbook, took out the change purse and dropped it into his sack.

'This cheap tramp won't have any more,' Chris said. 'Don't waste time . . . Stay in here one hour, or we'll blow your brains out.'

They went out, and the door slammed. JoAnn thought, Jeezus, Chris Damato has really been watching the TV. None of the baddies talked better out of the side of their mouth or had their eyes more like a snake. He ought to go to Hollywood, or New York, or wherever they made the TV shows, and then his dad could be real proud of him.

She returned to the window. The wind was blowing up. Those fellows were nuts, making a holdup in this weather, and no one able to go anywhere.

What the world needed was fewer nutty people. And more chewing gum.

Charlie Tyson hurled the last shovelful of snow far out over the edge of the ramp, and came inside the New Boat House. He

293

threw down the shovel and then, looking up, saw Bob Gardner giving him the hairy eyeball.

'O.K., O.K., admiral, don't shoot me this time,' he called. He picked up the shovel, wiped it dry and placed it with ostentatious care in its place on the rack.

Precisely 0941, and the goddam ramp cleared for the ninth time since they got here yesterday afternoon. Bob Gardner was sitting in the stern of the 36-footer, whittling. Dave Lerroux was polishing some brass. Ritchie was out of sight, probably gone back to sleep in the survivors' compartment, the bastard. That guy could sleep anywhere, any time. The 36-footer, secure on its cradle, looked twice life size.

'What's the news?' Charlie called up to Gardner. 'Didn't Salt Horse come down while I was digging out there?'

Gardner said, 'Yep. He thinks the sea'll come through on the afternoon tide.'

'That's about three o'clock?'

'1516.'

The small door at the back of the boathouse opened and two men came in. Another man appeared at the front, where the wide, high doors to the launching ramp stood open. The two men who had come through the back door were Joe Steele and Stan Jenkins.

Steele pulled his hand out of his coat pocket and showed a service pistol. 'Don't try anything funny,' he said. 'We're taking the boat.'

'You're sure heading for trouble,' Bob Gardner said mildly.

'Shut up. Get on board, Tyson. Everyone in the middle, there.'

Charlie followed Gardner and Lerroux up the ladder, trying to stir his brains out of the mud they seemed to have got bogged down in. There must be something he could do . . . but Steele was coming right up behind him, and Jenkins had a gun out now. Ritchie came out of the survivors' compartment.

'Launch her,' Steele said, 'fast.'

Now there might be a chance, Charlie thought. Bob might be able to let the boat down so fast that . . .

The man in the big doorway spoke. 'I'll let her down.' He came into the boathouse and Charlie, looking at him for the first time, saw that it was Randall.

'Go ahead,' Bob Gardner said, 'only, like I said, you're sure heading for trouble. You most of all, Fred.'

'Can it.'

With Randall in charge, the cradle began to grind down the rails. In a couple of minutes the 36-footer was afloat alongside the jetty. Randall jumped in and took the wheel. Joe Steele waved his gun. 'Get up in the middle there, and keep still.'

The motor kicked into life. The four crewmen stood in the well, hands in pockets, staring at the three men on the coxswain's flat. Charlie noticed that Randall would not meet his eye. Joe Steele kept looking at his watch. Snow settled fast on Bob Gardner's bleached hair, and the boat crashed heavily against the jetty as it rolled in the waves.

Bob Gardner said, 'Where do you think you're going, Fred?'

'Shut up!' Joe Steele snapped; but Randall answered, 'We're getting out, you goddam fools. Monomoy's going under, but we're not.'

Then men came fast along the jetty from the landward end. For a wild moment Charlie thought they were rescuers, but Joe Steele cried, 'Run, for Christ's sake!' and the men broke into a run, and came tumbling into the boat: Caroline Merchant, Joe's sister; Begg, Rooney, Worrell, Howard, all with sacks and boxes; and Bill Vernon, a grin spread like jam over his ugly face; and some way behind, Chris Damato, running easily along the jetty, a gun in his hand.

Another figure appeared, also running, but this man was older, and fat, and awkward on his feet. Charlie heard him yelling, 'Stop, stop! Cristoforo, for God's sake, stop!'

Chris Damato laughed, and fired his gun into the air, and kept running. Then he seemed to lose his footing, and stumbled. Charlie saw the expression on his face change, from wild joy to surprise, to disbelief, then – just as he fell – to a black hate, the teeth suddenly grinding together. He fell, sliding forward on his face.

Pete Worrell had a rifle raised. 'The bastard shot him,' he cried. He aimed the rifle carefully at the fat man standing there, fifty feet away, a pistol smoking in his hand.

Joe Steele knocked the rifle barrel down. 'Cut it out! He's done us a good turn. This boat's going to be crowded as it is. Let's get going, Fred.'

The boat began to move away from the jetty as Randall put her in gear. Joe Steele turned to the crewmen. 'You – jump!'

Bob Gardner stepped to the rail and jumped. Lerroux and Ritchie followed. Charlie, poised ready to jump, turned and yelled at them, 'You'll all drown, you silly bastards!' Then he jumped. The sea was an icy bear, embracing him, but the jetty was close and the other three all round, all swimming strongly.

Frank Damato knelt beside his son. Why was he lying there, only eighteen years old, a big red stain spreading out from him across the snowy planks and dripping down between them into the sea? There was a terrible noise in his own chest, salt burning his eyes, pain flooding up from deep in his belly. The boy's back rose six inches and collapsed. Blood gushed from his mouth, but all other movement stopped.

Frank felt hands on him. People were here, cold, wet men, dripping water over him; other men: Nelson, Chief Remington, Walter Crampton. 'You saw,' Frank Damato cried, 'you saw?'

'No. I didn't see.'

'They held up the hotel,' Frank sobbed. 'They locked the patrolmen in a room and took away their guns, didn't they?'

'They did.'

'They held a hostage and said they'd kill him!'

'They did.'

'I had to shoot! I am a policeman!' He searched their eyes. Didn't they understand what it was to be a cop? George Zanakis was there. Frank grabbed his hand, 'I had to do it, didn't I?'

The artist said, 'I don't know, Frank. No one will ever know. No one ever does.'

Frank turned to Walter Crampton. 'Walter, you tell me!' But Crampton said, 'It could have been me,' and turned away.

Frank collapsed slowly over the body of his son, and only from a long distance heard his wife's cold, impersonal voice: 'I tolda him. I tolda you.'

Charlotte Quimby, crouched over her fire on the parking lot, heard the faint scream in the sky and looked up in fear. Snow fell in large flakes and the wind blew sand and spray into the fire, so that smoke and sparks billowed stinging into her eyes. The screaming grew louder, then faded.

A couple of men stood near, waiting for coffee. They peered upward from under their parka hoods. 'That was a jet,' one said. 'Trying to find us.'

'What for?' Charlotte asked.

'To drop the dynamite, I guess.'

Minutes passed. The roaring scream returned, louder and

lower in the hurrying cloud wrack. One of the men said, 'He ought to be able to see something on radar . . . these new bomb-sights, the way they talk about them he should be able to drop the stuff smack dab on to this parking lot . . . He's going back west now.'

They waited. Charlotte energetically scooped up snow and stuffed it into her pot. One had to have something to do, every minute.

One man said, 'There he is . . . way south . . .'

The other said, 'If it was a bomb, yeah, he could drop it down the Coast Guard chimney from ten miles up, but this is boxes, with parachutes, and they won't fall straight, so he has to come low . . .'

Charlotte peered into her pot. All that snow had melted already, but it didn't seem to have raised the level of the water one little bit. She began to scoop up more.

The noise came sudden and fast, loud and low, so that the men crouched, dropping their cups. Black lightning swept apocalyptic through the cloud base, the whine rose to a full roaring scream, deafening in intensity and painful in pitch.

There was silence, and falling snow.

'The clouds aren't no more than fifty feet above the dune,' the man said. He paused, his head cocked. Other men had come, and all stared out to sea. Charlotte stared with them, but saw only the indigo murk, the slanting snow, and the marching grey-white waves.

A man's arm flung out, a voice yelled, 'Look!' For a moment, between blink and blink, she saw the spread wings, the glittering nose, the round engine pods hanging among the wave tops. The nose lifted and the giant dart streaked over, a long black oblong in its belly, and the frantic bellow of sound beating her to her knees.

A man shouted, 'I didn't see anything come out!'

Another said, 'I did . . . it fell way over, though. Fell in Long-ships Bay, that's what happened.'

No one spoke any more, and they all looked cold and afraid; all except Elliott King, who cried, 'Five minutes' coffee break, everyone! Then we'll *really* have to get to work for a change . . . Any coffee for me, Charlotte?'

'Certainly, Mr King,' she said.

She poured it carefully for him, and handed it to him with a pleasant smile. Mr King was no threat to her Harold *now*. A lady could afford to be generous, in the circumstances, and when a lady could afford generosity she should always do so, because it was nicer, and more feminine.

Nelson Pryor stood alone near the south-east corner of the Coast Guard station, looking down into the Gap. At the back of the parking lot Harold Morgan was supervising the unloading of a Highway Department truck. That load was food – brought up from the small stock left in the Longships in order to be stowed ready on the Great Dune. If the final disaster didn't come, the food would have to be carried back again. But in that case, people would be feeling too thankful to grumble about the wasted effort.

Maybe. There was nothing like being a politician to learn the depths of man's ingratitude and his capacity to complain.

The obvious place to store the food was in the station, right here on the dune crest. But if the sea came through the Gap, it wouldn't be more than an hour or two before it undermined the station, so they were stowing the food a couple of hundred feet north of the station, close to the Coast Guard camp. Remington had put a pair of sentries over his camp – but they were unarmed: because Boatswain's Mate Randall had stolen the arms and Joe Steele had gone off with them. Good riddance, Nelson muttered to himself. If that bunch had stayed, the time would have come, up here on the dune, when he'd have had to use police and Coast Guard to put down a riot – selfish, bullying, women-and-children-last kind of riot.

Chief Remington's calmness in the face of that disaster had amazed him, for disaster was sure as hell the label the Coast Guard were going to pin on it – arms, ammunition, and a 36-footer gone. Robbery, violence, death, desertion – you name it, the Coast Guard was involved in it, and Remington was the responsible officer in command. Nelson had expected a real explosion from Remington or, more likely, a breakdown. But Remington had only said he was sorry for Frank Damato. It only went to show, you never knew a guy until one of you was dead. And then only maybe.

God knew where Randall had holed up during the night. It looked as if he'd met Steele earlier, and Steele had fixed the whole plan. After dark they'd dug into the Evans home. As Arthur was a bank president, they probably thought the house would be full of jewels and thousand-dollar bills. They must have been mad when they saw that the Evans's lived very simply.

And as for that ape Vernon, leaving his wife and snot-nosed brats behind, Christ . . . !

The hell with them!

Five minutes to twelve, and sure enough, Chief Remington just came out of the station to stand beside him, without a word. The cloud base had lifted a little, but only to a hundred feet or so. Between the flurries of snow the middle part of the town spread itself out like a crazy little map below there. Charlotte Quimby was crouching over her smoky little fire, and the usual four or five men were waiting for coffee. The opposite slope of the Gap was pockmarked with men working to shovel sand down on to the parking lot. The *Goya* stretched its great steel wall seaward. There was a bulldozer buried in the sand the other side of it. Elliott had worked like that King Canute, but the ocean beat him and he'd finally burst into tears. The doc had given him a big shot of a sedative and Dorothy was looking after him.

Nelson said, 'It looks bad, John.'

Remington said, 'I've compared the marks. At three and a half hours before high tide, the level was only one foot short of the last tide at full. It's going to come over this time.'

Nelson said, 'O.K. . . . We'll move now, then. Everyone out of the hotel . . . the rescue teams through the streets . . . boats to put out to sea. I'll tell them.'

Remington said, 'All right, Nelson. We'll be here. Anything you want, just ask . . . Good luck to us all.'

Nelson stuck out his hand, grinning suddenly. 'And I'll bring up a couple of bottles of bourbon. Good luck.'

Jim Carpenter, his arms full of rolled canvas, kicked at the door of his room, and called, 'Barbara, open up!'

After a time the door opened and his wife stood there, blonde, beautiful, properly made up, her hair done, a nail file in one hand. 'Time to go,' he said briefly. 'Everything packed?'

She nodded. 'In the suitcase, and rolled up in the blankets there . . . Is it really time to go? I thought high tide wasn't till after three.'

'We've got to go. Where are the kids?'

'In the kindergarten room. We pick them up from the teachers, someone said . . . What have you got there?'

'Paintings.'

'The one you were doing of that girl? Jim, I absolutely refuse to let you take that.'

299

Jim carefully put down his roll. George Zanakis had told him he was an amateur and would never be anything else because painting was only a means of escape for him. O.K., so he wasn't looking for immortality. So he didn't know anything about art. But he knew what he wanted. He wanted to watch his hand moving and the line following, the colour coming, and slowly a woman being born full grown on the canvas, mysterious, frank, her surfaces as obvious, and as subtle, as those a yacht designer worked with.

He said, 'That painting's pretty good, for me. I've been able to *say* something about JoAnn, about her being a whore and a mother at the same time.' He opened the suitcase. 'What's this?'

'Hair curlers.'

'And this?'

'Eye make-up . . . eye brush . . . setting lotion. That's my nail polish . . . *Jim*, what are you doing?'

'I'm going to throw this lot out the window.'

'Jim, you can't!'

'You want these on the *dune*?' he cried.

She said, 'Why *should* I look like a frump? Just because it rains, or snows. We don't give up putting on lipstick . . .'

Jim stared at her, and after a while restored the bottles and brushes and packets to the suitcase. 'O.K.,' he said, 'I'll carry the blankets and canvas, and you take the suitcase.'

His wife glanced in the mirror, primped up her back hair, and said, 'If you think Mrs Mordent isn't going to be properly turned out . . . ! Ready now.'

'Everything's packed,' Florence Day said. 'We should be going.'

The Reverend Arthur Day knew her nerves were on edge, but enough had remained of her Southern drawl so that she always sounded calm, almost lackadaisical. For himself, he felt hot and sweaty inside his clothes. He had worked all morning in the Gap, as well as a man of his age and physical condition could. The men in charge had found a hundred excuses not to give him a spade or shovel, and at first he thought it was due to resentment. After all, at a time like this everyone would feel better with that faith in divine good intentions which he had publicly disavowed. But he soon understood that they didn't give him a tool because it would be a waste, with strong and experienced men available. They must have seen how badly he needed to do something, so, from time to time, for a few minutes, he had been allotted a shovel. Now he was back in the hotel, with snow and sand on his boots.

He said, 'You go down, dear, and wait for me in the lobby. I won't be a minute.'

Florence said, 'Mercy sake, what now?'

'I want to change my boots,' he said; 'these are wet and cold.'

She said, 'I'll put out a pair . . . and socks. Bring the others down. You may need them later.'

'Thank you.'

When she had gone he sat on the bed and painfully, because his back was stiff, bent even more unwillingly than usual, changed boots and socks. Then he opened the wardrobe and looked on the top shelf. The front of the shelf was littered with broken porcelain fragments where those wicked, stupid youths had smashed two vases during their holdup – out of sheer wanton destructiveness, as far as he could tell. Behind the litter three small undamaged vases shone in the gloom at the back of the shelf. So Florence had not packed them. He reached out his hand to stroke the surface of the nearest vase. Beautiful . . . and it had an extra meaning now. During his years of growing doubt it had served as a friend and rescuer. To turn from the questions he could not answer, from the trusting faces of his congregation, to the cool colours and impervious surfaces of the porcelain – that had saved his reason. Now it was not an escape that he needed, but a job, and porcelain could provide it. The intensity of his need to escape from the doubts about God had turned him into an expert on porcelain. He knew of half a dozen big antique dealers who would be eager to employ him. Or, supposing he set up on his own . . . . ?

He put the smallest vase in his right-hand coat pocket and the next smallest in his left. They would be the beginning. That is, if he and they survived destruction. It was strange. Monomoy had never seemed to him to possess any of the attributes of Gomorrah.

Ready to go now. Florence had left his prayer book on the bureau top. People would expect him to say prayers over the dead. The language was still beautiful . . . more beautiful, really, now that he could separate the ridiculous meaning from the beautiful music. He slipped the book into his trousers pocket and went out, carefully locking the door behind him.

A faded light lay in bars across the corridor, for most people, on leaving, seemed to have left their doors open. Peering into the rooms as he passed, the minister saw stripped beds, abandoned toys, a broken garter belt, a football, a television set . . . At the end of the corridor a spiderlike shape blocked the window, casting a pale shadow on the boards. As the Reverend Day approached, the figure became a human being, arms outstretched, pressing against the sides of the window. A woman, he thought. Then, from its size, and the head, he knew it was Father Bradford. Aha! Bradford had turned, like Lot's wife, for a last look over the town. A roll of blankets lay on one side of him, and on the other a suitcase and a small satinwood box. That would contain chalice, paten, pall, purificator, corporal, burse, chalice veil, a pyx, a flask of wine. And in the suitcase perhaps amice, alb, cincture chasuble, maniple . . . how beautiful, how beautiful the words!

He crept close and stood, looking past the other man's shoulder. What was the view? To the right the Coast Guard station and lighthouse were painted a dim grey-gold. Small dark figures climbed out of the Gap like Israelites ascending Jacob's ladder. To the left Longships Bay was etched in steep sharp waves, grey and white. A hundred yards from the shore visibility ended, for there the wind had lifted the wave tops and formed a curtain of water and snow. Along the line of the shore one ought to see the water tower, but it was not there. It must, indeed, have fallen down.

Fair in the centre of the view the white steeple of Monomoy Old Church thrust into the clouds.

'All going.'

The priest's voice was low. Arthur Day did not know whether Bradford spoke to himself or to him, knowing that he stood at his elbow. 'Two and a half centuries of labour, and faith. Everything our forefathers did. That lovely church . . .'

God of our fathers, the Reverend Mr Day thought, it is not Father Bradford who looks over the doomed town, but the Governor, surveying the work of his own hands, his own faith.

Arthur Day said, 'Suppose the Old Church survives. It would be a miracle, wouldn't it?' A powerful excitement throbbed in him, and the words that came were not of his choice, but were put into his soul from above. 'It would be a miracle!' he repeated.

'Yes,' the young priest said, 'it would be a miracle.'

'A miracle made for *you*, Father! The Old Church needs

302

you. For you, it will be saved. Without you, it will be destroyed. You believe, don't you?'

'I believe,' the priest whispered.

'*What* do you believe? In the love of God, or the infallibility of a good, fat Italian? In Jesus, or the Donation of Constantine – which you know is a forgery? These are your people, not the poles and Czechs and Portuguese who sneer at you . . .'

The priest cried out like an animal, no words distinguishable, his hands pushing outward against the sides of the window, never turning his head.

Arthur Day said, 'The Old Church has been empty of the Holy Ghost for years. It's *your* church, by right, by birth . . . If it is standing at this time tomorrow, will you accept the miracle? Accept that God saved it for you? You've changed your faith once, do it again! It's *faith* that matters, not *which* faith . . .'

'If the Old Church is standing tomorrow,' Father Bradford said, each word wrung slowly from him.

'If it's standing tomorrow!' Arthur Day cried.

The priest's arms slipped down the sides of the window and his head sank on to his chest. Arthur Day went carefully on his way downstairs.

Elaine Handforth walked north along South Commerce Street, carrying a heavy leather suitcase. A patrolman followed, loaded down with blankets, sheets, and a second leather suitcase, pair to the first. As Elaine walked slowly on, her grey hair blowing out from under her red hunter's cap, she mentally ran through a list of current problems.

First, of course, was the fate of West Village. As Walter pointed out, it was built on a sizeable dune. Otherwise, it could not have survived the hurricanes of '38 and '56, in her own memory. That was true. Still, something must be done to find out how it was faring.

Second, on looking round the Longships just now she had noticed at least a hundred blankets in the storeroom. They should be taken to the dune.

Dogfood? Birdseed?

At least one of the generating sets should be taken up the dune, by means of winches if necessary, as light would be vital in certain types of emergency.

Dr Burroughs was showing his years. This final phase of the emergency had found him quite incapable of lucid thought or proper preparation. He must be eased into retirement, not as a practitioner but as chairman of the Board of Health. As to his

303

successor, there were certain drawbacks to having Mr Miller elected. She would have to discuss the matter with Nelson . . .

Before turning up Boat Street she paused, noticing many people moving down North Commerce between the tremendous snow walls. 'Who are all those people?' she asked the patrolman.

'People from the houses, ma'am,' he answered. 'People who didn't come into the Longships. But they're all in the same boat now.' He set down his burdens and wiped his forehead.

'Will no one be trapped in their house?' Elaine asked.

'I guess not. We had just about all the real old and sick in the Longships. We can get at the rest somehow, what with fire ladders, ropes, snowshoes, and that . . . but some of them don't aim to leave, the lieutenant told me. They're sitting tight. Some of 'em say. The Lord's will be done, and some of 'em say, It ain't going to wash away *this* house. And some of 'em are drunk.'

Elaine led up Boat Street. The people's behaviour was very easy to understand, and quite justified. It was almost impossible to accept that Monomoy was about to end its existence. That there would be no Old Church, no Green, no Longships Hotel, no Monomoy House. *No Monomoy Handforths* . . . Ah. See, she. herself had failed to notice such an elementary. obvious fact. The unfortunate necessity of yesterday wasn't a necessity at all. Of course, one had not known that until just now, when it finally became certain that the ocean would come through the Gap.

She climbed slowly up the winding footpath to the dune-top. Men and women trudged ahead of her, bowed and loaded. It looked like the Retreat from Moscow, only this was a whole people, not just an army. Off to the right, where the snow ridge dropped sharply away to the ocean, a small movement caught her eye. Carefully she put down her suitcase. 'Johnny, do you see a bird? There.'

Patrolman Gilligan said, 'Where? Yes, I see it.'

'I don't have my glasses, but I *think* it's a very rare visitor. What colour is its throat'?

'Black, ma'am.'

'I thought so. Outer tail feathers white? Parallel browny lines on the back?'

'Wait a moment, I can't see . . . Yes, I think so.'

'A Lapland longspur, then, without a doubt. We have made quite a find, for Monomoy, you know. We can congratulate ourselves.'

'Yes, ma'am.'

'Now, where should we go, do you think?'

'Mr. Pryor's coming. I guess he'll tell us.'

Elaine Handforth waited, casually surveying the scene. The snow on top of the dune had never become very deep owing to its exposed position. Now it was trampled and soiled by the passage and repassage of many feet. Tents and shelters of every size, shape, and colour spread along the narrow flat crest and a little way down the easier lee slope. The people were here in their hundreds, and more coming. She heard shouts under the roar of the ocean, and laughter, and a woman crying.

Nelson was with her then, and with him the tall Negro girl, Louise Lincoln, and a taller, thinner man of about thirty, whom she did not recognize.

'We've made a place for you,' the girl said. 'Here, take my arm.'

Elaine rested on the girl's arm with a sigh. 'Thank you, my dear. It's quite a tiring climb. Now, if this young man will be so good as to take my suitcase, we'll soon be there.'

Walter Crampton carried only one load, which he could not set down, for it was his wife. Many had offered to help, but he had refused them all. He felt stronger now, as he reached the parking lot in the Gap, than when he left the Longships; and Daisy felt lighter.

As he started up the steps toward the Coast Guard station, she whispered, 'Wait. Let me look.'

He turned round so that she could see – see the Old Boat House with its reinforcement of sand; the barricade of sand and driftwood; the men at work, with shovels flying; the red flowers of Mrs Quimby's fire; the line of men and women and children climbing the steps; the everlasting fall of the snow.

'Stop there,' she said. 'There. Where I can see.'

Her eyes fastened on the lip of the Gap, near the Coast Guard station.

Walter said, 'But, Daisy, our shelter's ready, beyond the station.'

'Later,' she said.

He began to trudge up the path. At the Gap, where the others went on round the west side of the station, he turned east.

'Here,' she said.

George Zanakis appeared over the crest of the upper slope, his grey hair flying. He carried a big, square board, and a wooden case, and dragged a roll of blankets behind him.

'What are you doing here?' he shouted, almost truculently, as he came close.

'She wants to stay here,' Walter said.

'And I want to paint.' He looked at Daisy, almost angrily. Suddenly his face cleared. He shouted, 'Here, take these blankets. Make her comfortable. Then run along and get yours, and a tarpaulin or tent or something.'

Walter spread the blankets, and set Daisy down on them, then wrapped her well. Zanakis set up his board a few yards to leeward, and hurriedly squeezed paints on to a small palette. The wooden case, full of brushes, bottles, and paint tubes, lay open beside him, and his lips kept moving.

Daisy's right hand crept out from the shelter of the blankets, and fell to the sand. The bonelike fingers scrabbled, gathered a dozen grains . . . the wrist jerked with unexpected force, the grains of sand rolled down the slope toward the Gap and the barricade below.

Walter stood up. 'Reckon I'd better get to work down there,' he said. 'First, I'll bring the tarpaulin, and our things.'

She whispered a word, which was blown away by the wind.

George Zanakis shouted, 'Go on down, Walter! I want her alone on that slope.' As an afterthought he added, 'I'll look after her.'

Walter paused behind the artist as he passed. The big board, a canvas thumbtacked firmly to it, was held down by Zanakis' left hand against the lifting force of the wind. Down in the bottom left-hand corner the signature was there, big and black – ZANAKIS; and immediately above, taking shape as he watched, the intensely leaning shape of Daisy, one hand out, throwing sand.

'This is it!' Zanakis shouted. 'This is it! At the very end, a beginning!'

Snow and sand blew across the board, grains of sand clinging in the thick paint, but Zanakis ignored them, and shouted, 'Here on the dune it'll be safe. It will be found!'

Walter went on, and along the dune crest, toward the place where he had stacked their cases, bedding, and tarpaulin.

Lynn Garland waited in the manager's room, her bundle ready beside her on the floor. The desk was tidy, the cover on the typewriter, the papers put away in the proper drawers, the door open.

He would come for her, she knew; and a few minutes after

306

half past twelve she heard the thud of boots in the corridor, several pairs, boots that came on in step. They stopped outside the door, and she saw three Coast Guardsmen, and John. John turned to the men, 'O.K., you fellows go ahead.'

The men nodded and went on down the corridor. John came into the office and took her by the shoulders and kissed her. 'Ready?'

'Yes,' she said. She picked up her bundle, but he held out his hand for it, and after a hesitation she gave it to him. 'What are those men doing?' she asked.

'Rescuing the Charter,' he said.

She said, 'Why, *John*! The D.A.R. will give you another medal!' She felt a strong disinclination to move. Once she started walking, where would it end? Out that door – for the last time; down the corridor, across the lobby, out into the drive – for the last time; along the streets, between the snow walls – for the last time.

'Let's go,' he said.

'Wait . . . John, will those men get away . . . escape?'

'The ones who pirated the 36-footer? I don't think so. In normal times the Navy would have them at once – or one of our big cutters – or the Air Force. No one can do anything now . . . because it isn't important enough. That makes me feel crazy, just saying it, you know. I can hardly believe that it's me saying the pirating of a 36-footer, *my* 36-footer, right under my nose, isn't important.'

'Will they reach shore, though?' she persisted.

'You'd like to be with them? I bet there are plenty who would. . . . No, frankly, I don't think they'll reach shore. The 36-footer's damned nearly unsinkable, but not quite. Randall's a lousy coxswain. They'll be turned over half a dozen times, that's for sure, and that means broken bones, some lost overboard – I don't think they'll make it, but of course there's a chance.'

'What did Mr Helm say when you reported it all to him?'

'*Umph.*'

Police Sergeant Barnes came in. 'Where's Mr Carpenter, miss?' he asked.

'On the dune. Why?'

'Jordan and me have been searching the hotel, like he told us to. We've come across several rooms with doors locked.'

'Everyone was told to leave them *un*locked.'

'Sure. But some were locked. Like Reverend Day's, and . . .'

'I saw both of them up on the dune just now,' John said.

307

'Yeah. Well, Mr Carpenter gave us the master key, and we've been able to get into all the locked rooms except one. Number 303. That's Mrs Bryant and Mrs Keahon, on the list.'

'I saw Mrs Keahon on the dune,' John said. 'We'd better break in the door, you mean.'

'Yeah. Will you do it? . . . Thanks. I got the hell of a lot to do. There's a fire axe just outside 300.'

He went out. John said to her, 'I'd like you to come with me, in case . . .'

He set off at a quick long striding pace. She followed, feeling a little sick.

Captain Alejandro Lacoma, master mariner, sat on a straight-backed chair at the back of the dais in the grand ballroom. In *The Iceman Cometh* 'Harry Hope, the proprietor of a saloon and rooming-house' sat on it, to mark him as a man of at least that much property, compared with his guests and customers. The Spanish sailors perched on bar stools or leaned against the bar, looking generally towards their captain but not with any great show of attention, for some were rolling cigarettes, some cleaning their fingernails with their seamen's knives, and one playing a solitaire on the bar with small, tattered cards.

The captain said, 'It is an interesting question, Pedro, but I am not sure that we have understood enough to be able to answer it. I did not know that you, for example, understood any English.'

Pedro was short and dark and about twenty-five. Every one of them was short and dark and about twenty-five, but some came from Galicia and some from Malaga. Pedro Garcia was a Gallego, and had a scar on his chin. He said, 'I understand English well, captain, having worked in Gibraltar for a time, but it was not convenient to let it be known, for various reasons.'

'Of course,' the captain agreed.

'Well, I have been explaining the play to these others, day by day, and José María asked me this question, and I said we should put it to our captain.'

José María bore a tattooed crucifix on the back of his right hand. The captain now said to him, 'Let us hear your question again, José María, that we may give it proper attention.'

José María spoke haltingly, with gestures: 'Supposing these people asked permission to stage this same play in Spain. Supposing one possessed due authority to decide, yes, or no. What should one's answer be? Not necessarily according to the wishes of the church – nor according to the dictates of the state, for as we all know there can be no agreement on these things – but as men of conscience, as husbands, and fathers. That is my question.'

Paco Martínez with the blue eyes said, 'There is selfishness.'

'Lust and pimping,' said Antonio.

They all chimed in: 'A madness for money.'

'An insane pride of blood.'

'Delusion and self-illusion.'

'Vanity.'

'Betrayal – by venality, and by stupidity.'

'Loss of faith – of manhood – or virtue.'

The captain said, 'Do you think that the playwright is implying that these faults are especially prevalent in the United States? Or do *you* think so?'

José María said earnestly, 'No, no, captain! The playwright points at all men, certainly including us. He says – with skill, I think, although a trifle long-windedly – that life is essentially degrading . . .'

'That mankind is wicked,' Paco Martinez said.

'And weak.'

'Unable to face reality.'

'Or to take action to change it if he is able.'

José María said, 'Captain, we cannot dispute that at the end of the play everyone escapes to unreality, either to a past that will never return or to a future that will never arrive.'

The captain said, 'But they *stay*, man! Only one attempts to evade his humanity, and that is the salesman himself, Mr Hickey. He kills himself.'

Antonio said, 'I do not understand why he does that, I confess.'

José María said, 'It is because the reality which *he* could not face was love.'

The captain said, 'I agree with that interpretation, José María. So the playwright, at the very end, shows one character who destroys himself because he has rejected love. But one must ask oneself, placed in this imaginary situation which José María has posed, whether that is enough to justify the rest. What is the proper judgment?'

John Remington stopped outside Room 303. Rattling the handle, calling Alice by name, banging on the door, had no effect. Through the keyhole he saw the faded carpet, the window, and the corner of a bed.

'Nothing for it,' he said, and raised the axe.

After half a dozen blows the door broke free of its hinges and fell inward. One bed was stripped. Alice Bryant lay on the other, under the bedclothes. Her face was grey and greasy. Lynn already had her wrist, at the pulse.

'It's quite strong,' she said.

'She didn't take enough,' John said. There was a bottle of sleeping pills on the bedside table, a water flask beside it, and an empty whisky bottle rolling on the floor.

As they pulled back the bedclothes, Alice Bryant rolled over and began to vomit. She vomited continuously for five minutes.

Nelson Pryor and Jim Carpenter came in, followed by Frank Damato. 'What's that god-awful noise?' Nelson began; then he was in the room, and watching the half-unconscious woman in her convulsions. 'Just about saving her life, that, I guess,' he said. 'Poor Alice. When she stops, Frank, you and Jim take her up to the dune, to Dr Miller.'

Frank Damato looked half his previous size. His eyes were swollen and his lips cracked. He said, 'Yes, Nelson.'

The rest of them left the room. 'That's everybody out,' Nelson said, 'except those crazy Spaniards. They're in the ballroom, sitting round the stage bar, chewing the fat. Not a thing to worry about.'

'They have their blankets rolled and ready,' John Remington said.

They reached the ground floor and Nelson stopped at one of the big glass doors to the ballroom. 'There they are,' he said. 'Look at them! Lynn, tell 'em it is time to evacuate this humble, unworthy hotel, as it is about to be swept away by the ocean. Tell 'em we're trying to save their lives, even if we can't save anything else. Tell 'em every man can help.'

Captain Lacoma listened carefully and when Lynn had finished bowed, and said, 'You would wish that my men repair now to the dune, then? To whom should they report for orders?'

'Mr Carpenter will be up there soon,' Lynn said. 'But will you not accompany them yourself?'

The captain spoke a word to his men, and they got up and went out. Nelson said, 'What's he saying? We haven't got all day.'

The captain said, in English, 'Excellency, we have been debating a matter of judgment, about the drama that was being rehearsed. Should it be allowed to be performed? Now . . .'

310

'You speak English?' Nelson said incredulously.

'A little, as you hear.'

'Why in hell . . .' Jesus, what that guy must have seen and heard . . . My God, he understands me *now*!

'I had reasons, Excellency . . . As I was saying, we were discussing the drama that has been rehearsed. I had thought our debate was a small thing, a way of passing the time and occupying the mind. Now, suddenly, it has struck me that we should debate a real, as opposed to an imagined, problem. We are persons of dignity, concerned with truth and justice. The question is of the first importance. Pray do me the honour . . .' He indicated the empty chairs with a sweep of his hand.

Nelson Pryor said, 'For God's sake, captain . . .'

The captain said, 'I do not make my meaning clear. I mean, I can perhaps save Monomoy from this destruction which threatens it. The question I ask myself is, Should I? I invite you to debate that question with me.'

John Remington said, 'You can save the town? And you're wondering whether you should? You? We saved you, didn't we? Who the hell are you to ask—'

'Hold it, John,' Nelson Pryor said. He turned to the captain. 'You mean, you'd like to know what we would do if we were in your shoes, eh?'

'Yes, Excellency,' the captain said. 'What we *should* do. What is correct.'

'How can you save us?' John Remington burst out. Lynn's hand dropped on his arm and held him tight. She muttered, 'Darling, listen . . .'

Nelson Pryor sank into a chair. 'What did you all decide about *The Iceman*?'

'We had not come to the final decision. In my opinion the vote would have been against it.'

'But this is different, eh? We are involved in the . . . the catastrophe here, if it happens.'

'We were also involved in the play. Moral questions are equally real whether posed in theory or in practice.'

Nelson said, 'When a decision involves life or death, captain, is there a choice? Isn't it wrong to deny life? Wrong not only by the laws of Christianity, but by civil law. It has to become murder – or suicide.'

'Excellency, I suggest not. In sentencing a murderer, for example, the judge chooses between life and death. In war, the soldier must often ask of himself whether, in such-and-such a

311

circumstance, it is proper for him to live or to die. Similar choices arise even in sport – certainly in the *corrida de toros*. Ordinary self-respect demands that we extend the same appreciation of what is proper to our own circumstances. Our judgment must be impartial, and true, for we shall certainly answer for it in an appropriate place . . . in the hereafter, according to the Christians, within ourselves, as others believe. Do you agree?'

'Yes,' Nelson said unwillingly.

'Then what is your verdict?'

Nelson looked at Lynn. 'What do you say?'

She thought he was playing for time; but time was an enemy. She said, 'I think . . . I think we are full of wickedness. But I don't think we're so drearily bad, so bad without a future . . . bad without gaiety, without hope, as O'Neill's characters are.'

'Not only Mr O'Neill's,' the captain said. 'I was a young officer on that vessel, the *Vera*, about which your American lady wrote a book. I saw some folly on that ship, she saw *only* folly . . .'

Lynn said eagerly, 'I think there's more love in the world – in Monomoy – than there is in *The Iceman* or *Ship of Fools*.'

The captain said, 'Señorita, even the animals know love. Among the horseshoe crabs there is love and self-sacrifice.'

John Remington said, 'We've got skills that ought not to be lost . . . records going back hundreds of years . . . things we've made, like the Old Church, Monomoy House, the Charter House . . . paintings, sculptures . . . books, poems . . .'

'We have all those,' Nelson said. 'Unfortunately, they have all been used . . .'

'To further the very evils which are the justification for a death sentence,' the captain said. 'Can any just and intelligent person suppose that we are less wicked than Sodom? What a pettiness of vice and folly was theirs, compared with ours!'

Nelson said, 'You're right, captain. You're right. But I believe we should vote the other way. Only, I can't think why.' His hands were locked within each other on the table, motionless before him. He looked at John Remington. 'I'm not afraid, John . . . afraid to die, I mean, if we have to. Well, of course we have to, if not now, soon. That's something to remember, isn't it, when you're tempted to start howling and begging? . . . I just think we've forgotten something. There *is* a reason to vote for Monomoy, and people . . . only I'm too stupid to think of it.'

He stared at Lynn. They all sat in silence.

Nelson shook his head. 'It's something to do with the difference between a play and what's happening to us. Not that the

312

right and wrong of it are different. I agree with the captain there. It's—'

Lynn interrupted. 'I know! The play has an ending.'

'That's it,' Nelson said. He spoke fast: 'And you don't write a review until the ending's reached – right? Here, there hasn't been an ending. We're still acting . . . and in the process, I guess, writing. We're writing it here – on the dune – in the houses – even in that stolen boat.'

Captain Lacoma said, 'You are suggesting that we defer consideration, because—'

Nelson interrupted. 'I say that if you don't try to save us, when you can, you are in fact bringing down the curtain while the play is still being performed.'

After a time the Spanish captain said, 'In my opinion, Excellency, you are right . . . Señorita?'

'I think so,' Lynn said. 'Yes, I think Mr Pryor's right. We have failed in everything, *so far*. I haven't given up.'

'Captain Remington?'

John said, 'We've just got to do the best we can, as long as we can.'

Captain Lacoma stood up. 'There are one hundred tons of dynamite in the rear of C hold of my ship. All necessary detonators, fuse, and explosives are in D hold, in crates labelled "canned food." You appreciate that there is no guarantee these things *will* save us. I only say that, if used in time, they should help.'

'The manifest . . .' John Remington began.

The captain said, 'Our manifest was quite false. In fact we carry arms and explosives for underground forces both of the extreme right and of the extreme left, in Spain . . . You wonder why I did not reveal this information earlier? Sir, we would prefer, even now, that it should not be divulged, if possible. We wish to return to Spain and continue our lives and serve our ideals there, each in his own way . . . Now, since there is an element of urgency in the situation, perhaps we should go?'

Nelson Pryor waited, arms folded, near the south-east corner of the Coast Guard station. Standing on the dune there, a little apart from anyone else, he must look like Napoleon surveying the ruins of Moscow. Let them laugh. His hands were cold and one earmuff did not fit properly, so that ear was cold, too.

On the deck of the *Goya* men scurried hither and thither like ants. Ropes hung from her stern and a continuous chain of people passed packages up and along the dune to the parking lot. Every few minutes the men on deck had to cling to railing or stanchion as bigger waves swept up the steel wall and over the top. The same waves reached within a foot or eighteen inches of the black-top in the Gap, each time scouring out more sand from under it. Already several square feet had broken off and quickly vanished.

Elliott was working, at the head of a dozen men, to place dynamite charges under the whole south wall of the Coast Guard station. When they blew them, the station and its concrete foundations would fall into the Gap. Monomoy would have a better chance. If it were done in time.

Another team was working under one of the Spanish sailors to set charges which would blow the *Goya* itself apart, and so remove a main contributory cause of the danger to the Gap. If it were done in time.

Those men could not be seen, for they were working deep in the stranded hull, John Remington with them.

All along the dune the people were on the move again, because Elliott had said no one must be within half a mile when they blew the charges. The time was coming when someone would have to blow the whistle, stop all work, and send the labourers and charge setters to safety.

Walter Crampton passed, Daisy in his arms, her eyes closed; George Zanakis, a board held high over his head, the worked surface downward to protect it from the weather; Barbara Carpenter, all dressed up for a skating party, maybe; Father Bradford, looking as though he had seen the devil; Harriet Ibbotson and that goddam mongrel of hers; and old Warren Mercer, helped along by his wife – wonder how he'd greet the union organizers next time; Mrs Handforth, followed by Louise Lincoln and Robert; Lynn Garland, looking mad because she was in a group of Coast Guard wives and children, being shepherded along by Bob Gardner and a couple of seamen; his own daughter, with Charlie Tyson; now his wife was tugging at his sleeve. 'Nelson . . . Nelson, it's time we went. Elliott wants us to go now, along to the safe place.'

'The safe place? Where's that?' Nelson said.

A quarter to three. Maybe they'd make it, maybe not. He hoped so with a sudden painful longing, that made him grab Mary round the shoulders, and hold her tight. This storm was an Act of God for some, although men, including himself, had helped to turn it from an inconvenience into a disaster. It wasn't too different from the way men had changed the atom from a powerful tool to something just about like the ocean at the Gap there. But the Spanish captain was right, as far as Lynn Garland had been able to tell him what they'd all been yakking about: Man could be wiped out by an Act of God, and on the available evidence, he deserved to be. But as long as the silly bastard kept trying, he *might* be allowed to write his own ending.